Belles' Letters 2

Don Noble
Jennifer Horne,
editors

Livingston Press
The University of West Alabama

ISBN 13: 978-160489-183-6, trade paper

Library of Congress Control Number: 2016963818

Typesetting and page layout: Sarah Coffey, Joe Taylor
Proofreading: Andrea Burroughs, Sarah Coffey, Shelby Parrish,
Alyssa Wright-Brown, Cici Denson, Joe Taylor, and Tricia Taylor
Cover design and photo : Amanda Nolin
Acknowledgments: Stories by the following authors originally appeared in these journals or books: Marian Carcache, "Wingflicks," *Chinaberries & Crows*, Solomon & George, 2012, and *The Moon and the Stars,* Solomon & George, 2013; Katherine Clark, chapter excerpt from *The Headmaster's Darlings,* University of South Carolina Press, Story River Books, 2015; Vicki Covington, "Magnolia," *The New Yorker,* March 24, 1986; Jennifer S. Davis, "Detritus," *Indiana Review,* Summer 2007, and *Our Former Lives in Art,* Random House, 2007; Fannie Flagg, "Rome, Italy," *Stories from the Blue Moon Cafe II,* MacAdam/ Cage, 2003; Anita Garner, "No Shadow of Turning," *Undeniable Truths,* Rank Stranger Press, 2009; Gail Godwin, "Dream Children," *Dream Children,* Knopf, 1976; Shirley Ann Grau, "The Lovely April," *Selected Stories,* Louisiana State University Press, 2003; Carolyn Haines, "Neighborhood Watch," *Damn Near Dead 2,* Busted Flush Press, 2010; Jennifer Horne, "The Other Grandparents," *Tell the World You're a Wildflower,* University of Alabama Press, 2014; Suzanne Hudson, "The Seamstress," *Stories from the Blue Moon Café II*, MacAdam/Cage, 2003, and *All the Way to Memphis,* River's Edge Media, 2014; Angela Jackson-Brown, "Something in the Wash," *New Southerner* Fiction Award, *New Southerner,* December 2009; Nanci Kincaid, "Why Dogs Die," *Five Points,* Spring 2006; Cassandra King, chapter excerpt from *The Same Sweet Girls,* Hachette Books, 2005; Patricia Mayer, "Clara," *Two Legs, Bad: Dog Town Tales,* Livingston Press, 2015; Sena Jeter Naslund, "How Do You Do, Mister Cat?," *Georgia Review,* Spring/Summer 1990, *The Animal Way to Love,* Ampersand Press, 1993, *The Disobedience of Water,* David R. Godine, 1999; Jennifer Paddock, "Something Temporary," excerpted from *A Secret Word,* Simon & Schuster, 2004; Judith Richards, excerpt from *Thelonius Rising,* River's Edge Media, 2014; Michelle Richmond, "Scales," under the title "Logorrhea" in *Logorrhea: Good Words Make Good Stories,* Bantam Books, 2007, and *Hum,* University of Alabama Press, FC2, 2014; Elise Sanguinetti, "To You, Frère Twig," *Mademoiselle,* 1960; Lee Smith, "Desire on Domino Island," *Me and My Baby View the Eclipse,* G. P. Putnam's Sons, 1990; T. K. Thorne, "Jim," *Thirty Three An[niversary] Anthology,* Negative Capability Press, 2014, and winner, Chattahoochee Valley Writer's Conference 2008 Short Story Contest; Betty Jean Tucker, "Callie," *On a Darkling Plain: Stories from the Great Depression,* Livingston Press, 2014; Sue Walker, "Good Grief," *Blind Mule*; Theodora Ziolkowski, "Spores," in the chapbook *Mother Tongues,* Spring 2015, winner of *The Cupboard's* "Fifth-Ever Contest."

The Press and the editors gratefully acknowledge a grant from the Alabama State Council on the Arts that helped make this book possible.
These are works of fiction.
Surely you know the rest: any resemblance
To persons living or dead is coincidental.
Livingston Press is part of The University of West Alabama.

Table of Contents

This book is dedicated to the memory of
Edel Elise Ayers Sanguinetti, 1924-2014

Belles' Letters 2

Introduction

This volume is *Belles 2*. so of course there was a *Belles 1*.

In 1999, Joe Taylor and Tina M. Jones of the Livingston Press at the University of West Alabama, collaborated on a volume of twenty-one short stories and five excerpts from novels by Alabama women. In her foreword, Jones writes that, as a girl, she, like many others, had thought that Scarlett O'Hara and her many manifestations were "the epitome of Southern womanhood."

Eventually she realized that Scarlett—and her plantation life—represented only a small segment of Southern culture. Jones' hope was that the volume *Belles' Letters* (a playful southern version of *belles-lettres)* would help showcase the enormous range of the Southern female experience.

And, she said, these Alabama women writers would be "allowed a voice all their own. They do not have to share their pages with anyone but themselves. They are free to tell their stories."

Belles' Letters was a big success and, startlingly, eighteen years have passed since then, and hundreds of new stories have been written. Writers new at that time are veterans now, and there are of course voices being heard for the first time.

A couple of years ago, Joe Taylor decided it was time for another collection. Although it has probably become easier over the years for women to publish their work, we believe there is still room for a volume that contradicts any lingering stereotypes of how women write and what they write about.

To serve as editors of this new volume, Joe asked Don Noble, who keeps up with new Alabama fiction by way of a weekly book review on Alabama Public Radio, and had edited two volumes of Alabama fiction for Livingston: *Climbing Mt. Cheaha: Emerging Alabama Writers* (2004) and *A State of Laughter: Comic Fiction from Alabama* (2008), and Jennifer Horne, herself the author of a volume of fiction, *Tell the World You're a Wildflower (2014),* editor of a poetry anthology, *Working the Dirt: An Anthology of Southern Poets* (2003), and the co-editor, with Wendy Reed, of two volumes of essays by southern women on spirituality, *All Out of Faith* (2006) and *Circling Faith* (2012).

With Taylor, Noble and Horne set the ground rules:

Every contributor had to have a strong Alabama connection.

There would be no stories repeated from previous Livingston Press collections.

Each story was to be of some length—no flash fiction— but not so long as to qualify as a novella.

We favored short stories over excerpts but made a few exceptions in order to include some stand-alone sections from longer works by established Alabama writers. For reasons of space, this volume by no means includes all of the extraordinary women writing and publishing today.

The stories were to be only from living authors, and each author was asked to contribute a few words on the origin or "inspiration" for the story and some biographical information. The one deceased author included is Elise Sanguinetti, to whom this volume is dedicated.

The stories included here were chosen by Horne and Noble, either from work solicited from established authors, some previously printed in volumes or literary journals, or from entries in response to a call, online and in print, by Joe Taylor for story submissions.

Where other things were somewhat equal, we chose stories set in Alabama or with a strong Alabama connection in content.

The resulting volume boasts a rich assortment of subject matter, themes, locale, tone, and style.

As might be expected, a number of stories are love stories—first loves, lost loves, strange loves, from the most transient, feckless, grotesque, even abusive, to the permanent and heartwarming. We even include a send-up of the romance novel.

Likewise, there are many stories of family relationships, especially mother-daughter, mother-son, and wife-husband. Communication between generations is, as always, an issue.

It would not be Alabama without a number of treatments of religion, from angels to ghosts to snakes and a little magic.

Although many of the stories are contemporary, some reach back as far as the Depression; a few focus on race relations, but in a gentler, less violent vein than would have been the case in the past. We are in

Don Noble & Jennifer Horne

the twenty-first century and there will be stories of drug abuse as well as alcohol.

The stories range geographically from the Gulf Coast to north Alabama, from the inner city to the countryside, but with perhaps fewer outdoor and hunting stories than would be found in a volume of male writers. Several stories are set in small towns. The social/economic classes and their often humorous, sometimes sad interactions are all represented.

As in all Southern fiction, a number of dogs make their appearances.

The editors and publisher wish to thank the Alabama State Council on the Arts for the grant which enabled us to offer each contributor a small honorarium. We also thank all of our contributors, many of them truly distinguished and well-established, not to say famous, writers, such as Pulitzer Prize winner Shirley Ann Grau, Harper Lee Award winners Fannie Flagg, Carolyn Haines, and Sena Jeter Naslund, and best-selling authors such as Gail Godwin, Lee Smith, Nanci Kincaid, and Michelle Richmond, for graciously accepting these small honoraria and for taking the time to compose the short introductory pieces that give readers insight into the writing process.

We hope that, like the first volume, this collection will make readers aware of the great variety and quality of fiction being written by Alabama women, that it will stimulate, engage, entertain, and move its readers, and that readers will seek out other works by the writers they particularly like.

Putting together an anthology is an inexact science, and editors are always aware of potential omissions and lapses of taste. Let us close here by quoting somewhat tongue-in-cheek from the preface to a 1931 volume, *The New Yorker Scrapbook:* "This is a singularly straightforward book, designed to hurt the feelings of all writers not represented in it, without materially adding anything to the happiness of those who are. We knew long ago that such a book would some day be compiled. Luckily it contains only prose, and its pages are arranged in no particular order. A book of poems arranged in order of merit will be what will eventually throw us out of business."

Elise Sanguinetti

Over the years Elise Sanguinetti's novels and my acquaintanceship with her have given me a great deal of pleasure, and it has always been my belief that Sanguinetti was deserving of a lot more public attention than she received. I hope dedicating to her this book of stories by her peers will redress this balance in some small way.

Elise Sanguinetti was a true daughter of Anniston and Calhoun County.

Born January 24, 1924, she attended public school through eighth grade, then Ashley Hall School for girls in Charleston, graduating in 1942. She had her freshman year at St. Olaf College in Minnesota but, due to family finances, was forced to leave and return to Alabama.

Sanguinetti transferred to the University of Alabama and graduated in 1947 with a degree in French and English.

Sanguinetti had already decided on a career in writing while at Ashley Hall; at UA she studied under the famously successful creative writing teacher Hudson Strode, who was the mentor to a collection of novelists: Babs and Borden Deal, Helen Norris, Harriet Hassell, and Winston Groom.

Sanguinetti was close friends with Nelle Harper Lee, and the two collaborated in editing the school humor magazine *Rammer-Jammer*.

These two small-town Alabama girls had a lot in common, especially their dedication to writing, but were in some ways very different: Elise Ayers was a Tri-Delt with little irony and Nelle Lee a most reluctant and ill-fitting sister of Chi Omega.

Over the decades, the two would correspond, with Lee offering encouragement and advice to Sanguinetti on work in progress. In a letter of Lee's which came up for public auction in 1990 she wrote: "And speaking of Alabama writers, to my mind the finest we have is Elise Sanguinetti. If you don't know her novels, read them."

After graduation, Sanguinetti, who had always had a powerful interest in her Scandinavian roots, especially Norway, instilled by her Norwegian-born mother, Edel Ytterboe Ayers, studied for a term at the University of Oslo, Norway.

She and her mother kept up a strong interest in St. Olaf's, and Elise was awarded the St. Olaf "Distinguished Alumna Award" in 1993.

From the time of her graduation in '47 until about 1955, Sanguinetti wrote innumerable articles, features, and reviews for the *Anniston Star*, which she and her brother H. Brandt Ayers later inherited in 1977, after the death of their mother.

Married to Phillip Sanguinetti in 1950, Elise travelled with Phil as his work as a chemical engineer took them to St. Louis, Pittsburgh, and even Germany, before returning to Alabama.

It was in Pittsburgh that Elise wrote and had published in *Mademoiselle* magazine in 1960 her first fiction, "To You, Frère Twig," preceded in the magazine by this "Editor's NOTE: Elise Sanguinetti— a MLLE discovery—has that rare sense of humorous perception about adolescence which made *Catcher in the Rye* a classic. Here, with one of the funniest stories we've ever read or published, her first fiction appearance anywhere."

The story is comic and poignant. Narrated by Felicia Whitfield, twelve years old, herself moving into a confusing adolescence, we watch young Arthur, fourteen, modelled of course on Elise's younger brother, Brandt, sent away from home to prep school in distant Connecticut. At first terrified and a long way from home, Arthur not only adjusts, but in only three months develops a Yankee accent and Yankee attitudes.

It is perplexing to consider that Sanguinetti, in spite of this triumphant debut, never published another short story. It is believed she wrote many, but declined to submit them.

The answer may be that "Frère Twig" immediately inspired *The Last of the Whitfields*, which would be published in 1962 and enjoyed good sales and a warm critical response. McGraw-Hill's cover for *The Last of the Whitfields* speaks volumes. The publisher inserted the subtitle "A happy (but significant) novel of the South."

Sanguinetti's publishers understood what she was up to.

Most assuredly sensitive to racial struggles in the South and in her own hometown of Anniston, where there had just been the famous Freedom Rider bus burning, Sanguinetti nevertheless believed that a wide swath of Southern life was being ignored or misrepresented to the rest of the country in the Southern novels of her era. In Erskine Caldwell's *Tobacco Road*, for example, we see poor white Southern families, ignorant and even depraved. In Faulkner's *The Sound and the Fury*, the white family is depicted as dysfunctional, even mentally unbalanced; in *Absalom, Absalom!*, the Sutpen family is enmeshed in racial strife, injustice, miscegenation, and violence.

Sanguinetti also thought the northern press was misrepresenting Southern life and the Southern family. In *Whitfields*, a Yankee writer, Mr. Bob Hopper of *News Review*, comes to fictional Ashton, Georgia (based on Anniston, Alabama). He stays with the family, interviews people around town, gets to know them, but he never truly understands them.

Dominated by his preconceptions, he makes the white Ashtonians into caricatures, benighted in their thinking, with heavy drawls. Hopper can see only what reinforces the ideas he already held, missing the deep goodwill the Whitfields and their friends hold for their town and for African-Americans, however paternalistic it may seem to us now.

The Whitfields are not bigots. Their town is experiencing a most difficult time, with demonstrations and the turmoil of integration, but the novel is just as much about family life and its stresses. Young Arthur, like any teenager, has his growing pains. His mother and father may be perplexed by his behavior but their affection triumphs and Arthur grows up.

The shifting of subject and setting demonstrated in Sanguinetti's work would be carried through by writers such as Walker Percy who, in *The Last Gentleman* and *Love in the Ruins,* moved the Southern novel out of the swamp and into the country club.

Middle-class life in the Deep South was not all grim. Sanguinetti's novel was widely praised for its refreshing humor.

Whitfields was followed by three more novels, *The New Girl* (1964), *The Dowager* (1968), and *McBee's Station* (1971).

These novels, in their different ways, are most assuredly Southern fiction, but Sanguinetti was working a different field from most of her contemporaries. In *The New Girl,* Felicia, like her brother a small-town child, must learn to navigate the ways of a sophisticated, not to say Machiavellian, girls boarding school in Charleston.

The Dowager follows the travails of Cousin Winky as she deals with the labyrinthine complexities of Charleston society, and *McBee's Station* portrays Letitia Graham McBee, an older woman coping with societal change as she tries to hang onto the comfortable ways of the past.

Sanguinetti, after this astonishing blast of productivity—four novels in nine years—published no more fiction, devoting her efforts to the *Anniston Star* and civic work in Anniston. She was inducted into the Alabama Academy of Distinguished Authors in 1982.

Elise Sanguinetti passed away on Sunday, November 16, 2014. She was ninety years old.

There are plans for the reissuance of her four novels, and one hopes that a new wave of readers will come to enjoy and admire this fine writer.

—Don Noble

To You, Frère Twig

Elise Sanguinetti

Last year my brother Arthur changed, and Mother doesn't say that about the "twig" any more. The twig has been with us for ever so long, ever since Arthur's first day at school, when he came home with a drawing of a red and blue apple; on the red side he had written "blue" and on the blue side "red." I remember Mother sadly showing this to Father and in that strange, far-sounding voice saying, "You know, Allison, 'as the twig is bent, so is the tree.' " She had looked at Arthur, and then Arthur, a blond, frowning boy with glasses, had looked up at her almost wonderingly. But she only shook her head and sighed a sigh that somehow seemed to last through all those terrible years Arthur crept his way through the Ashton Grammar School. And the great "change" occurred.

Actually, I don't suppose it happened overnight, this change. It just seemed that way. But I think I knew from the beginning, when I first heard what they were going to do to him, that something tremendous would happen. I'm the girl, you see. (This means things, I've found out.) But I knew first—even before Arthur did—that they were going to send him away. I heard them talking, Mother and Father. This was after that school play when Arthur embarrassed us so by forgetting all his lines and just standing up there in the middle of the stage staring at everybody. Of course, everyone laughed—everyone except us and we had to sit there, tall and straight, listening to the laughing and watching Arthur all red-faced and wide-eyed. Later I heard Mother saying that "something has *got* to be done about him now." And Father said he guessed so too. Then Mother started talking about that school in Connecticut.

I listened to them and I was almost afraid. It seemed a terrible thing they were talking about. My own parents! Doing away with Arthur! If only he'd made better grades, I thought. Or got some "interests," like Mother had wanted him to. Still, I must say, I rather enjoyed some of Arthur's troubles; it gave me a sort of warm feeling, knowing I was thin and quick and different from him. Even so, it seemed a dreadful thing they were planning to do—sending him away, abandoning him more or less. So one night after dinner I told him what they were going to do to him. "You're gonna get sent away, Arthur," I said. And I remember the look of him, standing there in the middle of his blue-striped room—his face moonfaced and his spectacled eyes looking back at me, unblinking and round. I knew how afraid he was. And I felt closer to him then than I ever had before.

Arthur was fourteen when he finally got sent away. Connecticut is a long way away from Georgia, but my mother said "a change of atmosphere" was good for a child. So on a crisp blue September day we went down to the train station and saw Arthur, all name-taped and dressed in his new brown suit, off to the unknown spaces of Connecticut. He sat down in the green Pullman seat beside the window and I looked at him up there, bundled up in his suit and still chubby, and I thought how small he seemed and how tremendous the train was. Somehow I felt that Arthur, alone and unarmed, was going off to be killed. As his hand waved timidly good-by and he tried to smile, the train began to move and I looked up at Mother; her eyes were filled with tears, but she was trying to smile too. I thought, Oh, Arthur … and sadly watched the great black train until it had rounded the bend, carrying Arthur away, I thought, forever.

Naturally, we missed him those first few days. To me it was as if someone had died and there were pathetic reminders of the person everywhere—a shoe, Arthur's cub scout uniform, an old rope. Mother, I think, missed him more than anyone else did. After the third day she started waiting for the mailman, hoping to hear "some word." But it wasn't until the end of the second week that some word finally arrived. It was written in pencil and on slick theme paper, and since it was the first time Arthur had ever written a letter home, there was something sad to me about the "Dear Mother and Dad." In a jerky scrawl he had written:

I got here alright. I had five cheese sandwiches on the train and nearly missed the other train in New York. But I didn't.

My roomate's name is Bob Leyden and he comes from a place called Marble Head, Massichusits. It's real hard hear. We have to wash windows on Saturday—everybody does. Mr. Sykes said window washing can be fun, but it isn't. I've gotten to know a lot of the other boys but I don't like my roomate. Wish I was home and there only 84 days until Christmas. They think I talk funny up here. I gotta go.

Elise Sanguinetti

Love,
Arthur

Arthur hadn't been in school long before we starting receiving slick little envelopes from Mr. Sykes, the school's headmaster. Mr. Sykes never used the word "I" but always "we." And it seemed every letter began either "We fear" or "We are sorry" or "We believe." Anyway, Mr. Sykes and "they" quite soon decided Arthur had to go back a grade. "…Arthur just doesn't seem to have had the fundamental training some of the other boys have had," wrote Mr. Sykes. This caused no end of talk at home and Mother said: "He just can't keep up that's all! I told you. I've always said: 'As the twig is bent, so is the tree!'" And she kept saying this, over and over, as other letters from the headmaster arrived those first few weeks. That was all we ever talked about—Arthur and *school*—Arthur and twigs.

I thought Arthur's next letter home would have been a poem of gloom. But it wasn't at all. It was almost jubilant, for Arthur.

…Now I got this new roommate. His name is Knox Campbell and he's from New York City and goes to night clubs all the time. I think his folks are real rich because he's got this picture of his house and it looks like a castle. He says his father makes those things like that one you've got Mother, up in the attic—that kind of dummy thing you used to fit clothes on when Hattie would come in and so. He's in all my classes and we go around together all the time. He doesn't like Mr. Sykes either. Well, I gotta go.

He signed his name "A." And Father wanted to know why he'd signed his name like that. Mother said it was just probably something he had learned.

But Arthur seemed to be learning strange new things all the time. Suddenly we received a letter from him and his handwriting was completely changed—and unreadable. It was more of a printing than anything else and I'm sure the letter had taken him a long time to write. He asked us how we liked it. And he said he hoped we did, because this was the way he was going to write all the time now. Knox, his roommate, wrote that way, he said. Knox also said everybody at Harvard wrote that way. And Father said if they did he didn't understand how anybody ever got out of Harvard. Mother said she thought Arthur's new handwriting was "quite interesting."

Yet it was Arthur's next letters that seemed to interest Father, and I'm sure this was because every one of them had some mention of money in them. We were all quite shocked and, I must say, hurt when Arthur wrote us his clothes weren't right. "They don't wear the same kind of things up here as they do down there," he wrote in his new handwriting.

...Knox says some of my suits are kind of hicky and he said when you get to be almost fifteen it's stupid to wear ties that have scotty dogs all over them. He says his mother knows this store in New York City and if you'll just send me the money she can charge and I can pay her back. I can get my shoes here all right. They call them white bucks but they don't have any down there in Ashton so don't go around trying to find them. Knox says he guesses I'll need about hundred dollars for all this. Well, I gotta go.

Love,
A.

Mother read this letter out loud and because of Arthur's new handwriting she read white "lucks" instead of "bucks." And when Father heard this he stood up and in a loud voice said: "White '*lucks*'! What in the world has come over that boy? White '*lucks*,' my eye. A hundred dollars to make a sis out of my boy. Nothing doing!"

Nevertheless, Arthur was happy with all his new clothes. He wrote us he was really glad he'd got them because Knox had asked him to visit him in New York for Thanksgiving vacation and that they would probably be going to a lot of night clubs and he didn't want to look "hicky." He said he'd write us and tell us how much he'd need. Father said Mother could sell that dummy up in the attic and then send the money to Arthur. But Mother said to remember that it was Arthur's birthday and that it was interesting, she thought, for young boys to have "experiences."

"Like night clubs?" Father asked.

"Now, Allison," Mother answered. "*You* know better than that."

"Well, I don't know," Father said. "That Knox boy doesn't sound too bright to me. White 'lucks'!" And he shook his head and left the room.

Elise Sanguinetti

Still, I think it was during this period, listening to all the talk about Arthur's New York trip and thinking of him sitting in some great huge silver night club, that I began to feel forgotten. My own life in comparison seemed to be an endless line of cold sun and cracked sidewalks along which I would walk the way from school to home.

Then, to add to all this, Arthur's letter describing his visit to New York was three sheets of theme paper packed with joy. When I got home from my music lesson Mother had just finished reading it. I saw it in her hand, the folded pages all wadded up and half-sticking out of the envelope. She seemed happier than I'd ever seen her "We've had the grandest letter from Arthur!" she said. "I'll read it to you when your father comes."

"That's all right," I said. "I'll read it now."

"Oh, no. Let's wait until he comes. He likes to be with us when we read Arthur's letter."

So that night we all sat down in the library and Mother read it aloud:

…First off, we went up on the train. We stayed in the club car most of the way and then we ate. But guess what? A chaufer met us at the train. He was white and looks like Uncle Alex. We got in this huge black cadilack, in the back, and then we drove and drove until we got to this huge gray house made out of stone and it was Knox's house. Knox's Dad is really rich but he isn't really Knox's Dad. Knox said his real Dad was dead but he acts real nice. Mrs. Campbell is sure pretty. She's Knox's real mother. He told me all about it. But I can't tell. I had a room all to myself and this real high bed. We ate in the hugest dining room you ever saw. At dinner Mr. Campbell said I had a good vocabulary for a boy my age and he asked me what I was going to do and I said I guessed I'd be a lumberman like you. Mrs. Campbell was always talking about me and how polite I was. She said she was glad Knox was getting Georgia influence from me. She said he needed manners. Anyway that night we all got dressed up and Mr. Campbell put on this top hat and a coat that had velvet around the collar and Mrs. Campbell put on this blue dress and long fur coat and they took Knox and me to the—STORK CLUB! We sat in stripped seats and Mr. Campbell told this waiter he knows to bring us some cherry wine. Knox drank and got blotto! But I didn't. There was a man in there that's been married 15 times—a real old man and Mrs. Campbell said he was going to get married again. The Stork Club is real small, and not like the ones you see in the movies. But afterwards we went to Kopa and it's even smaller. Mr. Campbell said Knox couldn't

have another glass of cherry and I couldn't either. So we got a coke in there but Knox said they always put whiskey in the cokes anyway and he was really getting blotto, but I didn't. That was the best night.

But long about the last we had this dance. We didn't have it till then because I told them about me not being able to dance. But Mrs. Campbell showed me how until I got so I could do it pretty good. She used to dance in a night club and she really knows how. Anyway, all these girls came! Knox's girl is a real dame. Sue. But there was one better than her. Rose. Knox said he thought she had the hots for me and she would write. I haven't gotten one yet though. Northern girls are a whole lot different from southern ones. They're much more grown up and they hit you all the time. Knox said one thought the way I talked was cute. But I don't think she'll write. You ought to hear the letters Knox gets from his girls—at the end. Know what I mean? Anyway, Mrs. Campbell said I could come back any time at all. I think I will. And, oh yeah, she was glad I knew how to tip. They've got these white women for maids—two. And I gave them fifty cents a peace. I told Mrs. Campbell about how mad you get, Mother, when Aunt Jane and Uncle Arthur come and never give Velvet and Extra one dime. Anyway Knox says he wants me to come up in the summer but Mr. Campbell said Knox had to go to camp again. Knox says he's not going because he's too old and I don't blame him. Well, that's all. There's a whole lot more, but I gotta go.

Love,
A.

Everybody was smiling about Arthur—that is, everybody but me. I started walking around the room with my hip out of joint, but they didn't even say anything about *that.*

Anyway, Arthur's next letter caused Mother no end of worry and Father said he thought Arthur had gone "crazy."

The letter arrived on a Saturday and was written in ink this time. Mother discovered it on the hall table. "Well, a letter from Arthur," she said. Almost absent-mindedly she unfolded the letter and began to read. Suddenly her expression began to change and she frowned. "Whaaat?" she exclaimed. "Why—" She looked up at the ceiling. "Aaaaaallison!" she called to Father.

"What's the matter?" I asked.

"I—I don't know. Go get your father!"

Elise Sanguinetti

I told Father to hurry up and come downstairs, that Arthur had done something again.

"What now?" he asked wearily.

"I don't know," I said. I was so excited I could scarcely breathe.

We found Mother seated forward on the sofa in the library.

"What *now*?" Father asked again.

"I don't know," Mother replied. She looked up at us. "I just don't know."

Arthur's letter was the queerest thing I'd ever heard. In the first place, he began "Fond Parents" instead of his usual "Dear Mother and Dad." But it was the rest of the letter that really upset us. Mother had some difficulty reading it because even though it was a better example of Arthur's new handwriting he had placed little round circles over every *i* instead of just plain dots and, though pretty, the circles were so large in places that it made the upper line hard to read. Arthur's first sentence nearly jolted us out of the room. "I sit here in darkness, alone, and I am paralysed."

Father bolted forward in his chair. "What?"

"No, now just wait a minute," Mother said. She began the letter again:

...I sit here in darkness, alone, and I am paralysed. My heart is a cold gray stone and I am paralysed with gloom. I walk about in darkness always and my feet go SLUSH, SLUSH, SLUSH and gloom o'ertakes me. No one knows about all this but I. Even when the sun goes down I watch it SINK, SINK, SINK and darkness comes. For darkness and blackness are my kin folks, like you all, and I can tell it to the like of you. But nobody else! The moon rises up. RISE, RISE, RISE. But it's yellow and no kin. So, like the black ghost that I am I walk with my heavy gray stone and my feet go SLUSH, SLUSH, SLUSH! Farewell.

Your Obedient Son,   *A.*

For a time we just stared at each other. Finally Mother said: "Do you suppose it would be a good idea for us to send this to the school authorities?"

"I wouldn't be sending that around to *any*body," Father said. "It's too nutty!"

Father was smiling, but I wasn't. The idea that Arthur really might be crazy pricked me with a sort of kittenish fear and a horrible picture formed in my mind of Arthur, chained to a great iron chair in the attic, howling mad, and I shuddered, vowing I'd never think of that again. Father made it all seem better when he suggested perhaps Arthur was suffering from an unrequited love. I asked him what that was and he said it was when one party does and the other doesn't.

Nevertheless, this was the end of Arthur's gloom letters, and as time went on his letters became shorter and shorter and some of the time he even forgot to write in his new handwriting. Exams were coming on, he said, and he was really studying. He'd be glad to get home for Christmas. "It'll be divine to get out!" he wrote.

"*Divine?*" Father said. "He talks like a sis!"

The day Arthur finally did get out Mother and I had a sort of argument. I didn't want to go to the train station to meet Arthur. Mother said she had never heard of such disloyalty. "Here your brother has been away for three months and you don't even want to go to the train to meet him!" She told me to go right upstairs and put on my blue dress; we were leaving for the station in a few minutes.

Actually, I think I was almost afraid to see Arthur. He had done so many things, been to so many places, and I—I was still just me.

At the station Mother kept saying: "I wonder if he's changed. My, how exciting it is!"

The train came in and the three of us stood there, smiling, as each passenger descended, waiting for the moment when Arthur's familiar round face would suddenly appear and we could appropriately jolt into joy. When the last passenger came down we stood there, still smiling somehow, and Mother said: "I wonder where he is?" Father asked the porter if there had been a young schoolboy on the car. And the porter said there had been. But at just that moment Arthur appeared at the door. At least I thought it was Arthur. I looked at him again.

He certainly looked different. In the first place he had lost weight, a lot of weight, and his hair was cut very short all over. He was wearing his dark blue suit and right away I noticed his white shoes and the newspaper tucked under his arm. But the funny thing was he wasn't smiling or anything. He

Elise Sanguinetti

didn't even seem very glad to se us. He came down the train steps, slowly, and Mother rushed up to him and hugged him. He halfway reacted to this, smiling only slightly. Then he suddenly backed away from her and looked into her face as if he were examining it. "Wellll, hellooo, therrrre, Motherrrr," he said in the strangest accent I'd ever heard. Then he looked at Father. "How arrre you, sir?" He shook Father's hand. "And, Felicia," he said, looking at me as if I were a mere child. He straightened his shoulders and looked about. "Wellll, I see the little town is just about the same." He sighed an almost tired sigh.

We walked to the car in silence. Arthur sat up front with Father and I could see him moving his head, glancing at everything. "Nooo," he said, "nothing has really changed."

"You've gotten a new way of talking up there, haven't you, Arthur?" Father asked.

"Why, nooo," Arthur replied. "I don't reallly think sooo."

Anyway, that's when Arthur came home sophisticated. He didn't have any expression on his face and he yawned all the time. He was sophisticated for six days and then this boy who lives near us said Arthur had gone up north and got "daft." See, our town is small and nobody's ever been sent up north before. Nobody's ever come home rolling their *r*'s and talking about night clubs all the time either.

But the worst thing was that he genuflected in the Episcopal Church and this was horrifying because our church is very small and low. Finally Mother told him that since no one else seemed to be doing that she thought it was a good idea for him to follow the service as he always had. He didn't stop, though, until he nearly knocked his kneecap off on the pew in front of him. Boys genuflected all over the place at school, he said.

I suppose you could say Arthur's growing sincere was just an outgrowth of all these other things. Mother thought so. At times she gets very partial to Arthur. But then when it happened nobody really cared because what he did was so horrifyingly embarrassing that it really didn't matter how it started. This was his second semester in Connecticut and Father said he thought Arthur had "really gone crazy."

The first thing that happened was that we got this letter from Arthur saying he was bringing the most unpopular boy in the entire school home with him for Easter. His name was Seymour Yates and the reason he was so unpopular was because he "wets the bed all the time." Somehow it had become Arthur's duty to be nice to Seymour: "…Only last week the Head (Mr. Sykes) thanked me for my spirit in aiding the handicapped." At the end of the letter he said for Mother not to worry because "old Yates" had these rubber pads he took around with him all the time.

Mother was furious. She said she didn't have enough sheets to be changing them all the time and it did look as if Arthur could be a little more considerate of his own family. "Why can't Arthur help out some normal boy?" she asked. The very next day, though, she went downtown and bought six extra sheets. Then she had Velvet string an extra rope between the two oak trees in our back yard. "We may have some additional washing to do next week," was all she told Velvet. I guess that was why she was sort of upset when Arthur's next letter came. I mean she had gone to all that trouble and everything Arthur wrote that Seymour wasn't coming:

…His parents said he couldn't come because he's got to go to this doctor that the Head recommended. The Head told Mr. and Mrs. Yates that if Seymour didn't get cured he believed it was a good idea for them to keep him home until he did. You ought to see all these alarm clocks and everything he's got. I'm like the Head, though. He says he thinks it's cruel the way all the boys tease poor old Yates. And yesterday the Head told me privately that I stand a good chance of getting the Amos T. Caldwalder because I've started showing all this character. He said all the faculty had been noticing me and he hoped I don't flunk anything. I told the Head how I had always believed in the helpless and down-trodden and everything. You have to if you want to get the Amos T. Caldwalder award. It's the highest award any boy can get. Well, I've gotta go.

Your Servant, As Always
A.

Father was more interested in why Arthur had signed himself "Your Servant" than he was in the character award. "He's never shown any signs in that direction before."

"It's just probably something else he's learned," Mother explained and then she told Velvet she could pack away the extra sheets.

On Thursday we all had to go down to the train station to meet Arthur. There're only two trains that pass through our town, the one going and the one coming. Arthur was on the one coming and as usually he was the last passenger to get off. Right away I noticed something different about him. At first I thought it was his glasses but I remembered he had gotten the horn-rimmed ones Christmas and I guess I wasn't used to them yet. He was walking toward us with his hands folded in front of him, and as he got closer I noticed the peculiar look in his eyes—a kind of blue-eyed gleaming I'd never seen before. He came up and took Mother's hand with *both* of his, putting his left hand on the top of Mother's, not shaking it or anything, just resting it there like the minister does on your head when you're confirmed. "Mother," he said softly, as if he hadn't seen her for one million years. "Are you all right, Mother?"

Mother looked down at their hands and then at Arthur. "Why, of course," she answered weakly and then she broke into a wide smile. Arthur ignored the smile and then looked sadly at Father. He tried to shake hands the same way with him.

"A manly shake, Arthur," Father ordered, dismissing Arthur's prayerful left and practically shaking off his right.

Arthur folded his hands back in front of him and looked at me as if I were some pathetic child. "How are your studies, Felicia?"

"They're all right, I guess." I started brushing my bangs back with my hand and rolling my eyes upward. You had to do something; it was so emb*arr*assing!

One thing, though, his socks were still all wide and stretched at the top, which showed he'd forgotten to wash them again.

We didn't say much until we got to the car. Arthur sat up front and stared out the window. "The town of my youth," he commented as we passed this parking lot of broken-down cars.

Father just glanced at him and didn't say anything. Mother started talking about his character award. "That's so *fine*, Arthur! We really are proud of you."

"Well, I haven't gotten it yet," Arthur explained, turning all the way around to smile at her. "I really don't deserve it. It's just like Albert Schweitzer says—'A thoroughbred doesn't need the ear of corn.' "

"Did *he* say that?" Mother asked.

"Uh-huh. We've taken up old Schweitzer in English." He turned back to Father. "Such a great man. If only there were more like him in the world."

Nobody said much else until we got home. Then Arthur started acting really batty. About our two Negro servants—Velvet and Extra. We're not rich or anything. Extra is Velvet's forty-six-year-old son. He's not a real butler or chauffeur or anything; he does everything. Arthur is his best friend; he told me that one time when he was making this Ping-pong table for them to play on. Anyway, when we got to the house Extra and Velvet both came out to welcome Arthur home. They're practically nutty over Arthur. Right away they came all beaming-glad up to the car and Arthur, instead of waving and carrying on like he always does, just slowly got out of the car and then gave Velvet that same handshake and look he gave Mother. "Poor Velvet. Are you well?" he asked her.

I guess Velvet thought Mother had been telling him something, because she started backing away and saying, "Whatsamatter with you, Arthur? Somebody been talkin' to you 'bout my blood again?"

Arthur said no, he just wanted to know how she was, that was all. Then he turned to Extra. "And Extra—" he said in this stupid, half-crying voice.

Extra just stared at him, then reached down for Arthur's luggage.

"Oh, no," Arthur protested. "Let me. I never want to consider myself too good to carry my own bags."

Extra got that white-eyed look he gets when Velvet start fussing at him.

"Now, you rest," Arthur commanded Extra.

"Let's go inside," Father said. And when I caught Velvet's eye, I glanced at Arthur and then pointed my finger at my brain.

"Lawdy mer-ceeee," Velvet said and we all went into the house.

That night after dinner Arthur bored us all to death, talking for hours about Knox Campbell and Albert Schweitzer. He hated Knox Campbell now because Knox didn't care a thing in this world for anything except football and all these girls he had in New York. Albert Schweitzer wasn't like that. Knox was always making people do things for him, but a man like Albert Schweitzer wouldn't let a flea work for him if he could help it. Arthur thought we ought to fire Velvet and Extra. "How would *you* like to be some slave in somebody's house?" he asked Father.

Elise Sanguinetti

Mother asked what Velvet and Extra would live on if they didn't work.

"Pay them *any*way," Arthur answered. "Do unto others like you would have them do unto you. That's what Albert Schweitzer said."

"Somebody else said that too," Father said.

"I've got to go to bed," I sighed. Boring, boring, boring. Arthur was so boring I was almost sorry he had come home. I liked him better when he flipped through worthless magazines all the time.

"Yes, Felicia. You go right on up," Mother said in this worried voice.

I said good night and walked out of the room with my hip out of joint.

"And don't *do* that any more," Mother called. "You may *freeze* that way."

"Okay, I won't," I replied and went on up the stairs.

I don't know how long they stayed downstairs. It must have been late because Arthur didn't get up until eleven o'clock the next morning. Father wanted to know if we thought Albert Schweitzer slept that late. But Mother said for Father not to be "flip" about Arthur. "He's just feeling his way, that's all."

"I wish he'd hurry and find it then," Father grumbled.

"Well, let's not worry about him," Mother said. "I really think he might be coming into his own."

She kept saying that more and more as Arthur started staying up in his room typing on his typewriter.

"What's he *do*ing up there?" I asked Mother.

"Just thinking," she answered. "Thinking."

The thing was that Arthur thought too much, because two days after Easter, Father got this telephone call. We were all having lunch and Extra came and told Father that someone wanted him on the telephone. We always answer the telephone during meals. A lot of people don't but we think it's rude not to.

Anyway, we heard Father say: "What? What are you talking about, Charlie?"

Mother put down her fork and listened. "It must be old Mr. Henry. Wonder what he wants with Allison?"

Arthur stopped eating and his eyes behind his glasses got round and unblinking.

"It's rude to listen to other people when they're talking on the phone,"

I said.

But then Father's voice got louder. "I never wrote anything for your newspaper in all my life," he shouted. "Yes. Yes. I know. Well, you go down there and *stop* the press then! Somebody's just trying to make a—what do you *mean* you can't stop it?"

"Heavens!" Mother exclaimed. "Allison shouldn't talk to such an old man like that."

"I guess he's gotten something wrong again," I said. Everybody in Ashton knows about Mr. Henry. He's editor of our weekly newspaper—the Ashton *Star*—and he's always getting things wrong.

Father came back in the room and his face was redder than his tie. "Somebody wrote some damn fool letter to the paper and signed *my* name!"

"Don't say that, Allison," Mother said.

"Don't say what?"

"*You* know. I've never heard you say that word before—'dim,'" she explained, using an *i* instead of an *a*.

Father looked at her. "*That* was Charlie Henry! He wanted to tell me he had edited the *stronger* points in my letter. Dimmit, Charlie Henry ought to retire. He's too old."

"What was it about?" Mother asked.

"I don't know. I didn't ask him." Father stood up. "Now I've got to go *read* what I've written for the whole town to see."

"Poor Mr. Henry," Arthur said. "I guess he does get things confused. He must be talking about *my* letter."

Father just stared at Arthur. There was a white line round his mouth and I was frightened. "*You!*" he shouted. "Why in the name of heaven did you sign *my* name then?"

"I didn't," Arthur replied sadly. "I signed my initials and last name. I guess they are the same. Never thought of that."

Father didn't say anything. He walked out of the room and in a few minutes the back door slammed. Soon we heard the car whizzing down the driveway.

"Oh, Arthur," Mother said in her "bent twig" tone. "Why do you want to do these things?"

"I didn't think a simple thing like a letter would cause all this," Arthur

Elise Sanguinetti

explained, looking up at the ceiling. His eyes were magnified behind the glasses.

That afternoon the paper arrived. Mother got it first and I followed her into the library. The two of us sat there while she hurriedly and mumblingly read Arthur's letter out loud. It was the strangest thing I had ever heard and every now and then Mother kept saying "Mercy" and "oh, dear." I kept thinking of people all over Ashton reading the letter and I decided then and there I'd never go out of the house again. Arthur had written:

Every morning I go to my little bench beneath the spreading Chinaberry tree and there I sit me down to contemplate the worms. ["Mercy, I hope they don't think Allison wrote that!"] *Who would make a slave of these poorly creatures—working and loving and knocking out their brains? Once of a morning I watched the worms from my little bench and I thought: "I am for you, worm." Yes I am for them. So, too, am I for the other down-trodden of the world—prostitutes and opium eaters and* ["'Mercy!"] *yes, for the lowliest bum. They are my friends. They are your friends. Ashton, Georgia is full of them. They are the town's worms.* ["Oh, dear."]

We must all go toward the centril flame. ["He spelled 'central' wrong."] *This means LIFE. You travel though a dark passage and then in the midst of the jungle there is this little rustling of leaves. Behold! The Centril flame. It behooves us. Be kind, even to little worms. These are my thoughts as I sit upon my little bench. Bums, too, march down the aisle of LIFE. The flame burneth!*

Sincerely,
A. T. WHITFIELD
1 WOODLAND ROAD

We heard the back door close. It was Father. "He's sick," he yelled as he came into the library. "He's crazy as a bat bug! If anybody thought I wrote that rot, they're crazier than he is."

Mother put her handkerchief to her nose. "Now, don't, Allison! Don't let Arthur hear you. He's very proud of the letter, I know."

" 'Sitting on my little bench'!" Father quoted Arthur. "Where is he?"

"I don't know," Mother whispered without moving her handkerchief.

"Maybe he's looking at the worms," I said. Mother looked at me.

"Don't tease him, Felicia. His thought really is quite fine."

"Fine my foot!" Father shouted and stormed out of the room.

Arthur came home just in time for dinner. He had had a new haircut which made the two bumps on the back of his head more noticeable. Also he had his gleaming, simple look again. Father started to say something to him but Mother shushed him. "Not, now, Allison. We want to have a peaceful dinner." Arthur himself brought up the letter. He wanted to know how we liked it. And when no one answered he said he had first written it at school. It was an English theme and he had gotten a C-minus on it. The English teacher had written that he appreciated Arthur's "sentiment" but that his spelling and punctuation were atrocious. Arthur had corrected that, though, before he sent it to the paper.

"That's good," Father said and Mother shushed him again. I guess seeing how proud and everything Arthur was nobody could really say very much. Besides, he had to leave the next day for school. We wouldn't see him again until we went up to get him in June.

The next day we all watched in silence as Arthur boarded the train for Connecticut. He didn't much want to go back, he said. "Best vacation I ever had." As the train rounded the bend and we could see Arthur still waving, I looked up at Father and he was smiling. "My son, my son," he sighed, shaking his head.

We didn't hear very much from Arthur after that. He was studying hard, he wrote, and he had been put on the tennis team. Pretty boring letters and I didn't pay much attention to them. But as May came on and then June we started packing and getting ready for the trip and Connecticut. Arthur had written he wanted us there in time for Class Day. "That's when they give out all the awards."

"We can't disappoint him," Mother said. So on Thursday, Class Day, the three of us were ushered into the school chapel and we sat near the back with all the other families. Arthur and the rest of the boys sat up front. I could just see the back of Arthur's head and I noticed he wasn't grinning and whispering like the rest of the boys. He was looking straight ahead and I knew he was waiting for the moment when his name was called out and he could walk up and receive the Amos T. Caldwalder award. I hoped he would get it. On the trip up Mother told us she prayed that "something grand"

Elise Sanguinetti

would happen to Arthur. "He does deserve something," she said.

How sad the world is! How tragic it is! Arthur didn't get the Amos T. Caldwalder award. Instead, a tall thin boy with a brown crew cut walked down the aisle and shook the Headmaster's hand. The Headmaster even patted him on the back and you could tell by the way the boy was hanging his head that he had all this character. But poor Arthur. I could see the two bumps on the back of his head, which showed he had even cut his hair for the occasion. He didn't look to the left or right and the back of his neck was red. Mother looked down at the gloves in her hand and I guess maybe we felt even worse than Arthur did. He had wanted it so very much.

Arthur's name was called out for being the boy who washed the most windows and "with the best spirit" for the year 1959/60. We congratulated him heartily for this and never mentioned the other award. He was putting up a brave front, beaming and introducing us to his friends. Seymour Yates was there and by the way he was grinning and everything I guess he had been cured. But Arthur said he'd grown tired of old Yates. "He's gotten this new thing now. He keeps thinking he's going to stop breathing and has to run to the window all the time." "How really unfortunate for him," Mother replied. And then Arthur's English teacher came up. His name was Mr. Wilson and he was a tall, sandy-haired man who talked like an Englishman. I was afraid he was going to tell us Arthur hadn't passed, so I kept looking up at the sky. But he started saying these very startling things and I looked him square in the eye. He wanted to tell us he had rarely taught a more interesting "case" than Arthur. He said—and he really believed it—that Arthur (ARTHUR!) was going to be a writer!

"Of course he has a long way to go," Mr. Wilson continued. "There's a little matter of grammar and spelling," he added, patting Arthur on the back.

"Well, that's certainly interesting," Mother said and somehow she sounded a little sad.

They talked some more about this and when Mr. Wilson left we all turned to Arthur. He was happier than I had ever seen him and then he told us he had decided to get a job on the newspaper this summer. He was sure Mr. Henry would let him do something and besides Mr. Wilson had told him that being a newspaper reporter was the best way in the world to become a writer.

I thought I heard Father sigh, but I wasn't sure because somewhere, far away, while Arthur was talking I heard the sound of a train whistle. It sounded long and lonely in the morning sun and all at once I formed this picture in my find. I could see our house in Georgia—a hundred years from now. Thousands of people were flocking to it and, inside, all the rooms were marked off with ropes. People were coming to see the place where Arthur Whitfield lived. *My* brother!

All at once I felt a kind of crying inside and I thought, Oh, Arthur, Arthur. You're going to show everybody yet. You're going to be famous! You're going to be a great, famous man, Arthur! I smiled at him, full of pride and crying. The twig, I knew, was lost forever.

Elise Sanguinetti

Peas

Emma Bolden

I've taught English and creative writing in the South for many years now, and in every class, my students and I end up wandering in the fog of Southern vernacular. One subject always emerges: the usage of the word "y'all," especially in contrast to the term "all y'all." I invariably find myself repeating an explanation I've heard all of my life: " 'all y'all' is the phrase your mother uses when she's talking about a bad trait shared by your father's side of the family." In many ways, "Peas" is built around this idea and how a pre-teen girl comes to recognize and respect it. I remember studying Mendel and Punnett Squares while I was wandering in the fog of my own adolescence, squinting through the low-hanging clouds in an attempt to more clearly see who I was and why I was who I was. Like most adolescents, I also walked around in a state of constant low-key rebellion, always on the lookout for new ways to safely but surely separate myself from my parents. The narrator of "Peas" navigates the same inscrutable landscape, landing finally in the place where I found myself landing, over and over again: the realization that difference means little when it comes to love, and that familial love can survive differences and rebellions, even when one's family seems far more like all y'all than y'all.

In fourth grade, I learned that Gregor Mendel liked to look at peas. When he got tired of looking at peas, he made a breed of bee so vicious that he had to kill them all. I also learned that Mrs. Lucas didn't like it when I asked too many questions about those bees or the way that Mendel killed them. According to Mrs. Lucas, my questions were a distraction and I needed to sit myself down and stay quiet and just listen up good. I was already sitting, so I tried to sit myself down a little more. I stayed quiet and just listened up good as Mrs. Lucas told us how our parents' genes played four-square, bouncing traits back and forth until all of the genes except one were out. I didn't like it.

"Punnett squares! I used to be really good at those," my mother said. I was sitting on the edge of the garden tub so she could help me with my homework while I watched her put hot rollers in her hair. I'd been trying to find a way to inherit my mother's green eyes. Every time, every way I worked the square, my father's genes dominated. Hers receded.

"I'm not doing this right," I said. She took my pen and bowed her head over my notebook. I wrinkled my nose at the smell of her hairspray and watched her work the square as seriously as Amanda Lee worked a game of MASH. I was bad at both. I didn't understand why I couldn't just choose a Mercedes instead of a dump truck, or curly hair instead of straight.

My mother made the clicking sound that meant she was really thinking. "No, that's right," she said, pointing at the square I wanted to be wrong. "Green's recessive. Brown's dominant." She turned back to the mirror, and I watched as she watched herself spread foundation over her cheeks. "I'm still not sure this is working," she said.

"The square?"

"No, the foundation." I tried to make the noise that she made when she was acknowledging something, a funny little tickling sound in the throat. She'd been trying for years to find a foundation that masked the pinks in her cheeks. The woman at the Clinique counter had recommended a yellowish tone, then jabbed her make-up brush in my direction: "Now, this wouldn't work for her. She's completely different. Her skin's so sallow." I smiled the fake smile I used in family photographs and turned away to draw a face on my hand with lipstick and blue eyeliner.

The lady at the Clinique counter was right, though: my mother and I were different, even opposites, in terms of our bodies. Her body was proportional. My body was not. It was short-legged and long-torsoed, which made shopping for the uniform skirts I had to wear every day at Our Lady of the Mount Roman Catholic School embarrassing to the point of impossible. I'd pull the skirt up over the bulge of my thighs, feeling the fabric scratch its way up to my waist, then open the door to show my mother and the sales clerk. They'd tilt their heads in opposite directions, clicking their tongues and scratching their chins until my face got so hot that I had to close the door. I'd refuse to smile or say *m'am* until I was in enough trouble to make my mother tell the version of myself called by her first, middle, and last name that we were leaving immediately and I had best be nice to the lady at the register or else I'd be in even more trouble than I already was, Lord have mercy, was I raised in a fricking barn? It was humiliating, but it was less humiliating than having to stand inside the dressing room doorframe inside of a body that was wide and narrow and large and small in all the wrong places and in ways that my mother could never understand. Her body was the same as her sisters' bodies, her mother's and her grandmothers' bodies, her great and great-great grandmothers' bodies. I imagined them all standing in their long, lean bodies in one long, lean line. I imagined myself in my body, strange and squat and plopped a small distance from them, the disappointing dot at the end of a long and graceful exclamation point.

I followed my mother's work on the Punnett Square, clucking my tongue and tapping my finger against the letters she'd left behind. "Are all of my genes from Dad?"

"Of course not." My mother pointed with her powder puff to the divot where her neck met her collarbone. "There's this mole — and this one." She pushed my right foot on the arch, where it tickled. I was in a mood and wanted to pout, so I pushed my teeth together to keep the laughter in. My cousins all had a mole there. So did my mother and her sisters. One Christmas, we took off our new winter shoes and our wool socks and pointed our feet towards each other. There it was, on every foot, the mole that said that like it or not, we all belonged together in that room, sweating under our red and green sweaters.

"That's just a mole. It isn't, like, eyes or anything." My mother shook her head then opened her eyes wide to put on mascara, clicking a little tune with her tongue against her teeth.

The next day, we learned how Gregor Mendel decided if our earlobes were attached. He also decided if our hairlines pointed downwards and if we could make a tube by folding up the sides of our tongues. My friend Brooke could fold her tongue five times. It was the most impressive thing I'd ever seen. I hated her for it. When I slid into the passenger seat of my mother's burgundy Buick after the three p.m. bell, she asked how my school day was. I answered by glaring at the dashboard.

"Why yes, I had a lovely day," she said in a faux-Montgomery-high-

Southern accent. "Thank you so very much for asking."

I made a *hmph* sound and asked, "Can you roll your tongue?"

"What?"

"Can you roll your tongue? Like in a tube?"

"Oh." She stuck out her tongue. It stayed flat. "Nope." I sighed and pushed my back against the passenger seat, satisfyingly angry with the confirmation that it was all her fault.

Every drive home, I was allowed to ask my mother one question, which she had to answer, no matter what. Most of my questions were about what Amanda Lee told me at recess: "Can you get pregnant from a swimming pool?" "When you get your period, do you really bleed from both of your eyes?" My mother would shake her head and say, "Somebody needs to give that child a book." Since the questions about genetics were technically homework, I figured I could ask two. "Are your earlobes attached?"

"What does that even mean?" We were stopped at a stoplight, so she looked at herself in the rearview mirror to check her lipstick, like she did when we'd finally found an open spot and parked at the mall.

"Does the skin connect your ear lobe to your face," I said with a purposeful slowness, "or does it just hang there?"

"I don't know." She leaned over and I smelled her hairspray again. "You check."

I brushed the hair from her face, careful not to pull at her hoop earrings. "Nope," I said. "They're not attached." I wiggled her earlobe with my thumb, then did the same to mine. "We match."

"Well, I guess I really am your mother, then," she said, flicking a splinter of red lipstick off of her front tooth. "I was worried for a second."

Born and raised in Alabama, Emma Bolden is the author of Maleficae, *a book-length series of poems about the witch trials in early modern Europe (GenPop Books, 2013), and* medi(t)ations *(Noctuary Press, 2016). She's also the author of four chapbooks of poetry*—How to Recognize a Lady *(part of* Edge by Edge, *Toadlily Press);* The Mariner's Wife *(Finishing*

Emma Bolden

Line Press); The Sad Epistles *(Dancing Girl Press); and* This Is Our Hollywood *(in The Chapbook)—and one of nonfiction—*Geography *V (Winged City Press). Her work has appeared in* The Rumpus, The Toast, Prairie Schooner, Conduit, the Indiana Review, Harpur Palate, the Greensboro Review, Redivider, Verse, Feminist Studies, The Journal, Guernica, *and* Copper Nickel, *among other journals. She was the winner of the 2014 Barthelme Prize for Short Prose from Gulf Coast Magazine, the Spoon River Poetry Review's 2014 Editor's Prize Contest, and the Press 53/Prime Number Magazine 2014 Award for Flash Nonfiction. Her work was chosen for inclusion in* Best Small Fictions 2015 *and* Best American Poetry 2015.

The Twenty-Four Years

Julie Borden

Every Alabama woman sees the South through a different pair of eyes. "The Twenty-Four Years" describes a world inspired by my own experience as a synesthete—a world where numbers have color, where math fractures every person and idea into rainbow hues. Each day, I'm reminded of the importance of storytelling. If my experience of the South can differ on such a fundamental level, then what can the many perspectives of Alabama women collectively reveal about our region, our community, and ourselves?

I met twenty-four when I was eight years old. I was a mindfreak in the miniature, a tiny budding *synesthete*—though I wouldn't learn that term until I was sixteen years old. Back then, I had no words to describe the bright colors that flashed before my eyes when I added, multiplied, or even thought of a number. Learning my times tables was like mixing paint with an invisible palette. And so I knew, from a very young age, that twenty-four is an ugly number.

A buttercup erupts from the pavement, yellow petals bright and waxy. This is the color of the number four. A glass of milk with a single drop of red food coloring, stirred, to produce a dirty pink-white. This is the number two. Taken together, the pallid off-white and the sunny yellow form a repulsive, asymmetrical face: the number twenty-four.

Not until I was twelve—exactly half its own age—did I admit that twenty-four was my favorite number. By that time I'd joined my middle school math team, and I realized that twenty-four was divisible by practically every single-digit number. This was admirable, I decided, and significant. Twenty-four was more than its unsightly 2-and-4 exterior. It was 3 times 8—green grass times a rich, matte purple—and 4 times 6—buttercup yellow times denim blue—and a rainbow of other combinations. I could flick through these in my mind, layer by layer, watching them flash by like the shimmering scales of a fish in a pond.

Once let into my life, twenty-four was never far away. Through trial and error, I learned that twenty-four is the approximate number of seconds that I can hold my breath without pestering my lungs. Twenty-four is the number of cracks that I must jump on the way to the mailbox every afternoon. There are twenty-four inches in every two feet, which is the exact distance between the ground and the large freckle above my left knee. There are twenty-four major and minor scales in Western music, and the most common time signatures count out 2, 3, or 4 beats per measure— all divisors of twenty-four.

I spent endless nights with twenty-four in college, poring over research papers in dimly-lit corners of the library, counting every excruciating hour of consciousness in those twenty-four-hour days. My eyes throbbed with exhaustion, but when the birds started chirping around five AM, I would invariably close my books and plant myself in the dewy, lamp-lit grass outside the library. There I waited for the sunrise, a spectacle I couldn't have seen without twenty-four pushing me through the night. And when the sky finally brightened, the denim blue-6's and the buttercup-4's and the regal purple-8's and the 3-green grass illuminated the horizon—my little pieces of twenty-four—igniting the air all around me.

Julie Borden was born in Trussville, AL. In 2009, she left Alabama to pursue her B.A. in English Literature and Creative Writing at Rhodes College in Memphis, TN. She was awarded Rhodes' Allen Tate Creative Writing Award for Fiction in 2013, and two of her poems and the flash fiction "Love Tokens" appeared in the Spring 2013 issue of The Southwestern Review. *Upon completing her undergraduate education, she returned to her hometown and found employment at the University of Alabama at Birmingham.*

Wingflicks
Marian Carcache

Though the story is fiction, "Wingflicks" is probably more autobiographical than any other story I've written. I wrote it during a time of transition. I was no longer young, no longer married, no longer sure of what to do on the path I'd chosen to travel when the circumstances of my life had been different. Like Miranda, I had a foot in two worlds, but wasn't sure either could sustain me. Writing "Wingflicks" helped me sort the grain from the chaff and evolve into the person I wanted to be.

When my mama took me out of school and decided to teach me herself, she bought a botany book at a yard sale and we proceeded to plant things randomly in the backyard. It wasn't until she was satisfied with my knowledge of types of plants and categories of leaves—with the discovery that the cashew is from the poison ivy family and that morning glories, like potatoes, tomatoes, peppers, and eggplants, are nightshades— that she decided it was time to move on to the study of insects.

Her master plan was to work our way up to genetics, the discipline she believed held the key to all truths. "If you can figure out genetics," she said, "then maybe you can beat fate. It's like having a magical amulet that will free you from the spell of the wicked witch, let you out of Rapunzel's tower, turn you back from a frog to a prince." Her philosophy was that if genetically you come from Irish gypsies who were potato farmers or even sheep thieves you could embrace all the strength and spirit of adventure that those genes held, and still create a noble bloodline with your mind. "People used to buy the names of nobility for a price. Read Thomas Hardy," she said.

Mama had been a writer when she was younger and freer, but she had just stopped one day, defeated. She had thrown in the towel on the thing she was meant to be. I could see that, and so could she. With that background, she had no trouble teaching me literature, but sometimes I think she got lost in it. It was that side of Mama's personality, the side that got lost in thoughts, the side that concocted ideas about things other people didn't want to think about, that put division between her and the school system in the first place. It put a division between her and a lot of things, like an easier life. That's a whole other story, though. The one I started to tell was the one about what happened while we were still studying the bugs.

She had not allowed me to do the bug collection in fourth grade when I was still in public school, even though it was considered a huge project and counted a large percentage of that nine-weeks' grade. She did not believe it was okay to teach children to kill an iridescent beetle or a beautiful butterfly in order to make "points" in a teacher's book. The end result was that the teacher made an exception in my case and let me do a photography essay on bugs instead of having to kill real ones and pin them to foam board. My project was so good that it was sent to the nearby university and passed around to seniors studying to be teachers as an example of a "new idea." Furthermore, my project did not stink as did the others after a few days in the hot classroom. And my mother, whom the rest of the world thought of as odd, was once again a heroine in my eyes. But inside every heroine, I've learned since, is a vulnerable and scared girl trying to follow a cryptic trail of bread crumbs left behind by some old crone who may or may not be wise, who may or may not wish her well. Mama wanted things to be different for me. I see that now. Now I understand that if she made mistakes bringing me up, it was because she wanted things to be different for me. She wanted to leave a different kind of trail for me.

One day, a few weeks after we had started having school at home, I found her staring out the window with the botany book open on her lap. I couldn't tell whether or not she had been crying, but she was definitely deep in thought and a sad mood had settled on her heart. I lifted the book from her and read a passage she had highlighted: *Male cicadas have a pair of tymbals on the first abdominal segment. Their abdomen is a hollow, resonating chamber. The female produces timed wingflick signals of broad-frequency sound, something like a rustle or a pop. The wingflick has both a visual and an acoustic effect. As a matter of fact, their song sounds something like the word "pharaoh." Sadly, some of the females die only partially emerged from their nymphal skins.*

When Mama met Eddie Pharaoh, I think she was afraid of dying only partially emerged. Of course, she didn't put her feelings into those exact words, but Mama was beginning to show her age. She was still pretty to me, but in the way a rose is still pretty after it's been beaten down by rain or tossed about by the wind. She said she no longer recognized the face she saw in the mirror, and wasn't sure about anything anymore. She said life was beginning to take its toll. I could tell she sensed that there was something in Eddie that could make her sure again, that could help her find the key to what she had been searching for. But she'd been wrong about keys before.

My father, for example, was a mystery to me—someone she would not even talk about. It wasn't like it was with other kids who didn't have fathers around. My mother never seemed angry with him. She never talked badly about him. She just wouldn't talk about him at all.

Eddie Pharaoh had come with the spring. Mama said he appeared like a god in the middle of the road in front of our house. She was sitting on the porch alternating between pulling up briars from the flowerbed and making mosaic garden tiles from broken dishes, and had a clear view in all directions. She swears he didn't walk up from any direction; he just materialized and asked if she needed help with the yard work. Her hands were bleeding from either the briars or the broken glass, she said, and she noticed him staring at them. When she asked what he charged to mow, he said, "How about a cup of Java?" It wasn't long before Mama had fixed up an old camper in our backyard for Eddie Pharaoh to live in.

That first night that he stayed there, he built a fire in a barrel in front of the camper and pulled chairs around it. Then he brought out a guitar and began to play. When he noticed Mama and me looking out the back door at him, he motioned for us to come join him. He'd already arranged enough chairs around the barrel for the three of us. I looked at my Mama that night, illuminated by the flames from Eddie's fire, and saw the life coming back to her. I knew right then that no matter what else Eddie did or didn't do, he would see to it that my Mama didn't die partially emerged.

Later, Mama would tell me that the months we spent with Eddie Pharaoh were much more valuable than anything the school curriculum could have taught me. "You were learning about *life*, Memorie, about things that *mattered*, from Eddie Pharaoh—we were not just learning to take multiple choice tests." She went on for a while in her rambling way about what *we* learned from Eddie and I quit paying close attention to what she was saying, but this much I do remember. She said, "Descartes believed that to understand a rainbow, he had only to study a single droplet of water. Eddie was like a torrential downpour of experience, even if we *were* uprooted at the end."

That summer Eddie planted a corn patch behind our house, and he trained the wild muscadine vines onto arbors and tended to them so well that they bore a bumper crop of grapes that year. He told Mama that the corn was Silver Queen, and that she was a queen, too. He made her a crown of cornhusks and muscadine vine and crowned her: Miranda, Silver Queen of the Corn Patch. He taught her how to make wine in a churn. They made jelly, and even muscadine ice cream in a freezer with a crank. He said he had worked in agriculture in another life. What that actually turned out to mean was that he had joined the Peace Corps and taught people in poor countries to grow crops that would sustain them. Eddie had been a lot of places. The longer he stayed around, the more lives we heard about. He told Mama that he saw life as a river that should never stop moving or it would become a swamp. He said he had picked up the pieces of his life and put it back together again many times. He also told her that the day she invited him into our lives, she had saved his soul. He said when you've had to reinvent yourself as many times as he had, sometimes your soul got lost in the shuffle, but that she had found his and given it back to him. Mama looked radiant that night, as if she really were a silver queen. What she enjoyed most in life was saving things and putting broken pieces back together, making wholeness from fragments. That was the side of her that was grounded. I figured it probably came from the potato farmer DNA. I sometimes wondered if our lives would have been easier if she'd just planted her feet firmly on the ground, if she had just been content to nurture the roots instead of reaching for the stars, too.

Later that night, back inside our house, we crawled into the iron bed Mama had salvaged from a junk shop and painted gold. We were lying there enveloped in the purple mosquito net she had devised around us, when out of the blue, she said, "Memorie, have we ever talked about

Plato?" Then she told me about how Plato suggested that at one time we were all attached to another being, but that we got separated when Zeus got mad and threw a thunderbolt and now we spend the rest of our lives looking for the other half that would make us whole again. She didn't say that night that Eddie Pharaoh made her feel complete, but I knew where that train of thought had come from. I wanted to ask her if anybody ever *really* found their other half, but I guess I was afraid of what the answer would be, so I lay there silent.

The window was open from the top and I could hear Eddie's music playing in the back yard. Mama was silent, too, but I could tell from her breathing that she wasn't asleep yet either. Rod Stewart's gravelly voice came across the yard singing about a mandolin wind. I knew that if I looked over at her, I would see tears streaming down her face in the moonlight, so I didn't look. I just lay there listening till we both fell asleep with Eddie nearby, keeping watch over us. I wondered whom the tears were for, my daddy or Eddie Pharaoh. I suspected she realized, as I did, that Eddie had told us that night, whether he meant to or not, that one day he would be leaving us behind.

II

At least once a week I asked Mama to tell me the story of her and my father, but every time I asked, she answered, "That's one story better left untold." It was unlike Mama to hold things back, and even more importantly, it was unlike her not to be fair to me. The only reasonable explanation I could come up with for her not telling me about my own beginning, my own flesh and blood, was that he must be a serial killer or kidnapper or subway sniper. Maybe he was a terrorist or a thief of anthrax. In desperation, I finally asked her if he was some kind of monster that she didn't want me to know I had the DNA from, but she only answered, "Not at all," and then followed with what seemed a non-sequitur, "Sometimes we have no choice but to follow beauty, but also wisdom—that is why I could not leave you in the school system. It would have frustrated your destiny."

When I had had as much as I could take of what I had come to view as Mama's elaborate "bull," I went to find Eddie. His stories about his past lives were fantastic but, unlike Mama's ramblings, they had a substance, a foundation in something concrete. He had planted beans and drilled for water. He had also been a fire jumper. He had driven an earthmover in addition to reading the stars. As a matter of fact, he had said it was the stars that led him to us. And it *really had been* a meteor shower he had come here to observe.

"Do you think my father is in prison?" I asked, preparing myself to hear that I did, indeed, carry the DNA of the FBI's Most Wanted.

"I know he is," Eddie answered, "a prison of his own making."

Before I could dig for more information, Mama's voice cut the hot summer air like the howl of a banshee, causing Eddie and me both to jump. When it came to timing, she really did seem to have a second sight, to always know what I was up to. Eddie sent me packing, dying inside to know if he knew more about my father.

Mama was in the corn patch, holding that home school botany book from the yard sale, all charged up to do a lesson on *club fungi*. She was especially excited about rusts and smuts, having found some on the corn Eddie had planted. Mama put on a teacher voice and read from the book, "*a parasite is an organism that lives on another living organism.*" Then without one line of transition, she added, "a parasite is a thing neither you nor I would ever want to be, Memorie. Parasites are a blight." After that cryptic comment, we began our lesson from the book and our "hands-on experience," as she called it, in the garden.

That night, as I stretched out on the glider and put my head in Mama's lap, I watched the fire end of Eddie's Camel cigarette and felt the glider move slowly back and forth as Mama rocked it. The night air smelled like gardenia and honeysuckle and the crickets were busy somewhere in the night rubbing their hind legs together with all their might. I felt sorry that my poor Daddy was off in a prison of his own making instead of being there that night with us. But I also felt happy to be a part of what I saw happening between my Mama and Eddie.

III

After we went home and were in our own bed with the lights turned out, without prompting, my mama said, "Your father loved me, but broke my heart. And in doing so, he broke his own." We were both silent for a few minutes. I didn't dare speak for fear of breaking whatever spell had come over her and caused her to tell me something, anything. Finally, she continued, "The first time I saw him, we were both working a spring arts and crafts festival. I was selling mini ice sculptures and making enough money to get by. I had hit on the idea of freezing water that I had colored and flavored into shapes of things and selling them as novelty refreshment. It was a hot summer and people were buying my pretty frozen turquoise dolphins and pink lemonade mermaids to cool themselves down. He was blowing glass. He offered colored beads and glass animals for reasonable prices and his show really drew a crowd. Like everybody else, I was drawn to his performance. His gift for showmanship was remarkable. I couldn't take my eyes away as he heated the hollow tubes of glass until they were pliable and then gently blew into the open end as if he were blowing life into them at the same time he was shaping them into another, more interesting form, turning one more clear, hollow tube that was just like any other into something marvelous. There were winged horses and unicorns, crouching tigers and sleek panthers. To this day, I'm not sure whether it was the heat from his propane burner or some glitch in my own electrical hook-up, but I looked down to see myself standing in a liquid rainbow that was running from my booth to his. What was left of my inventory was running across the park. My booth was washing away and I didn't even care. When I looked at him, I felt like Dorothy, over the rainbow, face to face with a Wizard."

"What happened next?" I finally managed to ask.

"Well, first he shaped me into another, more interesting form, for which I will always be thankful," she answered and then grew silent.

"And then what?" I finally mustered the courage to ask.

"And then what always happens with wizards once you see behind the curtain," she answered, but gave no details.

IV

In the few months Eddie had been around, our whole world had transformed. Mama was still glowing and the thousand things wrong with the house had been repaired, one thing at a time. Even though we were in a

Marian Carcache

late summer drought, the vegetable garden flourished and there were even roses now running on a trellis at the end of Eddie's camper. Eddie had taught Mama to shoot a target almost at dead center so that she never had to feel powerless, he said. Best of all, though, she didn't cry into her pillow every night anymore after she thought I was asleep. And I was pretty sure by this time that my DNA was acceptable, that I was *not* the love child of a terrorist. Even though the days were becoming almost unbearably hot, the music floated from Eddie's camper every night on the sweetest, coolest summer breeze, and all seemed right with the world. Rod Stewart was wailing out to Maggie May that the morning sun showed her age, but that in his eyes, she was still everything—and my mama's heart seemed lighter than I had probably ever known it to be. She was such a serious mama about some things, but there were the contradictions that never added up: having birthday cake in the freezer most anytime because we loved frozen birthday cake icing, eating beignet with chicory coffee with the heaviest cream for supper at night, but limiting our nightshades and refusing to drink with meals so as not to put out the Fires of Digestion.

It was without warning that the hailstorm came in the hottest part of August. I heard it before I saw it. Hailstones the size of pomegranates were hitting the roof of our house. When I ran to the window to look out—this is the strange part—I saw colored hailstones that were shaped like mythological creatures. Jagged bolts of lightning were splitting the sky, and every now and then a lightning bolt would split one of the hailstones before it hit earth. Those that made it to the earth sizzled and melted as soon as they hit the ground. And only seconds later, the colored streak of water left behind evaporated without a trace. But the strangest thing was that for several seconds each hailstone that fell left a streaked aura in the sky, so the world outside the window looked like a special effect from a movie. The storm came and went in a matter of minutes, and then the afternoon cooled off cooler than it had been in weeks, and the aftermath was beautiful.

Except that when it was over, Eddie was gone—just like my daddy, just like any summer afternoon heat storm.

The camper was banged up pretty badly. We found craters in its roof that looked like a close-up shot of the surface of the moon. The glider had blown over, and the grill Eddie had used to cook on every night had been thrown into a tree and was mangled around the trunk. But the rose vine on the trellis at the end of the camper was untouched. It was covered with blood red roses the size of cabbages, and not a single bloom had shattered.

I begged Mama to call the police or to find Eddie on the Internet since she was so into *research*, but she said there was no need. She said men like Eddie don't want to be found, and that is what makes them rare and wonderful. "They're like the rainbow after a summer storm," she told me with tears in her eyes even as she tried to put on her bravest face. "Let's look up rainbows and find all the ways they are like Eddie," she said, grabbing the World Book. "Listen. *Rainbows are sunlight which has been spread out into a spectrum of colors and then diverted to the eye of the beholder by droplets of water.*" When I stared at her silently, she started to assure me that Eddie would return in his own good time, but I could only think of my daddy, in a prison of his own making, who had not put in an appearance, for whatever reason, in my lifetime—and I blamed her for letting Eddie go, too. I blamed her for sitting there with tears in her eyes doing nothing.

"Shut up," I screamed. "You never make people promise you anything, and you drag me into it with you."

Mama was quiet for a few minutes. Then she said, "You are absolutely right, Memorie. I won't try to bend other people's wills, because we are not parasites, you and I. We are not rusts and smuts who blight the lives of others. We want to be with people who *want* to be with us. So what would *you* advise me to do next?"

But she didn't wait for me to answer.

"Suppose I *did* know how to hold him here with us as tightly as a Venus flytrap holds an insect until it has squeezed the life out of it. Is that what we really want?"

"Yes," I screamed, "maybe that *is* what we want!"

Then just to hurt her I said, "Put me back in school so I can be like other people." Immediately I was sorry. I knew I had gone for her heart with that remark. If there was any way on earth for me to hurt her, it was to tell her that I wanted to be ordinary, that I wanted to be what she had set her heart against being. And I did realize that everything she said about Eddie leaving was true and that she could do little more than she was doing without crossing a line she didn't want to cross. She was making an effort to embrace the calm after the storm. She was standing knee-high in the debris it left behind, hoping for a rainbow—the way she had done my entire life.

The next morning, in a weak effort to make up, I said to her, "We're lucky, Mama. We've seen what must be one of the most spectacular light shows observed on earth."

"I've seen it twice now," she answered as she handed me a cup of coffee with heavy cream so thick that it sat on top and didn't sink, and a piece of frozen cake, an end piece with extra icing. "And I have no doubt that it's not the last light show on earth, especially not for you. So learn from it. It beats the hell out of the SAT as a learning experience."

After that summer, my mama put me back in school. She stopped talking about her theories concerning DNA, standardized tests, the legal definition of insanity in Texas—and she couldn't listen to Rod Stewart again for a long, long time. But she took out her word processor and started back writing fiction.

It was George Jones who kept her company late into the night for what must have seemed like an eternity to the timekeeper in her heart. To this day, I can still close my eyes and picture her out on the screened-in porch, typing away at her stories, a cup of coffee and piece of birthday cake on the table beside her, singing along with George Jones about it being "a good year for the roses."

But now there's Eddie, too, a little older, sitting there on the glider which they've pulled onto the porch, playing his guitar, keeping her company while she writes—adoring the woman he came back to and found wholly emerged.

Marian Carcache's short story collection, The Moon and the Stars, *was published by Solomon & George Publishers in 2013, and her novel,* The Tongues of Men and Angels, *followed in 2015. Her work has appeared in* Shenandoah, Chattahoochee Review, Southern Humanities Review, Bronte Society Transactions, Birmingham Arts Journal, *and other publications, and has been anthologized in* Due South, Belles' Letters, Crossroads: Stories of the Southern Literary Fantastic, and Climbing Mt. Cheaha: Emerging Alabama Writers. Under the Arbor, *an opera made from her short story and for which she wrote the libretto, appeared on PBS stations nationwide, was nominated for a regional Emmy, and was a finalist in the New York Festivals. She is recipient of the 2003-4 Alabama State Council on the Arts Fellowship Award for fiction, and three of her stories have been nominated for a Pushcart Prize. She grew up in rural Russell County, Alabama and now lives in Auburn where she is a member of the Mystic Order of East Alabama Fiction Writers and writes a weekly column for* The Citizen of East Alabama.

Wings

Ramey Channell

*Set in a rural neighborhood much like my own home in rural Alabama, "Wings"
is a story of mystery, revelation, and discovery, in the genre of magic realism.
This story was inspired by the subtle, ever-present influence of nature in all the
surprising and intriguing ways that nature presents itself, and by the breath-taking
experience of new discoveries, both physical and emotional. The basic element of this
story is the emotional connection and response that develops between two characters.
A marvelous story I read many years ago, "A Very Old Man with Enormous
Wings" by Gabriel Garcia Marquez, published in 1955, was an influence on my
writing and my perception of possibilities in real life and fiction.*

She began crying as soon as she realized what she had thought was
a pile of sticks and dead leaves was actually a living creature. Barely
living, maybe, but definitely some sort of … thing. Kneeling beside it, she
dared to place one hand on the brown, leathery carcass, and felt a slow
shallow breath, then another. She sat back and looked around, instinctively
searching for help, but there was no one else. She looked skyward, into
the clear autumn blue, and saw no help in that direction. Just a cold wind
wasting the few final dead leaves off the trees.

She wiped her wet eyes and cheeks with the back of her hand, pulled
her jacket off and placed it over the indecipherable collection of what
she guessed were bones, ligaments, sinew, a large knobby skull, partially
obscured by a thin ochre-colored wing. Perhaps because of the crying, she
had trouble focusing her vision. Not sure what she was seeing, she covered
it anyway, and ran back toward her house.

Other houses were nearby, and surely some of the neighbors were
home. Across the street, the retired couple would be going about their
early morning routine, and the young mother next door with two small
children — but Gloria intuitively rejected the idea of showing this to
anyone. She didn't even know what it was that she would be exposing to
the incredulous scrutiny of others.

The rusted red wheelbarrow was leaned against the side of the house nearest the woods. Her eyes were dry when she grabbed the wooden handles of the wheelbarrow and rushed back under the trees, thinking, "What if it's not still there? Well, what if it *is* still there?" But as soon as she saw the pile of surely some kind of body underneath her mustard colored corduroy jacket, she started sobbing. She rolled the wheelbarrow close to the prostrate thing on the ground, and hesitated, spreading her hands as if in supplication, afraid to touch it.

"Help me," she said. "Help me," addressing the bleak autumn woods around her.

When she got her hands underneath and began to lift, she discovered that it was actually much bigger than she had first thought. Folded and bent and crumpled limbs unfolded and thin almost papery wings expanded. It was surprisingly light, not too heavy for her to lift with no help. Her corduroy jacket slipped off and fell to the ground as she carefully deposited the thing into the metal wheelbarrow. There was an audible crackling sound like the unfolding and rustling of heavy paper. The wings fell away from the face. It was a *face*, brown and lined, almost hideous, but at the same time, not too frightening. Not too frightening, but her hands still shook as she snatched her coat off the ground and covered as much of the thing as she could.

Then she ran for her house, pushing the wheelbarrow and its occupant in a mad dash along the rocky bumpy trail.

When she reached the back porch steps, she moved the yellow jacket and placed her hand tentatively against the general location of where lungs and heart would be. There was a definite heartbeat, and regular slow breaths. Gloria felt a sudden surge of unexpected joy, rejoicing. The heartbeat against her hand had something she perceived as a musical quality, a chiming. Almost bell-like.

She ran up the wooden steps and threw open the back door. Her black and white tomcat strolled out, and he quickly vaulted down the steps, sprang into the red wheelbarrow, and sniffed the head, face, and wings of the unknown thing.

"Shoo, kitty! Shoo, kitty," she scolded, but the cat just looked at her, so she pushed him out of the wheelbarrow. He followed her as she carried

Ramey Channell

the creature through the back door and laid it on the floral cushions of the white wicker sofa. The dry wicker snapped and sighed, a noise very similar to the rustling sounds of flexing limbs and wings. The cat jumped onto the sofa and curled up against the thing resting there, and Gloria blinked her eyes, still having trouble focusing, and let him stay.

She first brought a cup of water, held it to the wide, thin mouth, and felt some calm, almost maternal, gratification to see a few drops being swallowed with no signs of difficulty. Then she didn't know what else to do, so she waited.

When she woke on the hardwood floor, leaning against the white wicker sofa, she gasped and shuffled backwards a few feet away from the startling creature resting there. The wings had opened out to an amazing size, one resting against the back of the sofa and one drooping gracefully down to the floor. The black and white cat purred softly as the enormous wings fanned open and closed, open and closed, stirring the air gently. One long, brown-leaf colored hand moved in a graceful gesture down the cat's sleek back, touching peacefully from head to tail, then back again.

Gloria fumbled for the cup of water and held it against the reclining thing's mouth. Somehow it no longer looked so much like a thing, and now looked surprisingly familiar, like *someone,* someone she had known a long time.

"Why are you crying?"

Gloria was surprised; she hadn't realized she was still crying.

"What are you?" she whispered.

"As you see," was the placid answer.

She blinked her eyes, squinted, and tried to take a closer look. Her vision blurred and spiraled. Tiny points of light flashed, blinked, haloing the reclining figure. The immense wings moved softly.

"Where did you come from?" she managed to ask, watching the movement of the wings and the softening of the brown-papery hand as it stroked the cat.

"Those woods where you found me."

Something about this answer made her unable to stop crying.

"Are you hurt?"

"Oh," a dismissive sigh. "Something struck me. I fell."

"Oh," she sobbed.

Gloria shook her head, not sure about the sadness that swept her, overwhelmed her. Sadness beyond belief, mixed with undeniable joy. And peace. For reasons she couldn't begin to understand, she thought about the sky at night. She saw the cold dark sky at night, filled with stars.

The graceful movement was like the movement of a dancer, rising and lifting. The cat jumped calmly to the floor and began washing himself. Standing at full height, the strange being glanced around the room, made a sweeping gesture with one hand, as if studying the surroundings. Still sitting on the floor, Gloria could clearly hear the musical, bell-like heartbeat.

She wondered if she had missed something, something important that had been spoken. She stood and held out both hands toward the sound of the chiming heartbeat, like warming her hands before a fire. She realized that she had left the door open, the room was cold and filled with a fresh outdoor fragrance, and a pulsing warmth spread outward from the audible chiming heartbeat of the being before her.

She felt herself trying to form a question. Perhaps she had actually spoken a question, but maybe not.

"Yes," was the melodic answer. The pulsing heartbeat reverberated as the strange winged being moved toward the door, leaving a trail of papery dust. "Always."

Ramey Channell's inspiration springs from a world where forests are inhabited by wondrous magical beings, back yards are visited by numinous creatures, and gardens are filled with echoes of enchanted song and laughter. As a child growing up in rural Alabama, she was spellbound by family stories of extraordinary beings and peculiar visitors, told in a setting so close to nature that the stories seemed natural and believable. An award-winning poet and author, her stories and poems have appeared in Aura Literary Arts Review, Alalitcom, Birmingham Arts Journal, Ordinary and Sacred as Blood: Alabama Women Speak, *and many other journals and collections. She was awarded the Barksdale-Maynard Award for her short story "Voltus Electricalus and Strata Illuminata." She has two published novels,* Sweet Music on Moonlight Ridge (2010) *and* The Witches of Moonlight Ridge (2016). *When she's not busy writing, you can find her in her studio or at the kitchen table, painting and drawing, or somewhere out in the yard sword fighting with her ten-year-old grandson.*

The Headmaster's Darlings: A Mountain Brook Novel
Chapter 11
Katherine Clark

This is my favorite chapter from The Headmaster's Darlings, *which is about an English teacher who is trying to educate not just his own students, but his entire community. In this scene where he addresses a ladies book club meeting, we see him at work outside the classroom at a social event attended by some of the mothers and grandmothers of his students. This chapter gives the clearest—and most comic— portrait of someone working within a frivolous society and its traditions while surreptitiously striving to change it for the better. My subject matter and themes found a culminating moment here, as we see most vividly what this schoolteacher is up against in his mission to change his world, and why he bothers. I particularly enjoyed writing this chapter, because when I was growing up in Mountain Brook, where the novel is set, my aunt invited me, her bookworm-ish niece, to accompany her to several of her book club meetings. I found them to be a lot less about literature than I had hoped ...*

Norman Laney hitched up his stomach, shifted in his chair, and seemed on the verge of launching into his talk, when suddenly he shook his head apologetically and said sheepishly, "I'm sorry. But I just can't do this with that man staring me in the face."

As he was the only man in the room, all the ladies turned in a twitter of curiosity to see who he could possibly be referring to. There was no man in the room. The ladies now looked at each other. Had Norman Laney lost his mind? They looked back at Norman, and when they followed his gaze, it led them to the framed photograph of the Haskins family with Ronald Reagan in the White House. This portrait occupied a place of prominence on the secretary in the Haskins' living room, on the wall directly opposite where the largest, sturdiest chair in the Haskins' household had been placed for Norman's use during the meeting of the book club.

Norman shook his head again and laughed in self-deprecation. "There are three things about myself I've never tried to hide," he said, smiling hugely. "I'm fat, I'm poor, and I'm a Democrat!"

The ladies erupted into laughter: Norman Laney was always a hoot. As far as they were concerned, he could lead every meeting of their monthly book club, if only he would.

"I mean, maybe he does something for you all," said Norman. "But he sure doesn't do anything for me."

The ladies positively cackled with glee, as Hailey Haskins scurried over to remove the photograph and place it in one of the drawers to the secretary. She was young; she didn't understand what she'd done wrong, why all the ladies were laughing, or what Norman Laney was talking about. It was a stroke of bad luck for her that he'd been asked to substitute for the other speaker who'd backed out. Norman Laney was such a wild card. Of course, this could turn out in her favor, especially if he told that hilarious Fannie Flagg story someone had recounted last week, about Norman Laney and Fannie Flagg in the back seat of a Buick driven by Miss Alabama's parents, all the way from Birmingham to Atlantic City to see Birmingham's own Miss Alabama, Delores Hodgens, compete for Miss America. Hailey Haskins had always loved watching Fannie Flagg on *Hollywood Squares*, and her opinion of Norman Laney had risen accordingly. Otherwise, she had never understood why some people were so crazy about the man.

But as for the photograph of Ronald Reagan: all she knew was that several of her husband's business partners at Hammond Coal had framed pictures of their family with Ronald Reagan in the White House, but not everybody did, so it seemed to her quite a score to have such a prized memento of their trip to Washington last year and their generous donations to the Republican Party every year.

Norman, on the other hand, understood quite well that he had a Fool's license and was expected to use it, that the ladies loved it when he was outrageous, when he said and did things no one else they knew would ever dream of saying or doing. It gave them something to recount to those who weren't there, as if they had witnessed something scandalous. And it gave them something to tell their husbands at the dinner table, as if they, too, had been out in the real world that day. But at the same time, Norman

Katherine Clark

thought, it wouldn't hurt if even one of these ladies had been made to think twice about Ronald Reagan and the Republicans. Norman considered himself an educator in the broadest sense of the word, and used any opportunity that came to hand for spreading enlightenment.

"Now. Have I ever told y'all my favorite story about Flannery O'Connor?"

The ladies shook their heads in happy anticipation. They would much rather hear Norman's stories than any talk about the book they had not had time to read.

"She was the guest speaker once at Birmingham-Southern when I was a student there. I won't say how long ago this was."

The ladies tittered as he knew they would.

"She was a pitiful looking thing then, on crutches," he continued. "The lupus had really hobbled her, though she could still get around. And the poor woman was afflicted with more than just a dread disease." He paused for effect, as if trying to find the right words. "Let's just say," he continued, "that her physical appearance created no mystery as to why she died an old maid."

The ladies laughed in appreciation, as their own major accomplishment in life had been to achieve marital status. Further, they all harbored the view that those women who "did" things, like Flannery O'Connor, were the ones who couldn't get a husband.

"But I adored her! I adored her!" Norman was quick to assure them. "After her talk, she took questions from the audience. This one young man stood up and said: "Miss O'Connor."" Here Norman adopted the officious manner of a self-satisfied know-it-all. "Miss O'Connor," he repeated in the new voice. "Do you think the shift away from teaching humanities in the public educational system has discouraged too many of our young people from pursuing creative writing?"

Now Norman changed into his Pratt City drawl, which was close enough to Flannery O'Connor's rural Georgia accent. "'Naw-aw-aw-aw,'" he said, dragging out that classic Southern syllable while endowing Flannery with a pronounced overbite. "'Naw-aw-aw-aw, I don't think the public educational system has discouraged *enough* of our young people from pursuing creative writing!'"

This time the ladies laughed because they knew they were expected to. This was obviously the punch line, though they didn't quite get it. Norman could tell that his story had fallen flat—he should have known this was not the right audience for it, which was undoubtedly why he'd never told it before to this particular group. But he just couldn't whip out his Fannie Flagg story for the ten thousandth time. He'd told it again last week at some other ladies' meeting club—he'd already forgotten which one it was, but he knew that many of those same ladies were sitting in front of him now. So he quickly veered into his prescribed talk, and the ladies switched into their dutiful listening mode, sitting a bit too still with their eyes a bit too absolutely focused on their speaker. (They did not want to be accused later of nodding off during Norman Laney's talk.) This part of the occasion was actually expected to be a bit dull, or it would not qualify as educational, and the ladies would not feel as if they'd earned the treats Hailey Haskins' maid was bringing in from the kitchen and placing on the table in the dining room as Norman Laney spoke about Flannery O'Connor's story "Everything that Rises Must Converge," in the living room.

It was only when he began his discussion of the violent confrontation between a white lady and a black woman on a Georgia bus that he realized his mistake. What four A.M. demon had driven him to pick this particular story when there were so many others in the collection? No doubt at that mystical hour of the night/day, he had flattered himself that Flannery needed him now every bit as much as she'd once needed her editor and publisher. Because it was the likes of him that took the ideas from her pages and crammed them through the thick skulls of those who would never read them. But at the un-magical hour of two-thirty in the afternoon, he was overcome with regret that he had chosen one of the more provocative stories, guaranteed to chafe the sensibilities of both the white ladies and the black help who were there for an event over which he alone presided at the moment. Why did he always have to take these huge risks and push things to the very brink, the absolute limit? His mother was right; this particular form of excess would be the undoing of him one day, if it had not undone him already.

Briefly he looked up from the book he was using, made a swift scan of the room, and quickly determined that he needn't worry, at least as far

Katherine Clark

as the white ladies were concerned. Years of slavery, racial injustice, the Civil Rights Movement, and the Montgomery bus boycott might as well not have happened. The burden of Southern history was not lying heavily on anyone's consciousness in the room today. In fact, there was very little consciousness at all. The eyelids of some of the ladies *were* actually flickering as he spoke, but apparently not in recognition that the story's themes had any bearing on the reality of their lives. Rather, they appeared to be dozing. Really, thought Norman with disgust, not even Cheever could have done justice to the mentality that lay sleeping before him. It was one thing not to understand why the plane had crashed near Philadelphia because it hadn't rained in Shady Hill. Surely it was quite another not to be aware of the race riots in Birmingham because you lived in Mountain Brook.

"Just as well," Norman tried to console himself. Perhaps some of his ideas or words would drift unnoticed into some of the sleeping brains and take root, sprout, even flourish and bloom despite the unfertilized soil. This was a phenomenon not unknown to him in his paying job as a teacher of young people. It was like scattering wildflower seeds in untended gardens. And given that he would never marry and have children, this was the only way that he would ever spread any of his own seeds. All he could do was throw whatever he had as far and wide as he could, and hope that some of it produced blossoms. Invariably it actually did, and sometimes in the most unexpected places. Seeds that landed in the cracks of the sidewalk, for example, could still produce beautiful flowers that were even more important than the ones in the garden because these offset and sometimes even redeemed the dull concrete. The seeds that lodged beneath the concrete were actually the most important of all, because these had the potential to break through the hardened crust and change the landscape. And this, after all, was his mission in life.

As soon as he had concluded, the ladies rose with a grateful sigh and followed quickly after their hostess, who knew that her moment had finally arrived. Only old Dot Trimble, bless her heart, came up to him instead.

It wasn't clear whether she had read the assigned book either, but she said, "It makes me so sad when a creative genius like Flannery O'Connor or Proust or Keats suffers from a terminal illness. I wonder why those who have so much to offer have to have their lives cut short. Then there's me, who has lived forever and never been a bit of good to anybody."

"Hush, darling," said Norman, leaning over to her good ear. "I'll tell you a secret." He lowered his voice. "If this house caught on fire in the next five minutes, and I had to choose one person to save from the burning building, it would be you." And this was true, too, or almost, since Libba Albritton was among the group, and she was taking him with her to New York in two days' time.

"You are nothing but a shameless flatterer," said Dot, delighted none-theless.

"Am not," said Norman firmly. "You know what else?" he said confidentially. "The longer she's gone, the more I miss Bella Whitmire."

Dot nodded sympathetically. She missed her dearest friend more than she missed her departed husband.

"I hate to sound like an old crank," said Norman, "but I think after your generation, they must have changed the baby formula and left out a key ingredient. Because the younger generations of ladies do not equal yours."

"It's your mother," said Dot graciously if somewhat inexplicably. "You put the younger generation next to her, and of course they don't measure up. No one does."

"You do, darling," he patted her hand. "You do."

By now they could hear the exclamations of delight coming from the dining room as the other ladies spied the food. When Norman and Dot Trimble joined them, he could see at a glance why. It was not the usual spread found at the other homes hosting the monthly book club meetings. Nothing offered on the table was homemade, and nothing came from Brody's, as far as he could tell. As the ladies quizzed their hostess, Norman learned that Hailey Haskins had ordered from that new bakery in Vestavia, of all places, and from a caterer who had recently opened up way out 280. He tried a lemon square. "Delicious!" he proclaimed with his mouth full, but only because Hailey Haskins had been eyeing him anxiously. His was the most important verdict in the room. But really, his mother's lemon squares were superior, and any good Southern hostess really should make her own. The food so proudly displayed on the starched linen tablecloth and the gleaming silver trays was just like the rest of the house: too perfect.

Even the lace cookies were somehow perfectly round instead of imperfect and irregular, as lace cookies were supposed to be.

He had never been to the Haskins home before, and it was the kind of Mountain Brook house he detested, furnished in that generic upper middle class taste produced by items of décor from shops specializing in bridal registries and expensive wedding gifts. There was no work of art and not a single book anywhere in the living room except for the large atlas on the coffee table. And no doubt that was there because some decorator had told Hailey she needed a book for the table, and Hailey had thought any big book would do. The walls had lavishly framed prints of ducks and birds. Obviously the prized object was the photograph of Reagan, and he had made her put that away. Everything else he could do his best to ignore, but he simply could not countenance that. He thought he also might point out to her as he was leaving that the shelves which flanked her fireplace were not for mass-produced though pricey knickknacks, but for books— preferably ones which had been read.

Alarmed to see Norman Laney scowling while standing empty-handed in front of a table full of food in her dining room, Hailey hurried over with a plate containing a choice selection of delicacies.

"Oh, thank you," he said with perfect politeness. "I've been trying to resist, because I really must get back to campus."

Hailey only nodded and left quickly, as if afraid to attempt a conversation she knew she would not be equal to. In a sense she was exactly like her house: perfect in a bland, generic way, and utterly lacking in any individual appeal or attraction. Everything about her figure was ultra petite and in exact proportion to everything else. "Cute" was the word that came to Norman's mind, and he hated cute. Not a single hair was out of place in her blonde bob, which was her generation's equivalent of the bouffant hairstyle favored by the older ladies. But her hair had been sprayed into place just as thoroughly, and the blonde was a single uniform shade with no alternation of high and lowlights. Clearly she was not capable of understanding the need for the subtle variations which produced the best effect. Her clothes were impeccable and her makeup was meticulous, especially as she refrained from eating any of the goodies which inevitably smeared the lipstick and left traces of powdered sugar in the strangest places. The diamond solitaire of her wedding ring was not over-large in and of itself, but was accompanied by so many stone-studded bands that her finger looked like it had been colonized by diamonds. It was what Norman privately called the Junior League ring finger. Even her very name had that cutesy effect. Of course, she could hardly be blamed for that, but with her, he couldn't help wondering if one of the things she had looked for in a husband was how well his name would go with hers. Norman despised cutesy names and could have throttled Bebe Bannon's parents, for example, who had given their daughter the stately and lovely name of Elizabeth, only to vulgarize it unforgivably.

Hailey was thirty to forty years younger than most of the ladies in this particular book club, who belonged to a generation of women who didn't read a book from cover to cover any more than they washed their own hair. But it was Adelaide Whitmire's book club, and therefore the only one Hailey had wanted to join. To a degree Norman pitied her, because she came from Opelika, Alabama, and had all the insecurity of the small town girl who needed to prove herself equal to Mountain Brook. Norman had once been in a similar position himself, when he needed to make it in Mountain Brook. But at least he'd had the good sense to know that the only way he was going to make it was by being who he was, and not by trying to pretend that he'd always been one of them.

This poor woman was trying too hard in all the wrong ways. As he bit into a beautiful but boring brownie, he was reminded of Food Rule #1 in the Deep South: Taste was more important than looks. Southerners would serve or eat the most hideous-looking glop as long as it tasted good. This food looked too good and didn't taste good enough. She was trying to impress them, trying to make her mark—instead of trying to feed them well. That was a costly mistake in more ways than one, as clearly all the food was expensive and designed to look like it. Then the way she hovered around the table—as if to facilitate and gauge her success—without eating, drinking, chatting, or seeming to enjoy herself in any way—was all wrong. As if she were merely part of the help. She would never make it in Mountain Brook this way.

He would have his work cut out for him with her children, who were currently in the lower school at Brook-Haven. Of course she had the per-

Katherine Clark

fect millionaire's family, a boy and a girl, whose first names both started with H. He'd have to see to it that they both took his "Art in the 20th Century" class. Perhaps some of its instruction would educate the parents as well as the children. Often he could reach the parents by reaching their children. Parents always had a second chance at education when their children were in school, and he did his best to make his lessons penetrate beyond the boundaries of his classroom. By the time he got through with the Haskins children, he sincerely hoped the parents would have something else on their living room wall besides ducks and birds, and something else on the shelves next to the mantel besides empty vases and glass figurines.

"We were wondering, Norman, if anybody had heard anything from poor Fee Keller."

It was Sissy Lockhart, one of his least favorite people, though everyone else loved her as much as they pitied her for the way her three daughters had turned out: one a suicide, one an alcoholic, and the other a serial divorcée who had lost custody of Sissy's only grandchildren two divorces ago. These grandchildren now lived in Louisiana, and if she ever saw them, no one heard about it. What everyone else loved was what he couldn't stand: the perpetual cheerfulness that never dimmed even as tragedy struck again and again and again. She was the party girl who never grew up, for whom disaster was no more than a bad grade on a test that would not deter her from attending the fraternity party tonight or dampen her spirits while there. If she had no other invitations, she would be at the Mountain Brook Country Club tonight playing bridge, as she did on any of her "free" nights. The dire struggles and sad fates of her grown children had impacted her no more than had their presence in her life as children, whose needs and desires had never curtailed her social schedule. To Norman, this was not a heroic sunny disposition. This was utter inner vacancy. This was the meaning of the word "vapid." Today she was clearly enjoying herself as much as always, her lipstick smudged beyond repair and her upper lip twinkling with sugar crystals.

"Haven't heard a word," said Norman, wiping his own mouth fiercely.

"You don't mean it," said Sissy, taking a large bite from a chocolate petit four, which left dark crumbs lodging contentedly in the corners of her mouth. "I thought if anybody knew anything, it would be you."

"Oh, I didn't say I didn't *know* anything," said Norman provocatively. "Just that I haven't heard from *her.*"

"Oh, so you *do* know something," said Sissy, placing her china dessert plate on the table. "Wait a minute." She turned around and snagged the arm of Grace Newcomb. "Norman knows something about Fee!"

This news travelled fast, and the ladies who had earlier avoided Norman on the subject of Flannery O'Connor now gathered near him as the subject had changed to Felicia Keller. Gossip trumped literature every time.

He shrugged noncommittally. "Finally I just picked up the phone and called her sister."

A collective "ah" rippled through the group.

"Said I was worried I hadn't heard from Fee and just wanted to check in."

As he paused, the anticipation of the ladies mounted almost palpably. "You all remember Monica."

The ladies murmured and nodded expectantly, though Monica had not lived in Birmingham since going away to college many many years ago— decades ago—and almost never came back to visit. Still, she had been "Zsa-Zsa Gabor," and as such, was of course utterly unforgettable.

"She's Monica van Hook now. As in van Hook Pharmaceuticals."

Everybody knew that. What they had not known was that Fee would just up and move in with her sister like that. She had told some of her "friends" that she would be visiting her sister at New Year's. They had thought nothing of it; she visited her sister fairly regularly throughout the year. But she had not told them she wasn't planning to come back. It was a bold, brave move that had taken them all by surprise.

"Monica just laughed and said she hardly heard from Fee either."

Now there was a collective gasp. The ladies didn't know what to expect at this point.

"I thought Fee was staying with her sister," said Libba Albritton sharply.

"Well, she is," said Norman. "But they're hardly under the same roof. And the guest house on the van Hook estate in Palm Beach is bigger than most residences in Mountain Brook, even on the most exclusive streets."

Katherine Clark

This sobering reminder of the larger world outside Mountain Brook actually silenced the ladies.

"No need to worry about Fee, I was told. She's the belle of the ball whose only concern is which invitations to accept. Supposedly she's got three suitors vying for her attention already. And one of them is a van Hook. A cousin of Monica's husband. His wife died last year. Apparently he is absolutely smitten with Fee and has been for some time. Long before his wife finally passed away. She'd had leukemia for years, I'm told, and lived like an invalid."

There was a moment of profound, thunderstruck silence before a buzz broke out all over the room as the ladies turned to one another for help in processing this startling information. But now that Fee was once again the object of male attention and desire, one thing was automatically established: it was no longer "poor" Fee but "darling" Fee. And no doubt about it: van Hook was a better name than Keller. The "van" conjured the notion of European aristocracy, if not royalty. And the van Hook fortune made Frank Keller look like a mere pauper.

"I just hope she *enjoys* herself," said Sissy to no one in particular and everyone at large. "That's what my mother told me, and I wish I'd listened. Just go out with all of them, keep them guessing, make each one think he's your favorite, and do it as long as you can get away with it. Because as soon as you pick one, you have to settle down with him, and then all the fun stops."

The ladies were glad to be able to vent their confused emotions into a big giggle.

"I just think it's absolutely grand that Fee is getting a second chance like this," continued Sissy. "She should make the most of it she can, and when it comes time to make a decision, pick the one with the most money and hope the good times last forever!"

This pronouncement was nothing more than a statement of the philosophy by which all the ladies had guided their young lives. However, they murmured in approval of Sissy's sweetness and uncomplicated good nature. She had suffered a series of mortal blows in her own life, and yet managed to be so kindhearted; it was a lesson to them all. Most were now dealing with some degree of envy that Fee had gained a second chance to make it work out even better for herself than it had her first time around. Most would have welcomed such a second chance themselves, if only because their lives as sought-after belles had been so much more fun than their lives as married women. Despite the joys they had known as wives, mothers and grandmothers, the happiest time of their lives had taken place when they were teenagers. The idea that a middle-aged woman could reprise that whirlwind girlhood of parties, dances, dates and dinners had never occurred to them. The fact that Felicia Keller was actually reliving those years, and they were not, was mildly devastating.

Norman popped a dark chocolate truffle in his mouth and decided on one cup of coffee before heading back to the school. Sissy Lockhart always depressed him, and just now he felt his spirits plummet to the point he even wondered if life weren't trying to usher him away from Mountain Brook for his own good as it had with Fee. Of course Fee had her faults— who didn't?—but nothing like the complete hollowness of Sissy Lockhart. At least Fee had raised her children, and had three successful sons to show for it. One on Wall Street, one in the MBA program at Northwestern in Chicago, and one a vice president in the Hong Kong office of a Fortune 500 company whose name momentarily escaped him.

True, it was much easier to raise sons than daughters in this Southern society, and Sissy's daughters had been caught in the very gears of social change, raised to live a life like their mother's, but unable either to embrace that existence or reject it fully. Mountain Brook could be treacherous for women. Fee was better off out of it and maybe he would be too if he took the job at Shelby State and used the extra money to buy a house somewhere outside of Mountain Brook. He often wondered why he even bothered with these people, why he didn't follow the advice he offered so forcefully to his students—to think big, to aim high, and above all, get out into that larger world.

But as he gazed around the dining room at the ladies who had put on their silk dresses and pearls and had their hair done for him, he was reminded of why he did bother. They had let him in to their world, misbegotten, malformed, misshapen beast that he was. They had accepted him and embraced him. Not all of them had, but enough had been able to see the worthiness of the soul buried beneath all those layers of fat. This proved there was at least a tiny spark of goodness buried beneath all those layers of injustice in a society engineered for the comfort and prosperity of the white and the rich. But that tiny spark was enough. Its mere existence showed that the whole society was capable of redemption, and now that he was in, his job was to be the agent of change and transformation. It was up to him to show them the path to salvation, and through their sons and daughters, he would deliver them from their own evil. After all, if they could overcome a prejudice against fat people, perhaps they could overcome their other prejudices as well.

Turning around, coffee cup in hand, he saw Adelaide Whitmire sidling up to him, her mouth in downturn as usual.

"I knew it was a mistake to let that girl into the book club," she grumbled.

"Why? What has she done? This looks perfectly lovely to me," said Norman, gesturing at the bounty laid out on the dining room table. When it came to Adelaide, he couldn't stop himself from playing devil's advocate.

"Before we started, I reminded her to ask for any questions and open up the discussion after your talk. You saw what happened. She completely forgot. As if the book club were just an excuse for a social occasion."

"Well, darling," he said mildly. "She's just nervous. It's her first time to be hostess. She'll learn."

Adelaide muttered something unintelligible.

"Was there something *you* wanted to say about Flannery O'Connor?" he asked innocently, popping another dark chocolate truffle into his mouth.

"And you were quite right to make her put that photograph up," said Adelaide.

"I've always said I wouldn't even want to be in the same room as Ronald Reagan," said Norman, "and I'm not about to start making exceptions now, not even for a photograph."

"It's terribly tacky," said Adelaide. "That sort of thing should be in the study, not in the living room."

Norman raised his eyebrows. "What makes you think these people have a study?" he asked. "I don't see any evidence anywhere that they've even read one book, let alone keep a collection of books in a room set aside for that purpose."

"At least he could put it in his office at work."

"Oh, I can think of other places to put that photograph," said Norman.

"Have you talked to Valerie lately?" said Adelaide. It was one of her many prerogatives in life to be able to change subjects abruptly without warning or preamble.

"No, I haven't. Why?" He sipped his coffee. At least this was good and strong. A New Orleans blend, with chicory.

"What about that teacher of yours? What's his name? Have you seen him?"

"Ellis. Mark Ellis. I see him every day." He took another slurp of coffee. And those dark chocolate truffles weren't bad either. Best thing on the table. He popped a third one into his mouth.

Adelaide clenched her jaw. "I need to know what's going on between them," she said.

"No, you don't," he said cheerfully.

"Norman, I insist you tell me everything you know right this minute."

"I don't know anything," he protested, setting his cup down on the sideboard. "And I don't want to know anything. We've been through this before. I make it a point never to get involved with anyone's love life. Those who've never managed to have a love life of their own have no business interfering in anyone else's."

Adelaide grimaced with displeasure.

"Libba only *thinks* it was Mark Ellis she saw with Valerie at Highlands Bar and Grill," he said soothingly. "But it could have been anybody. I didn't even know Libba had ever laid eyes on Ellis. If she has, it's only been once or twice, and she could easily be mistaken."

"Libba Albritton has eagle eyes," said Adelaide grimly. "She's never mistaken."

This was true.

"Look Adelaide," said Norman decisively. "You might as well accept reality. *If* Valerie *ever* gets married at all, it will be on her own terms to the man of her own choice."

"Dirk Pendarvis refuses to give me a copy of your contract," she said.

"That's probably because I shouldn't have given *him* a copy of it. It's not fair of me to abuse Dr. Plumlee's good faith in making me such a generous offer—"

"I think we should sue him. I hardly think it's legal for him to offer you a contract when you're under contract to us. Dirk laughed at me but I made him promise to look into it."

"You wouldn't really dream of going to that other place, would you, Norman?" said Grace Newcomb, breaking into the conversation which a scowling Adelaide tried to indicate was her own and hers alone. "What's the name of the place? I know they've offered you a lot more money—"

"Shelby State," he said.

"Shelby State," she echoed, nodding.

"Oh!" exclaimed Sissy. "I can't imagine Brook-Haven without you." As she bit into an almond cookie which crumbled awkwardly in unexpected ways, the other ladies nearby chimed in agreement.

"Shelby State has made Norman a very generous offer of a position in the English Department which the Brook-Haven School could never hope to match in terms of the salary," said Adelaide, drawing herself up to take command of the conversation. *She* was the one on the Board; *she* was the one who knew the details; *she* was the one who should be doing the talking.

"The only reason Norman would even consider the other position has nothing to do with money. The problem is the current headmaster at Brook-Haven School. He has urged Norman to take the other job—we're not sure why—but we suspect it's because Norman has been critical of his performance, and he wants Norman out of the picture. Naturally, this places Norman in a difficult predicament since the headmaster has made it publicly known he wants Norman to go."

"Can't you just fire the headmaster, then?" said Grace Newcomb, as the other ladies murmured their approval.

Adelaide held up her hand. "I can't go into confidential Board matters," she said grandly. "But I did ask the chair of our Board as much myself. And he said—" she paused and looked out over her audience— "we had to wait for the annual meeting and give the headmaster a chance to explain himself before any action is taken."

"I don't see why," said Libba emphatically. "He was clearly just hoping to shuttle Norman out quickly and quietly without much ado. Now it's blown up in his face and I don't see why we have to give him all this time to come up with some reason for wanting Norman out. He's had plenty of time to come up with some *very* creative reasons."

Adelaide drew herself up in preparation for launching another speech, but a babble of voices took over.

". . . never even met the man, have you?"

". . . don't believe I'd know him if I saw him."

". . . contract is up anyway at the end of this year."

". . . imagine why anyone wouldn't love Norman Laney."

". . . certainly isn't from around here."

Libba's voice broke through. "I think he should have been confronted immediately, and if he couldn't give a valid reason for setting himself up against Norman, he should have been advised that his contract would not be renewed at the end of this school year."

"Oh, Libba," said Sissy. "You are so smart."

"That might have left us without a headmaster in the middle of the year," said a prune-faced Adelaide.

Libba shrugged. "So what? Can't see that this man will be any great loss, whenever he leaves. Old Dr. Meacham meant for Norman to take over when he finally retired three years ago. Norman's the one who runs the school anyway. And *that's* why the headmaster wants him out. Meanwhile, we're giving him ample time to come up with something to say against Norman. This man could cause us a lot of trouble."

This time Adelaide's voice succeeded in rising above the babble. "We don't have to renew his contract no matter what," she stated flatly.

"Yes," agreed Libba. "But if he besmirches Norman's reputation, that could make it hard for Norman to become the headmaster."

That prospect silenced Adelaide, who had clearly never considered this angle before.

"But what could this man possibly say against Norman?" said Sissy.

"He could say I spend too much time off campus leading ladies' book clubs!" said Norman. "When I ought to be in the classroom teaching!"

There was general laughter followed by a cacophony of voices each coming up with their own theory.

"Didn't you take a month off last spring to prepare for the Shakespeare Festival?" said Grace.

"And I know you weren't supposed to use the gym last year when you read 'Christmas Memory,' " said Roberta Birdwell, wagging her finger playfully.

"Not to mention that picture of me in the new brochure is hardly a helpful advertisement for the school," said Norman.

"Is it true this headmaster person—whatever his name is—tried to call off the college tour this year?"

"What did Norman decide about that stomach surgery?" said Sissy.

"I didn't see that headmaster at the Sloss Furnaces exhibit last month."

"He certainly wasn't at the Orange Bowl Gallery opening when I went in September. That was one of the best shows Norman has had in a while."

"I think he must be jealous of Norman."

"He knows how much everyone adores Norman."

"Is Norman still taking me to Europe this summer?" said poor dear old deaf Dot Trimble, who could make out only that something was amiss—something about something being called off—and hoped it wasn't her trip to Europe.

"I just hope we haven't given this man the only weapon he needs," said Libba darkly. "Which is time. Time to come up with something to save his own skin at the expense of Norman's."

"It would take a lot to skin me," said Norman. "I dare anyone even to attempt it!" The ladies thought this was hilarious.

The only one not contributing to the raucous free-for-all was Hailey Haskins, who went around along with her hired help collecting soiled plates, crumpled napkins and lipstick-stained cups half full of cold coffee. Although pleased by a sense of success generated by the chattering voices, she would have preferred it if the ladies had continued to talk about her food, and where she got it, her home furnishings, and where they came from, as they had at the beginning of the social hour. Still, she was confident that her little party had given the ladies much enjoyment in the moment and much to talk about later, and that was the main thing. Her success today as a hostess would be known.

"But you *are* planning to stay at Brook-Haven?" insisted Grace. "The extra money offered by the other place isn't going to tempt *you*, is it?"

"Oh, what do I care about money?" said Norman, whose car would be in the shop for an estimated minimum of $800 in repairs while he was out of town the following week. "But I really can't remain at the school with a headmaster who apparently has taken it into his head to oppose me on so many important fronts. It's either him or me, but one of us has to go. So far the Board has given me every support . . . we'll just have to see what the headmaster has to say for himself next month."

"But honestly, Norman," said Sissy. "What could this man possibly say?"

"Well," sighed Norman. "I haven't murdered anybody and I haven't raped anybody, but otherwise, I'm probably guilty of everything else. So who knows? Now, ladies, I've got to fly, or the headmaster really *will* have something on me."

He blew kisses around the room and grabbed Adelaide's hand to give it a good-bye squeeze. He was also hoping that she, as this year's treasurer of the club, would remember to give him the $100 check he was due for being the speaker this month. But as she had forgotten to give him his check two months ago, he was not surprised when the idea never crossed her mind. It would only be at the end of the year, when there was a large, unexpected surplus in the account, that she would call him up to find out why, and he'd suggest that maybe she'd forgotten to pay the speakers. He would point out off-handedly that he, for example, had never received a check, and assure her that although it didn't matter so very much to *him,* maybe the others . . . except he was hoping to have that little extra for his trip to New York.

Well, he had to concede, even without the honorarium, the outing had been worthwhile and had served a purpose. Elizabeth Elder's game plan had now been executed in full. It only remained to be seen what, exactly, Tom Turbyfill was going to reveal, and whether this was enough to turn the tide against Norman Laney.

Katherine Clark was born in Tuscaloosa when her parents were attending the University of Alabama, and grew up in Birmingham. She attended high school

Katherine Clark

there at The Altamont School, then went on to earn her college degree from Harvard and a Ph.D. from Emory in American literature, with a dissertation on William Faulkner. She is the co-author of two oral biographies of Alabama characters: Motherwit: An Alabama Midwife's Story, *with Onnie Lee Logan, and* Milking the Moon: A Southerner's Story of Life on this Planet, *with Eugene Walter, which was a finalist for a National Book Critic's Circle award. Her debut novel,* The Headmaster's Darlings, *is the first in a series of Mountain Brook novels, based on the community in Birmingham where she grew up. It was the 2015 winner of the Willie Morris Award for Southern Fiction. The series is being published by Story River Books, the fiction imprint founded by Pat Conroy at the University of South Carolina Press. She has recently completed work on an oral biography of Pat Conroy, forthcoming from the University of South Carolina Press. After 15 years of teaching literature at the college level, mostly in New Orleans, Clark now devotes herself full time to writing. She lives on the Gulf Coast.*

Snakeskin

Loretta Cobb

"Snakeskin" is my favorite "little darling" ever, and its birth in this anthology should encourage any writer. The story is based on a chapter in my 2016 novel, How Can I Keep from Singing? *A variant on this chapter was originally set in San Antonio; I felt the characters were strong, the conflict was intense and the Texas setting was authentic. However, since I had to trim my novel for publication, any scenes outside Alabama had to go. As I was working on the novel, the late Jake Adam York solicited an Alabama story for the journal* Thicket; *being asked for a story made me feel more adventurous as a writer and willing to try braver, more experimental writing. Jake died before the story could be published, and so I am extra pleased that its publication here honors him and that encouragement.*

Bonita knows she hasn't imagined the voices. Not voices, really, but a wisdom that comes with waiting. Trees talk her through the wilderness of her childhood. In her 30's, she hikes through thick woods to a sanctuary of pine needles. She lies on autumn-damp leaves, listening, and gazes beyond blood-colored leaves to the sky. In her 50's the loss of her mother takes her to the cemetery—the comfort of its green, rolling hills and the knowledge that her mother lies there, attending.

Now, tree frogs outside the tent lull her to sleep. She sees the rounded curve, fuller now, of her sister Lucinda in moonlight. Lucinda sleeps soundly, certain that she remembers more accurately because she was three years older. All that wild summer burns like fire inside their heads, searing more because of the initial sweetness of denial.

I was as delirious as Mama with the romance of it. When Rhett came back, dusk full of honeysuckle and hot pink azaleas, I told Lucinda, "He's like a knight on a white horse!"

She grumbled, "More like Humpty Dumpty."

When Rhett took us to a movie as if we were a normal family, I sobbed over Geopetto's voice crying, "Pinoooooooochio!" At the age of eight, I knew about being severed. I wanted another "second chance." When Rhett kissed us goodnight at the door, he said, "Y'all run on upstairs. Pearl and I need to talk."

We are the golden throats of azaleas behind the porch swing, erect, full. We see the woman glance our way just before the man kisses the hollow of her throat.

I listened to them talk softly downstairs until I drifted into dreams of unicorns and ladies in silk. I woke up crying. I couldn't stop crying even after I was awake, but eventually I surrendered again to the dark unknown of sleep.

We are the lightning bugs. Our glow fills the girl's dream. We light her path, hovering at the edge of her life. Keeping watch. Sometimes, she rips us apart, making rings, or she smothers us in jars. The sacrifice is barely felt. We are timeless, never-ending.

As Spring teased the world into bloom, Rhett's letters became more frequent, Mama's delight in them greater. Lucinda laid them on Mama's pillow without comment. We raised the windows and set ice in front of the fan to keep cool. Mama slept in her slip, perspiration glistening her neck.

Elated after reading her mail one night, Mama reopened the letter at bedtime. She read over it several times. She smoothed the edges of the paper and ran her finger over the signature. Then she kissed us good night and went downstairs. Lucinda groaned and rolled over, tossing the sheet aside.

When Mama came to bed, she dipped a washcloth in the ice pitcher to cool her neck and the top of her breasts above the slip. I heard the match, smelled the sulphur, when she lit a cigarette, but I never opened my eyes to see the orange coal.

We are the leaves that strain to whisper, to cool the fevered heart.

Over the weekend, Mama talked to Rhett on the phone several times. On Sunday, she took Lucinda and me to the park for a picnic to tell us that we were moving to Mobile where Rhett lived now. I was thrilled, and even Lucinda couldn't hide her spark of interest.

Mama's posture was different, her gait changed, her eyes sprang back to life. The opposite happened to Lucinda who became flat, tight, cold; she already knew better than to trust joy. As usual, she was quiet, sullen.

Mama arranged for Uncle Clyde to handle the rental of our house and make the payments. "It's our only security," she told him.

"I know," he answered, strumming his Gibson and staring into the night that enveloped us. He was not eager to encourage Mama.

We are the stars who redden, then twinkle blue like a police car without the siren. If the girl could hear us . . .

The dome of the cavernous train terminal was surrounded by pigeons staining the red tiles. Inside, the stone walls reverberated every noise: chaotic passengers chattering, announcers mumbling over static, shoes ringing out their message of hurry hurry hurry. The bustle added to my thrill of traveling by train. With the help of a pot-bellied man stuffed behind the information desk, we found our track. We hugged our cousins, and Mama and Uncle Clyde said goodbye about 20 times, always thinking of one more thing to say.

Lucinda tugged at Mama's sleeve until Uncle Clyde said, "Pearl, you're gonna miss that train." Mama waved goodbye, her face streaming with tears. I climbed aboard the train, clinging to Mama like a kangaroo in her pouch. I was afraid the steps would be too big, and I wouldn't be fast enough. Suddenly the train would be moving, but I wouldn't. Brushing the sandy-colored curls back from my face, I saw my reflection like a framed photo. I wasn't sure I knew the freckled girl looking back. Through the glass window, the sun baked us, its glare relentless.

As soon as we heard the clackety-clack of the train in motion, a man in a cowboy hat sat down next to Mama. His eyes sagged, but they lit up when he saw Mama. He was late boarding and it was the only seat left, but it still made me mad. She didn't have any business sitting with that man on her way to be reunited with Rhett. I glared at the cowboy.

While we waited to transfer that afternoon, Mama shook her head and dug in her purse for a cigarette. Loose tobacco cluttered her red purse, a perfect match for the three-inch heels. Mama's belt was cinched so tight it looked as if it would cut her shirtwaist dress. She turned heads everywhere. When we boarded again, we went all the way to the back and piled our suitcases on the seat next to her.

"Shhh," she said, "Let's get some sleep. It's a long way yet and we don't want to be tired when we get there."

Lucinda smirked. Mama slept, but Lucinda and I were too excited. We played I SPY, watching for animals in the swampy wilderness, then slap Jack

Loretta Cobb

and gin rummy when the train began stopping at towns like Robertsdale and Bay Minette. On our map, we saw we were close to Mobile.

We are the owls hooting toward the girl who zooms toward Mobile, never hearing our question.

I hated for the train ride to be over, but my fervor when we arrived outweighed that concern. I was the first one to spot Rhett in the crowd! I set my suitcase down and ran. He picked me up and swirled me around like a princess. Then Lucinda got her hug, but Mama got a long kiss that embarrassed me.

"Let me get a taxi." Rhett disappeared into the crowded train station. We could see his bus driver's hat above his broad shoulders all the way to the sidewalk.

"He sure looks good in a uniform, doesn't he?" Mama said, more to herself than to us.

Lucinda quipped, "You got a thing for uniforms."

Mama ignored her, "He says we're gonna love the bungalow."

We rode through wide streets lined with live oaks and magnolias, the air thick enough to cut. When we arrived, I sprang around the room like a rabbit, squealing, "It's so modern!" The small cottage was furnished with a sectional sofa in the living room, blonde, glass-topped tables matching the sofa legs.

Lucinda, twirling her hair, offered restrained praise, "I'm glad we don't have all that dreary antique crap."

Our parents couldn't keep their eyes off each other . . . or their hands. "Y'all must be tired. Why don't we take a nap," Rhett suggested.

"I'm not sleepy," Lucinda declared.

"Me neither," I agreed.

"Well, y'all lie down and read or play some games cause I'm ready for a nap." Mama stretched, trying to look sleepy. They locked the bedroom door and didn't come out till late afternoon. I was disappointed they excluded us, but the thrill of our new place overshadowed the letdown. The back yard was filled with azaleas past their bloom, but terraced to provide an evergreen background for lilies of every color. The patio was lined with four-o-clocks drooping from thirst. I hummed as I watered them.

We're the blossoms singing back to the girl. We love her before she feeds us: the sweetness in her blue eyes, the mournful tune she hums. Mostly, we're treated like weeds because we tend to take over a garden.

It was a wonderful summer, the happiest family time we ever knew. The sunlit days were ordered by a structure unfamiliar in our lives and consistent rules Mama wasn't too drained to enforce. Rhett disappeared in his uniform at the same time every day and came home on schedule. We settled into the comfort, absorbed it like thirsty sponges. Lucinda and I had to work hard to find something to rebel against during this second honeymoon when our lives seemed smooth and normal.

I loved the danger, the thrill, of disobeying our parents by sneaking out for a walk while they slept. Rhett worked a three to eleven shift, so they stayed up late at night when he came in and slept late in the mornings. Lucinda's gray eyes had a glint. She loved rebellion. I was learning to. Escaping at dawn was compelling. I slipped into my shorts and followed my sister who had her fingers to her lips, "Shhh." Outside, she shrieked, her voice shrill, "Let's have some fun!"

The sky turned soft, like a yellow rose flushed at the edges. Dew sparkled in the spotless neighborhood while most houses were still dark, the residents asleep. A few blocks over, almost all the houses had columns and balconies and lots of wrought iron made to look like lace. The later it grew the more lights glowed in the early morning. "Look," I stooped to shake the dew off a sharp blade of grass, "like diamonds!"

"I think dew drops look like pearls," Lucinda countered. She always had a different opinion, but I didn't mind because we'd been so close all summer. We hardly ever fussed now or beat each other over the head with the hairbrush the way we used to.

I am the mosquito whirring at the girl's ear, just before I penetrate the milky skin at the bend of her knee.

Visiting with neighbors was something we had not done before. However, we could invite our Mobile friends in any time of day or overnight without worrying that our folks would be fussing or Rhett would come in drunk. That oasis summer was filled with shade trees draped by Spanish moss and the smell of freshly cut grass. The lawnmower, which came with the house, ran smooth as Rhett's face behind it.

One morning, I sensed a jarring regression when I whined from the

Loretta Cobb

doorway, "I'm hungry." Mama snapped, "There's corn flakes on the table. Fix it yourself this morning. Mama's real busy."

I ate the cold cereal without a banana or the strawberries we'd had all summer, wondering what I'd done to make her cross. She was like the old Pearl, not this new one who laughed all the time and made homemade rolls and pickles.

In her dressing room, Mama ran slender fingers over her cheekbones with a coat of Avon liquid make up. I wondered why she took such pains since the side without makeup was almost exactly like the one she had finished. When Mama used eye makeup, usually something important was going on. She lightly brushed her eyebrows with the sable brown pencil, then cut her eyes toward me.

"You always sneak up on me, Bonita. I swear you gonna be a private eye someday."

Then her eyes laughed at me through the mirror and I ran to give her a hug. "Mama's real nervous this morning for some reason," she explained.

"Is it that coffee thing they're having for you?" I asked.

"Why, yes," she answered, the painted brows raised in surprise. She piled dresses on the huge bed, making dust particles flutter in the ray of sunlight beaming through the window. She pulled at the white cotton blouse she chose several times until it was smooth across her stomach, which was flat as a pancake with the girdle on. Her flared red skirt matched the high heels and red handbag. She clipped on some red and white earrings and stood back to check out her image in the full length mirror. She straightened her shoulders. She knew she had it right. She asked tentatively, "Reckon I ought to take my hostess this chocolate pound cake or the pickles and squash relish?"

"Cake," Lucinda answered from our room where she sat at the vanity polishing her nails. Mama allowed her to wear a clear coat now.

"Yeah," I echoed. I had hoped she'd leave the cake for us. When she opened the door, the sunlight blinded me. I rubbed my eyes and said softly, "Hey, Mama." She turned back, the red highlights glistening in her auburn hair like a haloed angel. Her beauty took my breath away, "You look beautiful!" I whispered.

"Thank you, baby." For a moment a radiant smile replaced the worried, tight-lipped mask of shyness.

When she came back, all she told us was, "It was pretty nice." She took two aspirin and lay down with a headache for a few minutes, and by afternoon everything seemed normal again.

Rhett, on the other hand, found it easy to visit with the guys, watching sports. On his off-days, we packed a picnic and went to the zoo, laughing at the monkeys and shivering at the snakes.

Snakes: I guess you could say the first one that crawled into our piece of Eden showed up when Rhett started "drinking socially" one night. A crowd had gathered in some guy's den down the street to watch baseball while the women laughed and told stories, preparing for a cookout. Ripping through the night to play chase I was as happy for Mama as I was for myself. I saw her radiance in the glow of light framed by the kitchen window. She tore lettuce at the sink, dabbing at the corners of her eyes from the combination of fresh onion and good jokes. Every chorus of laughter from the women filled me with a surge of power that I didn't understand yet. I resisted being drawn to it as much as the game of tag. Just as I lost my concentration, a big thick hand grabbed me and a boy's changing voice shrieked, "Gotcha!" I tore out after him.

When the women called us to dinner, the aroma of charcoal-grilled burgers enticed us. After the children filled their plates and headed for the picnic tables in the carport, the men straggled in, craning their necks to keep an eye on the baseball game.

My eyes connected with Mama's as soon as I saw it. I could tell she had already noticed. I felt as if every light in the house focused on the silver Pabst Blue Ribbon in Rhett's hand. It gleamed in the fluorescent kitchen light as if it had some evil, magic power. From that very first drink, something in Mama and in me shut down. If we'd been light bulbs, we would have dimmed at that point and then burned out as it all unraveled. While we shuffled across the wet grass toward home that night, I heard Rhett say, his voice incredulous—already in denial—"But baby, the Pirates are probably going to the World Series. Who wouldn't have a few beers? I can handle it this time."

"Oh, yeah, sure," I heard her flat, lifeless answer. In a matter of days, our next door neighbor gave Rhett prescription drugs by the handful to

Loretta Cobb

help him cope. Daily, Lucinda and I were awakened by bickering.

Then one afternoon, he didn't come home till midnight. I overheard a new sound from the kitchen where Pearl made him drink coffee: I heard him sobbing. Listening, I felt a knife rip into my heart. Then, his sobs were replaced by a shrill, crazy laugh. We hadn't heard that since the last time pills were part of the dinner table conversation.

Mama lay in bed limp all day like a corpse. Her eyes were puffy, with dark circles underneath like purple bruises. She finally drug herself out of bed to the tub where she sat staring into nothing until late afternoon when she mustered energy to make sandwiches.

The next day Mama tried in vain to protect us from the madness overtaking our lives. Before we normally woke up, we heard her make a lot of phone calls but we couldn't figure out what was going on. We couldn't hear what she said after her practiced, overly formal beginning each time. "Yes," in her business tone, "Do you have a Lawrence Youngblood registered there?"

After a few days, Rhett came home sporadically, seemingly to pick a fight. Each night he was later, and then he didn't come home at all. Mama's worry escalated from hotels to hospitals. Her blank face became tight, her dimple wrinkle twisted into a question mark. While she called, I stood next to the bed where she filled the ashtray. She pressed the phone from her shoulder to her ear while she lit one cigarette off the other. "Yes, could you tell me if you have a patient by the name of Lawrence or Rhett Youngblood?" I held my breath, imagining him mangled in some bloody wreck, but the answer was always the same: No.

The stranger wore snakeskin boots when he came to take us for a ride. Mama told us his name was Hub and that Rhett used to work for him. Hub was tall, thin and very quiet. When we stopped for lunch at a pink stucco restaurant overlooking the bay, which Hub had carried on about, he barely touched his gumbo. Even when he wasn't swallowing, his Adam's apple worked hard. I watched a heron fish for its lunch among the reeds beyond the rusty boat tied to the pier.

I point my beak at the girl, shake my spiked tuft her way, fix her with my wild gaze. She admires my snowy feathers and graceful neck, but she ignores my soundless message: self-sufficiency.

Mama told us to go play the pinball machine so they could talk. Hub made calls in the phone booth. We played until we saw him put on his ten-gallon hat, which we recognized as a signal: time to go. His face was pinched up, puckered, like something was up: something dangerous.

"What's wrong, Mama?" I asked. "Has something happened to Rhett?" She looked surprised to see me there, as if she'd totally forgotten.

"Everything's all right, baby. I don't think anything has happened to Rhett." She gave the man a knowing look. Usually, when things were bad I pretended to be a puppy. I knew Mama loved me and would give me shelter, but she didn't remember I had sense sometimes.

"But why doesn't he come home? What's going on, Mama?" Lucinda joined in, her voice shrill, but the lips her question came out of tried to be sullen. Her eyes were a dark gray storm. Lucinda swears to this day Hub was a neighbor.

"Nothing, honey." Mama insisted. "Let's just enjoy our Sunday afternoon ride."

The snakeskin boots drove carefully, slowly, until we heard Hub shout, "I'll be dog; there they are. I told you!"

"Chase 'em," Mama said, in a meaner voice than I'd ever have recognized as hers.

Hub blew the horn, the sound of it startling, piercing. That's when I saw Rhett look out the back window of the car in front of us. His eyes were suddenly saucers and his mouth a round balloon. I had never seen him this frightened before. When Hub reached in the glove compartment for his pistol, I was paralyzed, not only beyond speech but beyond thought, even beyond barking.

Lucinda tried to look unconcerned. She sneered, staring out the window at the flat, thirsty grass. A tear slid down her cheek, which I focused on: like a boil, full and firmly packed at first, then runny and then going away.

While the car ahead of us sped around the sharp curves on the outskirts of town, we heard Rhett yell directions to the driver of the sleek red car.

When Rhett slid his arm protectively around the woman with brunette curls who ducked her head against him, Mama and Hub responded simultaneously. "Faster!" She screamed as he gunned the motor and rode the car's tail until the red car's brakes let out a deafening screech. We swerved

Loretta Cobb

into them when the driver slammed on the brakes, but Hub managed to hit them just hard enough to make them pull over to the side of the road. Mama pushed the car door open as if it were a trap door out of hell fire. She was out of the car before anybody could figure out what hit them.

By the time I got out, Rhett stood over her, yelling and pushing—his face red. Hub said, "Rhett, we don't need no pushin' and shovin', understand?"

Rhett didn't answer, but he quit shoving Mama. The brunette's blue eyeshadow was smeared under her sizzling blue eyes. Her dark red lips said, "Don't you start picking on Rhett."

That's all Mama needed. She jerked the woman by the rawhide tassels on her vest. Everybody else froze for a moment, but not Mama. She slammed that woman down in the ditch and jumped on top of her, beating the cowgirl with her fists in a rage I couldn't believe was coming out of my mother. The other woman tried to fight back, but all we could see were long fingernails the color of plums scratching Mama's back and yanking her lush auburn hair. Narrow streams of blood came through Mama's blouse.

The snakeskin boots pulled Mama off and held her back while the woman from the front seat of the other car restrained the cowgirl whose skirt was trimmed with silver studs that left imprints on Mama's arms. As the cowgirl's friend pulled her to her feet, we could see up that fancy skirt, all the way to her black panties.

Mama always wore white panties. I wondered if you'd call those silver things jewels. I wished people driving by would quit gawking. Lucinda glared at them. A few cars stopped and asked if we needed help, but Rhett waved them on, saying "I think we got it under control now."

I am the grass Carl Sandburg saw. New growth can heal a gash in weeks, fill it with the wonder of green.

The brunette cowgirl went home with Hub in his snakeskin boots. I hated to see him go, felt like I knew him well by then with his sad eyes, creased at the edges. The other couple drove us home in the red car, with Lucinda and me placed strategically between our parents on the back seat. Rhett made strained efforts at casual conversation with the couple in the front. "Boy, that's a good looking convertible on the corner."

"Umm hmm," they answered in unison.

Rhett tried again. "Y'all got plans for Labor Day?"

"Naw," the woman answered. The driver was busy with the rear view mirror, but there was nothing wrong with it.

Mama didn't say a word, but she was breathing so heavily it scared me. Her chest moved up and down in fast, rapid breaths, the wheezing worse and worse. By the time we got home, she was having a bad asthma attack and those whelps she called a nervous rash covered her.

"Y'all go on to bed now. I'll take care of her," Rhett said. He gave her a pill from his own pocket and then got her asthma pump. I hoped he wasn't poisoning her. Lucinda had a worse fear and she swears it's what really happened. In our room, Lucinda said, "I don't want to go to bed at six o'clock in the afternoon."

"Me neither," I said. "Wanna play a game of cootie?"

"No." She gazed out the window.

"Maybe we oughtta shake the piggy bank to be sure we get a popsicle tonight."

"You do it," she said, which I resented because it was bad enough the way she'd always eat her popsicle fast and then want a bite of mine. Now she wouldn't even help get the money together. I shook the bright yellow ceramic pig.

Lucinda must have stood at that window half an hour. Then she said, "I think I'll get my clothes ready for school tomorrow." She must have ironed that white blouse for twenty minutes.

Lucinda stirs across the tent, sees that I'm awake. "I can't believe you talked me into this, baby. It's too hot for camping."

Though we're at the top of Mt. Cheaha, it is so hot we have to dip cloths in the cooler and lay them across our naked chests to survive the oppressive heat. I tell her where my thoughts have been.

"Lord God, Bonita, you are so hopeless," she sighs. "Such a romantic and way too forgiving. I told you what Rhett did. Once we were asleep, he turned on the gas oven. We'd all have been dead if Hub had not come by to return Mama's purse. He smelled the gas, climbed in our bedroom window and opened up the house. I don't know why he never reported Rhett for that."

Loretta Cobb

She rubs her eyes, "I reckon if you write long enough, you can tell on him. You're full of bull, but I love you anyway." With that, Lucinda yawns, unzips the window, and pats my arm. "I need some air, and you need some sleep," she coos. Her breasts are slack now. Her hair, once spun gold, is threaded with silver just visible in the moonlight.

As the chirping chorus of Alabama crickets, we can make the girl miss her youth and have her believe in serenity beyond memory.

By some miracle, or—if Lucinda is right—through Hub's discretion, Mama seemed functional the next morning. Rhett stayed in bed, but she made waffles, the batter dripping out of the old waffle iron to join years of crusted batter that left black streaks on the outside. She heated the maple syrup, its aroma leading me to the table. The crisp waffle and gooey sweetness of syrup satisfied my hunger. Lucinda and I had eaten peanut butter and crackers for supper. Mama tried hard to be cheerful, pretend nothing had happened. Lucinda picked at her food. We went inside the gigantic high school to Lucinda's home room where Mama made a list of all the supplies needed. We never shopped for them though because when we got home Mama and Rhett had a long talk with the door closed. When she finally came out she screeched in an unnaturally cheerful voice, "Guess what girls! We're going home."

Stingers erect, we're the bumblebees that buzz outside the busy busy busy. We try to warn the four o-clocks of coming thirst, but they are busy, too, craning for a glimpse of the girl.

Since our bungalow was fully furnished, it didn't take us long to get our things together and simply walk away. Making our way from another false Eden wasn't easy, but I was relieved not to have to go to a new school. I'd be going back to the school in East Lake where I had friends, and so would Lucinda who seemed more relieved than I was. "That junior high was bigger than any high school in Birmingham," she said as we folded our clothes and put them in cardboard boxes to ship home.

Mama seemed relieved, too, almost happy as she went through the cupboards—figuring what was worth cramming in a suitcase and what had to be given away or trashed. Rhett, pale and shaky, didn't do much of anything but lie in bed. However, he pepped up in the evening for our last supper in Mobile.

We checked our things at the bus station and got all our business straight early enough to walk along the waterfront before we ate seafood at Rhett's favorite restaurant. Rhett had something hot that made his eyes sting, and Mama had a combination plate, which she shared with Lucinda and me because we only ordered shrimp cocktail. My sister's breasts peeped out of the tight cotton sweater enough to embarrass me. The youngest waiter kept smiling at Lucinda who was going to be 12 next week, but looked 16. I felt alone somehow, my mixed emotions like clothes tumbling in a dryer.

"Honey, aren't you ready to go?" Mama said, shaking me as if I'd fallen asleep.

I saw the colored lights from the ceiling reflecting in her hair, so beautiful. I wondered if she was a fallen angel or maybe a honky tonk angel. Is that what they'd look like? Would Lucinda become one?

"What? Oh, yeah, sure," I answered.

"Yes ma'am," Rhett said in the voice he always used when he needed to get his own habits cleaned up. I was worked up as we boarded the bus, expecting it to be as much fun as the train. It wasn't. Most people were asleep, with only a few reading lights scattered throughout the bus. We had a seat right in front of Mama and Rhett. He was asleep immediately, but she was restless.

I tried to see as much out the window as I could at night, but gave up quickly. When I woke up at dawn, the sky looked as if watery blood had been streaked against an eerie orange glow.

Lucinda read Mama's *True Confessions,* which she sneaked while Mama squeezed by people in the aisle. I entertained myself by making "photos" in my head of all the people framed by the bus's windows. These stories were all sad, unlike the ones I had thought up on the train.

We got off the bus, wrinkled and sagging like balloons not yet popped but allowing the air to leak a little at a time. In that moment, as we left the bus, I somehow knew we'd never rise as high as we had at the beginning of that summer. I could read defeat in Uncle Clyde's eyes, too, felt the sting of his pity. No matter how good he'd been to wire us money to come home, I didn't want him to pity us. More accurately, I didn't want to deserve his pity.

Loretta Cobb

He stooped down and kissed my head, "And how's this sweet little thing been all summer?"

Clearing my throat, I locked my arms around his neck, "Where's that old guitar, Uncle Clyde? We want to hear a song." Tittering relieved the tension, and then we got busy with luggage to cover the shame we carried—almost as visible, as palpable, as our bags.

None of us had anything else to say as we made our way down the familiar streets to his cottage where transplanted wild flowers bloomed in colorful profusion.

We are the wild flowers Clyde sings about after lunch. We dance, toss our heads for the girl. We want her to see there's strength in not caring where you grow. Anywhere you plop down Queen Anne's lace, it will spring up to grace the ditch.

Loretta Douglas Cobb grew up in Birmingham, Alabama. She graduated with honors in English from Alabama College (now UM) in Montevallo and earned her M.A. in English from the Bread Loaf School of English at Middlebury College. She worked as a junior high teacher and on the staff at UM, where she published numerous academic articles and established a study skills and tutoring program which grew into the Harbert Writing Center. After her retirement in '95, Loretta began a new career as a writer, freelancing for the Birmingham News *and writing fiction. Her first story, "Seeing it Through," appeared in the first* Belles' Letters, *followed by a collection of stories,* The Ocean Was Salt. *Her work was included in the anthologies* Climbing Mt. Cheaha *and* Working the Dirt, *and her story "Feeling Salty" was short-listed in the Irish International Competition for the literary magazine* Fish. *For the last decade Loretta has been part of the Alabama Readers' Theater, entertaining annually at literary festivals and for the International Scott and Zelda Fitzgerald Conference in 2014. Her first novel,* How Can I Keep from Singing?, *was published in 2016. Married to the writer Bill Cobb, she has one daughter and two grandchildren.*

Magnolia
Vicki Covington

I wrote "Magnolia" on a vacation to the beach. Our firstborn daughter was four months old. I was breastfeeding her. hose were the days before laptops and smart phones. So in order to write, I nursed her on the left side and wrote the entire story with my right hand on a yellow legal pad. When we got back home, I sent it to Daniel Menaker at The New Yorker. *He had read a dozen or so stories of mine by then and rejected them with long letters. He wasn't just an editor; he was a mentor. I sent "Magnolia" to him. I was, at that time, still working as a therapist. I awaited Menaker's rejection letter. One day, while I was leading a group for recovering women, Dennis abruptly stormed in. He knew not to interrupt a session. So I feared something bad had occurred. But he was carrying Ashley. So I knew she was all right. Then I saw what was in his hand: a FedEx envelope from 25 West 43rd Street, NY. Editors don't overnight rejection slips. So I knew before I opened it, that my life was going to change. They wanted to buy the story.*

The reason I drive this blue Mercedes is because my baby son, Jackie, gave it to me. Jackie used to be a preacher. Now he teaches college in west Florida. He has a sailboat, cars, and a second wife with natural-blonde hair. He was born during the Depression and needs his toys. My older two hate to hear that—they think I indulge Jackie. "Born during the Depression," they mock. Jackie almost lost his life in a boating accident after he got divorced and left the church. But that's another story.

Saturday is my day to take Mrs. Fraley to buy groceries. She's my age, but I call her Mrs. Fraley because I work as a waitress for her son at the restaurant. A family restaurant is a nice thing to have. I wait tables on Sundays for the church people. It makes for a busy weekend, since I take Mrs. Fraley to buy groceries on Saturdays. I am the only one my age who can still drive. It's a blessing I don't take lightly. God moves in mysterious ways, as witnessed by Jackie giving me this car. At first, I was thinking of all that money that might have gone to the poor. I see now that this car is a vehicle of God that carries old people to grocery stores.

Right as I was leaving to get Mrs. Fraley last Saturday, the phone rang.

It wasn't Mrs. Fraley. It was Lila, calling from the nursing home.

"Come get me," she said.

"What's wrong?"

"Something needs to be done."

"What is it, Lila?"

"I'll tell you when you get here."

So I went to the garage and cranked up the car. I decided to see about Lila before going to get Mrs. Fraley. The nursing home is just a few minutes away.

The place is new. Lila's son put her there after she started behaving oddly. When I got there, I went straight to Lila's room. She was standing by a bureau doing her hair.

"Well, forevermore!" I declared.

"What?"

"Oh, Lila."

"What?" She pouted, knowing what I was talking about. She was wearing a light-green evening dress. Lila's got balls of fat in places. The dress made her look like a bunch of big grapes. "The ladies' auxiliary sent used clothes."

Why don't they sort through them, I wondered. Sending an evening gown to an old lady isn't funny.

I led her by the elbow down the hall past wheelchairs, old people, and struggling plants. We sat by a Coke machine.

"I want my car," she said.

"No, Lila. Ben said no car."

Ben is her son. He told me not to let Lila have her car. "She'll wreck it," he said. It's a Plymouth.

"Take me to my house. I just want to see if it's still there."

"I'm sure it's there, Lila."

"Take me."

"Well, it's my day to get Mrs. Fraley," I said.

"Take me to the car first."

"No. We'll have to get Mrs. Fraley first."

"Then you'll take me?"

I stared at her.

"I'd do it for you," she said. Her eyes were the color of weak tea.

Lila and I have the same birthday. We graduated from high school together in 1923. She married Hal Ray. I married Scotty. Hal Ray was an ordinary man. Scotty was a drunk. He was born in England, and his family crossed over when he was a baby. Scotty was a tiny man. His eyes were very blue. Jackie asked me once if his daddy was a good lover. My older two would never ask a question like that.

I steered Lila to the nurses' station and checked her out till lunch. Then we went to get Mrs. Fraley. On the way, Lila dabbed her face with a violet handkerchief.

"Why are you crying, Lila?"

"Hal Ray."

"Don't cry, Lila."

Hal Ray died several years ago. There are two kinds of widows: those who go on living and those who don't. Maybe I was lucky to have lost Scotty when I was fifty—young enough to keep going. My older two knew him for a drunk. Jackie believes he was only misunderstood. I'm the only one with the real story. It begins with the fact that I loved Scotty. What kind of woman can love a drunk? I slept with that question for years.

We drove to Mrs. Fraley's. She was standing on the porch, clutching her black patent-leather purse. Mrs. Fraley's hair is like cotton balls.

"Who's with you?" she called, holding the wrought-iron rail, taking the steps with care.

"Lila."

I held Mrs. Fraley's hand as she settled into the back seat.

"Thanks, sugar."

"Pleasant day," I said.

"That's right, sugar."

"Lila needed to get out, didn't you Lila?"

"We're going to get my car," Lila said to Mrs. Fraley.

"O.K., sugar."

"First we're going to the grocery store," I reminded Lila. "To do Mrs. Fraley's shopping."

"Don't mind me," Mrs. Fraley said. "We can do Lila's business first if needs be."

I glanced at Mrs. Fraley through the rearview mirror. Her eyes sparkled as she looked out the window.

"Daffodils," she said.

"My car's parked in the back yard," Lila said.

"O.K."

"Ben parked it there."

"How is Ben?" Mrs. Fraley asked. "And your grandbabies?"

"My grandbabies are at Auburn."

"That's good, sugar. What're they studying?"

"Ben shouldn't have parked the car in the yard."

"Ben knows what's best," I said to Lila.

"What if somebody stole it?"

"We'll take care of it."

"Have they put pets in your home?" Mrs. Fraley asked her.

"The grass will die under the car," Lila said.

"Mrs. Fraley asked you a question, Lila."

"That's O.K., sugar. I was just wondering if they got pets at her home. They're putting them in the homes. It's good therapy."

"It's an idea," I said. "Wouldn't you like a puppy, Lila?"

Suddenly Lila turned to face Mrs. Fraley in the back seat. "The reason I got on this dress is because the auxiliary sent it."

"It's right pretty," Mrs. Fraley said.

Lila turned back around. "I'm worried," she said.

"We'll be there directly."

Lila jiggled her car keys between her breasts.

"Well, forevermore," I said.

"What?"

"You need a purse."

"Hal Ray told me this is the safest place for keys."

"Well, he was right about that," Mrs. Fraley said.

I pulled the car into the parking lot and helped Mrs. Fraley heave herself from the back seat. She took a grocery list from her purse. Her sparkly eyes were bright as ever. I squeezed her hand, thinking what a great morning it was to be alive.

When Scotty died, I had no place to go. We never had a home in the true sense of the word. We moved here and there. Scotty got us a little service station. It wasn't much of a family business—just one pump—but it belonged to us. The only thing we ever owned except for a cow. My older two helped pump gas. Scotty sat in back and drank with his friends. Jackie was only a baby. Lila and Hal Ray let me live in a garage apartment behind their house after Scotty died. I cried a lot. After a few months, Lila began calling my older two. "You've got to do something about your mother," she told them. My older two, to this day, hold it against Lila that she had this attitude. I started working for Mrs. Fraley's son at the restaurant after a year.

"Oh, I look a fright," Lila said as we pulled into her driveway.

"Nobody's caring, sug," Mrs. Fraley said.

"Your ice cream will melt," Lila said to her.

"I didn't buy ice cream, sugar. Here, have one of these," Mrs. Fraley said, holding out a handful of lemon drops.

"Look," Lila said. "It's there."

Her old Plymouth stood amidst spring weeds. I helped Lila from the car. Mrs. Fraley wanted to stay in back with her lemon drops and grocery sacks.

Lila walked to her Plymouth, unlocked it, and sat in the driver's seat.

"Please, just let me sit here."

"Don't crank it."

Lila stared ahead to the pasture behind her house. I walked around the place. The nandinas had grown tall and branched haphazardly onto the porch. Lila's home was always freshly painted when Hal Ray was alive. It was a perfect white box. In the spring, butterflies danced along the hedge.

I heard the old Plymouth start up. Lila made it roar.

"Roll down the window." I motioned to her.

She did.

"I'm going to drive it," she said.

"No, you're not."

"Just to the corner and back."

"No. Ben said no."

Lila clutched the steering wheel and gazed ahead to the pasture with those watery brown eyes of hers.

"Give me the keys, Lila."

Obediently, she turned off the ignition. "Let me sit here," she said.

I took her keys and walked across the weedy lawn to what was left of the garage apartment where I lived after Scotty died. I peered in. It was empty. It was a mess of cobwebs. I went to the fence and looked into the pasture. When I lived here, Lila and Hal Ray had a horse. The horse was a friend to me. I gave him apples and sugar from my hand. All I felt was that horse's tongue; the rest of life was numb. Scotty had been a drunk, but in the winter his body was warm in bed—even though I didn't touch it. Scotty smiled at me—even though he didn't speak. His blue eyes were like mute friends to me. The smell of liquor was a kind of perfume that dabbed me. Don't get me wrong—I hated it. But misery becomes an animal that lives in your house. It rubs your legs, crawls into your lap, sheds itself in summer all over your pillow and hands. And when it dies, you miss its claws. That's why I was numb. But the horse nudged me. In the morning, I looked at that horse and thought, This horse is brown; its tongue is like sandpaper. Hearing it neigh, I knew I still had ears. We shared the apples. I wore the same dress every day. It was the color of chocolate. Lila believed I was going crazy because of this. "Your mother won't change clothes," she'd tell my older two. The truth was I liked that dress. It was almost the same color as the horse. I'd stand in the pasture and look up. The land was flat and made the sky a big blue dome over me. I knew I was one solitary woman on this earth.

Death knocked Scotty's feet from under him. We'd been standing in front of Jackie's place in Florida, and a neighbor had taken a snapshot of Scotty with Jackie's kids. Scotty dropped to the grass, knees buckling like he'd been shot. That's how a heart attack works. Jackie held him. Later, we went through his wallet. It was empty. We kept hoping for a keepsake— something to save, a memory—but it was empty. It was good that Lila had the garage apartment. Hal Ray brought me hot meals. I had a bed, a rocker, a thermometer that hung over the sink. It had a rainbow above the hundred-degree mark. Lila was like a bumblebee—always darting all over the place, bringing ladies from the church, praying for me, baking me pies, trying to cheer me. I was Lila's project, her charity work. She felt that being married to a drunk had tainted and scarred my character. Oh, my older two hated that. The desire to both thank her and forgive her daily is a blessing I don't take lightly.

I shuffled through the dandelions in Lila's pasture. It's so futile trying to dig this type weed up, once it's deep. I wonder why people try. The sky promised only blue for the day. It was no secret spring was coming. Daffodils dotted the land, and specks of gold grew up the forsythia fingers.

I went back to Lila's car. "Come on, let's go, Lila," I said.

"I don't want to leave."

I opened the Plymouth door and took her hand. Like a fretful child, she accepted. "Let's don't go yet."

"Mrs. Fraley might be getting annoyed," I reminded her.

I led her leisurely over the property, past the place where she once planted pansies this time of year. Nut grass grew over the rocks that had formed a square garden.

"Tell Ben to take me out of that home."

"He will when you're better."

"I want to come home."

"It'd be hard keeping up the yard."

"Listen," she said, stomping her foot. "I'm going for a ride in my car."

"No."

"I want my keys."

"There's no place for you to go."

"I'm going to the corner and back."

"No."

"I'm getting a lawyer."

"Ben owns the car, Lila."

"I'm calling a lawyer. I know one."

"It's no use fussing over this. Nothing will change."

Suddenly she took my wrist and jerked it hard, causing the keys to spring loose. When I bent to pick them up, she stepped on my fingers. I winced. I held the keys tight. Lila grabbed my hand, trying to pry my fingers. Her nails were hard as weapons. They dug into my skin.

We stood there. Gradually, Lila's hands went soft. I glanced over to where Mrs. Fraley sat in my back seat sucking a lemon drop, content. Side by side, Lila and I ambled over to her magnolia tree, where a mockingbird was perched. "Let's sit a minute," I said.

In order to make the magnolia a shade tree, you have to cut the lowest branches when it's young. You do this once a season. If you're smart, you do it in December so you'll have green on your table at Christmas when the family sits to carve a turkey. You decorate in this way. It is natural and festive. Magnolia leaves are not delicate. They only grow strong and handsome. Scotty and I helped Lila and Hal Ray plant this tree. It didn't bloom for many years.

Vicki Covington's work includes four novels, Gathering Home, Bird of Paradise, Night Ride Home, *and* The Last Hotel for Women—*all from Simon & Schuster. Her short stories have appeared in various literary magazines. With Dennis Covington, she wrote a memoir,* Cleaving—The Story of a Marriage, *which was published by Northpoint Press (Farrar, Straus, & Giroux). The University of Alabama Press published a collection of her short essays titled* Women in a Man's World, Crying. *For a few years, she wrote a column for the* Oxford American *magazine, titled "Meditations for Bad Girls." She has been the recipient of a fellowship from the National Endowment for the Arts and an individual artist grant from the Alabama State Council on the Arts. She was born and grew up in Birmingham, Alabama, and lived there all her life until 2009 when she moved to Texas. She now enjoys playing with her three grandchildren who live only blocks away. After years of silence, the Muse returned to her and she has a contract on a new novel,* Once in a Blue Moon, *which will be released in Spring 2017.*

Detritus

Jennifer S. Davis

I am fond of Southern short stories that I describe as "walk-the-margins-of-real-ism" stories, strange narratives in which the events of the story could technically happen, but probably wouldn't. To me, this kind of story is often representative of the absurdities and paradoxes that make the South so fascinating and compelling and gobsmackingly frustrating. "Detritus" is one of my favorite stories I have written because of its absurd, fable-esque qualities. It is an amalgam of character sketches I forced together, the plot emerging from a need to make sense of why these particular characters would exist on the same page. Also, my mother complained that my stories were dark and depressing. She requested a happy story. I guess this is my version of happy.

The day our father left us for good to pursue his dream of becoming a professional bass fisherman, it snowed ten inches in Edna, Alabama. We thought the world was ending or a new one beginning. I had never seen snow before. I was thirteen.

That morning our mother laid beneath an old mulberry tree in the backyard wearing nothing but a nightgown and slippers, until the leafing arms of the tree, that just the day before had swirled in the gusty spring breeze as if writhing in prayer, grew weighted with snow and drooped toward earth in a humbled slouch, the tips grazing our mother's slippered feet.

"It's a sign," our mother said.

"Nimbostratus, Noah," Lucie said to me. She peered at our mother through the frosted kitchen window. "That's what them clouds are called. Nimbostratus."

For an eleven-year-old, everyone considered Lucie freakishly smart, which made what Molly was an even greater tragedy, although at the time she was simply our sister who did not speak.

None of us owned real winter clothing. So we improvised. Lucie squeezed on several pairs of her Sunday tights under a bunny jumpsuit our mother bought her the previous Easter. I made a scarf out of a table runner. We raided our father's drawers and pilfered his wool socks to use as mittens, figuring he wouldn't need them in the balmy paradise of Southern Florida, where he said the bass grew fat and sleek as seals. We wrapped Molly, a little lump of a toddler, in the heaviest bedspread we could find, then hurled ourselves out the front door and into an alien landscape. The snow: magical against our faces. Lucie propped Molly against the cragged trunk of the mulberry tree, then we pranced like nymphs, singing *Frosty the Snowman* until the words didn't sound like words anymore. Our mother remained perfectly still, her palms lifted toward the snow-heavy sky in supplication.

Around noon, Pete Fundak skidded over on snowshoes fashioned from pot lids and rope. "What's up with your mom?" he said, wiping frozen mucus from his thin mustache. Pete was only fifteen, but he somehow looked like a grown man, and the senior girls at school *ahhhed* over his sulky, pained, I-come-from-a-screwed-up-home glower. I was barely taller than Lucie and wouldn't see the dark facial fuzz of full-blown puberty for another couple of years. Pete and I had been best friends since he blew up a frog in my mailbox in first grade. I worked hard not to be envious.

"A sign," Lucie said from the middle of her cartwheel, her pink bunny ears dipped in snow.

"Oh," Pete said, not surprised, because our mother saw many signs in the world, although usually on a much smaller scale: a dancing tomato in a TV commercial meant Jesus wanted us to eat our vegetables; an eyelash in an eye meant that Jesus wanted Lucie to sit still long enough to have her bangs trimmed on the back porch before the she went blind. Pete had a father he'd never met and a mother who weighed four hundred pounds. He wasn't one to point fingers.

"Want to go sliding down the gully?" he asked, and we left Molly under the tree and my mother staring into sky and Lucie spinning in the snow and passed the morning slipping down the gully behind Pete's house on soggy cardboard boxes.

When our fingers and toes grew too numb to grasp the roots twined across the banks of the gully to heft ourselves over the lip of the ledge, we went to Pete's house for lunch. His mother made pickle and mustard sandwiches, moving from fridge to counter in a lurching blur while seated in an armless office chair Pete rigged with training wheels we found on a rusty bike tossed into the gully. Mrs. Fundak was too fat to stand for more than a few minutes. When she tried, she teetered like a life-sized Weeble Wobble.

"Good eating, boys?" she asked, her mouth full of Wonderbread. Pete hung his head. His mouth moved over his sandwich mechanically.

"Yes, ma'am," I answered, taking pride in my manners. The rolls of fat on Mrs. Fundak's face parted to reveal the glistening smile of a model. "You see," she said to Pete. "That's called politeness. That's called respect."

"May we be excused?" Pete asked.

"Now that's more like it," Mrs. Fundak nodded.

Outside, Pete kicked a frozen lizard against the trunk of a pine, waited for it to bounce back to his foot, then kicked it again. "I hate her," he said. "I mean I really hate her."

"Hate is not an option." I repeated what my mother told me every time my father had left for work and failed to return. Secretly, I envied Pete's situation. Because his mother was so fat, she could rarely catch him to punish him, and since she couldn't drive, he'd been behind the wheel running her errands since he could see over the dashboard.

"Maybe she'll die," Pete considered. He lobbed the prostrate lizard across the front yard. "Dying is definitely an option."

By the time I arrived home, the sun was a yolky smear against a blanket of shapeless clouds. My mother: a bulge of snow beneath the benevolent arms of mulberry tree. I found Lucie and Molly in the kitchen sitting at an empty table, Molly's placid face resting on the edge of the table like an expectant puppy.

"We're hungry," Lucie said, having long since spoken for Molly until we usually asked Lucie what Molly was thinking without addressing Molly at all.

The front door swung open, and there stood our mother, her dark hair white with snow. But her face flushed rosy and apple-cheeked, like she'd passed the day roasting by a fire. She held her hands in front of her,

Jennifer S. Davis

turned them over then back again as if she'd gotten herself a new pair.

"It's the passion," she said, smiling at us, and when our mother smiled, even we recognized that she was beautiful by anyone's standards. "Do you understand what I am saying? He's lit a fire inside of me." Then she laughed, jubilant, until Lucie and I started laughing from her laughter.

Here's what Jesus said to our mother under the mulberry tree: *Paint that door. Make that door speak to those with closed hearts.*

She'd woken with the bed empty beside her, which wasn't unusual, but this time she found a note from our father that said something along the lines of *When I get famous I'll send money, don't forget to change the oil in the truck and have a good life.* We weren't surprised. We'd found the note on her bedroom floor, had been expecting it for some time. But what we hadn't expected was our mother's reaction. She decided to get her ducks in a row, clean up ship, start afresh, and chose to begin this new life by stripping and varnishing the front door (Rome wasn't built in a day, she reminded us), something she'd been asking our father to do for years. It was an important step, she explained. A sign of her independence. Only when she laid her hands on the door, she felt a surge of dizzying energy. That's when she heard Him for the first time: *Paint that door. Make that door speak to those with closed hearts.*

Jesus didn't mean with varnish, she was sure of that, but like a painting in a museum. And when she opened the door to day, she saw nothing but resplendent white, a new world, everything clean and erased, a blank canvas, and she believed.

"A door," our mother said, "is more than a door. So it makes sense. It's an opening and a closing. A beginning and an ending. A choice. He's standing at the door knocking. You see?"

She said all of this and more, then walked into her bedroom, shutting the door behind her.

Nothing was ever the same for us, as you'd expect.

The next day dawned surprisingly warm, the snow melted to mud, and we wondered aloud how anything so wondrous could have happened to the forgotten town of Edna.

Our mother packed us in the truck and drove two towns over to the art store, spent the week's grocery money on tiny tubes of paint she smeared into a heavenly world all over our old front door. When the paint ran out, she glued on buttons and scraps of fabric, things she'd been saving for years with no reason as to why.

"You see," she said, her hands layered in paint, "my whole life was preparation for this moment." Her eyes glazed filmy and feverish, and there was a kind of fire behind them that most people spend a lifetime searching for.

Here's what we thought: if only she'd make some black-eyed peas and macaroni and cornbread and banana pudding. But our mother didn't think about things like eating and bathing and cleaning after the day Jesus told her to paint that door. She said she was being fed by the hand of the Lord. Didn't we understand that?

It's hard to explain exactly what my mother painted onto those doors. Not anything with a name. Just an explosion of colors that filled you until a heat spread from your belly to your limbs to your fingertips and made you want to raise your hands to the Spirit, and that's usually what they did. Believers from Tennessee and Georgia and Louisiana and sometimes farther started pilgrimaging to our house in expensive cars and pleated skirts and Sunday hats, dazed with bliss after laying their eyes upon the Lord's hand in my mother's work.

They left with a door strapped on top of their cars. Sometimes two. She couldn't make them fast enough. Locals hauled in truckloads of donated doors salvaged from old houses that rich people tore down. They brought paint and buckets of buttons and bundles of scrap fabric and anything shiny or precious that could be spared. My mother scraped the old lead paint off the doors, got them even and smooth as the quiet water my father loved to slice his boat into in the early hours of the morning, then painted herself ragged.

"The woman's done lost her mind," Pete's mother said when we wandered over for supper each evening, Molly tagged on Lucie's hip. "I'd call social services but they'd probably just stick you in a home with some nutso who locked you in the basement."

The doors sold for more money than we'd ever seen. Lucie begged my mother to enroll her in the gifted school in Birmingham, begged her to

Jennifer S. Davis

send Molly to specialists. "Why?" my mother said. "What other book do you need besides the Bible? Why would Molly need to be anything other than what God made her?"

In those early days, whatever money my mother earned, she gave to Full Gospel Baptist. I know this is true, because nothing changed in our home. Not one new chair, not a dress for Lucie, not a toy for Molly.

Over a year later, during the midst of an unforgiving heat wave that kept Edna cooling itself in front of the few air conditioners in town, Bobby Alan Moon brought my mother his wisp of a daughter. *Please*, he pleaded with my mother. *Help her*.

My mother stopped painting, closed her eyes. "It has begun," she said. But how could we have known?

The doctors in Mobile called Ray Moon *challenged*. What the people of Edna said was *she ain't right*. I guess it depends on how you look at it, but watching her standing in our door on that late June morning, her father pulling out of our driveway as fast as his car would take him, her pale arms clutching a shiny new Samsonite, I thought, something is wrong here.

Ray had a condition. She'd been in a car wreck when she was just fourteen, less than a year before she turned up at our door, and something in her brain died, the part that told right from wrong. According to my mother, that part shriveled like bad fruit and rotted away leaving room for the devil to fill and he did.

"Frontal lobe damage," Lucie said. "That's what's wrong with her. No impulse control. Nothing so dramatic as the devil."

None of us listened to Lucie. Our eyes were glued on Ray Moon.

She stood in our doorway for hours that first day, staring off into the distance, her fingers still wrapped around the handle of the suitcase. She wore a fine dress, lavender silk with black piping on the hem, and Lucie couldn't help but gawk, because the style was more suited to Lucie's age and Lucie never had much and wanted all. Ray saw none of us. Her pale eyes: the color of smoke fading.

Lucie and I made dinner with limp vegetables Mrs. Fundak sent us. Lucie walked with a plateful over to Ray. She finally set her suitcase down, bending only at the waist. The heels of her black maryjanes were punched together like a soldier. She put her hands out for the plate, but did not look at Lucie, and my sister, scared as a mouse, put the plate into Ray's outstretched hands.

"Thank you," Ray said, her first words to us. Her voice shocked us with its sweetness. She smelled of flowers, the scent overwhelming.

Ray's hands didn't so much as let go of the plate as collapse. My mother's plate struck the floor, food splattering the linoleum and the hem of Ray's beautiful dress, and not a chip, not a sliver came off that plate. It spun at her feet, whirring a thin sound, then stopped. "Why does he hate me?" she asked. "What have I done?"

"Take her and make her right," Bobby Alan Moon had said to my mother. "Fill her with whatever has filled you."

There is no cross you cannot bear. Ray Moon was ours.

We put Ray in Lucie's and Molly's room and they moved in with me, which made us irritable. We climbed over each other like crabs in a bucket. "You must be bigger than that," my mother said. "You must be strong."

For the first two days, Ray thrashed on Lucie's bed, still in her food-splattered dress, her long gold hair tangled over the pillow, her hands gouging her body, horrifying wails erupting from her throat. She wouldn't eat or speak or acknowledge us.

We fumbled through our days, drunk from the cloying smell of her. Lucie became sullen and listless, uninterested in her books. "Why bother?" she said.

Little Molly covered her ears every time Ray moaned or howled in agony. At the time, we were not aware of Molly's special kind of genius, didn't understand her hypersensitivity to loud sounds she could not control. She climbed from our bed in the night and hid in the shed. She slept curled around the garden tools. We found her there in the morning, tapping out elaborate rhythms on the blade of a shovel or axe.

"Let it be," our mother said about Ray. "We don't indulge spoiled children. She'll come around when she's wanting something."

Sure enough, the morning of the third day Ray sat up, taut-backed and rigid, flipped her legs over the bed, grabbed her Samsonite suitcase from the closet, and locked herself in our only bathroom for several hours.

When she came out, her breasts wrapped in scraps of purple fabric,

Jennifer S. Davis

her concave belly bare and glistening, a tiny black skirt low on her hips, her mouth as red and round as a fireball, I knew we were in for trouble.

"Why hi," she said, looking straight at me. "Got anything to eat?" She smacked her lips like old men do before Thanksgiving dinner.

"Gimme a break," Lucie said. She'd caught me staring at Ray's breasts. "Those ain't nothing but fat."

"Lucie," my mother said. "We don't speak of such things in this house." My mother stood in the kitchen, a paintbrush in each hand, blues dripping onto the floor. "Of course," she said to Ray, "you will have to change into something more appropriate."

Ray threw her head back, released a long, trebling keen. Then she shoved her hand down her skirt and began kneading wildly. "I hurt," she moaned.

"Oh goodness," my mother said. "You have to stop that."

"I sure am hungry," Ray said.

My mother gave her one of my father's t-shirts to wear over her outfit and told me to take her over to Pete's house for some lunch. Mrs. Fundak made us a huge pot of macaroni and cheese with a block of cheddar melted on top.

Pete couldn't stop staring at Ray, kept whispering to me, *look at the size of them tits*. When Ray caught him looking, she blinked longingly.

"How old are you, girl?" Mrs. Fundak asked.

"Fifteen," Ray Moon said, cheddar cheese smeared on her chin. "This is good."

"What's that smell?" Pete said. He pushed his nostrils in the air.

"You're awful developed for fifteen," Mrs. Fundak said. "I mean, there ain't nothing wrong with that. But you should be careful. I was early developed, and it got me nothing but trouble." She sniggered. "Fun, but trouble."

"More," said Ray Moon, pushing her plate toward the bowl of coagulating pasta.

"It's not polite to ask for seconds in someone else's home," Mrs. Fundak said. "Look, Pete. You see how rude that is. Pete's not polite, either." Mrs. Fundak stared pointedly at Pete. "You see, boy? You see how ugly rude is?"

"May we be excused," Pete said.

"Well," Mrs. Fundak said, rolling back a bit in her chair. "Now that's more like it."

We took Ray outside to show her the gully, and she immediately slid down its worn, dusty bank, squealing with pleasure the whole way, her skirt hiked up around her waist, her butt cheeks stained red from the dirt. There was something awe inspiring in her lack of fear.

"I bet she'll do anything we tell her to," Pete said.

"You know why the dirt here is so red?" Ray yelled from the gully. "Iron. The soil is rich in iron. A lot of pregnant women like to eat it. That's called geophagy."

Pete looked at me, stunned. "I thought she was retarded," he said.

"Not all of her," I said. "Just the part that tells right and wrong."

"Well hot damn," Pete said. "Hey Ray," he yelled down the gully. "Take off your shirt and show us what you got."

Without hesitation, Ray pulled my father's white T-shirt over her head, then untied the purple scarf.

"Like this?" she said, radiant. Her breasts were as round and flawless as those in the dirty magazines we found on the side of the road near the Conoco, and I felt myself harden, no matter how much I willed my body to still.

"Oh my God," Pete said. Then, "Do us a little dance." Ray began pirouetting, her long, slender legs perfectly poised. She looked like she'd had some training.

"Watch this." Pete picked up a few pebbles, began pelting them at Ray as she twirled tornados of red dust.

"Ow," Ray giggled. She rubbed her shoulder where a rock had hit her, gyrating her hips and humming the entire time.

I slapped the rocks out of Pete's hands. "What are you doing that for?" I said, knowing I should have said something sooner. "That ain't right."

Pete shrugged, kicked a clump of dirt over the edge of the gully where it fell at Ray's dancing feet.

"Look around," Pete said. "There ain't much right."

Jennifer S. Davis

My mother sent Ray to Bible School with the rest of us in July, but she was so disruptive—exposing herself in craft class, putting her hands down her skirt during youth fellowship, letting boys fondle her breasts behind the juice machines at lunch—my mother was asked to withdraw her. She put Ray to prepping doors, and Ray chipped and sanded faithfully, the soft heart curve of her bottom peeking from under her skirt as she worked.

"Ray," my mother would say when she saw her pressing herself against some poor man there to get drunk in the spirit. "Remember who you are. You are a child of God." We found Ray naked in the shed with more than one of the believers from Tennessee, Georgia, Louisiana, and sometimes farther.

"I've done something wrong?" she'd say when my mother hauled her off the men and out of the shed. "I'm bad?" she'd ask. The men whimpered as if they'd been wronged, covered themselves with cupped hands.

For obvious reasons, my mother decided to keep Ray home when classes started in mid-August. After school, Ray and I sat on a bench in the front yard and talked. She told me about before the accident, how she'd been an honors student and a cheerleader, how she'd had an ant farm that won the science fair, how she'd won a ribbon at dance camp for the best line kicks, how a boy named Cameron kissed her for the first time at the sixth grade homecoming dance.

I told her what I'd learned at school. How the core of the earth was partially made of iron, just like the red dirt pregnant women ate. Except the earth's core reached temperatures as high as 7000 degrees Celsius, which was about the temperature of hell, I figured. How some non-believer scientists thought animals around us evolved from previously existing animals, that people could have been monkeys or amoebas once.

"Oh I can believe that," Ray said. She leaned toward me confidentially, her hair tickling my forearm, her floral scent overwhelming. "When I was in that car wreck, I died for a few minutes. Like really dead. But I didn't see a tunnel of light or a bunch of angels in white robes like old people in church say. I was transformed into a bird with black-black wings that spread across a sky bluer than anything I'd ever imagined. And I flew. Just opened my wings and sailed across the world. Weightless. No pain.

No worries. Just flight. It was amazing." Her smoky eyes filled with tears. "Sometimes, well . . . sometimes I wish they hadn't bothered bringing me back."

"You were knocked out," I told her. "You weren't a bird."

"Oh no," she said. "You better believe it. I was a bird." She gave my hand a friendly pat, left it there, and I wondered, not for the first time, what it said about me that a girl who couldn't control her sexual impulses with strange men somehow had none for me.

"In mythology, birds are powerful creatures," she said.

"How about fish?" I asked. "Are they powerful, too? Because if my father gets what he wants, in heaven he'll be a large-mouthed bass."

I could see my mother out of the corner of my eye, the melancholy stoop of her back as she bent over yet another door. I hadn't realized I was so angry.

"People can only give you what they have to give," Ray said softly. "Your mother, your father, my father, Pete, Mrs. Fundak. You just have to learn to accept what they can spare you."

"Is that what you do?" I said. "Take it when Pete *gives it to you*." Immediately, I wanted to swallow my words. But there they were, bold-faced and obvious, my aching heart more responsibility than I could manage. I knew he came to her in the night; she didn't try to hide it. I watched them through my bedroom window, naked and intertwined in the soft grass beneath the mulberry tree.

Ray stood, regarded me coolly. "Now, there's no excuse for such hatefulness," she said finally. "You, of all people, have much more to offer."

And when she said it, I believed.

Under my mother's supervision, Ray seemed to be getting better. She quit rubbing herself at inappropriate times, stopped wailing and thrashing in her bed. Ray surprised everyone with memorization skills the doctors swore she would never recover, reciting long passages of scripture for my mother before bedtime.

"See," my mother said, pronouncing Ray practically cured. "The Word can do powerful things."

Jennifer S. Davis

"Whatever," Lucie muttered under her breath. "God ain't got anything to do with it. Her brain's healing. That's called *nature*."

And then, one morning Ray woke up and puked all over the fluffy green toilet cover.

"She's pregnant," Lucie said, a little too gleefully. "And *that* is definitely nature."

"No," my mother said. "It's the evil working itself out of her. It's bound to make the girl ill." She didn't look convinced.

When I finally mustered the courage to tell Pete that he might be a father, I found Mrs. Fundak sitting alone in her special chair on the porch.

"He's gone," she said. "Not a note. Nothing. He always was a rude boy. Got it from his father." She looked like she hadn't bathed in days. She was dressed in a half-buttoned nightgown. Her hair clung to her scalp. "Who's going to roll my hair? Help me into the tub?" She slapped her fat thighs and sighed. Then she whirled her chair around, scooted back into the house on tiny, spidery feet.

A week later, Ray was running for the bathroom two or three times a day. If she wasn't puking, she curled up in bed, crying. When Lucie found Ray laid out cold on the bathroom floor, my mother rinsed off her paintbrushes and closed up shop. She packed us into the truck, then tore out to Full Gospel Baptist for counseling and prayer.

"I don't understand," Lucie scowled. "What's Preacher Willie going to do about a baby? Shouldn't we be going to a hospital?"

"It's not what Preacher Willie's going to do. It's what God wants us to do," my mother said.

"Preacher Willie ain't God," Lucie said.

"Shut up, Lucie." My mother's hands twitched uncontrollably on the steering wheel.

Over the recent months, thanks to my mother's donations, Brother Willie had carpeted the sanctuary in a deep crimson, added a towering baptismal tank behind the altar, a new glassed-in nursery in the foyer.

"The Lord has been good to us," said Brother Willie. His entire office had been renovated—crimson carpet like the sanctuary, crimson velvet drapes, rose-colored stain-glassed windows that tinged the room a milky red.

"It looks like the inside of God's belly," Lucie said. "Or maybe Jonah in the whale." My mother whacked the back of her head, smiled serenely at Brother Willie.

"She'll have to get married," Preacher Willie said after my mother explained Ray's situation. He locked his watery eyes on Ray. She shuddered in the corner of the room. Her hands cradled her abdomen.

My mother stared blankly at Preacher Willie. She opened her mouth, but no sound came out.

That afternoon, my mother sat grimly at the kitchen table and flipped through the pages of her ear-marked Bible, the doors, for once, forgotten. After a few hours, she slammed the Bible shut, tucked it under her arm, and marched into Ray's room.

For days my mother sat at Ray's bedside, spooning special soups and teas in the girl's mouth. They clutched each other's hands, murmured low into the wee hours. The sweet scent of Ray radiated from the room. The doors and windows were kept open day and night.

One morning, a loud shriek exploded from Ray's room. We heard glass breaking. Furniture being overturned.

"Here it comes," Lucie squealed.

"Here what comes?" I said.

"The baby, you idiot."

"What baby?" I asked.

Molly crawled into the corner.

"A baby takes nine months to make," I said.

"Not one you want to get rid of." Lucie slit her eyes narrow. "What do you think all them teas have been for?"

We peered into Ray's room. It looked like a tornado had hit, knickknacks broken on the floor, the sheets slung from the bed, the nightstand on its side. And standing in the middle of the room with a writhing blanket in her hands was our mother.

Ray smiled at me. "I told you so," she said.

"If that's what a new baby's like," Lucie said, nodding at the thrashing blanket in our mother's hands, "I don't ever want to have me one."

"That's not a baby," my mother said, loosening the blanket so we

Jennifer S. Davis

could see "It's a bird. It came in through the window and wouldn't go back out. I had a time catching it. " And sure enough, you could just make out a long, charcoal beak in the folds of the blanket, its shiny, darting eyes.

"Lovely, isn't it?" my mother said wistfully. "I've never touched a live one." She squatted on the floor next to Molly, who placed her hand tentatively against the stunned bird's inky black head.

"Bird," my mother said, enunciating slowly. Molly chortled, patted the bird's head like a dog's. "Bird," Molly repeated, her first word, and we all stared at her in wonder. She smiled the same sad smile she was born with.

After everyone had a chance to stroke the bird, my mother walked reluctantly to the front door and opened the blanket. The bird lurched from her hands. In a matter of seconds, it was nothing more than a fluttering black gap against the day's sky.

"What about the baby?" Lucie said.

My mother held up a round gumball-sized pebble with stony protruding spikes. It looked like something from my earth science book, a shrunken, undiscovered planet.

"That's what's left of the baby?" For once, Lucie seemed confused.

"A kidney stone," my mother smiled. "The wounded soul is like any other living thing; it will push out rot sooner or later."

"Like your toe will push out a splinter left in too long?" I asked.

"Exactly," my mother said.

I peered into Ray's bedroom, where she leaned against a wall of pillows. The drapes billowed lazily in the morning breeze. Ray smiled tranquilly. "Did you see it, the bird?" She looked triumphant, as if something momentous about the mystery of the world had been revealed.

The next day, Bobby Ray Moon collected his daughter with little fanfare, like he was picking her up from summer camp. He shoved a wad of bills in my mother's hand, and for once, perhaps understanding that she was worthy of better, my mother put the money in the bank instead of the collection plate at Full Gospel Baptist.

Time passed, as it will.

My mother saved enough money to move us to Birmingham, where her artwork was displayed in galleries to much critical acclaim. She enrolled Lucie in the gifted school, and my sister, who found others like herself, flourished. She eventually became a doctor and opened a clinic in Edna, where she felt she was needed most. My mother bought Molly a piano so she could put her twitching fingers to work, and although she's never spoken a complete sentence to this day, she tells epic stories with her music.

And eventually my shoulders broadened and my voice deepened and I became man enough to have my heart shattered soundly more than once, which is all we can ask for in life, those small moments of hope in the initial throes of love when all is still possible.

I never heard of Ray Moon again after the day she left our house wearing the same lavender dress in which she arrived. But I like to think she lives her life as fearlessly as that broken girl left on our doorstep, carrying with her, as do those who knew her one long-ago summer, the understanding that with faith, all that is lost and dark within us might somehow find a way to emerge into the inchoate world and take flight.

Jennifer S. Davis grew up in Dadeville, Alabama, and her writing often explores the everyday absurdities of the American South. She is the author of two collections of short stories, Her Kind of Want, *winner of the Iowa Award for Short Fiction, and* Our Former Lives in Art *(Random House), which was included by Barnes and Noble in the Discover Great New Writers Series. She has published fiction in such journals as* Tin House, Paris Review, One Story, The Oxford American, Epoch, Georgia Review, *and* Zoetrope. *She lives in Baton Rouge with her husband and three young sons and teaches in the MFA program at LSU.*

Jennifer S. Davis

Rome, Italy

Fannie Flagg

What I would want for the reader most of all is to bring them into a world and give them some laughs and maybe make them say, oh, that happened to me—I understand that, oh yes, I've done that. And, basically just sort of have a laugh at the human condition, which is pretty funny, you know.

Mrs. Lenore Simmons Krackenberry, a large, imposing woman with a scarf flowing behind her, was escorted into a private room at the Vatican and apologetically informed that her audience with the pope would be limited to five minutes. She smiled good-naturedly at the young man and in a deep Southern drawl so thick you could cut it with a knife said, "Honey, five minutes is all I need. He's busy. I'm busy. So that's just fine."

She sat with a lace handkerchief on her head bearing the initials LSK and admired the tapestries hanging on the walls while she waited. She had decided to spend her "Soak Up Culture Month" in Italy this year, so she could kill two birds with one stone, and this was one of those birds.

In a few minutes she was ushered into a room where the pope was sitting with his interpreter standing by his side. She walked up and said, "Well, how do you do. I'm Lenore Simmons Krackenberry all the way from Selma, Alabama. And I know one of your darling archbishops from Mobile, Archbishop Oscar Lipscomb. We are both on the board of the International Coalition of Christians and Jews, and while I was in town I wanted to drop by and chat with you about this birth control thing."

The small, thin, nervous man by his side turned to the pope and said in Italian, "Your Holiness, I am afraid I cannot understand what she has said; her English is very poor."

The pope smiled and nodded at Lenore. She smiled back and continued, "Now look, I know you all are against it, but really, you need to change those little rules. I think you really need to get behind this thing and tell all your people to stop breeding so much. Too many people are going hungry.

"Not to mention the overpopulation problem. Why just look at Bangladesh, those poor people are starving to death … I'm head of the Selma chapter of Planned Parenthood and we think it's just cruel to bring children into the world just to have them starve to death. If you can't feed them you shouldn't have them … don't you agree?"

The interpreter said, "I believe the lady is speaking of a drum that is free … or something of this nature."

The pope nodded and smiled. Lenore Simmons Krackenberry smiled back, and asked the interpreter, "What did he say?"

"His Holiness appreciates your interest in this matter."

"Oh? Well good. Tell him I love his outfit, and tell him he should come to Mobile sometime for Mardi Gras. We have all kinds of lovely clothes he would like. Brocades, silks … the King and Queen of Mardi Gras outfits alone cost over one hundred thousand dollars. And we would love to have him. Tell him he could have his own float if he wanted."

The interpreter pulled a long white handkerchief out of the pocket of his cassock and wiped his brow and said, "Your Holiness, I am sorry. But I am sure she will not be much longer."

Lenore looked at the pope. "Your palace is just lovely. I'm a Presbyterian myself but I can certainly appreciate all the time and effort you go to to keep it looking so nice."

The interpreter said, "She says something about …" He faltered, "I cannot be sure …"

The pope smiled pleasantly and nodded at her. Lenore glanced at her watch.

"Well, I'm going to run now … but I did want to put that bug in your ear while I was here…"

The interpreter smiled, "I think she is finished." The pope smiled again and said something pleasant in Italian.

"What did he say?" asked Mrs. Krackenberry, smiling and nodding back.

"His Holiness would like to thank you for your visit. He is always most happy to receive Americans and would like to give you his blessing."

Fannie Flagg

"Oh ... well, how sweet."

The pope made the sign of the cross and gave her a long blessing in Latin. When he finished she did a small Magnolia Trail Maiden curtsy and said, "I loved meeting you. And do come to Selma sometimes, we would just love to have you. Now, if you come, you be sure to call me, I'm in the book ... and I'll tell Archbishop Lipscomb you said hello ... Arrivederci!"

Lenore walked out and met her friend, Mrs. Pearl Jeff, who had come to Rome with her and who was waiting outside.

Mrs. Jeff said, "Well, did you meet him?"

"I sure did, and honey, he is just precious, the cutest jolliest thing. He couldn't have been nicer."

"What happened? Tell me everything."

"Well we chatted for a few minutes, of course, to be polite. And then I told him what I thought and he seemed to agree."

"Oh, what did he say?"

"Well, he didn't say much. He just more or less listened. You know, he doesn't speak a word of English. I had to be interpreted. But at the end he said a little something in Italian. Now you mark my words, I bet we see a big change in that birth control policy in the near future."

"Really?" said Mrs. Jeff in awe.

Lenore waved away a pigeon that was flying over her head. "Oh, yes, and I invited him to come to Selma. I told him we would love to have him."

"Ohhh, do you think he might come?"

Lenore looked at Pearl. "Well I don't know why in the world he shouldn't. He loves America."

Fannie Flagg's career started in the fifth grade when she wrote, directed, and starred in her first play entitled The Whoopee Girls, and she has not stopped since. At age nineteen she began writing and producing television specials, and later wrote and appeared on Candid Camera. She then went on to distinguish herself as an actress and a writer in television, films, and the theater. She is the New York

Times *bestselling author of* Daisy Fay and the Miracle Man; Fried Green Tomatoes at the Whistle Stop Cafe; Welcome to the World, Baby Girl!; Standing in the Rainbow; A Redbird Christmas; *and* Can't Wait to Get to Heaven. *Flagg's script for the movie* Fried Green Tomatoes *was nominated for an Academy Award and the Writers Guild of America Award and won the highly regarded Scripter Award for best screenplay of the year. Flagg lives happily in California and Alabama.*

Fannie Flagg

No Shadow of Turning

Anita Miller Garner

The best road route from Florence to Mobile is actually not through Alabama at all but through a deserted region of East Mississippi. On a road trip using this route to Mobile, my husband and I found ourselves in a tiny Mississippi town at an odd hour, looking for gas in a thunderstorm. We went inside a WalMart—almost deserted due to the time of day and the weather—and when I glanced up, I looked right into the face of a beautiful young woman who glanced down quickly to avoid eye contact, embarrassed it seemed. Her left eye and cheek were bruised. I think she had gone to that deserted Walmart in the thunderstorm hoping no one would see her. I think she had not run into a door or fallen down the steps or tripped over the dog. Someone had done this to her—probably a loved one. Then when I discovered that Lauderdale County, Alabama, leads the nation in domestic abuse, I knew I had to write this story. The detail of the tattoo came from Al Young who told it when he visited UNA and Pam Kingsbury and I took him to lunch at Sweet Basil Cafe. He said it would be a great detail for a story, so I told him it fit perfectly a story I was writing and that I was going to steal it, and he smiled, generously.

What, after all, do any of us know about those we love?

Darlene feels that thought circle her brain like the red-tailed hawk she watches soaring high above a distant field beyond the edges of Plantation Hills subdivision. She steps back from the clothesline to survey her work. Ten pairs of little boy jeans line up like the bottom halves of paper dolls.

"I just married him too fast is all," Anna Linda says. Darlene watches Anna Linda pour onto the ground the spent sludge from her coffee cup, Anna Linda's striped hair—alternate platinum and cherry red as cough drops—lit by the afternoon sun.

According to Anna Linda, her husband Petey Parsons jerks her around in just about every room of their house. Pushes her down in the kitchen for leaving dirty dishes in the sink then drags her across the floor by the hair. Kicks the leg of her plastic lawn chair as she sits on the deck and shells peas for his supper. When he is too tired to devil her, he just sits in his big brown recliner, watches her fold laundry in front of the TV, and tells her she is frigid in one breath while in the next breath yells he knows she is unfaithful.

Darlene is required only to listen to Anna Linda's arguments with herself, not respond, as Anna Linda describes the latest Petey episode. As usual, in this version of the story, it is all Anna Linda's fault. Today it is because she married Petey too soon.

"You got to make a man wait," Anna Linda says. "I should a known that." She stares at something in the sky, and Darlene turns to see a half moon lit high in the west in the daylight sky. "What a man needs," Anna Linda says, "is mystery."

Darlene's boys, Jeremy and his younger shadow Jason, run out the back door and stand at attention on the grass, waiting for Anna Linda to stop talking just long enough to breathe so they can ask Darlene permission, quick, before Anna Linda starts in again, answering her own questions, no pause.

Jason squirms before he blurts out "Mama, can we go see Awesome's baby?"

Jeremy slaps the back of his younger brother's head and looks, as always, to Darlene for approval, the older son who was first in Darlene's heart and who struggles to keep that position. "Don't interrupt people, Jason."

Awesome is a mare at the farm down the road from Plantation Hills, just a short bike ride away. Darlene has seen Awesome's colt lying in the morning sun in the field on her way home from driving the boys to school, before she returns home to put clothes in the washer and turn on the dishwasher, before she drives to the almost empty house on Normandy Lane and watches Charles Wayne Murphy close the living room drapes before he comes to her in the bedroom of the house he has had listed for sale now for three months and takes off his clothes.

"Just for a little while," Jason pleads.

"We'll be careful," Jeremy adds with authority.

When Darlene says yes, the boys vanish.

Anna Linda continues. "Does Jack ever treat you like Petey treats me? Push you around?"

Darlene thinks about it, the way her husband treats her, as if she is a

Anita Miller Garner

keepsake sofa from a favorite, dead grandmother, too lumpy to keep but too cherished to throw away. She tries to put together a sentence.

Anna Linda interrupts Darlene's thoughts. "Because I can't even ride with Petey to his mama's house without him figuring out a way to make me cry. I know he's gonna do it before we even get in the car, but I can't help myself. I know by the time we get there my mascara will be run halfway down my face. God, his family must think I'm ugly. What can I say?" She pauses briefly to sigh. "I love the man."

Darlene met Charles Wayne Murphy over a year ago at Tiger's Gym, and as far as she can figure, no one knows they are having an affair.

She went to the gym after Jack added her to his membership and told her it would do her good to get out, and anyway, he said, maybe she would drop a few inches. Darlene stood at the mirror, turned sideways, and held her breath. After the birth of Jeremy and then four years later Jason, her stomach was no longer flat.

She had no fancy workout clothes, so she wore her usual loose jeans and sneakers. She was surprised to find how much she liked the elliptical machine, the stationary bike, the burn in her shoulders and sudden hot sweat she felt on the rowing machine. After two months of bench presses, she could lift half her body weight. When she soaped her arms in the shower, she could feel the new, firm curves of her biceps.

Mid mornings when she went to the gym, mostly there were just young mothers in an aerobics class and retired men drinking coffee around the table up front by the windows. Charles Wayne Murphy was older than Darlene, in his forties, in real estate, and could come to the gym any time that suited him, he told her the day he spotted for her. He and Darlene had been the only two people in the weight room. Darlene lay flat on her back and strained to lift the barbell. She felt her face flush from the effort.

"Damn, girl," Charles Wayne had said, standing there ready in case she got in trouble. "Don't hold it in. Breathe out."

Darlene slowly let go of her breath but still struggled. She lowered the weights.

Charles Wayne stood so close she could feel the heat of his body. "Breathe in again," he coached her. "Now push," he said. "Grunt. Loud.

Push that bar up."

Darlene let out a high-pitched moan from her gut, like a cry from an animal hit in the road. She pushed from her center, lifting. This time she kept the barbell steady, under control.

Later, as she left the gym, she waved to Charles Wayne as he stood talking by the front counter. He called out to her to wait and came over to where she stood. When she reached out to shake his hand, he pulled her to him and gave her a friendly hug instead.

"Thanks," she said, "for helping me." He smelled of soap and clean sweat. A hint of bar smoke on his jacket.

"Anytime." He grinned. And then, "I could show you some things. If you're interested."

Darlene and Anna Linda sit near the clothesline at the picnic table Jack made with the five thousand dollars worth of wood-working equipment from Sears that takes up most of the space in the garage. Jack made the picnic table and chairs as well as a bar in the basement room where he put a big screen TV and a long shelf all down one wall that holds his signed Jack Daniels bottle collection that Darlene dusts, one bottle from each of their annual pilgrimages to Lynchburg to the fall barbecue cook-off. When she dusts them, she thinks with a laugh *Like sands through the hourglass, these are the days of our lives*. When the shelf is finally full, she wonders if she will still be alive to dust it.

Anna Linda sits crying in the rough chair, her legs drawn up like a little girl. How can she be sure, she asks, if Petey really loves her? She has been at Darlene's so long now that Darlene wonders if Anna Linda will be able to make it home in time to heat up leftovers in a way they appear to be a good thing to Petey Parsons, something Petey Parsons will eat and not complain about. Darlene has venison chili in the slow cooker, one of Petey's favorites, and decides she will send some of it home with Anna Linda.

Anna Linda shifts forward, lifts the back hem of her shirt, pushes down the back of her pants, and asks Darlene if there is a bruise in the middle of her lower back. She reveals a small tattoo of a red butterfly below the panty line. Darlene knows her face must reflect her curious

Anita Miller Garner

surprise. Although Anna Linda had never mentioned it to her, Darlene had heard about the tattoo, yet she had never seen it.

"Oh, that," Anna Linda says, wiping a tear. "Petey saw that on the internet. He set it up for me to get it. Stayed with me the whole time. Even held my hand. But now he's jealous of the tattoo guy." Anna Linda's eyes pool with fresh tears. "He says I flirted with the man. That's just crazy. I was in too much pain to flirt. Anybody would know that. And besides, that's been months ago."

Darlene's mind wanders as Anna Linda gives the details about what each element of the tattoo means, about how if you know how to read the codes, the tattoo tells all the ways Anna Linda is willing to do it. For instance, the initials P.P. above the butterfly mean that Anna Linda will only perform those sexual acts with Petey Parsons, she says. Darlene watches the hawk sail down the street now, headed for the tall cedar on the vacant lot that was supposed to be a park. Darlene has watched the hawk for months, watched it hunt ground squirrels and field mice in the tall, wild grass. She wonders why the hawk flies above the streets, following the grid on its way to and fro, as if riding in an invisible car high up in the air. She wonders why it does not fly over the houses. She thinks of asking Anna Linda if she, too, has noticed this.

"Every night he brings his pistol into the bedroom and puts it right under his pillow," Anna Linda says. "He says he keeps it there in case he hears prowlers. What if I get up to pee in the middle of the night and he thinks I'm a prowler?"

Darlene hears tires squeal and the *boom boom boom* of a car's sound system. She looks through the chain link gate to the street in front and catches a glimpse of the shiny black SUV with the windows down, laughing teenagers in the front and back seats. Twice more she hears the tires squeal in the distance and realizes the driver is accelerating so fast the tires of the SUV slip as the driver struggles to make the turns, trying to make his way out of the maze of Plantation Hills.

They had met so many times in the house on Normandy Lane that it seemed impossible to Darlene that the neighbors had not figured out what was going on. Charles Wayne Murphy told her to park her car in a different spot every time and to always back her car into the driveway when she parked directly beside the house. That way, he said, no one could read her license plate. He told her to remove the dealer advertisement plate she had on the front, the one the car dealer stuck on, without asking, when Jack bought the car.

"What will I tell Jack if he asks why it's missing?"

"Tell him you guess it fell off."

Not that Darlene and Charles Wayne talk that much. When Darlene thinks of Charles Wayne Murphy as she sorts laundry or makes the boys' beds, she does not think of what Charles Wayne says as much as she thinks of his muscular shoulders, the urgency of his tongue, the new language her body has learned from his.

Once he asked, cautiously, "What do you tell your girlfriends?"

She thought about it. "I don't have girlfriends."

"You talk to other women, though, don't you? All you girls talk."

"Anna Linda talks to me."

"And what do you say back?"

Most of the time the questions he posed were physical, asked with his eyes as he guided her through the hours spent in the daylight that sifted through the curtains on Normandy Lane.

What Darlene learned she liked was risk. Like making out in high school in a parked car. The risk of being caught. Without telling anyone, she flushed her birth control pills down the toilet, punching each pill out of the foil pack to watch it hit the water. She kept the pink plastic package in the usual spot in her drawer in case Jack checked. Two boys, he said, were plenty.

"Take a deep breath," Charles Wayne said when he could tell that she was close. "Now let it out." Darlene could hear his voice change to something higher pitched and soft like pleading. "Let it out."

To Darlene, hearing her own voice echoing in the almost empty house felt like something she had been trying to say for a long time but had never known how until that moment.

The sun is almost ready to set. Darlene and Anna Linda leave the back yard and go into the kitchen, Darlene to pack some chili into a plastic container, Anna Linda to drink the last cup of coffee in the pot. Darlene hears a car door slam shut and looks out the window to see Petey Parsons' red truck in the driveway, Petey Parsons himself bounding up the front walk, his face contorted. When Darlene opens the front door before he's even knocked, she fears that Petey has snapped and will have his pistol in his hand. In the distance, she hears two sirens.

Petey's face, however, is not tied up in anger but in urgent pain. He grabs Darlene's arm and starts guiding her back down the sidewalk to his truck. "Come on, Darlene," he says with concern. Anna Linda stands in the open doorway, her mouth open, her eyes large. Petey yells to her, "Damn it, Anna Linda, come on."

Petey was headed home when he came upon the two boys at the scene, Jeremy screaming hysterically, hovering over a smaller body by the side of the road. A mangled bike with training wheels still lay on the blacktop. A man in a delivery truck had already called 911 on his cell phone to report the hit and run. Petey drove as fast as he could to Darlene's house.

Already, in such a short time, cars are backed up. Petey Parsons drives around the cars and through the tall, dry grass on the side of the road so fast that Darlene's head bumps the headliner in the cab. They have arrived before the ambulance as well as the sheriff.

Darlene feels it takes half a lifetime for the truck to come to a stop and for her to get out and run to her boys. Jeremy's face is so changed by panic and fear that he is hardly recognizable as the same child who stood before her at the clothesline just a short while ago. Jason, on the ground, looks asleep, as she has seen him a thousand times on the sofa in front of the TV at night or in his bed in the mornings. At the sound of her voice, Jeremy has moved aside now so that she can cover Jason's body with her own, keep him warm with the blood coursing through her body. She kisses his warm forehead and smells in his hair the little boy scent of fresh air and sweat from playing hard. She is aware of a loud siren approaching, but she can't let it concern her. She is there to love her child back to life if it comes to that.

"Ma'am," a man says quickly as he takes her arm and moves her out of the way.

Who can make sense of the rush of people, the flashing lights, a man in uniform asking her questions when all Darlene wants is to see her son and know what they are doing with him?

And Jeremy, her little man, saying over and over "I'm sorry, Mama. I'm sorry," a constant whispered chant through his tears as he stands by her side, sometimes adding "he wouldn't listen to me."

Two men ease Jason onto a stretcher, but when Darlene tries to climb into the back of the ambulance along with them, a deputy, one of Jack's old high school buddies, puts his arm around her. "Come on, Darlene, let me give you a ride. We'll lead the way for the ambulance. I've called Jack already." Darlene looks to Jeremy, who is being led by Anna Linda and Petey Parsons back to Petey's red truck.

One time they did talk.

They were dressing to leave when there was a sudden downpour on Normandy Lane and neither Darlene nor Charles Wayne Murphy had brought an umbrella. There was time to kill.

"Tell me about that hot friend of yours with that red striped hair."

Darlene had never thought of Anna Linda as hot. She thought of her as sad.

"She cries a lot."

"She was in front of me at the Jiffy Mart the other day. She dropped a quarter, and when she bent down to get it, her shirt hiked up and those jeans of hers just about slid off. She had on these black thong panties and this butterfly tattooed real low on her back. I mean *real* low."

"I don't know anything about that."

Darlene told Charles Wayne about the only thing she could think of that was Anna Linda's, and that was Anna Linda's angel garden. Everything else in Anna Linda's house was Petey's, but the angel garden was hers alone. Anna Linda had taken Petey's pickup truck across the state line all the way to the curb market in Saltillo that sold yard decorations at good prices and loaded up the bed of the truck with concrete saints painted in bright colors and plain, unpainted gray concrete angels, one of each kind the market had. One large girl angel standing tall. A pair of chubby little angels kneeling together, joined by a glob of concrete. A small child angel with a concrete Bible beneath its hands clasped in prayer. When Anna

Linda arrived back home, Petey Parsons got up out of his recliner long enough to help her unload, but the labor of making the garden had been left up totally to Anna Linda. She planted perennials so in case she died the garden would go on living in her memory, she said. When Anna Linda's mama cat rolled over on two of her newborn kittens and smothered them, Anna Linda invited Darlene and the boys over for a funeral in the angel garden. Jeremy and Jason picked the blossoms off a confederate rose and laid them on the tiny graves.

When she finished telling the story, Charles Wayne's sweet distant smile told her he liked thinking of Anna Linda, black thong and all, in a garden of concrete love.

All of this and none of this is in Darlene's brain now. She is on the way to an emergency room where she will find out if her baby will live. If this turns out wrong, she thinks, nothing else she ever does in her life will matter.

The deputy drives fast, racing through intersections, the siren screaming nonstop. Darlene turns around to look, and the ambulance is right behind them, lights flashing.

"The way I see it," the deputy begins, "the vehicle hit the bike and threw that boy to the shoulder of the road." Darlene can see that he is nervous but trying to be positive. "Could be it just knocked him out is all." He keeps his eyes on the road and does not look at her as he says this. Darlene does not think he believes these words.

Cars scatter, some pulling over on the shoulder to let them by. Darlene studies the ambulance trailing behind them, but there is nothing she can determine. The deputy calls out to the dispatcher on the police radio the name of each intersection as they approach it.

When they arrive at the hospital, the deputy parks and Darlene watches the ambulance pull directly up to the emergency room bay. She bounds out of the police car, headed toward the opening doors of the ambulance when she sees Jack already standing at the edge of the platform, watching the action around the van's back doors, turning to look down at her, his eyes sharp with impatience.

A man wearing scrubs comes out of the hospital doors and asks a question just as one of the men who loaded Jason emerges from the back of the ambulance. Darlene is too far away to hear the words clearly that they have said, so a couple of seconds pass before her mind can process the words *didn't make it.*

She does not cry out but instead stumbles in the twilight to the cold pavement, twisting her right leg under her in the process and scratching her palms as she falls on the asphalt's grit. Her hands break her fall so that she does not bump her head, but she lays her cheek onto the rough black surface anyway, a cold pillow of darkness as her mind hums in pain. Her leg and hands throb, so she closes her eyes, too numb for tears. She forgets time, purpose. She is consumed by the knot of ache deep inside her.

Eventually she hears someone approach and feels the soft touch of an arm around her as she lies there. Anna Linda's perfume is like warm vanilla. Her voice is soft.

"Come on. Let me help you. Jason will want to see you."

Darlene sits up slowly and looks into Anna Linda's eyes, thinking Anna Linda must not know, realizing this is the first of a thousand people she will have to tell this to for the rest of her life. "Jason's gone." She makes herself repeat the words that she had heard. "He didn't make it."

Darlene sees the confusion in Anna Linda's eyes before Anna Linda speaks. "Is that what you think, hon?"

"I heard them say it. He didn't make it."

"I saw him myself just now, Darlene, as they were taking him. His eyes were open. He was complaining." Anna Linda gives a little laugh and hugs Darlene tight. "He's not gone."

Darlene hugs Anna Linda back, a sudden rush of relief taking away her breath. She is happier than she can ever remember being in her life, happier even than the days her babies were born. When the two women stand up and start walking toward the lighted bay, Anna Linda begins to wail in big sloppy sobs. Darlene tries to comfort her by stroking her hair. "This may just turn out to be," Darlene says, hearing the joy quiver in her own voice, "the very best day of my life."

At first she does not see him in front of Petey Parsons in the edge of shadows out from the bright lights of the bay. Petey Parsons stands with the half moon lit up behind him, the grass dark at his feet, his right hand

Anita Miller Garner

resting on one of Jeremy's shaking shoulders. Jeremy, her own child, looks at her, Darlene thinks, as if she is someone he cannot recognize, his glare holding something deeper than impatience, something born of betrayal, something closer to hatred than love. Before he looks away with tears in his eyes, he crosses his arms. She knows Jeremy cannot not understand how she can be so happy when Jason has caused so much trouble. "He wouldn't listen to me," Petey says to her. "I tried to talk some sense into him, and he just wouldn't listen."

Somewhere the sun shines brightly, no shadow of turning, Darlene thinks. The reflection of the moon tells her so, shining on all their wasteful lives. Somewhere inside in a hallway she knows Jack waits to tell her with one look all the ways she has failed. Still, the constellations tell her the story of her own fear that even doubt can't kill off, and that story is that through it all she keeps looking up.

When Jeremy runs off into the dark parking lot, Darlene knows he is mad and hurt. Petey Parsons shrugs.

But nothing, not even that, can break her feeling of simple careless plain dumb luck.

A(nita) M(iller) Garner received the M.F.A. in Fiction from the University of Alabama before teaching Southern literature and fiction writing for ten years at Virginia Commonwealth University. She has served as poetry editor of the New Virginia Review *and as a fiction editor of* storySouth. *Currently she is Professor of English and Creative Writing in the new graduate program in Professional Writing at the University of North Alabama. Her collection of short fiction,* Undeniable Truths, *was published by Rank Stranger Press in 2009. A second collection,* Southland, *is forthcoming. A former Alabama State Council on the Arts Fellowship Recipient, she currently reads fiction for Mindbridge Press in the Shoals and blogs about Southern culture at www.amgarner.blogspot.com.*

Dream Children

Gail Godwin

In the summer of my thirty-sixth year, I made a daring change in my life and moved to a farming community in the Hudson Valley. After a lifetime of living in apartments, dormitories, and cities, I rented a two hundred and fifty year old stone house, all but empty. During the weekdays I was alone and soon began having a different sort of dream experience. On the edge of sleep, I rose from the bed, floated down the stairs, and encountered the unexpected. The rooms were different, there were people, or sometimes just one person, waiting for me at the foot of the stairs. These encounters always began in trepidation because I didn't know if I would meet a friend or foe. During my more sinister "float-downs," the house was in a more primitive state and the people moved about the landscape unaware of me. They seemed further removed in time. The other thing that happened during this period was that a friend had miscarried for the seventh time. While she was in the hospital a nurse mistakenly laid a newborn baby in her arms and said, "Here is your baby boy." "Dream Children" is a weaving of one woman's deep country dream interrupted on weekends by dinners and house guests and city gossip. But the woman clings fast to the secret of her night visits and buttresses their validity by reading of people like herself who can commute between worlds. She accepts that dream and reality aren't competitors, but reciprocal sources of consciousness. Her discovery marked the start of my ghost-story quest. From then on, my characters meet their ghosts: Cate in A Mother and Two Daughters, *ten year old Helen in* Flora, *and eleven year old Marcus in my forthcoming novel,* Grief Cottage, *which is my first ghost novel.*

*T*he worst thing. Such a terrible thing to happen to a young woman. It's a wonder she didn't go mad.

As she went about her errands, a cheerful, neat young woman, a wife, wearing pants with permanent creases and safari jackets and high-necked sweaters that folded chastely just below the line of the small gold hoops she wore in her ears, she imagined people saying this, or thinking it to themselves. But nobody knew. Nobody knew anything, other than that she and her husband had moved here a year ago, as so many couples were moving farther away from the city, the husband commuting, or staying in town during the week—as hers did. There was nobody here, in this quaint, unspoiled village, nestled in the foothills of the mountains, who could have looked at her and guessed that anything out of the ordinary, predictable, auspicious spectrum of things that happen to bright, attractive young women had happened to her. She always returned her books to the local library on time; she bought liquor at the local liquor store only on Friday, before she went to meet her husband's bus from the city. He was something in television, a producer? So many ambitious young couples moving to this Dutch farming village, founded in 1690, to restore ruined fieldstone houses and plant herb gardens and keep their own horses and discover the relief of finding oneself insignificant in Nature for the first time!

A terrible thing. So freakish. If you read it in a story or saw it on TV, you'd say no, this sort of thing could never happen in an American hospital.

DePuy, who owned the old Patroon farm adjacent to her land, frequently glimpsed her racing her horse in the early morning, when the mists still lay on the fields, sometimes just before the sun came up and there was a frost on everything. "One woodchuck hole and she and that stallion will both have to be put out of their misery," he told his wife. "She's too reckless. I'll bet you her old man doesn't know she goes streaking to hell across the fields like that." Mrs. DePuy nodded, silent, and went about her business. She, too, watched that other woman ride, a woman not much younger than herself, but with an aura of romance—of tragedy, perhaps. The way she looked: like those heroines in English novels who ride off their bad tempers and unrequited love affairs, clenching their thighs against the flanks of spirited horses with murderous red eyes. Mrs. DePuy, who had ridden since the age of three, recognized something beyond recklessness in that elegant young woman, in her crisp checked shirts and her dove-gray jodhpurs. *She has nothing to fear anymore*, thought the farmer's wife, with sure feminine instinct; she both envied and pitied her. "What she needs is children," remarked DePuy.

"A Dry Sack, a Remy Martin, and ... let's see, a half-gallon of the Chablis, and I think I'd better take a Scotch ... and the Mouton-Cadet ... and maybe a dry vermouth." Mrs. Frye, another farmer's wife, who runs the liquor sore, asks if her husband is bringing company for the weekend. "He sure is; we couldn't drink all that by ourselves," and the young woman laughs, her lovely teeth exposed, her small gold earrings quivering in the light. "You know, I saw his name—on the television the other night," says Mrs. Frye. "It was at the beginning of that new comedy show, the one with the woman who used to be on another show with her husband and little girl, only they divorced, you know the one?" "Of course I do. It's one of my husband's shows. Ill tell him you watched it." Mrs. Frye puts the bottles in an empty box, carefully inserting wedges of cardboard between them. Through the window of her store she sees her customer's pert bottle-green car, some sort of little foreign car with the engine running, filled with groceries and weekend parcels, and that big silver-blue dog sitting up in the front seat just like a human being. "I think that kind of thing is so sad," says Mrs. Frye; "families breaking up, poor little children having to divide their loyalties." "I couldn't agree more," replies the young woman, nodding gravely. Such a personable, polite girl! "Are you sure you can carry that, dear? I can get Earl from the back…" But the girl has it hoisted on her shoulder in a flash, is airily maneuvering between unopened cartons stacked in the aisle, in her pretty boots. Her perfume lingers in Mrs. Frye's store for a half-hour after she has driven away.

After dinner, her husband and his friends drank brandy. She lay in front of the fire, stroking the dog, and listening to Victoria Darrow, the news commentator, in person. A few minutes ago, they had all watched Victoria on TV. "That's right; thirty-nine!" Victoria now whispered to her. "What? That's kind of you. I'm photogenic, thank God, or I'd have been put out to pasture long before … I look five, maybe seven years younger on the screen … but the point I'm getting at is, I went to this doctor and he said, 'If you want to do this thing, you'd better go home today and get started.' He told me—did you know this? Did you know that a woman is born with all the eggs she'll ever have, and when she gets to my age, the ones that are left have been rattling around so long they're a little shopworn; then every time you fly you get an extra dose of radioactivity, so those poor eggs. He told me when a woman over forty comes into his office pregnant, his heart sinks; that's why he quit practicing obstetrics, he said; he could still remember the screams of a woman whose baby he delivered … she was having natural childbirth and she kept saying, 'Why won't you let me see it, I insist on seeing it,' and so he had to, and he says

Gail Godwin

he can still hear her screaming."

"Oh, what was—what was wrong with it?"

But she never got the answer. Her husband, white around the lips, was standing over Victoria ominously, offering the Remy Martin bottle. "Vicky, let me pour you some more," he said. And to his wife, "I think Blue Boy needs to go out."

"Yes, yes, of course. Please excuse me, Victoria. I'll just be …"

Her husband followed her to the kitchen, his hand on the back of her neck. "Are you okay? That stupid yammering bitch. She and her twenty-six-year-old lover! I wish I'd never brought them, but she's been hinting around the studio for weeks."

"But I like them, I like having them. I'm fine. Please go back. I'll take the dog out and come back. Please …"

"All right. If you're sure you're okay." He backed away, hands dangling at his sides. A handsome man, wearing a pink shirt with Guatemalan embroidery. Thick black hair and a face rather boyish, but cunning. Last weekend she had sat beside him, alone in this house, just the two of them, and watched him on television: a documentary, in several parts, in which TV "examines itself." There was his double, sitting in an armchair in his executive office, coolly replying to the questions of Victoria Darrow. *Do you personally watch all the programs you produce, Mr. McNair?"* She watched the man on the screen, how he moved his lips when he spoke, but kept the rest of his face, his body perfectly still. Funny, she had never noticed this before. He managed to say that he did and did not watch all the programs he produced.

Now, in the kitchen, she looked at him backing away, a little like a renegade in one of his own shows—a desperate man, perhaps, who has just killed somebody and is backing away, hands dangling loosely at his sides, Mr. McNair, her husband. That man on the screen. Once a lover above her in bed. That friend who held her hand in the hospital. One hand in hers, the other holding the stopwatch. For a brief instant, all the images coalesce and she feels something again. But once outside, under the galaxies of autumn-sharp stars, the intelligent dog at her heels like some smart gray ghost, she is glad to be free of all that. She walks quickly over the damp grass to the barn, to look in on her horse. She understands something: her husband, Victoria Darrow lead double lives that seem perfectly normal to them. But if she told her husband that she, too, is in two lives, he would become alarmed; he would sell this house and make her move back to the city where he could keep an eye on her welfare.

She is discovering people like herself, down through the centuries, all over the world. She scours books with titles like *The Timeless Moment*, *The Sleeping Prophet*, *Between Two Worlds*, *Silent Union: A Record of Unwilled Communication*; collecting evidence, weaving a sort of underworld net of colleagues around her.

A rainy fall day. Too wet to ride. The silver dog asleep beside her in her special alcove, a padded window seat filled with pillows and books. She is looking down on the fields of dried lithrium, and the fir trees beyond, and the mountains gauzy with fog and rain, thinking, in a kind of terror and ecstasy, about all these connections. A book lies face down on her lap. She has just read the following:

> Theodore Dreiser and his friend John Cowper Powys had been dining at Dreiser's place on West Fifty Seventh Street. As Powys made ready to leave and catch his train to the little town up the Hudson, where he was then living, he told Dreiser, "I'll appear before you here, later in the evening."
>
> Dreiser laughed. "Are you going to turn yourself into a ghost, or have you a spare key?" he asked. Powys said he would return "in some form," he didn't know exactly what kind.
>
> After his friend left, Dreiser sat up and read for two hours. Then he looked up and saw Powys standing in the doorway to the living room. It was Powys' features, his tall stature, even the loose tweed garments which he wore. Dreiser rose at once and strode towards the figure, saying, "Well, John, you kept your word. Come on in and tell me how you did it." But the figure vanished when Dreiser came within three feet of it.
>
> Dreiser then went to the telephone and called Powys' house in the country. Powys answered. Dreiser told him what had happened and Powys said, "I told you I'd be there

and you oughtn't to be surprised."

But he refused to discuss how he had done it, if, indeed, he knew how.

"But don't you get frightened, up here all by yourself, alone with all these creaky sounds?" asked Victoria the next morning.

"No, I guess I'm used to them," she replied, breaking eggs into a bowl. "I know what each one means. The wood expanding and contracting … the wind getting caught between the shutter and the latch… Sometimes small animals get lost in the stone walls and scratch around till they find their way out … or die."

"Ugh. But don't you imagine things? I would, in a house like this. How old? That's almost three hundred years of lived lives, people suffering and shouting and making love and giving birth, under this roof… You'd think there'd be a few ghosts around."

"I don't know," said her hostess blandly. "I haven't heard any. But of course, I have Blue Boy, so I don't get scared." She whisked the eggs, unable to face Victoria. She and her husband had lain awake last night, embarrassed at the sounds coming from the next room. No ghostly moans, those. "Why can't that bitch control herself, or at least lower her voice," he said angrily. He stroked his wife's arm, both of them pretending not to remember. She had bled for an entire year afterward, until the doctor said they would have to remove everything. "I'm empty," she had said when her husband had tried again, after she was healed. "I'm sorry, I just don't feel anything." Now they lay tenderly together on these weekends, like childhood friends, like effigies on a lovers' tomb, their mutual sorrow like a sword between them. She assumed he had another life, or lives, in town. As she had here. Nobody is just one person, she had learned.

"I'm sure I would imagine things," said Victoria. "I would see things and hear things inside my head much worse than an ordinary murderer or rapist."

The wind caught in the shutter latch … a small animal dislodging pieces of fieldstone in its terror, sending them tumbling down the inner walls, from attic to cellar … a sound like a child rattling a jar full of marbles, or small stones…

"I have so little imagination," she said humbly, warming the butter in the omelet pan. She could feel Victoria Darrow's professional curiosity waning from her dull country life, focusing elsewhere.

Cunning!

As a child of nine, she had gone through a phase of walking in her sleep. One summer night, they found her bed empty, and after an hour's hysterical search they had found her in her nightgown, curled up on the flagstones beside the fishpond. She woke, baffled, in her father's tense clutch, the stars all over the sky, her mother repeating over and over again to the night at large, "Oh, my God, she could have drowned!" They took her to a child psychiatrist, a pretty Austrian woman who spoke to her with the same vocabulary she used on grownups, putting the child instantly at ease. "It is not at all uncommon what you did. I have known so many children who take little night journeys from their beds, and then they awaken and don't know what all the fuss is about! Usually these journeys are quite harmless, because children are surrounded by a magical reality that keeps them safe. Yes, the race of children possesses magically sagacious powers! But the grownups, they tend to forget how it once was for them. They worry, they are afraid of so many things. You do not want your mother and father, who love you so anxiously, to live in fear of you going to live with the fishes." She had giggled at the thought. The woman's steady gray-green eyes were trained on her carefully, suspending her in a kind of bubble. Then she had rejoined her parents, a dutiful "child" again, holding a hand up to each of them. The night journeys had stopped.

A thunderstorm one night last spring. Blue Boy whining in his insulated house below the garage. She had lain there, strangely elated by the nearness of the thunderclaps that tore at the sky, followed by instantaneous flashes of jagged light. Wondering shouldn't she go down and let the dog in; he hated storms. Then dozing off again…

She woke. The storm had stopped. The dark air was quiet. Something had changed, some small thing—what? She had to think hard before she found it: the hall light, which she kept burning during the week-nights when she was there alone, had gone out. She reached over and switched the button on her bedside lamp. Nothing. A tree must have fallen and hit a wire, causing the power to go off. This often happened here. No problem. The dog had stopped crying. She felt herself sinking into a delicious, deep reverie, the kind

Gail Godwin

that sometimes came just before morning, as if her being broke slowly into tiny pieces and spread itself over the world. It was a feeling she had not known until she had lived by herself in this house: this weightless though conscious state in which she lay, as if in a warm bath, and yet was able to send her thoughts anywhere, as if her mind contained the entire world.

And as she floated in this silent world, transparent and buoyed upon the dream layers of the mind, she heard a small rattling sound, like pebbles being shaken in a jar. The sound came distinctly from the guest room, a room so chosen by her husband and herself because it was the farthest room from their bedroom on this floor. It lay above what had been the old side of the house, built seventy-five years before the new side, which was completed in 1753. There was a bed in it, and a chair, and some plants in the window. Sometimes on weekends when she could not sleep, she went and read there, or meditated, to keep from waking her husband. It was the room where Victoria Darrow and her young lover would not sleep the following fall, because she would say quietly to her husband, "No … not that room. I—I've made up the bed in the other room." "What?" he would want to know. "The one next to ours? Right under our noses?"

She did not lie long listening to this sound before she understood it was one she had never heard in the house before. It had a peculiar regularity to its rhythm; there was nothing accidental about it, nothing influenced by the wind, or the nerves of some lost animal. *K-chunk, k-chunk, k-chunk*, it went. At intervals of exactly a half-minute apart. She still remembered how to time such things, such intervals. She was as good as any stopwatch when it came to timing certain intervals.

K-chunk, k-chunk, k-chunk. That determined regularity. Something willed, something poignantly repeated, as though the repetition was a means of consoling someone in the dark. Her skin began to prickle. Often, lying in such states of weightless reverie, she had practiced the trick of sending herself abroad, into rooms of the house, out into the night to check on Blue Boy, over to the barn to look in on her horse, who slept standing up. Once she had heard a rather frightening noise, as if someone in the basement had turned on a faucet, and so she forced herself to "go down," floating down two sets of stairs into the darkness, only to discover what she had known all the time: the hookup system between the hot-water tank and the pump, which sounded like someone turning on the water.

Now she went through the palpable, prickly darkness, without lights, down the chilly hall in her sleeveless gown, into the guest room. Although there was no light, not even a moon shining through the window, she could make out the shape of the bed and then the chair, the spider plants on the window, and a small dark shape in one corner, on the floor, which she and her husband had painted a light yellow.

K-chunk, k-chunk, k-chunk. The shape moved with the noise.

Now she knew what they meant, that "someone's hair stood on end." It was true. As she forced herself across the borders of a place she had never been, she felt, distinctly, every single hair on her head raise itself a millimeter or so from her scalp.

She knelt down and discovered him. He was kneeling, a little cold and scared, shaking a small jar filled with some kind of pebbles. (She later found out, in a subsequent visit, that they were small colored shells, of a triangular shape, called coquinas: she found them in a picture in a child's nature book at the library.) He was wearing pajamas a little too big for him, obviously hand-me-downs, and he was exactly two years older than the only time she had ever held him in her arms.

The two of them knelt in the corner of the room, taking each other in. His large eyes were the same as before: dark and unblinking. He held the small jar close to him, watching her. He was not afraid, but she knew better than to move too close.

She knelt, the tears streaming down her cheeks, but she made no sound, her eyes fastened on that small form. And then the hall light came on silently, as well as the lamp beside her bed, and with wet cheeks and pounding heart she could not be sure whether or not she had actually been out of the room.

But what did it matter, on the level where they had met? He traveled so much farther than she to reach that room. (*"Yes, the race of children possesses magically sagacious powers!"*)

She and her husband sat together on the flowered chintz sofa, watching the last of the series in which TV purportedly examined itself. She said, "Did you ever think that the whole thing is really a miracle? I mean, here we sit, eighty miles away from your studios, and we turn on a little machine and there

Gail Godwin

is Victoria, speaking to us as clearly as she did last weekend when she was in this very room. Why, it's magic, it's time travel and space travel right in front of our eyes, but because it's been 'discovered,' because the world understands that it's only little dots that transmit Victoria electrically to us, it's *all right*. We can bear it. Don't you sometimes wonder about all the miracles that haven't been officially approved yet? I mean, who knows, maybe in a hundred years everybody will take it for granted that they can send an image of themselves around in space by some perfectly natural means available to us now. I mean, when you think about it, what *is* space? What *is* time? Where do the so-called boundaries of each of us begin and end? Can anyone explain it?"

He was drinking Scotch and thinking how they had decided not to renew Victoria Darrow's contract. Somewhere on the edges of his mind hovered an anxious, growing certainty about his wife. At the local grocery store this morning, when he went to pick up a carton of milk and the paper, he had stopped to chat with DePuy. "I don't mean to interfere, but she doesn't know those fields," said the farmer. "Last year we had to shoot a mare, stumbled into one of those holes... It's madness, the way she rides."

And look at her now, her face so pale and shining, speaking of miracles and space travel, almost on the verge of tears...

And last night, his first night up from the city, he had wandered through the house, trying to drink himself into this slower weekend pace, and he had come across a pile of her books, stacked in the alcove where, it was obvious, she lay for hours, escaping into science fiction, and the occult.

Now his own face appeared on the screen. "I want to be fair," he was telling Victoria Darrow. "I want to be objective... Violence has always been part of the human makeup. I don't like it anymore than you do, but there it is. I think it's more a question of whether we want to face things as they are or escape into fantasies of how we would like them to be."

Beside him, his wife uttered a sudden bell-like laugh.

("... *It's madness, the way she rides.*")

He did want to be fair, objective. She had told him again and again that she liked her life here. And he—well, he had to admit he liked his own present setup.

"I am a pragmatist," he was telling Virginia Darrow on the screen. He decided to speak to his wife about her riding and leave her alone about the books. She had the right to some escape, if anyone did. But the titles: *Marvelous Manifestations, The Mind Travellers, A Doctor Looks at Spiritualism, The Other Side…* Something revolted in him, he couldn't help it; he felt an actual physical revulsion at this kind of thinking. Still it was better than some other escapes. His friend Barnett, the actor, who said at night he went from room to room, after his wife was asleep, collecting empty glasses. ("Once I found one by the Water Pik, a second on the ledge beside the tub, a third on the back of the john, and a fourth on the floor beside the john…")

He looked sideways at his wife, who was absorbed, it seemed, in watching him on the screen. Her face was tense, alert, animated. She did not look mad. She wore slim gray pants and a loose-knit pullover made of some silvery material, like a knight's chain mail. The lines of her profile were clear and silvery themselves, somehow sexless and pure, like a child's profile. He no longer felt lust when he looked at her, only a sad determination to protect her. He had a mistress in town, whom he loved, but he had explained, right from the beginning, that he considered himself married for the rest of his life. He told this woman the whole story. "And I am implicated in it. I could never leave her." An intelligent, sensitive woman, she had actually wept and said, "Of course not."

He always wore the same pajamas, a shade too big, but always clean. Obviously washed again and again in a machine that went through its cycles frequently. She imagined his "other mother," a harassed woman with several children, short on money, on time, on dreams—all the things she herself had too much of. The family lived, she believed, somewhere in Florida, probably on the west coast. She had worked that out from the little coquina shells: their bright colors, even in moonlight shining through a small window with spider plants in it. His face and arms had been suntanned early in the spring and late into the autumn. They never spoke or touched. She was not sure how much of this he understood. She tried and failed to remember where she herself had gone, in those little night journeys to the fishpond. Perhaps he never remembered afterward, when he woke up, clutching his jar, in a roomful of brothers and sisters. Or with a worried mother or father come to collect him, asleep by the sea. Once she had a very clear dream of the whole family, living in a trailer, with palm trees. But that was a dream; she recognized its

Gail Godwin

difference in quality from those truly magic times when, through his own childish powers, he somehow found a will strong enough, or innocent enough, to project himself upon her still-floating consciousness, as clearly and as believably as her own husband's image on the screen.

There had been six of those times in six months. She dared to look forward to more. So unafraid he was. The last time was the day after Victoria Darrow and her young lover and her own good husband had returned to the city. She had gone farther with the child than ever before. On a starry-clear, cold September Monday, she had coaxed him down the stairs and out of the house with her. He held to the banisters, a child unused to stairs, and yet she knew there was no danger; he floated in his own dream with her. She took him to see Blue Boy. Who disappointed her by whining and backing away in fear. And then to the barn to see the horse. Who perked up his ears and looked interested. There was no touching, of course, no touching or speaking. Later she wondered if horses, then, were more magical than dogs. If dogs were more "realistic." She was glad the family was poor, the mother harassed. They could not afford any expensive child psychiatrist who would hypnotize him out of his night journeys.

He loved her. She knew that. Even if he never remembered her in his other life.

"At last I was beginning to understand what Teilhard de Chardin meant when he said that man's true home is the mind. I understood that when the mystics tell us that the mind is a place, they *don't mean it as a metaphor*. I found these new powers developed with practice. I had to detach myself from my ordinary physical personality. The intelligent part of me had to remain wide awake, and move down into this world of thoughts, dreams and memories. After several such journeyings I understood something else: dream and reality aren't competitors, but reciprocal sources of consciousness." This she read in a "respectable book," by a "respectable man," a scientist, alive and living in England, only a few years older than herself. She looked down at the dog, sleeping on the rug. His lean silvery body actually ran as he slept! Suddenly his muzzle lifted, the savage teeth snapped. Where was he "really" now? Did the dream rabbit in his jaws know it was a dream? There was much to think about, between her trips to the nursery.

Gail Godwin

Would the boy grow, would she see his body slowly emerging from its child's shape, the arms and legs lengthening, the face thinning out into a man's—like a certain advertisement for bread she had seen on TV where a child grows up, in less than a half-minute of sponsor time, right before the viewer's eyes. Would he grow into a man, grow a beard ... outgrow the nursery region of his mind where they had been able to meet?

And yet, some daylight part of his mind must have retained an image of her from that single daylight time they had looked into each other's eyes.

The worst thing, such an awful thing to happen to a young woman... She was having this natural childbirth, you see, her husband in the delivery room with her, and the pains were coming a half-minute apart, and the doctor had just said, "This is going to be a breeze, Mrs. McNair," and they never knew exactly what went wrong, but all of a sudden the pains stopped and they had to go in after the baby without even time to give her a saddle block or any sort of anesthetic... They must have practically had to tear it out of her ... the husband fainted. The baby was born dead, and they gave her a heavy sedative to put her out all night.

When she woke the next morning, before she had time to remember what had happened, a nurse suddenly entered the room and laid a baby in her arms. "Here's your little boy," she said cheerfully, and the woman thought, with a profound, religious relief, *So that other nightmare was a dream,* and she had the child at her breast feeding him before the nurse realized her mistake and rushed back into the room, but they had to knock the poor woman out with more sedatives before she would let the child go. She was screaming and so was the little baby and they clung to each other till she passed out.

They would have let the nurse go, only it wasn't entirely her fault. The hospital was having a strike at the time; some of the nurses were outside picketing and this nurse had been working straight through for forty-eight hours, and when she was questioned afterward she said she had just mixed up the rooms, and yet, she said, when she had seen the woman and the baby clinging to each other like that, she had undergone a sort of revelation in her almost hallucinatory exhaustion: the nurse said she saw that all children and mothers were interchangeable, that nobody could own anybody or anything, anymore than you could own an idea that happened to be passing through the

Gail Godwin

air and caught on your mind, or anymore than you owned the rosebush that grew in your back yard. There were only mothers and children, she realized; though, afterward, the realization faded.

It was the kind of freakish thing that happens once in a million times, and it's a wonder the poor woman kept her sanity.

In the intervals, longer than those measured by any stopwatch, she waited for him. In what the world accepted as "time," she shopped for groceries, for clothes; she read; she waved from her bottle-green car to Mrs. Frye, trimming the hedge in front of the liquor store, to Mrs. DePuy, hanging out her children's pajamas in the back yard of the old Patroon farm. She rode her horse through the fields of the waning season, letting him have his head; she rode like the wind, a happy, happy woman. She rode faster than fear because she was a woman in a dream, a woman anxiously awaiting her child's sleep. The stallion's hoofs pounded the earth. Oiling his tractor, DePuy resented the foolish woman and almost wished for a woodchuck hole to break that arrogant ride. Wished deep in a violent level of himself he never knew he had. For he was a kind, distracted father and husband, a practical, hard-working man who would never descend deeply into himself. Her body, skimming through time, felt weightless to the horse.

Was she a woman riding a horse and dreaming she was a mother who anxiously awaited her child's sleep; or was she a mother dreaming of herself as a free spirit who could ride her horse like the wind because she had nothing to fear?

I am a happy woman, that's all I know. Who can explain such things?

Gail Godwin was born in Birmingham and raised there and in Asheville, N.C. Godwin studied at Peace Junior College, in Raleigh, North Carolina, UNC-Chapel Hill, and then received an MA and PhD in creative writing from the University

of Iowa. Her first novel, The Perfectionists, served as her dissertation. Godwin received early acclaim with the novels The Odd Woman (1974), Violet Clay (1978), and A Mother and Two Daughters (1982), all National Book Award Finalists. A Mother and Two Daughters has sold a million and a half copies. These and novels such as A Southern Family have established her as a major interpreter of Southern life, especially of women contesting their traditional roles. Five of her novels have been New York Times bestsellers. Godwin is an amazingly productive writer, with fifteen novels, two volumes of journals, a memoir about publishing, a history of the heart, and two volumes of stories, Mr. Bedford and the Muses (1983) and Dream Children (1976), from which this story is taken. For the 1975-76 year Godwin received both the John Simon Guggenheim Foundation Award and an NEA Grant. In 1987 she received the Janet Heidinger Kafka Prize for A Southern Family. Since 1976 Godwin has lived in Woodstock, NY. Still writing, she received the 2016 Alabama Library Association Author Award for Adult Fiction for the novel Flora and will publish Grief Cottage, a ghost novel, in 2017.

Gail Godwin

The Lovely April

Shirley Ann Grau

I've long made a practice of not reading my short stories or novels once I have finished and they are published. I don't know why I adopted this practice but I have observed it religiously. As a result I have long ago forgotten not only titles but plots and timbre. When I did re-read "April" I found I was reading a story I did not recognize (an odd feeling). It was both a love story and a fairy tale, neither of which I have ever written. The characters or situations are not based on my friends or family. On what then? I finally decided that, like most writers my memory is cluttered with many many bits of future fiction, jumbled together, men and women, unnamed streets, untold stories, quiet fields when the cotton is making, the buzz of Saturday night crowds on streets in dusty sad towns. Mr. Robin had slipped away from them. To me. Though I haven't heard from him lately.

My father sat on the edge of a baggage truck and waited for the afternoon train. The sun was getting low into the last quarter of sky: there was no shade at all under the wall-less shed of the railroad station, except in the little room that had a sign, "Agent" in sun-cracked paint letters.

Hal Beecham came out of that office, tugging mailbags. "Hi, Doc," he said. "You expecting anybody?"

"Yes."

Beecham cocked his head, listening. "There she comes, all right."

"On time."

"You waiting for somebody?"

My father laughed. The sound bounced around among the heat waves that were rising from the black asphalt street.

"You know what I'm doing here as well as I do."

Hal Beecham lifted his sandy eyebrows. "Me?"

"Sure."

Hal Beecham dragged the mailbags out onto the platform. "You never told me."

My father did not answer.

"Well," Beecham admitted, staring down at his dirty white buck shoes, "I reckon I did hear some talk."

"I reckon you did," my father said.

Beecham wiped the sweat from his chin. "People get to talking."

My father snorted, very softly.

"You know his name?" Beecham studied the broken dirty nails of his left hand.

My father snorted again. "Mr. Robin."

Beecham stared, his eyes squinting and his mouth pursed. "Mr. what?"

"That isn't his name. He just wants to be called that."

"I get it," he winked. "I get it."

"I bet you knew that much already, just from the town talking."

"I didn't know his name . . ." Beecham said shyly.

My father wasn't happy about the whole business. But he was doing it as a favor to Mr. Robin's father, who was an old friend and a man you couldn't say no to, anyway.

There were two houses on our block: ours and one other, a small one that hadn't been lived in for years. Mr. Robin's father had that one fixed up so his son could live there, along with a cook and a colored butler. Although everybody always called Henry Stanford a butler, his job was really nothing more than keeping an eye on Mr. Robin. Because Mr. Robin did strange things sometimes, especially in the spring. "The lovely April," he called it.

His name was Mr. Richard Carlysle Peters. He was a little man, not much more than five feet tall, and very slight, almost scrawny, except for a little round stomach, like a pillow stuck out in front. He had a little face that could have been thirty-five or seventy; a little jutting cleft chin and a pug nose that turned up sharp at the end; the usual sort of blue eyes and lots of curly, almost tow-colored hair. He'd forget to go to the barber, and nobody remembered to tell him very often, so his hair was always sticking out in wisps over the back of his coat collar or curling into his ears. He had one peculiar gesture: he would run his fingers over his ears and back to his neck, just at the hairline, brushing up the long curls, at the same time giving his head a little tossing jerk—just exactly the way a girl does when her hair gets in her way and she shakes it back.

Shirley Ann Grau

Though Mr. Robin didn't look it at all, his family were important people. His uncle was governor of Carolina, elected just the year past. His father was a judge and about the richest man in the state. Mr. Robin was the exception. He wasn't nice-looking or smart or even clever. He went to school for a while, but he'd fall asleep in class sometimes and never pay attention, any time. When he was in the fifth grade (they'd promoted him because his father was an important man), he got roughed up by some bigger boys who'd yelled "pansy" at him. He would never tell who had done it, though it was almost a month before he got over the bruises and cuts.

One thing—Stan Watson, who was in seventh grade, a tough little kid, disappeared a week later. They finally found him in one of the small, old-fashioned freezers in the woods of a vacant lot behind the ice factory. The lid was locked.

Mr. Robin didn't go back to school. Each morning his mother would hand him the satchel with his books and stand by the front door and watch him trudge off down the street. She'd watch until he turned the corner and then she'd go back in with a sigh and send a servant after him. Sometimes he kept walking until he was out of the town. When he found a spot of grass that looked particularly soft he would put his satchel down very carefully and stretch out. He wouldn't sleep. He'd just stare right straight up at the sky. If there were clouds, his eyes would move very slowly, following them across the circle sweep of his vision. If it started raining, he'd find a tree with thick, twisted branches for a shelter. He never seemed to mind.

In winter he had to do something different; it was too cold to be outside. Mornings there was always a heavy frost, and he would walk looking back over his shoulder to see the dark tracks his own feet had made. Usually he'd head straight for the movie house——it was empty that time of day. He'd sit down at the piano in front and pick out little tunes with one finger. Nobody stopped him. After all, there was always his mother's servant standing close by, watching.

That was how he grew up. And somewhere in those years, nobody quite knew how, he got the name of Mr. Robin.

Until he was well into his twenties, almost out of them in fact, he kept up the pretense of going to school. He still carried the same little satchel. He had never opened it; by this time the lock was rusted and stuck. Each day, just as he came in the door, his mother would ask, "How was school?" and he would say, "Lovely." That was one of his favorite words.

Mr. Robin's mother died one hot July day. He went to her and said, "Mama?" in a kind of hesitant whisper, but she was too far gone to hear. His father took his shoulder in one hand and with the other pointed him stiffly out of the room. Mr. Robin left and was gone for two days, the days of her wake. Nobody knew where he was; nobody had thought to tell a servant to follow him, the way she did.

He turned up all rumpled and dirty, in time for the funeral. Nobody told him what to do or watched out for him, but he did everything exactly right. He washed and shaved and put on a white linen suit and a white starched shirt and a black tie. He brushed his curly light hair until it stayed in place and then to be sure he poured hair tonic on it.

People stared at him and wondered what was going on in his head, but he didn't seem to notice anything. He nodded to his uncles and his two cousins who'd come back from college in Stanton. Then he looked at the broad bands of black crepe on their arms and he said very quietly, "I want one of those."

After all the services were over, his father moved to a hotel. For a week or so he stayed there, getting over the worst of his grief (he cried, people said; he cried for his wife, a hard shrewd man like that) while he tried to figure out what to do with his son.

He finally decided to set him up in a small town, where there was someone who could be trusted to keep a supervising eye on the whole thing.

That was how Mr. Robin came to us.

Of course, everybody in town was watching. They were surprised and disappointed, too, when Mr. Robin got off the train quietly and said how do you do to my father, calmly and just a little bored. That night there were lights in a house that hadn't been occupied for years, but the shades were drawn, and at nine o'clock the lights went out.

The next morning Mr. Robin's cook went into town to the grocery, while the butler, Henry Stanford, fixed a hammock between two pecan trees in the front yard. But Mr. Robin didn't appear. Maybe he was unhappy

Shirley Ann Grau

and sulking or maybe the change had just confused him; for five or six days nobody saw him.

Then one Friday afternoon, my mother found him in our kitchen. He was leaning against the doorjamb, his thin legs crossed, his arms folded, and his little mouth pursed. My mother stopped so suddenly that she almost lost her balance on the waxed kitchen floor.

Mr. Robin straightened himself and bowed very slowly from the waist. "Good evening, madam," he said, and his soft voice had just a hint of an English accent. (He had got that from his mother, along with his blue eyes and blond curly hair. She had come from Staffordshire.) "I am Mr. Robin."

"But I've met you before," my mother said. " The first day you came."

Mr. Robin sighed, very slightly.

"Do you remember?" she insisted.

"I forgot such a lovely lady." His soft light voice was really sad.

My mother smiled and one of her fingers caught up the stray hair at the nape of her neck. "What a nice compliment."

Mr. Robin smiled, too, and his blue eyes opened even wider. "Oh, I say that to everybody," he added earnestly.

My mother gasped and then laughed aloud.

Mr. Robin said, "I hope you don't mind my being in your kitchen."

Our cook, Oriole, had come in the dining room door and stood staring.

"It is so nice in here," Mr. Robin said. "Not lonesome like it is in my house."

"Oriole," my mother said, "would it worry you if Mr. Robin visited our kitchen?"

"No'm."

Mr. Robin bowed formally, the way his mother had taught him to do, years ago, when she had tried to teach him to dance.

And so all the rest of the summer, Mr. Robin hung around the kitchen.

Sometimes he'd move out to the yard and sit under the big sycamore. Leaning back against the white-and-brown-streaked trunk, he looked even littler and fuzzier than usual.

But most times he'd be on the kitchen step, just outside the screen door. He'd sit quietly there, staring off across the narrow valley to the ridges on the west. Even on the clearest day their rocky slopes were blurred and

Shirley Ann Grau

indistinct; the usual summer fires were burning there.

"The little people," he announced aloud one day.

"The what?" Oriole opened the screen door and stuck her head out.

"The little people."

"That what I thought you say."

Mr. Robin nodded toward the smoky ridges. "They're doing all that burning up there."

Oriole leaned against the door, one hand on her hip. "That right?"

Mr. Robin lifted his light-colored eyebrows until they arched up into his hair, peaked like gables. "What would you say if I told you I was one?"

Oriole laughed in her deep voice. "I say you plain better not start no fires around me." She held open the door. "You just come in and tell me some more stories."

"Poor little fellow," my mother said. "He's found somebody to talk to."

He had. He spent all his time back there. Once, because it was a dark, near-fall day, and fall days are always sad (like the dead cotton fields, brown and rattling with only a shred or two of white blowing in the wind), Oriole decided to sing "Garlands of Flowers." It was a Creole tune she'd learned from her first husband, who'd come from New Orleans. She sang it very well.

Maybe it was the day and maybe it was the song, but both Oriole and Mr. Robin began to cry. My mother heard the sniffling and went out to see. Mr. Robin rushed past her, toward his own house, his blue eyes red and wet.

"We was singing a funeral tune." Oriole blew her nose and smiled and went back to work.

Oriole was a big woman, deep-black colored and bowlegged. She'd thrown out two or three husbands because they got funny and laughed at those bowlegs. That was one thing she couldn't stand—being laughed at. And when she said thrown out she meant just exactly that. She was a powerful woman, a match for a man in any sort of fight. You could see how her dress pulled over the lumps of back muscle; and when she kneaded dough you could see the muscles in her forearms knot and unknot like pieces of rope.

Shirley Ann Grau

She had a little house a mile or so down the road, a good solid house with one room and a lean-to for a kitchen and a woodshed out back; but still an old house: her mammy and pappy had lived there until they died. She owned the little piece of farmland too, but that was just cut-over fields. And the only hard cash she had was what she got from my mother every Saturday morning.

All her husbands had been big, good-looking fellows who could have had just about any girl they wanted. And there were lots younger and prettier than Oriole. She had a funny way with men. Days when she'd got rid of a husband——she'd had some legally and some not——she'd whistle in the kitchen like a mockingbird.

Along toward real fall, when it got to be too damp and windy for sitting outside, Mr. Robin caught cold. My father told his servants to make him stay inside for a week.

For that whole week there wasn't a sound from the kitchen. Oriole cooked and washed the dishes like always. But she didn't bother whistling or singing. And when she carried the dishes into the dining room she walked sort of stiffly.

It wasn't that she was in a bad humor, but she was so quiet and listless that my mother finally went back to talk to her.

"You're not sick, are you, Oriole? Do you want Dr. Addams to have a look at you?"

"No'm." Oriole kept right on fixing the meat for dinner, her black arms moving slowly up and down.

She looked out the window where you could see a few white specks of Mr. Robin's house through the thick trunks of the bare pecan trees.

"I ain't never missed a man yet."

"Don't you fret," my mother said. "He'll be all right."

"And I reckon he ain't even a man." Oriole blushed under her black skin.

By the end of the week, Mr. Robin was back in the kitchen. This time he brought something with him, a yellow upholstered stool that he carried from his own kitchen. He carefully selected a place: under the window, next to the porcelain-topped table. And he settled down for the cold months.

That was the winter it snowed. Two days before Christmas the gray sky broke. White snow covered the ground, making little drifts of an inch or so against the walls and the hedges.

Mr. Robin got Christmas presents from his family. They, remembering what he liked most of all, got together and filled a box——big almost as a laundry box, and so heavy that Henry Stanford grunted when he lifted it from the mail sack. There was only food in the box——candies and cakes and heavy jelly pastries wrapped carefully in waxed paper.

For a while, sitting on the floor in his living room, Mr. Robin studied his box. Then he put the cover back on and rushed across the snow-crusted yard.

He forgot his overcoat and his hat. It was very cold outside and there was a stiff wind. He began to run; by the time he'd got to our house he was almost exhausted. He kicked at the door.

Oriole opened it quickly. "Lord," she said. "Looks like all the devils in hell chasing after you." She grinned; her single gold tooth flashed. "You come on in."

While she cooked dinner, Mr. Robin sat on his yellow stool and ate most of the candy. He put the box down and his puffy blue eyes followed Oriole around for a few minutes. He got to his feet very slowly, gave a funny little clucking sound, and reached for the door handle. Oriole held his head while he was sick on the snowy grass in the yard. They came back inside, shivering, both of them. Mr. Robin sat down very weakly on his chair and leaned back against the wall and closed his eyes and hardly moved the rest of the day.

Pretty soon winter was over; and the spring rains were beginning. You could feel how excited Mr. Robin was. Then the rain stopped bit by bit and the sky got clear, the bright clear blue that is soft and hard all at once, the way the sky is only in spring. The ground began to dry and drain and very suddenly you could see things coming to life.

He was a different man in spring. His face suddenly got a peaked look; there was a little pointed chin where there had been a soft round one. His tousled curly hair fluffed up to little points around his face.

Some people began to wonder if his left foot was a hoof, until Mr.

Shirley Ann Grau

Robin one evening walked barefoot through the red clover field kicking at the round flowers so that the heavy dew splashed up in thick drops. His feet were small and fat and white and perfectly usual.

One afternoon my father came on Mr. Robin lying full-length on the ground in the wide rows between the turnips in our garden.

My father said, "Good afternoon."

Mr. Robin did not answer or move.

"It must be chilly on the ground."

"No," said Mr. Robin.

"Well," my father said, "how are you feeling?"

"I'm feeling fine," Mr. Robin said and his voice was as light and soft as the rustling wind. "I'm feeling real extra fine."

"It must be the weather." My father's eyes studied him carefully.

"I'm feeling extra fine."

That should have warned my father. After all, in the report he had of Mr. Robin in the big file in his office, there was a history of things that always happened when Mr. Robin was feeling fine.

The first thing was the green paint. The very next day, about midmorning, he covered his whole face with green paint.

Henry Stanford, still laughing so hard he couldn't speak, brought Mr. Robin up to my father's office. Mr. Robin was wearing an injured expression. His little mouth was pursed into a perfect circle, but he would say nothing.

A few days later Henry caught him half a block down the street, his clothes on wrong side out, his tie fastened firmly behind his neck and his black derby perched backward on his little head.

"For all the trouble," my father laughed, "he's such a nice little helpless fellow. You can't help liking him."

My father wasn't so sure about liking him a week later when Mr. Robin slipped upstairs into our bathroom and, using my father's own razor and soap, shaved off all his hair, until there was just a pink lumpy dome with ears that stood out like handles.

Oriole spent nearly two hours cleaning up the mess; there were soap-sticky wads of hair on floors and walls and doors.

My father got angry dark splotches on his cheeks. "What did you think you were doing?" my father asked Mr. Robin in a voice that was far from gentle.

Mr. Robin smiled right back at him. Smiled so bright that little wrinkles ran up over his face and crinkled along his bare skull and moved the little patches of adhesive tape covering the small nicks he had given himself.

For this, Mr. Robin was to stay in his own house for five days.

Oriole didn't say one single word during the time Mr. Robin was gone. She did the cooking and the cleaning she had to do, and then walked dismally home, stumping along on the dirt road like her feet had suddenly got too heavy for her.

"Sometimes," my mother told my father, "she's as crazy as he is."

My father grinned. "Maybe," he said, "only I don't think so. I just don't think so," he repeated.

My mother sat down in the rocking chair by the window and tipped herself back and forth, "What's the matter, then?"

My father's grin got wider. "She's in love."

My mother stopped rocking so suddenly that her heels made a sharp click on the floor. "She's what?"

"She's in love."

"With Mr. Robin?"

My father nodded. My mother kept staring at him. You could see she didn't believe a word.

"Yes," he said. "That's it." He was not talking to her now. The words were directed to the polished leather of the shoes he had propped up in front of him. "She's in love. He's in love. That's it."

"But that poor little thing is hardly a man," my mother said.

My father puffed out his cheeks.

"That's what makes it so perfect for her. She doesn't like men."

My mother gave an unbelieving sigh.

Mr. Robin decided he did not like being kept in the house. The very first day he escaped six or seven times. Until the cook shook her finger threateningly and shouted at him. Then he retired to his room and sulked. He wouldn't come out or eat all the next day. And the following day he escaped again. It happened like this.

Very early Sunday morning—before it had really got light and there was just that trembling uncertain glow to the sky, like always in spring—

Shirley Ann Grau

Hank Miller and his clanking little truck drove up to Mr. Robin's. (The town was too small for a regular garbage collection; Hank did most of the hauling.) He loaded the big cans on his truck and went inside to collect his money from Henry Stanford. Mr. Robin slipped into a can that was almost half empty and pulled the top on after him. He rode off with the truck.

About midmorning we located him. He had gone to church.

It was a dark church. The only windows were high up in the walls and covered with dark stained glass. The walls themselves and the pews were all dark wood that had been rubbed and polished for so many years that it gave out a dark light of its own.

And there was Mr. Robin. He was sitting in the very first row on the left side and he was sitting very quietly, not making a sound. Just wearing his black derby hat.

There was a sermon, but nobody listened. They were all watching Mr. Robin's hat. That was how we found him so quickly. Everybody's attention was like a finger pointing at him.

"Wait here," my father said. "I guess I better go get him."

His shoes had rubber soles so that there was just the faintest brushing sound. But at each row heads turned to him—it was like in passing each pew, he pulled a wire that swung all the heads. Up in the pulpit the minister was still preaching. Maybe he didn't quite know what he was saying.

Finally my father reached the front pew where Mr. Robin sat all alone. (Nobody ever occupied that pew; it was the one in which Jeff Davis had sat when he'd rode past this way during the war.)

My father sat down and pushed himself along the polished wood until he was next to Mr. Robin, who was looking straight ahead with a kind of puzzled intentness. Since he had no hair, the hat sat far down on his head, resting very gently on the back of his ears. If he were able to pull those ears flat against his head, he would disappear, and then there would be just the hat left sitting on the smooth waxed wood of the pew. Mr. Robin would be out somewhere, under a tree, staring up at the clouds. Or in our kitchen with Oriole.

My father slipped his arm through Mr. Robin's and he whispered something to him. For a couple of seconds Mr. Robin didn't move. Then he lifted both his hands and carefully, with elaborate ceremonious gestures, he took off his hat.

The whole congregation gasped. Even the minister gave a kind of gurgle and stopped.

Under Mr. Robin's hat there was his shaved bare head, white as a china cup but lumpy. And on top of that head was a pancake, a regular-sized pancake, and on it was a fried egg, all white and yellow.

It was very quiet. Seemed like nobody was breathing. Holding Mr. Robin's arm tightly, my father got up and rushed for the door. The pancake slipped to the floor with a gentle plop.

It seemed like that was all there'd be of Mr. Robin.

His father wrote and said that he was sending for him on the twenty-second, which was the coming Friday.

My father shook his head. "I'm glad it's over. It just wasn't working for him here."

"Poor Oriole," my mother said. "She'll miss him."

"No use telling her just yet," my father said. "Tell her after he's gone. It'll be easier."

The kitchen door swung closed just a tiny bit. Oriole had been listening. It wasn't going to be any surprise to her.

And the next day she asked my father to buy her little farm.

"All right," my father said. "But where'll you go?"

"I got people of mine I'd like to see."

My father stared at the black motionless face, its eyes shiny bright in the sunlight. "Let's just call it a loan," he said, "You can buy the place back from me when you want it again."

"I ain't going to want it," she said. "I ain't coming back."

So he gave her $350 for the little square of fallow ground and the little wood house. She rolled the bills and slipped them into the pocket of her dress.

"You're not going to carry that money around. . ."

"Yes, sir."

"You'll get robbed."

She just grinned.

"Look," he said. "You're strong and you can take care of yourself

Shirley Ann Grau

against most men alone, but what if there's two?"

Oriole pulled out the razor that dangled on a string around her neck.

"Okay," my father said and shrugged his shoulders. "Okay."

On Friday, the twenty-second, Mr. Robin's father came, a very tall, very thin man with white hair that was balding all across the top of his narrow skull. His eyes were large and a very dark blue, fringed with almost red lashes. He had no resemblance at all to Mr. Robin.

Judge Oliver Peters and Mr. Robin spent the afternoon in our living room. My mother got out the sherry and the little biscuits she kept for special occasions, along with the high silvery tones of her laugh.

While they were there, chatting politely, Oriole went to Mr. Robin's house.

"I came for them," she said to Henry Stanford, and pointed to the bags, all packed and ready, standing on the porch. "He said I got to get them."

Henry Stanford looked at her, all fixed up in a new white dress that crackled with starch, and said, "Sure."

Henry noticed that she had a new bright blue wagon, with a young mule between the poles. He saw Oriole flip Mr. Robin's bags into the back, which seemed to be filled with household goods, pots and stoves and such.

As Oriole was driving off, he called, "Why ain't you taking a car?"

And Oriole yelled right back at him, "We ain't needing a car."

So Henry sat down again and dozed off. He was still dozing later on when my father and Judge Oliver Peters came to pick up the bags on the way to the station.

My father turned red with anger when he learned what had happened. But Judge Peters put one hand on his arm. "My dear doctor," he said. "There's nothing valuable in them. The bags aren't important; and the train is. Send them along when you find them."

Mr. Robin and his father got on the train, after shaking hands with my father, and settled down in their seats. Judge Oliver Peters took out a sheaf of papers from his briefcase and began to study them——he had a very important meeting the following morning. Mr. Robin sat down very quietly and stared out the window. He and his father never did talk.

The train hadn't gone more than five miles or so before it came grinding to a halt. Oliver Peters fastened his papers together with a big brass clip and put them inside the case. "What the hell is wrong now?" Holding his briefcase in one hand, he swung down the steps.

"You best watch out, sir," the conductor called.

Oliver Peters paid no attention. He kept right on walking, noticing now that he was passing little red warning flags, stuck at intervals along the track. When he reached the engine he saw what had happened.

There was a large gray granite monument planted squarely on the track. Oliver Peters walked over and looked at it. On one side, upside down now so that he had to twist his head to the side to read it, was an inscription: "This road was built in 1862 by General Cornelius Greenleaf, commandant of the Confederate arsenal at Cheehaw."

Oliver Peters looked around. There, a hundred yards to the north, was the road. The hunk of granite had been dragged from there to the tracks.

"Just you look at these mule tracks," a trainman said, pushing back his striped gray cap and wiping his forehead with one grimy hand.

"Why did they do it?" Oliver Peters demanded.

"Mister," the man said, "there ain't no telling."

The engineer laughed; he was a tall, thin man, with a long scar down one cheek and crisscrossing it the little blue scars of inexpert stitches. "They put out warning flags for us a mile back——just like the rule book says."

Judge Oliver Peters rubbed his forehead and frowned. He stood back and watched while the train crew found a heavy sapling and used it as a pole to topple the monument off the tracks. They left it lying on the roadbed.

Oliver Peters sauntered back to his compartment. He planted his chin on his hand and stared morosely out the window, watching the landscape begin to move. Half an hour later, he noticed that his son was gone.

My father said, "She knows this country with her eyes shut. She'll head straight for those high ridges."

It was late twilight now and even the heavy cement base of the granite marker looked soft and indistinct. Henry Stanford was searching the ground a couple of hundred yards away, following the imprints of the mule's hoofs.

"Hey," he called. "Here."

My father followed his shout down a little gully with soft, sloping sides,

Shirley Ann Grau

covered thick with red clover. Henry was pointing down at the ground.

"Look," he said.

In that light you had to bend far over to be sure what you were seeing——the beginnings of wheel marks, thin and not too wavering: a new wagon.

"She stopped here out of sight," Henry said.

We followed, far as we could, until we got to the stretches of pine where the needles were too soft to hold a trace.

It was night now, cool, the way nights always are in spring, with a good wind off the hills and a flat, bright sliver of moon lifting up in the east.

"They could be traveling on a night bright as this," my father said.

We stood for a minute and listened to the sounds that came down on the spring wind: birds' flutter and the scurry of little animals and the swish of pines. You could almost hear the steady beat of the mule's hoofs and the creak of that new wagon, moving.

Born in New Orleans, Shirley Ann Grau spent her childhood from 1938-1945 in Montgomery, the family not returning to New Orleans until Grau's senior year of high school. Her 1965 Pulitzer Prize for fiction, the novel The Keepers of the House *(1964), is set on a plantation outside of Montgomery, although the town and state are never explicitly named. Narrated by Abigail Howland,* Keepers *is the story of her grandfather's mixed-race love affair, the children of that union, and the violent response by local bigots when the truth is known. After college at Sophie Newcomb, Grau in 1955 married Tulane philosophy professor James K. Feibleman. They and their children divide their time between Metairie and Martha's Vineyard. There were three volumes of fiction before* Keepers: The Black Prince and Other Stories *(1955), which one reviewer called the best collection since J. D. Salinger's* Nine Stories, *and the novels* The Hard Blue Sky *(1958) and* The House on Coliseum Street *(1961). The Hard Blue Sky powerfully depicts hurricane season in Louisiana and, oddly enough, Ms. Grau was flooded out by Katrina in 2005. After* Keepers of the House, *Grau has published six more volumes of fiction: three novels,* The Condor Passes *(1971),* Evidence of Love *(1977), and* Roadwalkers *(1995), and three collections of stories,* The Wind Shifting West *(1973), from which "The Lovely April" is taken,* Nine Women, *and, most recently,* Selected Stories *(2003).*

Neighborhood Watch

Carolyn Haines

I came to write "Neighborhood Watch" for David Thompson, who was the owner of Busted Flush Press and the heart of Murder by the Book bookstore in Houston, TX. David died unexpectedly in the fall of 2010. He was tireless in his promotion of crime fiction and authors. Busted Flush Press was at the forefront of publishing in 2010—as David's vision led him to bring backlists for authors he loved back into print. He also published a number of popular anthologies. "Neighborhood Watch" was written for Damn Near Dead 2, *a collection of stories featuring sleuths who might be considered "over the hill." The collection was published shortly before David died.*

Penmanship had never been her strong suit, but in these days of computer communications, Yvonne knew not to underestimate the power of a hand-written letter.

The black ink flowed across the ecru notepaper in daring loops and swirls.

Dear President Obama,

My sense of irony has been keenly exercised since the brutal murder of my daughter, Rainbow Saffron King. Are you aware that any moron with an IQ in the single digits can buy a gun, yet I have to take a test to keep my driver's license? My neighbors, who are inbred Okies with six toes and rabbit red eyes, all have automatic weapons. Even as I write they are playing shuffleboard in their front yard with weapons trained on my front door.

My poor little Rainbow was planting a vegetable garden to feed the poor when a stray bullet zipped through her heart. Though the police ruled it an accidental shooting and told me there are no laws in Alabama prohibiting folks from shooting weapons in their front yards, I believe Rainbow's death to be a murder. Can you please get those worthless buffoons sitting in Congress to do some work and change the gun laws of this country? A big gun does not make a man's penis a single bit bigger.

Yours truly,

Grace Montcrieff King

Without a moment's hesitation Yvonne copied down the address of her archenemy, Grace Montcrieff King, and sealed the envelope. If the CIA came looking for the author of the note, they'd find plenty to keep them busy at Grace's address.

Yvonne put the note beside two others, already stamped and waiting only on the arrival of Jeffrey, the postman, before winging their way to the White House. She'd written notes to the prior resident of America's first house—with no response. She had higher hopes for the new occupant of 1600 Pennsylvania Avenue. He appeared to have some gumption.

She checked the clock in the kitchen, noting she had forty minutes until Jeffrey was due. She swallowed a handful of vitamins with a glass of filtered water. There was time for one more note. From the kitchen drawer she brought out high-powered military field glasses and focused on the yellow Victorian half a block away. Grace was out in her yard, tending the roses that were her pride and joy.

Yvonne took in every detail. Grace had been to the hairdresser. Her coppery curls feathered around her face, and the color was fresh and perky. At the end of the month, Grace's hair would be faded, sliding toward the natural gray. Grace was at least sixty-two, though she lied and claimed to be only fifty-eight.

Grace lied about many things.

Most especially about her husbands.

After three glasses of wine at a dinner party, Grace had confessed to Yvonne that she'd gone to the altar five times and hoped to make it six. No dummy, Yvonne had searched out Grace's marriage licenses and come up with only two, Anthony Montcrieff, whose name Grace clung to like a favorite pair of panties, and Barney King, her current spouse, who was in assisted living. But Grace was honey to fly-brained men, there was no denying that. Men buzzed around her, intoxicated by her come hither flirtations.

To that end, Grace performed Yoga stretches in the window of her second story turret, where any passerby could watch the contortions, which were right amazing for a woman her age.

Old Marshall Binghamton, who owned the property at the end of the road with the fine view of Mobile Bay, walked past Grace's house at least twice a day, eyes out on stems, hoping to catch a glimpse of her antics. Deviant old bastard. When his timing was good and he saw Grace bending and twisting, he'd stop dead on the sidewalk, breathing noisily through his mouth, and sometimes trembling. Oh, he had fantasies of what he wanted to do to Grace.

Which reminded Yvonne to get busy with her letter.

Dear President Obama,

Please consider the injustice of health care in our country today. Insurance companies are villainous in their callous decisions to provide health coverage to policies valuing the penis. Viagra is paid for by insurance policies but birth control pills are not. So men are allowed to have their pleasure (even if too senile to remember it) while young women must risk pregnancy? Foul! I say FOUL!

This is just one example of gender-biased health care in this country.

Please level the playing field of sexual misconduct for male and female alike. What's good for the goose is good for the gander. Force insurance companies to cover birth control pills so my teenage daughter can safely continue with her relationship with a sixty-nine-year-old man we are hoping will soon die in a moment of sexual bliss. (He's loaded and she's his beneficiary, the old fool.) But until he croaks, she needs someone to pay for her Yaz because she spends all her money on butt floss undies.

God bless you,

Mable Graham

She signed the note—written on a different type of note card and in a small cramped hand—with a flourish. Mable lived two blocks over and was normally her partner in the weekly bridge games held in the neighborhood. Mable was a good egg, except for her support of the Reverend Bewley Birchwood, a televangelist who promised gold and glory for those who contributed to his TV ministry. To Yvonne's way of thinking, a little CIA intervention might save Mable a shitload of money.

Yvonne placed the stamp, one featuring the black Michael Jackson, on the envelope just as she heard Jeffrey's footsteps on her stoop. She gathered her out-going mail and went to open the door.

Jeffrey had already dumped his mail sack in anticipation of her invitation for a glass of iced tea. It was their routine. He'd make his report

Carolyn Haines

of the neighborhood while he cooled off a little. She admired a man who walked a mail route even in the August heat. The Daphne, Alabama, post office had offered him one of the riding carts, but he said he was holding out for an electric scooter. The truth was, Jeffrey was a conservation nut and walking also gave him an optimal opportunity to keep up with the neighbors.

"Binghamton had a young woman down at his boat dock today." Jeffrey followed Yvonne into the kitchen and took his chair. "She looked to be mid-forties or so. Good figure. She was friendly enough. Blond, about five-five. Beauty mark on her left cheek. It's not even ten o'clock and she had what looked like a Bloody Mary in her hand. Made me think of a good-time girl. Could give Grace a run for her money."

"Grace may have a few more wrinkles, but I'd put my bet on her. She knows every angle in that game." Yvonne could never get over the naiveté of men like Jeffrey. They thought it all came down to a bouncy ass and silicone tits. Grace knew moves that would curl Jeffrey's toes, and most of them had nothing to do with the bedroom.

"Old Binghamton seemed mighty smitten. Had that mouth-open, quivery action goin' on." Jeffrey did a fine imitation as he accepted the glass of tea.

"What about Lady Kelley?" Yvonne changed the subject. She didn't like Grace well enough to defend her.

"She's still sittin' in her chair in front of the TV. She won't come to the door, so I can't say if she's cryin' or not."

Lady had lost her husband to a heart attack. Her children had come to visit. Once. Six weeks ago. The ungrateful little miscreants had shown up at the funeral, all weepy and full of woe. Once the will was read and they got their cut, they were gone. Lady, so called because of her genteel personality, had been stripped of financial control. The oldest boy, a sweaty, overweight high school football coach, was in charge of everything. Rumor was the children intended to force the sale of Lady's house and move her to assisted living.

"I'll take her some muffins," Yvonne said as she refilled Jeffrey's glass. "If I hear those kids of hers are coming back, I'll put roofing tacks in the driveway."

Jeffrey wiped the sweat from his glass. "Everything else is quiet. I still say old Binghamton is gonna take up with the younger model. Who'd pass up a T-bird for an Edsel? "

Yvonne had a good laugh. That Jeffrey, he sure knew how to get her tickled. At least once a day he came out with some jewel. She gave him the stamped notes, and he tucked them in his sack before he hefted it and continued on his way. If he saw anything noteworthy, he'd give her a call. Between the two of them, they looked out for the neighborhood.

She put on her athletic shoes, laced them tight, and went to the back yard to call Jethro, her Walker hound/Doberman cross. He'd shown up, starved and abused, in her yard four years before. She'd had him neutered, wormed, vaccinated, and socialized in a matter of weeks, and now he was the best companion imaginable. They walked each day, just before her story came on. Jethro helped her keep the neighborhood safe.

Yvonne didn't bother locking the front door. The neighbors knew each other and who should be allowed to come and go. Any funny stuff, someone would call the police.

Grace was still working in her roses when they marched by. Yvonne spoke—she was always courteous, that was how she was raised.

Jethro was past Grace's yard when Grace called out, "Have you heard Reg Gamble got into some trouble last night?"

It was just like Grace to hold out information until Yvonne had to turn around and walk back. It was a control thing with Grace. Yvonne considered pretending she hadn't heard, but Jethro did a one-eighty. Yvonne had no choice but to follow. Well, she had a little something to tell, too.

"No, I hadn't heard. I hope he isn't sick," Yvonne said, friendly as could be.

"Oh, no. Not unless you count sucking on a vodka bottle as sickness. Got drunk at the sports bar and got a DUI. Cops kept him in jail overnight. I heard he was pitching a hell fit, calling the officers names. His sister bailed him out this morning and took him to the Bradford Center to dry out." Grace's lavender eyes sparkled.

"That's too bad," Yvonne said. "Drinking is an illness, Grace. It's not some kind of moral weakness. Brain chemistry out of whack."

"Oh, posh!" Grace waved airily. "Reg is an old drunk. Mean as a snake when he's on the bottle. Don't try to make excuses for him."

Yvonne let it go. "I hear old Binghamton's got him some frisky blond company. I wondered how long he'd last as a single man. Once his wife died, every widow woman in Daphne took him a casserole. Looks to me like he wanted something more than hot tuna and noodles." Men had once called Yvonne's robust laughter naughty.

"Who is she?" Grace didn't hide her consternation.

"No clue." Yvonne caught a flash of calculation in Grace's expression. "Want to come along with me and Jethro for a walk?"

Grace dropped her leather gardening gloves in the dirt. She dusted her hands and came out the gate. "I need a good stretch."

They strolled down the sidewalk beneath the shade of the live oaks that made Bayside Manor, a gated retirement community, worth living in. The sidewalk was smooth and level, newly built to accommodate those fancy little scooters.

"How come you never married, Yvonne?" Grace rotated each shoulder as if her joints were unhinged.

"Who said I never married?" Yvonne was surprised at the question.

"Well, I just assumed . . . You don't wear a ring. You never talk about a husband or children."

"Some folks don't need a man to validate who they are. Not one in the present *or* one in the past. What's gone is gone, Grace. So how many times were you married?"

Grace looked confused. "Why do you ask?"

" 'Cause you brought it up? How many?"

"Three."

Yvonne nodded. Grace King was a liar. If she was breathing, she was lying. "I never hear you talk about children either."

"Oh, I couldn't have any. I had a delicate uterus. I miscarried three times. My pelvis is so narrow. The doctor said it might break me in two to carry a child, and I was married to Gerard then. A gynecologist. He said I should have it all taken out. He loved me so much he didn't want to risk me."

"Did he work for the health department?" Yvonne was deviling

Grace, but she couldn't stop herself.

"Of course not! He had a private practice and was the most sought after doctor in Louisville."

"What happened to him?"

"It was just tragic," Grace said. "He had a heart attack delivering a baby. Slipped right off his stool onto the floor and he was dead. Like to have broke my heart."

"Was he first, second, or third?"

"Second." Grace looked peeved. She pointed down to the end of the street where the land dropped steeply to the water of Mobile Bay. A wooden pier jutted out. The boat slip was empty. "Marshall's boat is gone."

"He's smarter than I thought," Yvonne said.

"What do you mean?"

"There's a storm brewing out on the open water." She pointed at the dull, flat clouds far on the horizon. "If he anchors the boat right, he can use the motion of the waves to add some punch to his amorous moves. Maybe that young blond won't kill him then."

Grace's mouth thinned into a narrow red line. "I need to get back to my garden." She turned abruptly and strode back the way they'd come.

Yvonne unleashed Jethro. He loved the water. Maybe he had some lab in him somewhere. They had DNA tests for dogs now. An owner could find out the lineage of a mutt. Then again, what difference did it make? Yvonne wasn't certain what her ancestry might include. She liked the water, too.

She sat on a bench and watched Jethro race down the steep steps to the pier. He didn't even hesitate as he launched himself straight off the end in a flying leap to splash in the water. It was good to be young, she thought, remembering her own days of jumping from creek banks into icy streams. Those had been good times.

Now, though, it was time for her program. She whistled up Jethro and headed home. *All My Children* was her lunchtime vice. She'd followed the boudoir antics of Erica Kane since she'd first appeared on the scene. Erica was close to sixty, though she looked no more than forty-five. On *AMC* a character could be a villain one week and a saint the next.

Carolyn Haines

Redemption was easy as pie on television.

The next day dawned hot and sticky. Clouds hung over the bay, thick and clotted with rain. A tropical depression was boring up the center of the Gulf of Mexico, and though it was unorganized, there was the chance it could blossom into a monster storm. The August waters, superheated by development all along the coastline, favored such.

Yvonne went out on her front porch and used the field glasses to check up and down the street. To her surprise, Grace was working in her rose garden. It was barely six o'clock in the morning, and Grace was not by nature an early riser.

Yvonne watched surreptitiously as she sipped her morning coffee. Grace was acting strange. She dug in the dirt with quiet fury, and when the sun was full up and Grace had pushed her hair back from her perspiration-dampened face, she dropped her gloves and headed down the street toward the bay.

She was checking up on Binghamton! Yvonne wondered herself if the old boy had made it home. With the storm brewing over the water, he should be docking in safe harbors—but perhaps Grace waiting on the pier was more dangerous than the Bermuda Triangle.

Yvonne took her coffee cup and binoculars inside and wrote a letter.

Dear President Obama,

Are you aware that in the Alabama halls of higher education, female assistant professors make an average of eight thousand dollars less than their male counterparts? Gender bias should not be allowed in institutions supported by state and federal dollars. When the worth—or lack of worth—of an employee is determined by male genitalia—or lack thereof—it's a sad comment on the education and values our young people are receiving.

Does a penis bestow a superior ability to teach? I have not found this to be true.

Please look into the wage disparities between genders in universities and colleges that accept federal dollars. While it is a fact in Alabama, it is likely true in other places.

Thank you,

Marshall Binghamton

She'd typewritten the letter and signed it with a scrawl that could have said anything. Marshall Binghamton would never support equal pay for equal work. He was a chauvinist through and through. Which is why it gave Yvonne an extra boost of pleasure to fold the letter and stuff it in an envelope.

Once it was stamped and ready for Jeffrey's arrival, she grabbed a bagel and Jethro's leash and called the dog. No point missing the fireworks if Binghamton happened to be docked. She wondered if Grace would be so bold as to knock on his front door. Maybe!

With Jethro for a beard and chewing the last of the bagel, she pushed her way through the thick air to the water. The Moon Dancer, Binghamton's boat, was snugged in the little boathouse. And Grace was nowhere to be seen.

Yvonne circled the cul de sac and tried to see past the shrubs to Binghamton's house, but the camellia bushes with their dense green leaves were too thick. Jethro tugged at his leash, but she didn't let him loose to rush to the water. The clouds looked threatening. And she had some errands to run before a big storm came through and knocked the power out for several days.

At the local library she got on the Internet and searched for ob-gyn Dr. Gerard in Louisville, Kentucky. She figured Grace was lying, but it was better to check. To her surprise, she found the obituary for Dr. Gerard DeLong, noted obstetrician, who died unexpectedly of a heart attack while delivering a child at Mercy Medical Hospital. He was survived by his wife, Eugracia DeWitt DeLong, and two children from a previous marriage.

Yvonne had not discovered the DeWitt name when she'd first looked into Grace's marriages, and she certainly wasn't familiar with Eugracia, an unusual derivative of Grace. She did a search for Eugracia DeWitt. What came up was the society page of the *Kansas City Register*. Eugracia and her husband, Roger DeWitt, were featured at a party for a local architect. There was no doubt that the woman in the photograph was her neighbor.

She searched for Roger DeWitt. The next mention was an obituary. Roger slipped from the roof of their Kansas City home and plunged to his death. Eugracia McKenzie DeWitt was his sole survivor. Gregor

Carolyn Haines

McKenzie, her third husband, was also deceased. Anaphylactic shock.

So Grace hadn't lied, exactly. Dr. Gerard DeLong, Roger DeWitt, Gregor McKenzie, Anthony Montcrieff, plus the latest, Barney King, a bank manager suffering from premature Alzheimer's Disease and living in a facility across the bay in Mobile. Barney had been institutionalized a few weeks before Yvonne moved into the neighborhood. Grace went to see him twice a week, though she said he didn't recognize her.

The doctors said he'd lost the will to live and could go at any minute, which would leave Grace free to pursue Marshall Binghamton full throttle. Yvonne almost felt a dollop of pity for Marshall, but she squished it.

On the way home, she braved the blustery weather and sudden sheets of rain and stopped at the store for coffee, apples, peanut butter, chicken and frozen dumplings to cook for Jethro, and a bottle of Jack Daniels. She allowed herself one tall Jack and water each evening, and with the storm approaching, she didn't want to be caught with a short supply.

She made it home just as Jeffrey was headed down her front walk. They went inside together, and he played fetch with Jethro while she put the chicken on to boil and made fresh tea. Jeffrey was about to pop with some information, but they had a ritual. When he was at the table, tea in hand, he grinned.

"Old Binghamton was out in his yard this morning when I delivered the mail."

She arched her eyebrows, interested but not too eager.

"Had a pair of red undies hanging from his robe pocket and strutting around like a rooster in a henhouse."

Yvonne poured herself some tea. She really wanted a Jack, but it wasn't even noon. "Did you see the blonde?"

Jeffrey shook his head. "No strange car in the drive, either. Could be she left before I got there."

"Grace is going to take this hard." Even knowing all she did about Grace, Yvonne still felt sympathy. It was humiliating to get beat out by a younger model, as if life experience had no value at all.

"She's dug up most of her front yard. Is she puttin' in a sprinkler system?" Jeffrey asked.

"Burying her high hopes, I think."

He drained his glass, put it on the counter and started back to the front door where his satchel waited. She handed him the letter.

"Only one?"

"Been a busy morning," she replied.

"That storm's comin' in fast. I'd better hotfoot it. I want to get home and make sure everything's secure. You need any help here?"

Yvonne thought about it. "I'm fine, Jeffrey. Thanks for asking."

Some of her neighbors sat in recliners and watched the Weather Channel day and night. Yvonne was determined not to fall into that trap. It was always heat or rain or wind or lightning. The weather bogeyman prowled the Gulf Coast, and it did no good to sit and watch for him. Either he'd come or not. She refused to let her last good years be mired in futile worry about Mother Nature's business.

She and Jethro made a round of the exterior of her house, checking to be sure there was nothing loose to fly through a window. Only one storm in recent history had come directly up Mobile Bay. Most skirted west to Biloxi or east to Pensacola. But if one did come, the bluffs of the Eastern Shore were high enough to prevent flooding. No one could do anything about the wind and rain.

When she stopped in her front yard to double latch the white wooden gate, she saw Grace still out in her yard throwing a shovelful of dirt on a mound already chest high.

"Come on, Jethro." Yvonne opened the gate and let the brisk wind blow her across the street. "Grace! Have you lost your mind? There's a storm coming. Stop digging up the front yard and get your house in order."

Grace looked up, eyes wild. "I have to finish this garden."

When Yvonne got close, she saw that Grace had chopped the root system of several of her prize roses. The woman had gone totally round the bend, and over an old mouth-breather who trembled in anticipation.

"Get a grip." Yvonne was brutal. "Give me that shovel." She took it from Grace's hands. "Now go inside and get ready for the storm. Have you checked on Barney?"

"No. No I haven't." Grace actually hung her head. "You're right. I'll do that now."

Carolyn Haines

"Are you okay?"

Grace nodded. "Thank you, Yvonne. I don't know what got into me."

She climbed the steps and entered her house. The wind quieted for a moment and Yvonne heard the lock click into place. She and Jethro continued down the street. At the end, she saw Marshall Binghamton out tying lines to hold his thrashing boat in place. Old fool.

She went to the pier and signaled for him to throw her a line. She helped him secure the boat. The water was so rough Jethro had no interest in a swim. He stayed Velcroed to her side.

"Hear you got a new friend," she said when Binghamton came off the boat, his legs shaky from exertion or possibly fear. He'd almost been thrown off the pitching boat several times.

"It's a free country," he said.

"I haven't heard that expression since 1958," she said. "What's her name?"

"Mind your own business." He stormed away through the thick hedges of his lawn and disappeared.

Yvonne almost shot him the bird. Rude old deviant. But she'd been raised better than that. She and Jethro went home. The local news station had gone to full weather coverage, not a good sign, and she decided to watch before the power went out.

Hurricane Francine churned straight toward Mobile on a course due north at sixteen miles an hour. She was a Cat 3 and might strengthen.

Yvonne snapped off the TV and unplugged it. She cooked the dumplings with the chicken and set them aside to cool for Jethro. If the power went out, they wouldn't keep long. He might as well enjoy them while they were fresh.

She made a pot of coffee and considered writing another letter, but her concentration was fragmented. Grace was on her mind. As if she'd conjured her up, Grace's car pulled out of the drive and left the neighborhood. The only places Grace went were the hair salon, the grocery, or to see Barney. Yvonne could only hope she was smart enough not to try to cross the seven-and-a-half-mile-long bay bridge with such a storm bearing down on them. The Jubilee Parkway was high enough to avoid the waves—for the moment—but the wind could flip a car over the rail. And the causeway was likely underwater by now.

Grace finished one cup of coffee and decided to chuck her discipline and have a Jack. Storms somehow called for a bit of drinking. The abandon was alluring—just throwing up her hands and saying, fuck it.

Drink clinking with ice, she went to the telephone table and pulled out the phone book. Only a dozen assisted living facilities in Mobile were listed. She'd never asked which one Barney was in, but she could make a few calls, see if she could get Grace on the phone and talk some sense into her about the storm. The weather was getting worse and worse.

Jethro settled at her feet as she made the first call. She hit pay dirt on the seventh. The receptionist knew Barney King. He'd been her family banker.

"Are you a relative?" she asked.

"I'm a friend of his wife's," Yvonne explained. "I need to speak with her. It's an emergency."

"Mr. King passed away last year," the woman said. "I'm sorry."

Yvonne put the phone down, momentarily stumped. When she picked up the receiver again, she called Louisville, Kentucky, information and asked for Andrew DeLong. She let the operator place the call for her.

Andrew was not at home, but his wife, Judy, had a moment to talk about Andrew's father, Gerard.

"He was a delightful man," she said. "He left a big hole in our family. We get cards from his patients every year saying how much they miss him."

"And his wife, Eugracia?"

"Eu-gracia? The name says it all. Once she had his money, we haven't seen or heard from her." There was a split second of silence. "Why are you asking?"

"She's my neighbor. I know her as Grace King." Yvonne's heart beat too fast and she sipped the bourbon.

"Tell her spouse to be careful. She's a black widow. Andrew thinks she tampered with Gerard's heart medicine."

Yvonne finished her drink in one long, smooth swallow. "Why would you say such a thing?"

"Because he believes it. And so do I."

"Do you have any proof?" Outside a gust of wind blew something heavy onto Grace's roof. The storm notched up, and the telephone line crackled.

"If we had proof, she'd be behind bars."

The streetlights had come on though it was only five o'clock. Tree limbs, pitched by the steadily increasing wind, cast strange shadows on the pavement. Yvonne sat at the window, binoculars focused on the yellow Victorian. Grace had returned home, and she was moving about the turret room on the second floor, but she wasn't doing Yoga. It looked like she was packing a bag.

She disappeared and the front door opened. She ran out into the rain. Her car backed out of the drive, and she drove toward the cul de sac at a reckless speed.

"Holy shit, Jethro," Yvonne said. She was well into her third Jack, but Jethro never judged her. "Do you think old Binghamton is in danger?"

Jethro didn't have an answer, but Yvonne knew who to ask. Jeffrey. The postman lived only a mile or two away. He was a single man who might enjoy a bit of adventure. She dialed.

"Francine is headed down our throats," Jeffrey said.

"Grace has five dead husbands. She drove down to old Binghamton's like a bat out of hell."

Jeffrey sighed. "Give me fifteen minutes and hope no trees have fallen across the road."

Yvonne found her ex-husband's storm slicker and his .38 that she kept clean, oiled, and in good working order. Marty Jarvis needed neither where he'd gone. She got the leg holster he'd used to carry his second piece.

She was waiting on the porch when Jeffrey pulled into her driveway in his old Pathfinder. Jethro moaned softly behind the closed front door, and Yvonne relented and let him out. He'd stay by her side.

The three of them took off at a brisk walk, the wind pushing them back, making it difficult to gain headway. Jeffrey probably wanted to tell her she was a fool, but she couldn't hear him above the howl of the wind.

When they got to the bluff, she saw the Moon Dancer had broken her aft lines and was slamming against the boathouse. The fiberglass hull wouldn't last long with that punishment. Yvonne was about to turn away when she saw the body floating by the boat.

"Grace!" She shouted into the gale and grabbed Jeffrey's shoulder and pointed.

The body bobbed in the swells, disappearing and then floating back, face down, arms spread. Through the sheets of rain, Yvonne could determine only that it was a female wearing white slacks and a red blouse.

"Po-lice!" Jeffrey pointed to the Binghamton house. "Call po-lice!" He pushed Yvonne in that direction. He started down the steep steps of the pier. Yvonne pulled her cell phone from her pocket. The storm whipped so fiercely reception was nil.

Yvonne grasped Jeffrey's slicker, but it slipped from her hands. He pointed at the house and made frantic dialing motions, then continued his treacherous descent down the wet stairs in the wind.

Yvonne ran. She did it without thought. Jethro right at her heels, she pushed open the cast iron gate, brushed through the camellia bushes and ran across the lawn to the white stucco house. Grace's car was in the driveway. At the door, Yvonne pounded with all her might. It occurred to her she liked neither Grace nor old Binghamton, yet she was risking her life, as was Jeffrey, to save one of them. She couldn't help the way she'd been brought up.

No one answered her banging, but the door wasn't locked. She stepped inside, calling Jethro to follow her. The hound shook, spraying the entrance hall with water. Yvonne crept forward, searching for a phone.

Jethro padded through the foyer toward a closed door. As Yvonne approached, she heard someone speaking. "She threw herself at me," old Binghamton said. "I had no choice."

Yvonne pulled the .38 from the holster on her calf. Jethro nudged the door open and she poked her head in. Old Binghamton and Grace faced each other across a beautiful oak kitchen table. Yvonne was a fool for good wood, and the table was solid and elegant. She forced her attention to the occupants of the room. Both held guns pointed at each other. Neither noticed her or Jethro.

"You killed her," Grace said.

"She was going to tell you." Old Binghamton's gun shifted left to right along with his trembling head. "She threw herself at me and I couldn't

Carolyn Haines

resist. She was going down to your house to tell you. I couldn't let her."

"You killed her." Grace sounded like a needle stuck on vinyl.

"There's a price to be paid for interfering in a man's happiness," Old Binghamton insisted.

Yvonne found herself in a quandary. If Grace was a murderer of husbands and Old Binghamton screwed and then killed women, who was she supposed to save? Neither seemed worth the effort.

She grasped Jethro's collar and backed away. The person she ought to be concerned about was her friend, Jeffrey. She found a telephone in a den and dialed 911. She reported the body in the bay and the pending gunfight. When the operator asked her name, she said, "Martha Stewart." She hung up and went back in the storm to find her friend.

Yvonne stood at her kitchen window. Sunlight filtered through the leaves of the live oaks. Across the street, two men unloaded a van full of furniture and carried it into the yellow Victorian that had once belonged to Grace Montcrieff King, black widow. Grace awaited trial for the murder of three of her five husbands. Old Binghamton had been charged with the murder of Lindy Morton.

Hurricane Francine had turned unexpectedly east, walloping Pensacola yet again but leaving Mobile Bay mostly unscathed. Four weeks had passed and songbirds flitted outside Yvonne's window. The first hint of fall spiked the air.

Grace sat down at the table and picked up her pen.

Dear President Obama,

America faces many hard issues, but none so dangerous as the continued overpopulation of the planet. Our tax codes, written and designed to keep an underclass of working poor available to feed the factories of wealthy industrialists, reward Americans for reproducing. The opposite should be true. Americans who do not reproduce should be given tax breaks, especially with the planet groaning under the weight of too many human beings.

This senseless tax structure goes back to the days when a man's virility was judged by the number of children he sired (regardless of his ability to feed and educate said children). It is just another example of policy based on the penis.

Please step forward into the 21ˢᵗ Century and stop this madness.
Yours truly,
Yvonne Jarvis

Along with the note card she inserted a newspaper clipping with a photo of her and Jeffrey Tatano, the postman, receiving the Baldwin County crime stoppers award for assisting in the capture of two murderers.

Carolyn Haines, a USA Today *bestselling author, writes the popular Sarah Booth Delaney mystery series.* Bone to be Wild *is the fifteenth in the series and was published by St. Martin's Press. She also writes dark fiction under the pseudonym R.B. Chesterton. When she isn't writing books, Haines is working as founder and chief stall cleaner at Good Fortune Farm Refuge, a 501c3 animal rescue. In 2010, Haines received the Harper Lee Award for Distinguished Writing, and in 2009 the Richard Wright Award for Literary Excellence. She has published over 70 books. She lives in Semmes, AL on a farm.*

Carolyn Haines

The Other Grandparents

Jennifer Horne

I love looking at old photographs and imagining the stories that go with them. I've written a one-of-a-kind chapbook with old photos pasted in to illustrate a story I made up from the pictures. Once in a village in Greece, after I'd spent an hour poring over a bin of old portraits, when I went to pay, the woman looked at me, smiling, and said, "For free." The Monroe County Museum Store in Monroeville, Alabama keeps a box of photographs of local people and events under a display table, and whenever I'm in there I squat down on the floor and browse through it, looking for material. The photo that inspired this story came from that box—the mysterious quality of the light, the man that just might possibly be Truman Capote, the dressed-up children reminding me of Capote's story "Children on Their Birthdays." "The Other Grandparents" ponders the question of which stories families tell and which they keep hidden, and what those choices tell us about our families.

My mother only this week told me the story of when Truman Capote came to her seventh birthday party. He didn't come to Arkansas where she grew up—not ever, that I know of. She was visiting cousins in Monroeville, Alabama, and, as the visit fell on her birthday, they threw her a party with the neighbor children in attendance. In a picture from that day my mother showed me, the girls are in frilly white dresses with anklet socks and sandals or patent-leather shoes. Mr. Capote is in the picture as well, speaking to my grandmother, who at that time of course was a pretty, still-young woman in a becoming dress. My mother's first cousin Jenny was a poised and precocious child, which makes me wonder whether Truman Capote got his inspiration for "Children on Their Birthdays" from that party. He, too, must have been visiting cousins in Monroeville. Thankfully, unlike Miss Bobbitt in the story, no one was hit by the six o'clock bus that day, but something did happen, something my mother both knows and does not know. What she knows is that Mr. Capote said something extraordinary to her mother, and that she was never quite the same afterwards. What she does not know, because she never found the

171

right moment to ask in the years before her mother died, is what he said, or why he was moved to say it. It seems possible to me that this black-and-white almost chiaroscuro photo was taken just as he was speaking to her and that it captured her psychic state. Her head seems light, fuzzy, almost immaterial, not a lack of focus or a flaw in the equipment but a true picture of how she felt. She is half-turned, in profile, while he is facing the camera, though with dark sunglasses that hide his eyes. He looks annoyed at the photographer or perhaps just at the glare of the afternoon light and the emptiness of his highball glass.

My mother, Susanna, said that her mother, Lucy, had taken her down to Alabama on the train, a long journey and not direct, to get away from her father for a little while. "She would take these breaks periodically," my mother told me, "when his goodness just got to be too much for her." My grandfather—named Franklin, after FDR—was ever patient, kind, temperate, helpful, easygoing, understanding, and loving. For a woman of my grandmother's temperament who needed to kick up her heels, kick off the traces, and in general just kick back every once in a while, his saintliness made her feel shallow and selfish, so when she felt a little evil coming on, she'd pack up a suitcase and take my mother to visit some cousins, of whom she had plenty, and she would smoke and drink and gossip and cackle until she got it out of her system and she could once again appreciate the many fine qualities of my grandfather.

After this trip, though, after whatever Mr. Capote said to her, she began, occasionally, to talk to herself in the morning while she made coffee, along the lines, my mother said, of someone arguing with herself: "Well, why don't you? But what good would it do now? Well, you won't ever know if you don't try, will you? Water under the bridge, my dear, water . . . under . . . bridge."

On the day she died, many years later, she uttered a cryptic statement that made my mother wonder further: "He was right—I wasn't as bad as I thought I was. That was true." Or "Tru." Of course it wasn't possible to know.

The birthday party was in July. They returned to Arkansas for the long, hot, lazy dog days when summer is ending and everything is dry but autumn has not yet come. School started the weekend after Labor Day,

Jennifer Horne

and the next weekend Lucy announced to Susanna that they were going on a picnic, and wouldn't that be fun. My grandfather was helping somebody with something that day and so did not go with them. Lucy packed a heavy picnic basket and put it in the back seat of the Chevrolet, and Susanna got in the front, buckled her seatbelt across her lap, the metal buckle already hot from the day's sun, and they pulled out of the driveway.

To Susanna's question about where they were going for their picnic, Lucy would say only that it would be a surprise in more ways than one. She seemed nervous but at the same time determined, her permed hair brushed high off her forehead, her lipstick making a red flag of her lips, her manicured nails tapping a repeated drum roll on the steering wheel at stoplights.

They drove out of town along the highway for several miles then turned off on a county road my mother didn't know. The road curved and rose, crossing dappled shadows of leaves and passing few houses.

Just about the time Susanna was about to have to ask her mother to stop so she could go, by the side of the road behind a bush if necessary, her mother said, "Morrison, 6300 County Road 14 West. That has to be it," and pulled into a driveway marked by a tilting, scarred mailbox, a hand-lettered "Keep Out" sign, and an old tire in which a few yellow and orange marigolds, grown leggy and sparse, eked out their lives.

My mother's part of the script was predictable. "We're stopping here? For a picnic?"

Several dogs of indeterminate breed came out from their dirt beds under a large privet hedge and began barking furiously, keeping them in the car.

Lucy looked at Susanna. "Do not, repeat, do not tell your father that we came here. Do you understand?

"Yes ma'am."

"We are here to visit your grandparents. Your *other* grandparents. I thought it was about time. Now mind your manners and don't embarrass me in front of my in-laws."

This was the first my mother, Susanna, had heard of her father's parents. Until then, it just hadn't come up.

The dogs had retreated somewhat and when Lucy and Susanna got out of the car they barked but without real enthusiasm.

"Don't look them in the eye and they won't bother us," said Lucy, taking the picnic basket from the backseat.

More privet hedge grew in random sproutings around the house, and on the screen door a patch of screen had come loose and flapped listlessly in the dull breeze.

Lucy knocked. A minute passed during which time small sounds came from inside, as of someone trying to move quietly, and a curtain twitched very slightly. Finally the door was opened by a scrawny but wiry woman, brows furrowed in protective defense of her home. She stood, silent, waiting for her visitors to speak first.

"Ruby?" said Lucy. "It's me, Lucy. And I've brought your granddaughter Susanna."

The woman's deep smoker's wrinkles went suddenly from frown to wide smile, then she clapped her hand over her mouth. "Haven't put my partials in yet! But Lucy, what a nice surprise. I thought you was some government lady from town. Come in, come in. Susanna, aren't you big?" And then, over her shoulder, "Hiram, you won't believe who's here!"

A sound came from behind her, the grunt of someone heaving himself up. As they entered the house, Hiram came forward. He was a fat man of the old-fashioned kind, pants pulled up over his round belly and held in place by suspenders, so that he resembled an egg with human features and clothes painted onto it.

His face, too, opened into a smile as he recognized Lucy. "Well, if it ain't my daughter-in-law! And this is your girl? Franklin's girl? Susanna? Honey, come over here and give your old granddaddy some sugar."

Susanna presented herself and kissed his proffered cheek. He smelled slightly smoky and dusty, like an old blanket from the attic.

"Ain't she pretty? And Lucy, you're a sight for sore eyes."

They sat down in the living room, a smallish and cluttered room redolent of smoke, cabbage, dog, and Pine Sol. It was a not unpleasant smell, my mother says. She sat quietly, taking in the room, while the grown-ups talked, then she remembered she had to pee.

"Excuse me, may I use the toilet please?" she asked, using her best manners.

Jennifer Horne

Ruby smiled. "You sure may, but it's out back. Don't mind the dogs—they won't hurt you. But rattle around a bit once you get inside to scare off any snakes." She smiled in a way that might be joking or might not. Susanna didn't know her well enough to say.

She didn't want to go after hearing about the out back and the snake part, but her mother was looking at her in a way that reminded Susanna of her promise not to embarrass her mother in front of her in-laws, and she was still young enough to worry about having an accident if she didn't go, so she walked back out the front door and around the back to where a small, unpainted outbuilding stood, and she lifted up the wooden latch and banged on the wall to scare the snakes and for the first time in her life sat down on a hole cut out of a board and, after a minute of tense waiting, let loose. It sounded different from the pleasant sound going in the toilet made, both farther down and duller, and when she was finished and looked for toilet paper there were only neatly cut squares of newsprint, which she used and dropped down into the dark hole as well. She had been taught always to wash her hands afterwards but saw nowhere to wash up, so she went back inside the house and rejoined the adults.

" . . . and he stays so busy with church work and Rotary activities and so on, he just barely has a moment to himself," her mother was saying.

So they had been talking about her father while she was gone.

"But I thought," Lucy said, shifting to a brighter register as she saw Susanna returning, "I should just bring Susanna along whether he could come or not, not even bother him with asking, so here we are! Oh, and I brought us a picnic. I thought maybe we could all eat it together. In here," she added, to make clear that she did not intend for them to go out into the yard.

The picnic basket held more than enough for the three adults and one child—ham, bread, potato salad, devilled eggs, lemon squares, apples, and a tub of chicken salad they didn't even touch. As soon as they finished, Lucy put all the perishables into the old squat refrigerator that sagged into the kitchen's linoleum "so that it won't spoil," had Susanna take the basket to the car, and then conveniently forgot to retrieve the rest of the food when they left.

As they were saying their goodbyes outside, Lucy said, "Oh, I left my pocketbook on the couch," and when she came back out she had a slight smile, a secret smile Susanna had not seen before.

"Well, bye y'all," said Ruby. "We sure was happy to see you. Come back again soon." She and Hiram waved as Lucy turned the car around, then headed back to the house. They were not the kind to keep waving until you were out of sight, apparently. As the car reached the highway, Susanna saw Ruby come running out of the house with an envelope in her hand, looking peeved.

"Mama, it's Grandma," Susanna said, looking out the back window. "I think she wants us to stop."

"Never mind," said Lucy. "I just left a little something for them. Now turn around and put your bottom on the seat."

On future visits—and there were several that fall that could be called picnic visits, as long as the weather held—Lucy became more devious about leaving money behind. She would give Susanna a check for twenty dollars and ask her to leave it on the mantel, or in the pocket of Ruby's housedress, or under her cigarette pack. But, she said, "Just don't leave it under the Lemon Pledge or it might take her months to find it."

My mother told me that she came to think of Ruby and Hiram as her secret grandparents. Her mother told her simply that her father and his parents had had some kind of falling out, and that Lucy would tell him at the right time, but until then it might just be best not to mention it. It would be a nice surprise for him when she told him, and Susanna ought to know her grandparents, said Lucy, seeing as they were the only ones she had living. Lucy's parents were by all accounts lovely people whom everyone still missed. They had died within a year of each other, her mother of cancer, her father of influenza, when Lucy was in her twenties. They had left Lucy with a small inheritance, enough to ensure her independence when she needed it, but somewhat "adrift on the seas of life" as she liked to put it. My grandfather was her anchor, though sometimes he may have seemed like a ball and chain.

Susanna was to discover that she had secret cousins as well as secret grandparents. One Saturday when they arrived, there was an unfamiliar car in the gravel driveway, an older model two-tone Chevrolet with faded paint.

Jennifer Horne

"Ah!" said Lucy in her bright voice. "More family!"

They hauled the large picnic basket, once again packed full, inside the house, where Susanna met her father Franklin's sister, her Aunt Bunny, so-called because she was born on Easter. Bunny had twin boys, Cletus and Clay, currently out in the woods somewhere trying to catch a snake. That first day they would torment my mother, in the way of boys, teasing her until she cried with the threat of making her eat dirt. The next time, she wore her pointy-toed shoes and kicked each one hard in the shins before they knew what had happened, after which a respectful détente prevailed.

Cletus and Clay did not so much eat as inhale, and Bunny would issue mild, ineffectual warnings to them that merely slowed their progress as their piglike eyes registered on her and then went back to surveying what was left to eat. After the first time with the boys, Lucy removed several packages from the basket in advance and hid them in the refrigerator or cupboards, out of the direct line of the boys' voraciousness.

Christmas came and went, and with cold weather their visits grew few, but they picked up again in the spring. One warm Saturday morning in May they had made their visit and were halfway home when Susanna became aware of a thudding sound. She looked at her mother who was clearly noticing it too but pretending not to, as though it might go away.

"Damn!" she said, giving the rarely-said word at least two syllables, heavily diphthonged. "You didn't hear that, Susanna," she added parenthetically. "Damn damn damn damn damn. Or that."

She pulled off on the shoulder in the shadow of a hillside, got out, and verified what she knew to be true: the presence of a flat tire, or, put another way, the absence of air in the right rear tire.

"Well, Susanna, your mother does not change tires, so we will just have to wait for a good Samaritan. How ironic."

They sat in the car with the windows down, ate the two slightly crumbled brownies left in the basket, shared a warm Coke, and sat some more.

"Mama," said Susanna.

"What," said Lucy.

"Why doesn't Daddy visit Mama Ruby and Papa Hiram?"

"He's just mad about some things that happened a long time ago. He'll get over it."

"What things?" Susanna's eyes, and her mother's, were both closed as they rested their heads on the back of the car seat and held still for the little breeze coming in the windows. It was easier to talk about such things with your eyes closed.

"If I tell you, you can't tell your father, or let him know you know. Are you grown up enough to do that?"

Susanna nodded. Who would turn back now? Even with their eyes closed, her mother knew she had nodded her agreement. The breeze blew a stray hair across Susanna's cheek, and the world seemed to have let out its breath.

My mother said this is the story Lucy told her:

"You can see they don't have a lot of money now. Well, they had even less then. Everybody was hurting because of the Great Depression. Somehow or another, Ruby got an idea in her head. And when Ruby gets an idea, watch out.

"She piled the kids in the car and started driving. After about an hour they reached a town, and she drove onto Main Street and parked. Of course the kids had been asking what they were doing, and she had put them off, but after she parked the car she told them they were going to play a little game, a Christmas game—did I say it was Christmastime, and cold?—and that the children, Franklin, Eddie, and Bunny, were to keep their mouths shut except for yes ma'am and no ma'am.

"They walked along the sidewalk, past tantalizing displays of toys in the department store window, to the local café, where they sat in a booth and she ordered a cup of coffee and one piece of pie with four forks. The waitress paused, then put in the order at the counter. Ruby put her head in her hands. Her shoulders began to shake slightly.

" 'Mama, what's wrong?' Franklin asked.

"She spread her fingers open so that he could see her right eye, and she winked. At that moment, Franklin says, he thought she'd gone crazy.

"The coffee and pie came, four forks, and she straightened up, brushed at her eyes, and thanked the waitress.

" 'Everything all right, ma'am?'

" 'Oh, yes, thank you,' said Ruby. 'It's just—well, this world is a vale of

Jennifer Horne

tears, ain't it, and we'll all be better in the sweet bye and bye.'

"The waitress paused. 'How 'bout I bring these children a glass of milk each, no charge?'

"Ruby began to pretend-weep again, softly, and this set off Eddie and Bunny.

" 'You are so kind. Thank you. I'm not usually like this, but I've been to see my mother in the hospital in Little Rock, and somebody stole money from my purse in the waiting room while we was all sleeping, and their daddy has had to take work down in Texas . . .'

"By this time she had attracted the attention of several of the other diners, and by the time she left the café they had been given a full meal, more pie, gas money, and an invitation for the children to pick out a toy each at the department store.

"Franklin, as the oldest, was mortified. Bunny never had much going on between her ears and just went along. And your Uncle Eddie, who you haven't met and I hope never will, just blossomed into his role—a born con man.

"On the drive home Ruby explained that people needed to feel the Christmas spirit, that she was doing them a favor by giving them a chance to help others less fortunate than themselves.

"Franklin took his toy and gave it to a little colored boy down the road. He tried to forget the whole thing, but the next year she did it again, in a different town. She changed up the story as it pleased her—her mother had died, her husband was in prison, one of the children needed treatment for scoliosis (Eddie particularly enjoyed stories in which he could play the lead). Each time, Franklin tried to get out of going, and each time his father forced him into the car. His evident misery actually worked to Ruby's advantage."

Susanna had been listening quietly the whole time, but she had a question that needed asking. "But Papa Hiram? Didn't he care? Wasn't he embarrassed?"

"I'm afraid not," her mother said. "Hiram is lazy as an old dog, always has been. He thought Ruby was 'right clever' to come up with her little scheme.

"One Christmas, when Franklin was thirteen and nearly big enough to resist his father, vowing to himself this was his last time, they went through the usual rigmarole and were in the process of being taken pity on by the local folk. Ruby decided to up the ante, just to make things more interesting for herself, and asked the café owner if she might possibly place a very quick call to her mother in the hospital, just to let her know they were going to be all right. He agreed, reluctantly—long-distance calls used to be a big deal, undertaken only for major life events like a birth or a death—and she called Hiram from the back office. Somehow or another the owner had gotten suspicious of her, and he picked up the phone on the counter and listened in.

"As she came out of the back, sniffling a little for effect, he met her and blocked her way. Franklin saw his mother's face go momentarily white before she recovered herself. The owner took her by the elbow, gently but firmly, and guided her to the booth to gather up the children and then out the door of the café, as she waved her thanks to the patrons. 'No charge!' he was saying as they walked outside, smiling so that he seemed to be wishing her a Merry Christmas and a safe journey. What he really said was, 'Lady, I'm not going to ruin people's Christmas by exposing you as a fraud, plus there's your children to consider, but if I ever see you or hear of you pulling this stunt again, I'll call the police on you, children or not, Christmas or not.'

"Your daddy fumed all the way home, humiliated, vowing to leave that family behind him and never return, which he did at age sixteen. Even though he ended up only thirty miles away from them, it might as well be a thousand."

"That's pretty bad, Mama," said Susanna.

"I know. They're not really very good people. They're just family. And family shouldn't be strangers to one another."

Just then the sheriff's car pulled up behind them. When the sheriff got to the window, he smiled. "Why Mrs. Jones! What're you doing out here?"

"Oh, Sheriff Clements, thank goodness you're here. I was trying to show Susanna that waterfall everybody talks about, but not being from here I got totally turned around and lost, and then we had a flat. I'm so glad to see a friendly face."

Jennifer Horne

The sheriff bent to look at the tire and came back to the window. "Looks like you picked up a nail somewhere. I'll change it out for you and then you can get it to the garage."

Lucy thanked him effusively and asked him if he could possibly not mention it to Franklin, as she felt so foolish having gotten lost.

"Well, all right. But you be careful next time and get your directions straight. There's some rough folks out there in these woods, some of 'em just as soon rob you or shoot at you as look at you."

Lucy took the car to the garage when they got into town, and they walked home. When she told Franklin later, at supper, that she'd had a flat tire on the highway, she didn't say where and he didn't ask. This is how Susanna learned about the sin of omission. Later, when she was grown, and had become my mother, she'd learn that when someone lets such an omission alone, it's because they are afraid of the answer their question might bring. She learned that with me, and she still blames herself for not asking, as though that would've kept me from developing a taste for wrong-side-of-town dives and pretty, heartless men who make you feel like a movie star one day and a smoked-out cigarette butt the next.

Susanna was a good child. She didn't like to lie, and her soul was at peace only when everyone around her was happy and harmonious. She loved to draw pictures of herself, Lucy, and Franklin, all smiling, in front of their house. One sunny Saturday morning she was lying on her stomach in her bedroom drawing and coloring when her father walked by the door and stopped to visit. Susanna had been working on Ruby's hair, which the silver crayon did not get quite right, and she was half in her own world of seeing and imagining.

"Who are you drawing?" he said. He was an awkward but loving father, and he wanted to show interest.

"Grandma Ruby and Grandpa Hi—" Susanna, of course, realized that she had accidentally given away their secret, and she froze, silent.

"Oh," said Franklin. "Well, keep drawing then."

She heard him walking down the hall to the kitchen where her mother was preparing lunch. The swinging door closed, its hinge squeaking.

Minutes passed, and she didn't hear anything, so she walked quietly down the hall and listened. There was a gap between the door and frame, so she put her eye to the cream-painted wood and peeked in. Her parents were sitting at the kitchen table facing each other, both of them in profile to her.

"I'm sorry, Franklin," Lucy was saying. "I should have told you. I just didn't want a fight. I thought Susanna should know them, and that she could handle it, but I shouldn't have made her keep a secret."

Her father looked tired. "To tell the truth, I'm sort of relieved. I thought something was up, and I was afraid it was something worse."

"Franklin! I wouldn't take Susanna if I were doing something like that." Seeing how it sounded, she added, "I wouldn't *do* something like that, period."

"OK. But why now? What made you decide to go now?"

Susanna had wondered that, too, but the ways of adults were mysterious.

"She called me," said Lucy. "Last summer. After we got back from Monroeville. Said she wanted to meet her grandchild, her only granddaughter. Drop by any time, she said, and would I mind bringing something for lunch, a little chicken or ham, as they were a little short this month. So I did take a picnic, like I said, but we just ate it inside. And I started leaving a little money each time, along with the leftovers from the picnic."

"You what?" Franklin said. "You what?"

Susanna began to worry that they would really fight. Her father lowered his head, put a hand to his brow, closed his eyes, and sighed deeply.

Her mother bit her plump red bottom lip.

When Franklin looked up he was smiling and shaking his head. "I've been sending her money every month since I was eighteen years old, all through our marriage, sent a money order yesterday. That old woman is *still* running her cons. I don't suppose she mentioned that to you?"

Seeing the question on Lucy's face, he said, "I know, I should have told you. I'm sorry. I was embarrassed about my sorry family and I didn't want to talk about it. So, she played us both for fools."

Susanna watched as they looked at each other for a long moment, each set of eyes a mirror to the other's.

"Fools in love," said Lucy.

He leaned across the table to kiss her and Susanna tiptoed back to her room, soul calm. The visits continued, but no longer secretly.

My mother told me all this sitting next to my hospital bed, occasionally leaning over to give·me sips of ice water from an articulated straw. "So much like your grandmother," she was saying, as I drifted back to sleep, her hand stroking my hair.

When I woke up, she was out of the room, gone to the cafeteria, I presumed, for coffee to fuel her vigil. I realized I was thirsty again and reached for my cup.

The minute I shifted in bed, my two broken ribs sent out warning flashes of pain, hot slivers in my sides. What a stupid, ridiculous, embarrassing, wasteful thing to do, drunkenly running off the road into a ditch, missing the turnoff to the driveway of the City Limits Bar and Grill in search of the latest pretty man I'd fallen too hard for, all the while telling myself what a free spirit I was, so unconventional and daring. It had been a year and a half since I'd finished college, and though I had gainful employment it was hardly what I'd dreamed of as an art major. Was this why my friends got married, to avoid the awful aloneness and disappointment of post-college life? Or even, like Karen, stay with a loser like Joel, just to be with *somebody*?

My brain clearing a little from the pain, I thought about the story. Why had she never told me that one? I thought I knew them all—the donkey in the back yard, the cigarettes taped behind the toilet, the red-headed twins who joined the circus, the church bazaar kleptomaniac, the lost letter from great-uncle Jack that literally fell out of the sky one Fourth of July.

Last words. Oscar Wilde's *bon mot* as he turned to the hideous wallpaper: "One of us has to go." Lucy's: "I wasn't as bad as I thought I was."

Ah, sweet Susanna. All of her stories had a message, and even in my state of fuzzy-headed self-pity I could see this one.

I could hear her voice now in the hallway, speaking to the nurse, thanking her on my behalf.

Maybe she was right, that I was like my grandmother. It would be a while, I thought, before I could know for sure.

Raised in Arkansas and a longtime resident of Alabama, Jennifer Horne is a writer, editor, and teacher who explores Southern identity and experience, especially women's, through prose, poetry, fiction, and anthologies and in classrooms and workshops across the South. She is the author of two poetry chapbooks and two poetry collections, Bottle Tree *and* Little Wanderer, *and the editor of* Working the Dirt: An Anthology of Southern Poets. *With Wendy Reed, she co-edited the essay collections* All Out of Faith: Southern Women on Spirituality *and* Circling Faith: Southern Women on Spirituality. *She's also written a collection of short stories in the voices of Southern women and girls,* Tell the World You're a Wildflower. *Jennifer is currently at work on a biography of writer Sara Mayfield. She has been the recipient of fellowships from the Alabama State Council on the Arts and the Seaside Institute in Florida, and in 2015 she gave the Rhoda Ellison Lecture at Huntingdon University in Montgomery, Alabama and was awarded the Druid City Literary Arts Award, given by the Tuscaloosa Arts Council.*

Jennifer Horne

The Seamstress

Suzanne Hudson

I had never been to a Mardi Gras ball, so my then-boyfriend granted that one on the old bucket list. As it happened, in front of an auditorium full of fancy folks, an important member of the society busted her butt during the lead-out/tableau. It was a thing of beauty and so inspirational, because once I got over being humiliated for her I wondered: What if she had that coming? What if she really deserved such a public come-uppance? I decided that she damn sure did, and I hope the reader gets the take-away that karma is, indeed, a bitch. And social climbers are, indeed, the scum of the earth. Enough said.

W ell, all I can say about that," Mrs. Clark Hogan Wilson pronounced, with the bearing of a robed, gaveled judge, and even more of the authority, "is that Sarah Jo Cooper never had any inkling about how to keep herself a cut above the riff-raff."

Mrs. Wilson, "Francie" to her most bosom of friends, lifted a dimpled little hand to brush a puff of parlor-dyed curls back from her forehead, revealing grooved wrinkles born of brow-knitting and, on a typical day, glaring as she sulked. Today, however, she was not sulking, riding instead the crest of an exhilarating wave of self-importance while she engaged in the gossip that nourished her. She stood on a four by four, raised platform, feeling that much higher than her handmaidens, while a seamstress altered the ball gown she was to wear a week from Friday.

She had just been regaled with the tale of Sarah Jo Cooper, who had left her husband of thirty-two years to ride off into the sunset with a drywall hanger who was renovating the antebellum home said husband had bought for her only a month prior. "Once trash, always trash," Mrs. Wilson said. "I believe I pointed that out to you at Mitzi Stanton's last dinner party if you'll recall. Do you recall that? Do you?"

"I most certainly do," her most recent best friend Camilla, Mrs. James Cunningham Dixon, replied, as the seamstress worked at pinning Mrs. Wilson's hem.

The seamstress, Celeste, had observed this cannibalistic friendship over the previous weeks of fittings and alterations as she constructed Mrs. Wilson's Mardi Gras gown. She had noted that Mrs. Dixon was tenacious about doing her duty as a hanger-on, bearing platters of giddy gossip for her mentor to consume. Gifted with an encyclopedic knowledge of maiden names and double first cousins, Mrs. Dixon could sniff out vague ancestral connections to any scandal and find genealogical secrets that would horrify the sensibility of a St. Louis streetwalker. She had even prodded Celeste, a deliberately private soul, for personal information, for a family history from which to gain a point of reference. She had been delighted when she discovered that Celeste had grown up with her own maternal third cousin, Martha Sams, in Brannon, Mississippi, south and west of Columbus, immediately seeing that cousin Martha could offer the lowdown on Celeste.

In addition to her role as Troubador of Troubles, Purveyor of Peccadilloes, Mrs. Dixon also undertook her task of Flatterer-in-Chief to Mrs. Wilson with an effusive fervor. "You are an excellent judge of character, Francie. It's pure power of perception. You simply *know* people through and through, and I do recall that you pointed that out to me about Sarah Jo Cooper. Saw right clear through her. I swear, you don't miss a beat," she gushed.

Mrs. Wilson picked a piece of lint from the velvet skirt of her gown and flicked it into the air. It dipped and danced like dwarfed confetti. "Of course you also recall that it was at Mitzi's tacky little dinner party," she said. "Do you recall that embarrassing nightmare of a party?"

"Absolutely do," Mrs. Dixon said. "It was right there at that selfsame party that you pointed out to me about Sarah Jo's flawed character. You pointed out to me how cozy she was with the help. How she had her head leaned in to that college boy bartender who—"

"The one in the tiki hut," Mrs. Wilson said. "Do you recall that tacky little tiki hut Mitzi had set up by the pool as an island bar?"

"Well of course. How could I not? It was the one with the young college boy bartending in it. A medical student, I think."

"It was a Hawaiian luau theme you see, Celeste. A luau is a Hawaiian feast, did you know?" Mrs. Wilson spoke down to the woman at her feet.

Suzanne Hudson

"All of our parties—well, the very best ones, anyway—they all have a theme. You know, the creation of a tableau, a setting, a dramatic flair."

"My, how elegant." Celeste, the seamstress, pulled another straight pin from her wrist cushion, working with the gold net material bunched at Mrs. Wilson's waist, draped down around the rich, deep purple velvet gown, the tips of her nimble fingers faintly aware of little sausage-like rolls of fatty flesh beneath the clingy fabric. "Now, Mrs. Wilson, it's important that you bring those shoes you plan to wear with this when you come for your next fitting. This netting is very tricky to hem and—"

"Yes yes yes," Mrs. Wilson said in her hurried, impatient voice. "But as I was saying just now, the theme is what makes the party, if you have the flair to make it work. Believe you me, there is nothing more pitiful than a flopped theme."

"Well you wouldn't know about that, Francie," Mrs. Dixon said, rummaging through an oversized handbag. "I'm telling you, Celeste, there is nothing like one of Francie's parties. They are the best, bar none. You should get to see one before you die, my hand to God. Do you want a Life Saver?" she held out the roll of candy, its foil wrapper peeled and hanging like tossed serpentine.

"No, thank you," Celeste said. The gold netting was stiff and unwieldy next to the supple purple velvet. "Would you lift your arm, please?"

Mrs. Wilson complied, sending the sprung flesh on the underside of her arm into a series of jiggles. "Like last August. I had an all black party last August. Not black *people*, you know, but a black décor, like a wake or a funeral, for Hogie's fiftieth birthday party. And he's way older than me, so don't you even think it. Do you recall that party, Camilla?"

"It was only the be-all end-all of birthday parties," Camilla gushed. Celeste pulled another straight pin from the red satin wrist cushion. Her own husband had not seen fifty, had died instead, at twenty-eight, leaving her with four small children, a Singer sewing machine, and an avalanche of debt, estranged from the family that could have helped her.

"And the all black party was such a hit that on New Year's I had an all white party, just like those jet setter folks do. You know, everything white— white food, like sour cream and cream cheese dips, and vanilla cakes and this divine, frothy white wine punch. Oh—and white flowers. You know, floating camellias and such. And white candles—white everything."

"It was nothing short of fabulous, Celeste," Mrs. Dixon, ever the sycophant, effused. "Francie throws the best parties of anyone in our circle, and you don't even get into our circle unless you know how to throw a grand party. Well, except for Mitzi Stanton, I guess."

"*Our* circle?" Mrs. Wilson lifted one eyebrow with arch indictment and let it soak in for a moment. Then she smiled with forced benevolence. "At any rate, it is no small feat to be a successful hostess, I am here to tell you. It takes quite a lot of thought and creativity. You can't believe all the little details you have to be mindful of. Just one tiny thing can cause a huge flop."

"My," Celeste said again.

"Right down to the guests," Mrs. Wilson went on. "You have to take care to have a complementary mix of temperaments and a code of dress. Of course, the guests at my white party were all required to wear white, so as not to disturb the theme. You have to be very specific on what to wear. Some people just don't have any finesse. Lord, my arm is tired. Can't I put it down?"

"Yes, ma'm." Celeste drew back and studied the netting she was attempting to drape as per instructions from Mrs. Wilson, who continued her pontification on the art of hostessing a successful party.

"If just one guest breaks the dress code, well, it simply sticks out like a sore thumb. It ruins the larger picture—the canvas, if you will. Anyway, I imagine I have just about done it all, party theme-wise."

"But whenever we think she's outdone herself, she comes up with a brand new twist. It's a flair, that's all. It's an inborn talent." Mrs. Dixon took a compact out of her purse and powdered down her nose. "I declare, I shine like a lighthouse beacon. And I don't have the first idea how to have my hair done for the ball." She scrutinized the stiffly layered flaps of frosty blonde, turning her head at sharp angles. "Good night alive, these highlights are all wrong."

Mrs. Dixon was in the process of moving from a social stratum just beneath that of Mrs. Wilson and into the one Mrs. Wilson presided over, so well-done highlights were of utmost importance. Mrs. Wilson herself was hoping to be elected president of her Mardi Gras society the next time

Suzanne Hudson

around, poised to launch up to the next social level, the one that every great once in a while pierced the true aristocracy of coastal Alabama.

Mrs. Dixon snapped the compact shut. "I do know one thing, though. Even a magnificent Mardi Gras ball hasn't got much on one of Francie's parties. Go on, Francie, and try to tell Celeste all the themes you've done just this past year," Mrs. Dixon urged.

"Well, let's see," Mrs. Wilson said. "I've done a Roaring Twenties party and a Screen Siren—that's where you come as a movie star. Hogie and I were Liz and Dick. Anyway, a Screen Siren party, a Beach Blanket Bingo party over the bay, a Monaco Casino party at the country club. Gosh, it must be a half dozen. And I'm here to tell the both of you that a Hawaiian luau with a tiki hut bar, a bunch of plastic leis, and Don Ho ukelele music comes a dime a dozen."

"Isn't that the gospel," Mrs. Dixon chimed in. "It's practically one of the commandments: 'Thou shalt not throw a Hawaiian luau.' But then, Mitzi Stanton has nothing near your sense of style, Francie. On top of that, she's a Jew. I don't think they even believe in the Ten Commandments, do they?"

"Yes," the seamstress said. "They do."

"Anyway, that was just fluff about the commandments," Mrs. Dixon said. "My main point was about Francie having oodles of style and Mitzi having not one blessed drop."

"Well at the risk of seeming big-headed, I certainly won't contradict that," Mrs. Wilson said. "And that is why I was elected parliamentarian and historian of the Merry Makers over Mitzi Stanton. The only reason we let her join in the first place was because her husband is Methodist and the premiere auto salesman in Mobile. A Jew and Mardi Gras is oil and water, so she had no business being an officer. The gall. But after that tacky little luau of hers, she might as well have just put a sign on wheels out front of her house saying, 'Mitzi Stanton has no flair whatsoever.' There was no way she could have avoided me beating her in that election."

"It was a landslide, Celeste," Mrs. Dixon said to the seamstress. "It was practically a unanimous mandate."

"Goodness." Celeste walked a slow circle around Mrs. Wilson, studying the fit of the sequined bodice. Mardi Gras sparkles of purple and gold winked promises from the roly-poly pudge of Mrs. Clark Hogan Wilson.

"Oh, absolutely. A landslide," Mrs. Wilson reiterated. "And an honor, of course. A position of leadership, which is where you ought to be if you have flair and a keen sense of style. I mean, the business of the Merry Makers is to have party after party. Leading up to the big party during Mardi Gras, of course. It takes a keen sense of style."

"Well, honey, that is you. That is just you all over," Mrs. Dixon cooed, retrieving an emery board from the handbag and commencing to sand the edges of her fingernails. "I swanee, my nails look like a scrub woman's." The scritch of the emery board punctuated a short silence before Mrs. Dixon remembered to re-focus on her friend. "Like I say, Francie, style is simply your calling card. You could have stepped right out of *Cosmopolitan* or *Vogue*." She craned her neck to see the seamstress, who again worked on the netting at Mrs. Wilson's back. "I'm sure you know, Celeste, that Mrs. Wilson will be showcased at the tableau. Which means, of course, that your dressmaking skills will be showcased."

"It's exciting all right," Celeste said. She had been hearing for months about how Mrs. Wilson would be presented as an officer of her Mardi Gras society at a grand processional, or tableau, before the ball. It was a huge event, the penultimate pinnacle of Mrs. Wilson's social history as one who jockeyed for every movement upward she could garner. "I will be proud to have you model my work."

"Oh, but Celeste, sweetie, it's as much how you *wear* a dress as how it's made," Mrs. Wilson said. "More, even. Let's face it. Anybody and their sister can make a dress. Lord, I bet retards make them in factories all the time. I mean, the real flair is in the *wearing* of it, don't you think?"

"Yes. Of course." Celeste, practiced in the art of appearing unruffled by insensitivity, began unpinning and re-pinning the gold netting around the back of the dress.

She had tried to tell Mrs. Wilson that the netting would clash with the texture of velvet and had urged her to pick a grainy satin for the skirt of her gown, but Mrs. Wilson would have none of it. Mrs. Wilson had been looking for a specific effect, "a Marie Antoinette effect," she had said, "all swooped out on the sides, you know, but add a part hanging down

Suzanne Hudson

the back. Almost a train, you know. A French queen for the Mardi Gras ball—*le bon temps*."

French like a New Orleans whore, Celeste had thought.

Mrs. Wilson had been coming to her dressmaking parlor for over twenty years, as had an entire parade of ladies and little girls carrying mounds of satin, Chantilly lace, dotted Swiss, *poi du sois*, crepe, velveteen—fabrics that cocooned their social stations in life like spun silk. She threaded embroidery into fine linen christening gowns, stitched the smocking across toddlers' dresses, sewed red and black velvet cuffs onto tartan plaid Christmas dresses, secured pastel netting over bridesmaids' skirts, and attached mother of pearl beads and Irish lace onto wedding gowns. She ran her tape measure around the busts, waists and hips of the women, down the lengths of their backs, an intimacy ripe with irony. She aided well-dressed ladies in elaborate deceptions, drawing and cutting patterns for designer copies—which was the most lucrative part of the business—and she deposited the women's folded bills and personal checks into her own burgeoning bank account. The stock market investments she made had doubled, tripled, then quadrupled the fees provided by the ladies who commanded her services.

In recent years she had begun to look forward to a very comfortable early retirement. Now, in the midst of her forties, she was finally winding down, putting the last of her children through college, coming upon her own time in life. And she had taken more abuse than she would have ever predicted when she ran away from home at the age of seventeen, from wealthy parents in the Mississippi Black Belt, just to be with the man who loved her briefly, and very well, indeed, before he died.

A couple of her clients were not just from old, but *very* old, money—Old Mobile aristocrats who would never deign to boast as Mrs. Wilson did, but who held on to a slick, sterling silver barrier of aloofness, a much more subtle, polite kind of reminder that Celeste's purpose in life was to be at their beck and call, which often meant kneeling at their feet. Unlike the social unfoldings of Mrs. Wilson's Mystic Order of Mirthful Merry Makers, their Mardi Gras functions were written up in vast detail in the *Mobile Press Register*. Their King and Queen were treated like the blue-blood royalty they were born to be, their expensive crowns bought and paid for by money seeded by robber barons, then aged in timber, shipping, and double deals. Celeste hated them, save for one or two, with a fierce purity. She hated the low esteem in which she was held by them. And, having refused her own inheritance, having put it aside for her grandchildren, she hated the inherited currency her customers bestowed upon her after she worked on the hems of their garments, bowed there at their feet like a penitent parishioner seeking absolution.

But she hated Mrs. Wilson and her ilk a million times more, hated their hungry grasps at that higher station in life she had shunned, their shallow little battles, the meager stakes they raised above their means. Mrs. Clark Hogan Wilson epitomized it all, and Celeste had watched her for over two decades, coming up a notch or two here, down one notch there, her long, futile climb tearing at what little potential for a soul had ever rested in her heart in the first place.

Mrs. Clark Hogan Wilson talked about the local aristocrats—the Fillinghams, Dolans, McColloughs—as if they were more than passing acquaintances of hers. "Who will be the next Queen of Carnival?" she would ask. "Of course, we knew Maxine Dolan would have it this year, but next year there's going to be a huge battle between Lexus Dolan and that Mary McCollough. Their daddies are likely to come to blows. Isn't it delicious?" Celeste thought this talk of hers analogous to those pathetic women who discussed TV soap opera characters as they would friends or family members, filling their empty lives with the escapades and tribulations of the fictional characters portrayed by third rate stars.

Mr. Clark Hogan Wilson was a merchant who had made it to the top of the floor covering market in town, complete with television commercials on the local stations—"Let Hogie make your home homey," the jingle went—bringing in plenty of money, though never enough, in Mrs. Wilson's eyes, to erase his lack of a college education. As she aged, she shaded the truth about her husband by degree, until he became "an honorary Kappa Sigma at the University," and "an honorary member of the Wolf Landing Hunting Club," and "an influential player in city politics."

No one seemed willing to call her on her lies. Celeste, as always, chose to keep her stoic, perfected silence and her fruitful livelihood, for the sake of her children. Sometimes, though, she felt as if she were treading silent black waters, gasping for air, grappling for a lifeboat captained by Mrs. Wilson, whose history was the antithesis of her own principled past, an impostor of a captain who all the while pushed down on her, shoving her head under the waves, beating her back from the vessel with an oar.

"It will be nothing short of magnificent, Celeste," Mrs. Dixon was saying.

"What is that?" Celeste silently cursed the stiff netting.

"The tableau, of course. The tableau." Mrs. Dixon squirmed and giggled like an antsy kindergartner. "I know it's supposed to be very top secret and all, Francie. And I know it's going to be my first time as a guest at the Mystic Merry Makers' Ball, but can't I please tell Celeste just a little? Just a little about the tableau?"

Celeste pulled another pin from the shiny red satin wrist cushion.

Mrs. Wilson sighed. "Oh, all right. But Celeste had better not go blabbing our secrets to just anybody, because not just anybody gets to come to our ball."

"Celeste won't tell, will you, Celeste?"

"No," the seamstress said.

"All right, then." She set her handbag on the floor and sat up very straight. "First of all, there will be the most elaborate costumes you can imagine. All two hundred and forty members will be in the processional. Their husbands will be seated along the edges of the arena, wearing dignified tuxedos, of course. And the members will wear these gorgeous costumes. But naturally *you* know they are gorgeous, because you made lots of them yourself."

"Yes, I did," said the seamstress.

"Anyway, the theme this year is 'Let the Good Times Roll All Around the World,' so each group of ten or twelve ladies will be dressed in costumes native to a particular country. And they'll do a dance to some taped music—related to that country, you know. And this will go on and on and on. Until the big moment."

Celeste fingered a sequin that had snagged loose from the bodice. "I'll have to fix this," she murmured.

"The big moment is when they introduce the five officers, one by one. And these spotlights follow them down from the stage and across the arena. And they do a Mardi Gras dance to some New Orleans jazz and the president introduces the queen and the queen commands the ball to begin and oh, I am so excited!"

"My goodness, Camilla, get a Xanax out of my purse and calm yourself," Mrs. Wilson said. "But I admit it will be a thrill to be followed across an arena by spotlights while hundreds of people seated in the audience watch. Kind of like being Miss America. And to think it might have been that Jewess Mitzi Stanton instead of me, if not for that tacky Hawaiian luau she threw. Goodness, I'm tired of standing on this step-stool."

"You can get dressed now," Celeste said. "I think I see what needs to be done."

Mrs. Dixon babbled on and on about the tableau while Mrs. Wilson changed clothes. "I mean, I've been to balls before, and they were nice. But this is the Mystic Order of Mirthful Merry Makers. They are known to have the best ball, besides the top two societies, of course. And you have to practically marry into those, you know."

Celeste almost said, "Yes, I know about marrying into even more money, because that is what my father expected, only I chose not to take my father's fortune and double it by merging assets with another family. I did not prostitute myself to a man I did not love." She often wanted to spit the truth at them, tell them what a sham it all was, their desperate bid for upward mobility. "When you marry for money, you earn every penny," her husband used to say, and Celeste knew that these women could have only reached their desired level by marrying into it, and they had certainly not done that. Too, marrying up would have been a long shot, at best, for women like them, shallow and unbeautiful as they were. No, the heart pine core of aristocracy they lusted after was a closed society, and they would never be allowed into the club. Not that club, the one in which she had been reared. Never that ultimate club.

Mrs. Dixon caught Celeste's gaze, pointed at a scrap of the gold netting on the floor, and mouthed the words, enough of a whisper that Celeste could hear her. "That just does not *go*," she whispered, shaking her head, wide-eyed.

Celeste shrugged.

Suzanne Hudson

"Remember to bring your shoes to your next fitting," Celeste said again, when Mrs. Wilson emerged from the hallway that served as a makeshift dressing room.

"Yes, I know. I don't have to be told a thing forty times," Mrs. Wilson huffed, rolling her eyes at her friend.

"Oh, Celeste," Mrs. Dixon said. "My cousin Martha is coming down from Brannon to visit this weekend. I'll tell her hello for you."

"Yes. Do that," the seamstress said.

"And I warn you, Miss Mysterious. My cousin Martha will give me the scoop on you and yours. So if you have some big old juicy secrets, well—look out."

"I certainly will," the seamstress said. "Goodness."

"I know what, Francie. You *must* do the dance," Mrs. Dixon said. "Before we go, you must do the dance for Celeste."

"Yes, our little Cinderella. Our poor little Cinderella who needs a fairy godmother to transform her for the ball," Mrs. Wilson said.

Celeste gathered the cast off gown into her arms, gold netting stiff and scratchy. "What sort of dance?"

"The Mardi Gras dance. You know the one. Like this." Mrs. Wilson began to strut, the familiar Mardi Gras strut so common on the streets of New Orleans and Mobile. "Da-da-*da*," she sang, dipping and swaying. "Da-da-*dadada*. Da-da-*da*. Da-da-*dadada*. And here comes the good part." She did a half turn and broke into a backward strut while Mrs. Dixon joined her in the song. And they both danced their way out the front door, laughing a rowdy chorus of anticipation while the seamstress pressed the crisp gold netting to her cheek and contemplated their reverie.

When Mrs. Wilson returned the following week for her final fitting, gold shoes in hand, she was sans her usual appendage, the fawning Mrs. Dixon. She was also oddly quiet, the sulk lines in her forehead grooved in a fixed petulance as she stood on the small platform. Celeste re-pinned the hem and double-checked each seam, the zipper, the hook and eye, the malignant gold netting all webbed out like a cancer around the skirt. The room was a jumble of sparkling gold, yellow, green, purple—fluffs of flounces, bolts of beaded and brocade fabrics for the Carnival season. Last minute gowns lay about in various stages of glitter, some gaudily playful with festive flashes of rhinestones, others like garish Las Vegas neon, ready to play out to a night all boozy and sour with stomach-turning dances and sloppy, slathered-on kisses from strangers.

"You don't wear your gown on the float, do you?" Celeste asked. "It could be a problem getting—"

"Well of course not," Mrs. Wilson snapped, breaking her silence in two. "Don't you know anything? We have to wear masks and costumes that go with the theme of the float. My God. Why would you even *have* a float if you weren't going to have costumes? Just why?"

Celeste tugged at the sequined shoulder strap. Mrs. Wilson's flaccid skin pooched around it; more flesh spilled in a bratwurst-like bulge over the top of the scoop-necked back. "This seems fine," the seamstress said.

"I'll tell you what *seems*," Mrs. Wilson snapped again. "It *seems* to me that you often ignore what I say. It seems to me that you often behave rudely. Like now. You do not show one bit of interest in the workings of the float."

"I never cared much for Mardi Gras parades. I only went when my children were small." Celeste made gentle rearrangements in the gold netting that swept around the sides of the velvet skirt.

"And I admit I don't care much for the parades, either, so don't think you're anything special," Mrs. Wilson said. Her voice had an angry, tense tone that Celeste had not heard before. "I don't want to be gobbed up in those hordes of people on the sidewalk, that's for sure. The unwashed masses." She shuddered. "I'm telling you, you get a birds' eye view of the dregs of Mobile from high up on a float."

Celeste uttered her favorite of her standard remarks. "Goodness."

"You can't tell me you wouldn't like to be a float rider. You can't tell me you wouldn't like folks to be yelling to you for beads or moon pies. It's like being a queen. It's like being Cleopatra coming down the Nile on a gilded barge. I don't understand anybody that wouldn't like that."

Celeste moved to the other side of Mrs. Wilson's skirt, to the other pouf of gold.

"No, I don't understand it one little bit," Mrs. Wilson went on. "Oh, I'm sure plenty of folks would say they didn't want to be a float rider, but those are the ones that are so jealous they wouldn't ever admit how

Suzanne Hudson

much they deep down want to take your place. But I can't for the life of me understand somebody that gets to be a float rider and then walks away from it like it's nothing. Like it's not worth a damn thing. Do you understand somebody like that?"

"Well, I suppose it's—"

"Somebody like that is just mean or crazy or stupid is what I think. Somebody like that maybe has brain cancer or some kind of schizophrenia to walk away from what counts."

Celeste knelt at Mrs. Wilson's back, checking the hem of the faux train, seeing how it lined up with the glittering three-inch heels she wore.

"It's a disgrace is what." Mrs. Wilson huffed and blew like a spooked pony. "It makes me want to spit to high heaven."

Celeste stood. "I'll send this over to Lawson's Dry Cleaning to have it pressed for you as soon as I get it hemmed. You can pick it up there on Thursday."

"You do that," Mrs. Wilson said in a voice thick with sarcasm. She stepped down, wobbling on her heels. Celeste caught her elbow, but the other woman jerked it away and stomped off to the hallway dressing room.

"I guess you see that Camilla Dixon, my little pilot fish, is no longer at my side," Mrs. Wilson, still boiling, shouted from the hallway. "She's like to have a breakdown, too, because I have officially uninvited her to the Merry Makers' Ball. As an officer I am allowed to do that. You see?"

"Oh?"

"Some people just don't know when to shut up. Some people say more than anybody wants to know, that's all."

"Yes. They do," the seamstress said.

"But not you. No. Never you. You don't do a damn thing to let on what cards you've been dealt, do you? You keep your trump hand right up against your chest, don't you?"

Celeste smiled. "I don't play cards."

Mrs. Wilson burst through the door, flushed and trembling. She flung the dress across the room. "See that you get this finished right away," she commanded.

"Of course," the seamstress said.

Mrs. Wilson snatched several bills from her purse. "I have your money.

And, oh—here's something else." She dug down into her handbag, coming out with a handful of throws. "Since you won't be at the parade," she said, and threw beads, bills, doubloons, and a lone moon pie across the room, the dinging and clattering of the cheap trinkets like a percussive curse against the hardwood floor.

Celeste watched her priss her chubby frame through the front door, where she turned and scowled her best, deepest-wrinkled sneer at the seamstress. "Camilla was right about one thing, though."

"Really?"

"Yes. Really. She was right about how you ought to experience at least one of my parties. Maybe you could serve *hors d'oeuvres* for me sometime, or pop out of a cake or something equally cheap, like what you have chosen in life."

"Oh, I don't know," Celeste said. "I'm really only good at sewing. That, I am quite good at. But you might consider asking my son, Hollis. He does a little private bartending to help with college expenses."

"Is that so? Well, I'm sure I am honored that you chose to reveal something about your personal life to little old me. A son. And in college, no less."

"Just finishing medical school," Celeste said. "But he won't be available much longer. He'll be doing his internship. And he's engaged, too. A very nice girl, very down to earth. Mary McCollough."

For a split second it seemed to Celeste that Mrs. Wilson's sneer would be wiped away by utter shock, but it held steady, set there in the grooves of her face, her eyes ripe with pure hatred.

"You go to your choosing and rot like a trashy beggar in hell," Mrs. Wilson said, slamming the door hard enough to rattle windowpanes in the adjoining room.

Celeste retrieved the throws and the cash, then picked up the mangled purple velvet with its clashing Marie Antoinette gold netting. She walked over to her time-worn Singer sewing machine, spread the skirt back and out, and then set to work on the hem, the stabbing and clicketing of the piston-borne needle sealing her resolve.

The Mardi Gras season came to a drunken climax on Fat Tuesday and faded into the confessions of a hungover Ash Wednesday, and the ladies who came into Celeste's place of business were abuzz with the tales of intrigue, subterfuge, strife, and backbiting that so often accompanies large-scale social gatherings.

But by far the most buzzed about tale was that of the bizarre and shocking occurrences at the Mystic Order of Mirthful Merry Makers' events. All along the parade route, it was told, Mrs. Clark Hogan Wilson would go missing for an inordinate while, only to be found in the Port-o-Potty hidden in the bowels of the float, miserably shoveling moon pie after moon pie into her jowly little face, eyes glazed over in a sugary chocolate-induced haze. She would be brought up to her place high at the top of the float, a facsimile of a pink Matterhorn with purple clouds towering above the crush of the crowd, above the minions who were corralled back like sheep by grilled metal barricades. She would throw a few handfuls from the large box hidden behind a cliff in the Matterhorn, then, when no one was noticing, would make her way again to the Port-o-Potty, another stash of chocolate moon pies hidden deep in her bra and in the folds of her emerald green satin Swiss Alps costume.

Mrs. Wilson's mood picked up later, most agreed, as the members of the Mystic Order of Mirthful Merry Makers retired to the Civic Center to prepare for their tableau. Everyone agreed it was a beautiful tableau this year, maybe even better than any society in town. The China Dolls, Flamenco Dancers, Hula Girls, Belly Dancers—group after group, they waltzed, twirled and waddled their way across the arena to the applause of the crowd, the ceremonial flash and swoop of spotlights, the twinkling of sequins on satin.

Then the arena fell silent as the officers, in various states of elegance and pre-eminence, took the stage. Mrs. Wilson was announced first, illuminated by three white lights that tossed the glitter of her sequined bodice out to the audience as she began her walk down the stairs to the Mardi Gras song. The three spotlights brushed her round frame, the deep purple velvet skirt netted over by gold. When she reached the arena floor, she broke into the traditional strut while the onlookers clapped hands to the rhythm.

And it was told all over town what happened when she turned to execute her signature flair, to strut her backward strut. It seemed, they said, to happen in slow motion, that the heel of one gold shoe caught in the netting, and, in that instant, all that followed became inevitable. Her arms flailed, the crowd sucked in a collective gale of a gasp, the other foot stepped back, even farther into the netting, pulling the first shoe completely off, and pulling her the rest of the way down. She tumbled to her ample buttocks with a padded thud, sitting in the middle of the arena floor, legs outspread, all dignity seared away. Even worse, the jolting force of her landing, it seemed, had liberated one lone moon pie from the brassiere prison where it had resided since her chocolate binge on the Merry Makers' float. The chocolate covered disc of cake and marshmallow hit the floor beside her, cellophane glinting as it spun in the Miss America spotlight. And it did a twirling little dance of its own before coming to a rest on the waxed floor of the arena next to her cast off shoe.

From the hushed audience came a twitter or two, but these were hurriedly shushed by others, who then twittered a bit themselves. A long forever of stunned silence passed before a couple of the tuxedoed men— not her husband, who was frozen with embarrassed horror—leapt to their feet to help her up. One of them gallantly and discreetly pocketed the moon pie in an effort to restore a fraction of dignity to the occasion. Then, like an awkward Prince Charming, he bent down to hold the sparkly gold shoe as she wiggled and worked her plump foot into it.

Of course, the music swelled again, and the processional went on. The other officers were introduced, and the president introduced the queen, and the queen commanded that the ball begin. And, after crying on the shoulders of her most bosom of friends, Mrs. Clark Hogan Wilson danced all evening with a smile fixed to her face, fixed like the grin of a stalked and trophied animal from a taxidermy establishment, attempting to make light of the ruination of her vertical advancement.

Efforts to put a gag order into effect for the members of the Mystic Order of Mirthful Merry Makers were futile, and the events of that evening were carried from function to function by wagging tongues, received with doubled-over laughter, and passed on. The story was unstoppable, and it grew exponentially, on its inevitable course of becoming a Mardi Gras Legend. The moon pie, too, became an icon, was auctioned off at charity events, passed from Mardi Gras society to Mardi Gras society and beyond, along with the tale of Mrs. Clark Hogan Wilson.

And the tale was told again and again, at bridge clubs and teas, in nail salons, beauty parlors, and shops. It was told at the country clubs of the nearly elite and at the exclusive clubs of the most elite. And it was told in the fitting room of the seamstress, Celeste, who knelt at the feet of the ladies, working the fine fabrics of their choosing. It was told over and over, while the seamstress, she with the most vindicated of hearts, turned bland bolts of material into crisp summer blouses edged in navy blue piping and full, cinch-waisted skirts swirling the colors of stained glass windows between her practiced and nimble fingers.

As a graduate student in creative writing in 1977, Suzanne Hudson won an international prize for short fiction in a contest judged by Kurt Vonnegut, Jr., and Toni Morrison. Twenty-three years later a short story collection, Opposable Thumbs, *was published and was a finalist for a John Gardner Fiction Book Award. She has since had short stories in* Stories from the Blue Moon Café, *volumes I, II, and IV,* The Alumni Grill, Climbing Mt. Cheaha, A Kudzu Christmas, State of Laughter, Men Undressed: Women Writers on the Male Sexual Experience, Delta Blues, *and* The Shoe Burnin': Stories of Southern Soul. *A second short fiction collection,* All the Way to Memphis, *came out in 2014. Her first novel,* In a Temple of Trees, *and her second novel,* In the Dark of the Moon, *are both being re-released. Hudson lives near Fairhope, Alabama, on Waterhole Branch with her husband, author Joe Formichella.*

That Which Passes

Laura Hunter

Fascination with M. C. Escher's convoluting graphic artwork is one factor that influenced the events of the story "That Which Passes." Life is determined by choices we make, some which force us to stop our comings and goings, our ascending, descending, trying to decipher optical illusions that manipulate our lives. But, for Ellen Parker, once choice breaks out of choosing mode and becomes a stand, she must live with what she has gained and lost.

Drained by early pregnancy and its intermittent nausea, Ellen slides back into sleep after Dick and Ricky leave for T-ball practice. At 10:17, the phone rings. She jerks upright. A twinge stabs her lower back. She circles her hand over her stomach and arches out her belly.

Coach Corley. He's canceled practice. Bad weather. Dick dropped Ricky off. Hasn't come back. Can she pick Ricky up or should he take the boy home with him? Storm's moving in fast. Had this call come earlier in her marriage, she would have folded accordion-like to the floor. But things change. These four years, she has watched Ricky grow from babyhood into a child who idolizes his father, and she shelters the both of them. Now this.

Ellen grasps the bathroom counter to steady herself. The reality of Dick leaving their son so he can sneak off with Abby Summerfield has her body no longer grounded. Were she to close her eyes, she would rise, oblivious, leaving her body clumped below. "Damn you, Dick Parker," she mutters.

In the kitchen, she shoves Dick's coffee cup and Ricky's half-eaten toast aside. Ellen wonders how little time passes each morning when Dick strokes her back, then showers and moves on to his lover. She takes a bag of artificially flavored popcorn and tosses it into the microwave. Punching in three minutes, she knows this baby does not need fake stuff. With all this turmoil, she does. She picks up the puffed paper bag and tears it open to release the steam.

The phone rings again. Caller ID lights up Abby Summerfield's name. "It's Dick," she says. "Something's hemorrhaging." In a town this size, Dick would have told her not to call an ambulance.

"Dear Lord, let this pass," Ellen whispers. She bites her lip and starts to hang up. "Shit," she says. Ellen needs to get her son before the storm breaks. Static from the rising storm shoots through the phone.

"Mrs. Parker?" Abby speaks. "Are you there?"

After a moment, Ellen asks, "Dick know you called?"

"No." Abby answers so quietly Ellen strains to hear.

"That's my Dickey," she says. "He would never want his public image soiled." She drops the phone into its cradle and locks the door.

***

Outside, the day is bad. Gummy air means severe storms are close. To the east, dense black clouds filter the air into an almost yellow. Tornado weather. Raised in the south, she knows storms rising from the east can be killers.

She stops at a drive-thru for Ricky's lunch and drives to the T-ball field. Ricky tears into his fries and chocolate milk. Greasy smells from the kiddy burger meal and butter-flavored popcorn saturate her hair and coat her skin like slime. Watching Ricky in the rearview mirror, she hopes he'll be asleep soon.

The storm announces itself with full force winds, as April storms tend to do in central Alabama. Wind whistles through the upper air. Sycamore leaves turn from green to silver, as wind twists their underside to face the on-coming storm. Ellen fights wind gusts, fearing she is losing control. Her back stiffens.

To smother the nausea that rises in her throat, she lowers her window, but a sudden drop in air pressure pushes heavy on her chest. Pregnancy heaves run chilling shivers down her arms. She swallows hard and combs buttery fingers through her tawny hair.

While brushing her hair earlier, she had recognized her color isn't the pale she had with Ricky during her first two months. Today's pasty complexion is more left-out raw potato. Maybe she'll call ob-gyn Monday, get her blood count checked. She fans a hand across her face to stir the humidity, but the humidity has settled, mashing its dampness into every living thing. It won't release its hold until after the storm. She closes the window and turns on the air-conditioner.

***

Tenth Street and Azalea Avenue. Ellen flips the blinker and turns left onto Tenth. She revs the Buick's motor, headed toward student apartments across from Bryant Cemetery. Once she turns, the slight cramp in her back lessens. She parks across from Abby Summerfield's apartment. A college co-ed, she has decided. Probably a bouncy one with long blonde hair. The panic in her voice this morning told Ellen she has no experience handling a man who can vomit after eating Mexican food.

As she opens the back car door, Ricky sets his milk on the floorboard, ready to follow.

"Stay here, Sweetheart. Mommy will be right back. I need a hug."

"I want to go." He starts to climb out. "Daddy didn't come back," he whines. "Coach had to wait. He got mad." He puffs his lips.

"Coach is not mad at you," she croons. "I'll be right back." She hands him a copy of *Where the Wild Things Are*. "Read the pictures."

"I know this one." He pushes the book toward her.

She shoves it back, harder than she had meant. "Read it anyway."

Ricky picks up his plastic milk bottle and sits down. She kisses his forehead and closes the door.

She takes her time crossing the street. Dogwood petals torn loose by the approaching storm fall round her like paper snippets dropped from the sky. Ellen loves dogwood blooms, their four white petals, tipped with a spot of sacrificial blood. They are whiter against dark clouds, these dogwood blooms. As soon as they fill the trees, in comes a storm and strips the trees naked.

Ellen knew where to come. Since moving outside Tuscaloosa a year ago, she has memorized Abby Summerfield's address from letters Dick collected over the last four years and hid in a shoebox inside his closet. The first time Ellen saw the Tuscaloosa address, Dick's business trips and his push to move north from Montgomery weakened a tie she believed had been steadfast.

The afternoon she discovered the letters, Ricky had cried out during his nap. She comforted him and returned to read the letters, one by one.

Laura Hunter

Their words almost drowned her when she read a familiar phrase. By the time she had read all the letters, shock had moved into numbness. Reading the scripted words brought the realization that this lie, this stowing of the letters, betrayed her as much as did his infidelity, simply because he had buried them inside their home. It was as if he brought this woman into their bedroom and allowed her to watch as they slept.

***

Rusted iron railing runs half the length of the flamingo-colored stucco building, separating the sidewalk from cinder block steps leading to the basement door. Standing on the top step, she braces her hand against the rough wall, then sits, her knees weak.

Across the street, Ricky waits. She questions her decision to leave him in the car. Spring storms are dangerous. Air so electrically charged it forces air back into your chest, boisterous thunder, then stark lightning, followed by rain so dense it seems more fog than water. Locals mark events by historical years when two-fisted snowstorms blow in on arctic air: tornadoes followed by snows from light smatterings that weaken stalks and droop blooms, to heavy cover, breaking tree limbs over power lines, enshrouding entire towns in darkness. Left behind these freak storms are new tulips, blood-red against dingy snow.

Ellen rises. Her body tingles as she counts each step to the landing. At the bottom, she doesn't knock. A gust of wind blows dogwood blossoms off the sidewalk and down the stairwell. She read once that a dogwood bloom is not a bloom at all, but a cluster of green buds surrounded by four white leaves that look like petals. The white leaves drop, and center berries grow into tiny, red fruit that perpetuates the life of the tree. She doesn't like the concept of four white leaves. She wants each to be one bloom complete. A leaf-petal, its tips near-black, totters on the edge of the step above her. Ellen stiffens her back and knocks.

Abby Summerfield opens the door as if she'd been waiting on the other side. Petite and stocky, she is older than Ellen by at least ten years, in her late thirties, early forties maybe. Age shows in her thin wrinkled neck. Cropped brown hair hits her chin when she moves her head. If she has an upper lip, it curls back into her mouth, invisible.

"I'm Abby," the woman says, lifting her hand slightly.

Ellen ignores her. "Where's my husband?"

"In there." She tips her head toward an arch at the top of three steps behind her.

Neither moves.

"I'll tell him you're here."

"No. I'll tell him," Ellen replies, her jaw tight.

"This is still my house, Mrs. Parker." Abby's eyes harden.

"Your house, yes. But he's my husband."

Abby Summerfield goes up to the bedroom.

Ellen moves inside, blinded for a moment by darkness. There are no windows. Behind her, wind sucks the door shut. A copper pyramid shade hangs low over a yellow Formica table that separates the strip kitchen from the rest of the room. No open jelly jars, no stained mugs or empty cereal boxes, not even a crumpled paper towel, nothing clutters the countertop.

On the table, a hodge-podge of jig-saw pieces face two metal chairs. An Escher, Dick's favorite. Stairways that lead nowhere and convolute onto themselves. Lizards following lizards following lizards' tails. Everything moving without going anywhere, everything turning in on itself. At home, Dick works the puzzles alone. Their spiraling patterns make Ellen dizzy. She stares at the puzzle pieces. "My God," she whispers. "Dick's at home here." The concept unnerves her, and her left breast responds, throbbing as if milk-full. She drops her keys and covers the breast with her hand. She forsakes it and grips her left wrist.

Before her, angular light throws stark shadows across the room. White ceramic angels, so white they look soft, some tall, others short, sit clustered on the sofa table. A shaped needlepoint angel with stiff gold wings and metallic halo fills the overstuffed navy chair. A cluster of wooden angels painted in Renaissance reds and blues stands guard on the bottom step leading to the arched access to the bedroom. Another, dressed in rose chiffon, topped with a tinsel halo and what looks like white chicken feather wings, hangs by fishing line from the ceiling. Navy carpet speckled with gray dots reverses Ellen's perspective, and she floats in an upside-down world.

Abby Summerfield appears at the top of the landing. "I collect," she says.

Laura Hunter

Ellen chews her inner lip.

Abby stops by a plywood angel propped against the wall. Washed, rather than painted, with blues and gold to make it appear old and valuable, it stands almost three feet tall.

Ellen recalls Ricky, alone in the car. "I need to make this quick," she says.

Abby steps into the living room to let Ellen pass, then she extends her hand.

Ellen steps back, palms held up flat. "Don't touch me." If she touches Abby Summerfield's skin, it will be scaly, like rat's tail.

"He makes me happy," Abby says.

Ellen glares. "Sounds like the same spiel he gives me." She moves past. "Almost every night," she adds.

Faint light strains through dirty transom glass across the top of the room, level with the street. Ellen glances up. If she stands on tiptoe, she can see her Buick's tires. A mattress on box springs rests on the floor, flush against an underground brick wall. Dick lies under a muslin comforter covered with over-sized purple pansies. Ellen glowers at him. "Couldn't you at least have pulled off your wedding band?"

"Don't start, Ellen," Dick says.

"So. This is why we moved to Tuscaloosa." Thunder moves closer. Or perhaps a transfer truck passes on the highway going south.

"Where's Ricky?"

"In the car."

"You brought him?" Blood dried on his lips cracks as he speaks.

"Should I leave him at the ballpark?"

Dick looks away. "I need help." He grinds his fist above his navel, swallowing, drinking his own spit. A yellow towel fills a green plastic bowl by the bed. Water, past red but not yet black, borders the towel. He has not bled like this before.

"Get up."

He shifts his legs. "I didn't mean for this to happen."

"Get caught? Or have an affair for five years?"

"It's not been . . ." He lifts himself up on his elbow.

"Don't lie, Dick. I've known about her for over a year," Ellen stares at him. Splats of rain ricochet off the transom windows.

"I thought I could go home." He tugs at the comforter to cover his nakedness. "Ricky'll never understand," Dick whimpers.

"And I will?" she asks. She turns her back on him.

"You're always there for me." Dick gulps. "I've always been there for you." Lowering his voice, he mimics her father the night he caught them in Dick's car. Her dad beating his fist against the car window. Neighbors' lights coming on. "But I didn't marry you because he said so." He stretches out his hand again. "Don't make me beg, Ellen. For God's sake, you're my wife." He sounds like Ricky whining for another bowl of ice cream.

Ellen speaks to the wall. "I'm more aware of that than you, obviously." A car passes down the street overhead, its tires splattering rain like water in hot grease. Earth's force magnifies itself and her rising fullness drains her face. She presses her hand against the brick for support and blinks, rather than let him see her cry.

"Put your pants on. I'm taking you to the hospital." After a moment, she says, "I'm pregnant."

"What?"

"I'm pregnant. Early December. A Christmas gift, you might say." She tries a chuckle but hiccups instead.

"I'm ready to go home." Dick moves a foot off the mattress. "Look at me."

Ellen doesn't move.

"I'm your husband. It's my right."

Like dirty dishwater tossed carelessly into the yard, his anger soils her. She resists the urge to brush something rank from her hair and clothes. Instead, she whirls and stalks forward. His rages usually have him standing over her. This time she, not Dick, speaks. "Your right? You think I have to take you in?" She lowers her voice.

Dick draws back his foot.

"Because I birthed your son?" Ellen leans directly into his face, surprising herself with her quietness. "You're wrong, Dick Parker. Going home has nothing to do with me having to take you in. You go home, not because I have to let you. You go home only if I want you to."

Her voice lowers to a scratchy whisper. "You go home because Ricky

Laura Hunter

needs you more than that woman does. And she can't have you simply because she's not got a man of her own." She waits for him to answer. "You go home only when I decide you're fit to be around our son." She drops down on the bed near Dick's feet. Realizing where she sits, she jumps up.

**

A blast of wind blows dogwood petals against the wet windows. One sticks, flattened like a lop-sided cross against the transom. For the first time, Ellen doubts her logic in getting pregnant. Early that night, Dick had lifted his face out of her hair and hovered above her. His arms, braced on the sheet, shimmered bronze like Monarch wings in candlelight. The man she had married ten years before smiled down at her and whispered, "I love you, Ellen." This is my husband, she thought. Out of his loins came my son, my sweet, sweet son. She opened herself to him, like a squash blossom, full and warmed by mid-day heat. The next morning, she knew she was pregnant. Ellen Parker has vested her life in the idea that whatever pleasure she knows comes to her through a hard wall of pain. The fire in her legs from Dick's touch, joy in her marriage after the humiliation of her father, and Ricky, her Ricky, after the sweat, the splintering, the ripping of birthing him. Now facing the daily waking walking hellfire of Abby Summerfield. She might as well be a *National Geographic* warrior walking a path of hot coals.

"Where's Ricky?" Dick puts a hand over his groin and draws the comforter closer with the other.

"I told you. Now, get up."

"He know where you are?" He rolls toward her.

"Get up, I said." Ellen lifts his head off the pillow with one arm and drags his legs off the mattress with the other. Her baby doesn't need this. "We're going to the hospital." She lowers her shoulders to lift him off the bed.

"Ellen?" Dick drapes an arm around her neck.

"Shut up, Dick." She clinches her jaw.

The mattress sits so low that, with his sock feet on the floor, Dick's knees stick up in the air like skinny, marionette legs. Ellen tugs his socks up from where they have wadded around his ankles. Same old Dick. Always wears his socks to bed. Sliding her arms under his armpits for leverage, Ellen inhales the stale oniony odor of their morning sex. She stifles a heave, refusing either of them the satisfaction of her vomit on their bold-faced pansies. Dick presses his face into her neck. His cheeks damp, she wonders if he's sweating or crying or both.

"I do love you." He speaks into her neck.

Ellen pulls at dead weight. "Stand up. I can't do this by myself."

"I'm trying." He collapses.

She picks his khakis off the floor and slips them over his feet.

"My shorts. I can't go without my shorts."

Ignoring him, she works the pants up over his knees and hips. She tries to lift him again. He tumbles back on the mattress, his slacks gaping open below his navel. His body looks older somehow than when he had left her this morning. Unable to move him, Ellen goes to the living room.

Sitting on the bottom step of the landing, Abby palms her forehead.

"Call an ambulance."

"He doesn't. . ." Abby starts.

"Do it anyway." Walking toward the door, she says, "I'm going to see about my son."

***

Ricky sleeps, one sock on, one sock off. His hair, shoe-polish brown like Dick's, sticks to his forehead. Asleep, he looks so much like Dick that she wants to shake him. Rain no more than sprinkles and a lull in the wind have fooled her into a false sense of change. When a sideways gust yanks her hair out from her head as if trying to drag her down the street, she realizes she continues to be deceived. She kisses her fingertips and brushes them against Ricky's head where his infant soft spot had been.

Back inside, Ellen drops cross-legged on the floor at the bed's foot. Staring at the blank wall, she waits in the quiet, the room darker now from lowered clouds. A hollowness inside her yearns for something. Perhaps a heavy swell of rain to break and begin the onslaught. Anything to make the storm official.

An empty beer bottle rolls under the iron railing, over the transom ledge, and shatters on the linoleum floor. Shards of brown glass tell her what she has been asking for.

Laura Hunter

Dick lifts his head. "What's that?"

"Storm," Ellen answers. "Lie back down." She hoists herself up on the mattress edge. "I'm going outside to Ricky. I don't want him to wake up and be scared."

"Don't go."

"I'm going, Dick." She exhales through her mouth. "Your . . . she's called the ambulance. Ricky and I'll meet you at the hospital." Weakness turns to weariness. "See that she's not there." Without looking back, she walks past Abby Summerfield, leaving the front door ajar.

***

Outside, with the early afternoon as dark as late evening, Ellen runs against stiff wind, grappling in her pocket for keys. She must have left them in the car. The ground is now clear of dogwood blooms. From the back seat, Ricky's face marks a tiny circle, much like a white balloon set on a flimsy stick and glued to the window.

She opens the door to Ricky's reprimand. "Mama, you left me."

"No, Baby, I'm here," she calls over whipping wind. She hears someone running toward her and looks around for help. Only a black limb. It somersaults down the street toward her. Ellen lifts Ricky. Slicing pain cuts across her back, encircling her belly as she picks up the child. Folding double, she sets Ricky back in the car and squeezes out the cramp. Blood rushes from her face and gushes down her thighs, leaving her faint. "Oh, God, no," she whispers. "Not my baby." Lightning breaches the sky as rain the color of unbleached bed sheets advances down the street. Somewhere a siren blasts. An ambulance. A tornado warning. She can't know which is which.

"I left my keys, Baby. Be right back." Ellen slams the car door and runs. Her hair, now soggy tendrils, slaps her face. Inside, she searches the dimness. "Keys." Ellen demands. Abby Summerfield, still seated on the step, reaches up and flips on an overhead light switch.

Ellen grabs her keys from the table. Puzzle pieces scatter over the floor. From outside, a pop resounds as if a bone has broken. Ellen dashes for the door and battles her way up the stairs, into leaves and limbs, fighting for the street. Before she reaches the highest step, she sees the Buick. Behind it, the old oak's rotten core stands exposed. A thick limb rests across the car, its trunk crushed like an empty aluminum can. Ellen runs, calling to Ricky, toward the car.

Out of the dark branches comes Ricky's panicked little boy voice. "Mama?"

Laura Hunter, born in the Alabama hill country of Walker County, lives outside Northport, Alabama. A graduate of the University of Alabama, she has an Educational Specialist degree in Secondary Teaching Methodology. During her teaching career, she taught high school and college level classes in composition, American and British literature. After retirement, she earned 18 non-degree credits in creative writing and 18 credits in Journalism and magazine writing with Pulitzer Prize winner Rick Bragg. Winner of state, national and international awards, her stories are published in the anthologies Belles' Letters, Climbing Mt. Cheaha *and* Motif. *Magazines that contain her works include* ALALITCOM, Crave Magazine, Explorations, Birmingham Arts Journal, Marrs Field Journal *and* Pithead Chapel. *Creative nonfiction has appeared in* Prime LifeStyle, Longleaf Style, *and* Motif. *She also has a story collection,* Hard as a Rock, *ready for publication. Her novel manuscript* Beloved Mother, *the story of three women in early 20th century Appalachia, has been submitted for publication consideration. In her spare time, Hunter works with a small writing group in Tuscaloosa. She gardens and reads, primarily Southern and Appalachian authors. Her writings reflect the perseverance of the downtrodden, those who refuse to give up, even against extreme odds.*

Something in the Wash

Angela Jackson-Brown

When I first started writing "Something in the Wash," I knew I wanted to write a story that would be empowering to the women in the story and hopefully, empowering to the women who read it. I grew up in a time in the South where I witnessed a lot of women whose husbands cheated on them, but one thing these women seemed to all have in common was they never allowed these infidelities to break them. In fact, many times they flipped the script and raised babies that came out of these infidelities or in even more extreme cases, they befriended these "other women." Having seen relationships like this in my own community, I knew that one day, I wanted to tell their stories.

1875

I knowed that was Preacher's boy soon as I laid eyes on him. He looked just like Preacher round the eyes and the mouth. He had them same sleepy eyes Preacher got and the same droopy mouth that make Preacher look like somebody done took his bottom lip and give it a good tug. Preacher was near 'bout seventy and I was a few years older than him, but you'd thank he was a young man by the way he carried on over the women.

The dew was still wet on the ground when she and that boy showed up. Preacher hadn't long finished eatin his breakfast and had left for the cotton fields when I heard the dogs barkin outside.

"Ya'll mutts hush up," I yelled out to 'em. But they kept on barkin, so finally I couldn't take the commotion no more and I went to the door and there that young girl and her little boy stood at my door.

Me and Preacher is sharecroppers. Livin on the land we use to be slaves on. We'd run up North and lived there 'til Freedom came. Seem like the land called us on back home, so we took what little bit of money we had and came back to Parsons, GA. We didn't have no hope that Preacher's mama, Ma Punk and my mama, Patience, were still alive, but it still hurt to come back and have to see them both buried out in there in the niggra cemetery. We talked about goin back North, but we was old and figured we might as well just stay on here in Parsons and work the land.

Preacher was like a lost spirit when us first run off when we was youngins. He'd seen too much. We all had, but slavery seemed to wear him down more than most. That's why we took off. But time didn't do much to make Preacher any better. I looked at the girl and boy standin in front of me. I wanted to close my door to them, but 'course me bein the righteous woman I was, I didn't do no such thing.

"Yes," I said, eyein her and the boy. I had the door just open wide enough for me to peer out at them. I ain't one to open my door to strangers, even if they is a woman and boy that look just like Preacher.

She was standin there holdin a little red suitcase and holdin the hand of the boy. He looked to be 'bout six or seven. She was wearin Sunday clothes on a Monday. She had on a bright, yellow dress that swept the ground, white gloves and a little yellow hat that was perched on her head all cockeyed.

She was that high-yaller type—thin lips, long, strangy black hair and skin so light she could pass for white if'n she wanted to. The boy was more dark, but not by much. He was the same complexion as Preacher and he was wearin his Sunday best too. She had him all dandied up in some blue knee britches and a starched, white shirt. He had a little straw hat sittin on top of his head too. You'd thank it was Easter Sunday the way they was dressed.

I reached up and tried to smooth down my hair. I'd taken off my headscarf 'cause I'd been drippin sweat in the head, and had planned to put on another one. I looked down at my housedress; it was all splotched. I'd never really paid it too much mind 'til just then.

"Hello, ma'am. My name is Pearl, and this boy here is my boy Lewis. Say hello, Lewis," she said puttin her arm around his shoulder, pushin him toward the door so close that his little nose was pressed against the screen.

"Hello, ma'am," he mumbled.

I nodded my head, still not openin the door. I couldn't speak. Seem like my tongue was all tied up in knots. I just kept lookin at them. Waitin, really. Kinda hopin she wasn't gone say what I already knowed she was gone say. She kinda shifted her weight from one foot to another. She looked like a scared child 'bout the face. She didn't hardly look like she

Angela Jackson-Brown

oughta be nobody's mama.

"Ma'am, you mind if me and this boy sit on your porch for a spell? We pretty much walked all the way here from my Pappy's place from up near Macon and we shore is tired," she said, takin a dainty little handkerchief from her pocket and dabbin at her face.

I wondered where Preacher had met her. He had taken to preachin again, so I'm thankin he probably met her at some revival meetin. My rheumatism kept me from goin with him most times. Don't speck, from the looks of it, he'd be wantin me to tag along anyhow.

Somehow I found my voice. "Course you can sit. Is ya'll hungry?"

I could tell they were, but neither one of them said so. They just plopped down on the steps, the boy inchin as close to her as he could without climbin on her lap. I didn't press them about eatin 'cause to be honest, I shore weren't in no mood to be cookin' for my husband's woman and child.

"Miss Apple…"

"What you call me?"

"Miss Apple. That's what they call you ain't it?" she asked, lookin up at me all confused.

When she said my name, I wanted to swang open that door and push her off my porch with what little strength I had left in my body. When she let my name flow off her lips like she knew me and all, well, I coulda balled up my fist and walloped her 'cross her mouth. I knew her knowin my name meant she and Preacher must have been closer than just a one time thang.

Somewhere between him layin down with her and gettin up, the two of them had talked. That somehow made all this worse. My spirit suddenly felt like it do when the preachin and singin at church is just right. I wanted to throw my arms in the air and shout at the top of my lungs, but I stayed quiet. I opened up the door and went out and sat in my rocker. It was mid-October and a bit cool, but I didn't feel no chill at all.

"Ma'am, can he go out there and play? You know—so we can talk," she said, lowerin her voice.

"That be alright," I said, and she whispered something in his ear. He nodded and then run out to the tree wheel swang Preacher put out in the yard for when some of the children from church would come over. Me and Preacher didn't have no children of our own. I'd carry a baby for a month or two and then it would slide right out as if there weren't nothin inside of me for it to latch hold to. Nothin grieved me more than not bein able to have some babies. I think if I'd had a baby or two then maybe Preacher and me woulda been a tad bit closer.

"He shore is a mannerable boy," I said to her. Not bein able to thank of anything else to say.

"Thank you. Ma'am, I didn't mean to come here and disrespect your house. But he and I don't have anywhere else to go. Miss Apple, he Mr. Preacher's boy. I was just sixteen when—Miss Apple?—Miss Apple?"

I slumped down in my chair. Hearin her say the words stole my breath. She hopped up and was fannin me with her handkerchief.

"Ma'am, do you need some water?" she asked. "I don't know where things are, but I could go look."

I shook my head. What I needed was a good dip of snuff to pack between my bottom lip and gums, but I had promised the Lord I wouldn't use no more snuff—not even to calm my nerves. I just commenced to rockin. She kept lookin at me like I had all of a sudden took sick.

"Ma'am, we don't have to talk about this if'n you don't want to. I reckon you can figure out the story. But right now, Lewis and I don't have nowhere to go and no money to get there," she said, her light brown eyes stretchin wide, battin real fast to keep the tears away. "Ma'am, I'm trying to get to Chicago. I hear niggras can do good for themselves up there. I was praying you and Mr. Preacher might see fit to spare us any little bit you can to help us on our journey."

I looked at that little gal like she was crazy. Where she think me and Preacher was gone get some money? There she come marchin up to my house dressed better than lots of whites around Parsons, and she think we suppose to give her money that ain't even ours to give. We be lucky to break even after everything said and done. Seed for next year's crop, a little muslin so I can make us some warm clothes for the winter, and some food staples we couldn't grow ourselves—once we paid for them things, the money would be gone. Preacher would get a nickel here and there when he'd go out and do them revival meetins, but that wasn't often since he had to be home to work the land. I clicked my teeth together and just

Angela Jackson-Brown

looked at her.

She kept on talkin like I wasn't lookin at her like she was outta her fool mind. "I know it's awful bold of me to be marchin up here in your face like this beggin for money, but I didn't know where else to go. Me and my folks had a fallin out. I promise, if'n ya'll help me and Lewis this one time, you won't never be bothered with us again."

Then, she burst into tears. Now you cryin, I thought to myself. Weren't cryin when you was beddin down another woman's husband, now was you? But the little thing looked so pitiful. I didn't know what to do except what any Christian woman would do and that was to get out of my seat and put my arms around her shoulders and pat.

"Maybe your folks take you back," I said and she boohooed even worse. I patted harder. "Never mind that, honey. Never mind. Why don't you tell me 'bout this pretty dress you wearin. You make this?"

Pearl dabbed at her eyes again. "No, ma'am. This dress used to belong to the white woman I did housework for back home. It was dingy as all get out when she gave it to me, but I washed it real good. And that suit Lewis got on. I made it with some left over scraps from the Easter suit of the little white boy I kept," she said smilin through her tears. I smiled back at her. One thang is for sure. No matter how upset a woman might be, you get her to talkin about her cookin, sewin, or cleanin, and she cheer right up.

"Ain't no need of ya'll rushin so. Chicago ain't goin nowhere. Come on in."

"You sure, ma'am?" she asked.

I nodded. She weren't gone get no money outta us, but I could at least make sure she and that boy had some food to eat 'fore they got on they way.

"Thank you, ma'am," she said, smilin, but not quite meetin my eye. "Lewis. Lewis, come here son."

"Where you say you from?"

"Near Macon. You ever been there?"

"No," I said, but then I started rememberin. I remembered the revival meetin Preacher did near Macon around the time the boy would have been got. I was down in the bed sick and a lady from our church had come and stayed with me. I even remember him sayin it was the best meetin he'd preached in years.

"Better than when you use to preach under that Chinaberry Tree?" I'd teased. When we was young, Preacher used to preach to all us slaves underneath this Chinaberry Tree that sat off near the fields where we picked cotton. After Freedom come, I heard some niggras went out there and cut down that tree.

"Don't talk about them days. Them days is gone," he'd said and had gone off in a huff. He didn't like talkin about slavery times none. Not even about his mama, Ma Punk—God bless her soul. I'd bring up them days or his mama, and he'd jump hot and be gone for hours.

"Your folks' house was where he stayed?" I asked. She looked at me and nodded. I reached over and patted her shoulders. Weren't no use in me bein mad at her. She was just a chile. Could be me and Preacher's grandchild or great-grandchild even. I looked at her and wondered how Preacher could have come to that—layin with a child. "Get that Lewis and let's go inside and get you two fed. I know ya'll hungry. Tell me 'gain how ya'll get this far?"

"Walked some—rode in the back of wagons the rest of the time. Couple nights we slept in a few barns. We cleaned up this morning at a creek down the road from here."

I nodded. "Well, come on in."

She called that boy Lewis again and he came runnin. They both followed me inside. Mine and Preacher's cabin wasn't much, but we'd done a lot to make it feel like home. We had the main room where I had my stove for cookin and keepin us warm at nights durin the winter months. We had a well outside that I would go to for water for cookin and washin dishes after we ate. I still had some biscuits, sausage and gravy left over from the breakfast I had made for Preacher. I fixed them both a plate and they ate like they hadn't ate in days.

I just watched them for a spell. I was wonderin why I wasn't more angry. Oh, I was plenty angry at Preacher, but this little chile and her son were growin on me. She and I talked and talked. Not 'bout nothin serious. Just woman stuff. We talked about clothes we had sewed lately and foods we liked to cook and then, we talked about washin.

Angela Jackson-Brown

Before I left the plantation Ma Punk taught me how to make lye soap, and since then, that is all I ever let touch our clothes. I mix up some lye, some hog grease, and water, and then I heat it all up in my cast-iron pot. I wash all my clothes by hand with water from the creek. People all over Parsons know how good I do with washin clothes. I take in wash for Miss Dorothy Parsons. She married to Mr. Jackson Parsons whose daddy, Little Jack Parson, weren't nothin but a little boy when me and Preacher run off 'fore slavery ended. But with my rheumatism, it be gettin harder and harder to take in wash.

I ask Pearl how she like to wash.

"I like to wash with lye soap like you, but I also like to put a little rose water in my wash. I make it myself. It make the clothes smell so good."

"It don't stain your wash?"

"Oh no, ma'am," she said, shakin her head, causin her hair to float 'cross her shoulders. "Only way you know it's in your clothes is by the smell. I make another kind of smell-good water with eucalyptus. I sometimes sprinkle a little of that on my sheets and pillowcases. It help to make you sleep better."

She reached into her purse and handed me two little bottles that looked like plain water. I opened one of 'em and could smell the scent of roses. It smelled better than the smell good stuff you could buy to dab on your neck.

"That be for you, Miss Apple," she said smilin and then duckin her head.

"Thank you, honey," I said. I put the little bottles of smell good stuff in my apron pocket. I knew I should be hurryin her and the boy off on their way. I should be tellin them to get out my house and leave me to some peace. But if the truth be told, I was enjoyin her company, and the boy weren't no trouble at all. He just sat out the way and played quiet to himself.

She smiled. "You're welcome, Miss Apple. Thank you for your kindness. I wasn't expecting you to be so nice."

I shrugged my shoulders. "Ain't no use me bein mean to you and that boy. Preacher the one who shoulda known better. You was just a chile. Still is next to him and me."

A look went 'cross her face like she'd just seen a haint or somethin. "He's going to be mad about Lewis and me being here."

I reached over 'cross the table and patted her hand, shockin myself at what I said next. "Don't you worry none. I'll take care of Preacher." Then I thought, how was I gone take care of Preacher? He and me was more like two strangers livin together. Too much had happened in Preacher's life that had him bitter and hard, 'specially towards me. He still preached on God's love, but you could tell by lookin at him that he didn't let that love inside himself. I knew little Pearl was just one of many. Half the niggra gals in Parsons had laid up with Preacher. I knew this. I tried not to let it pain me, cause I knew I didn't have nothin to make him want to come to my bed no more. I looked out the window, payin attention to where the sun was. "Time I get a pot of stew goin, and this wash ain't gonna take care of itself."

"May I help?" she asked.

I looked at her real hard. "You talk with good manners. You shoulda been a teacher. I'm sorry you got mixed up with Preacher. He always has been able to charm the birds out the trees."

I got up and started collectin the dishes so I could wash 'em. I had a pot of water boilin on the stove.

"They must be hurt—your mama and daddy, I mean. What with you and this boy takin off and all. Why did ya'll up and leave like that?"

She bowed her head and wiped away the tears. "They were real hurt when I—when this happened. I never would tell them who the daddy was. That caused tension. But then it got worse, because they weren't kind to Lewis. I didn't want him getting hurt anymore, so we left."

I shook my head. "Seem like they coulda took one look at that boy's face and knowed he was Preacher's boy, but I guess folks see what they want to see. And I can't see nobody bein unkind to that boy, but never mind all that," I said real fast 'cause she was lookin like she was 'bout to have a full-on cryin fit. "If'n you want to help me, you better slip on that apron I keep hanging on that coat hook over in the corner."

"Yes ma'am," she said and quickly got up.

We cleaned up the breakfast dishes and while I got the stew cookin, Pearl started in on the wash. After a while, I got tired, and sat a spell, but she kept workin. We both got quiet. She was all into what she was doin and I was watchin her like a mama bird watchin her chicks. I was makin sure she didn't do nothin wrong. But she didn't.

She tended to my wash like she was washin a newborn baby. I saw her reach into the water and gently washed the delicate clothes—my slip, my one good Sunday dress, and some of my underwear. I almost sighed. I ain't never seen nobody enjoy washin like that nor take such good care of what she was washin, except for me. If it weren't for Preacher and his doins, I could almost see me and Pearl growin close. I don't have what you'd call friends. I pretty much stay to myself. I have speakin friends, but no close friends.

After Pearl finished washin my things, she turned her attention to Preacher's good white shirt. Yesterday before church, he cut himself shavin and dribbled some blood on his shirt. I probably could have gotten it out if I had tended to it right then, but I wasn't 'bout to work on the Lord's day—shirt or no shirt.

"This stain won't come out, Miss Apple," Pearl said after several minutes of scrubbin.

I got up slowly from my chair and walked over to the sink where she was workin. Sweat was pourin down her face and even though she was wearin an apron over her dress, I could tell she had splotched it up a bit. I took the shirt from her tiny little hands. It was hard for me to believe hands that small had the power to wash. Hands that small ought to be playin a piano or writin words on a chalk board.

Her hands weren't nothin like mine. My hands were rough from years of field work. I wondered if Preacher had stroked her hands and said soft words to her when they lay together. I couldn't remember the last time he'd touched my hands. I tried to soften them a bit by puttin salve on them, but they never got soft.

"Let it be for a spell," I said, pushin the shirt deeper into the soapy water. "If it's gone come out, it'll come out in the wash. Why don't you and the boy go and rest in me and Preacher's room. I know ya'll tired. I'm gone wait on Preacher out on the porch. He be home for lunch soon."

She looked at me for a moment, and then gave me a tight hug. We stood there for a minute, just huggin, the smell of rose water and sweat fillin the air. She looked tired but not so scared. She left the room and soon I heard her and Lewis headin towards the back of the house.

I looked into the water at Preacher's shirt. The water had become slightly pink but the stain was still there.

I pulled the shirt out of the water and walked out to the porch with it drippin water the whole way. The dogs started barkin again, and this time, I knew they were lettin me know they had heard Preacher comin. I didn't look their way. I just sat down hard in my rocker with that shirt on my lap and waited for Preacher to come home.

Angela Jackson-Brown was born and raised in the little town of Ariton, AL, where she first developed her love of the written word. She is an award-winning writer, poet and playwright who teaches Creative Writing and English at Ball State University in Muncie, IN. She is a graduate of the Spalding low-residency MFA program in Creative Writing. She is the author of the novel Drinking from a Bitter Cup *and has published in numerous literary journals. Recently Angela's play,* Anna's Wings, *was selected to be a part of the IndyFringe 2016 DivaFest and this fall, her play* Flossie Bailey Takes a Stand *will be part of the Indiana Bicentennial Celebration at the Indiana Repertory Theatre. Currently, Angela is collaborating with musicians on a musical she wrote called* Underneath the Chinaberry Tree *and she and her agent are putting the finishing touches on her novel,* Shooting Across the Sky.

Why Dogs Die

Nanci Kincaid

"Why Dogs Die" is set in Alabama—although I don't think Alabama is mentioned. It seems particularly good for an anthology of women writers because, while it is narrated by a man, it's the story of the lives of the Southern women around him. The fact that he is so unaware of this is, of course, part of the story. The narrator believes he's talking about himself most of the time—and he is— but in doing so he's telling the bigger story of the women in his life. Humor may camouflage the harsher reality of the situation but it doesn't override the truth. (I hope it doesn't. It shouldn't.)

Stella says she's not coming to the hospital until I tell Mama the truth. She says it's bad enough that our marriage was a lie these last few years—but she's not about to turn our divorce into a lie too. That just goes to show you how much Stella has changed. So Mama will say to me like she always does, "Stella still hasn't been to see me."

"Night classes," I'll tell her. "You know Stella is taking those classes."

"Every night?" Mama will ask me. "When does she rest?"

So far, I'm the only son who isn't divorced. Mama sort of thinks of me as the *good* son, the one that turned out right. So that's one reason I hate to let her down. That and the fact that Stella wants me to tell Mama about Heather too. Heather works for me down at the branch bank. It's true, she's young, but her cash drawer tallies to the penny every night. That's how I first noticed her. She always balanced out. She's been divorced herself for about two years and it hasn't been easy. I just don't think it'll do Mama any good to hear everything Stella wants me to tell her. No need for Mama to get off on a bad foot with Heather first thing, is there?

"Divorce is not all that bad," I've tried to tell Mama in the past. "Look at Wallace and Vaughn. They both went on to re-marry two great women, didn't they? They're happier now than they've ever been, aren't they?"

But still Mama blames herself. "Their failure is my failure," she says. "I didn't raise you boys to give up like that."

"Well, in Vaughn's case, Mama, it was more like he was given-up on. Ginger just up and made a run for it and there was nothing he could do."

"Do you think your daddy is the easiest man in the world to live with? Do you think life with him has been a picnic?" This is Mama's refrain. She doesn't expect us to answer. "But did either one of us ever give up?" she asks. "What God has joined together, let no man put asunder."

"You ever think maybe God didn't join some people who get married, Mama? You ever think He might not have had a thing to do with it? Might have been against it from the start?"

"See, that's what's wrong with everything right there," she says, "that kind of talk."

It's generally understood that Wallace, Vaughn, and me don't want to hassle Mama too much with the gory details of our personal lives. Any woman who's lived with Daddy all these years has got enough on her plate. So we go easy on Mama whenever we can.

I'm on my way over to the house now, to check on Precious, Mama's dog. She's a miniature mix. Daddy is supposed to be taking care of her, but the truth is Daddy has no idea how to take care of anybody. It just doesn't occur to him, the needs of others. Since Mama's been in the hospital, Mrs. Pico next door has been bringing Daddy his supper every night. Mama calls her from the hospital to be sure. Here's Mama with her heart threatening to give out any minute, and she's busy trying to arrange for Daddy to get his three squares a day right on time.

Stella says Mama probably wouldn't be in the hospital now if Daddy would just evolve a little. It all started with that carpet Stella ripped out when we bought the house out at Highland Hills. Stella saw more potential in the place than I did. We were at that point, you know, where you think if you can just move into a better house, then you'll have a better marriage. Like if you can get sidetracked into house renovation it will distract you from the shambles your life is in. Like new copper plumbing and wiring for internet and state of the art stereo components will sort of rewire your relationship too—by technological osmosis. Stella is the one that insisted we get rid of that carpet. Sure it was ugly, but it wasn't but a couple months old. Hardly been walked on. I don't have a lot of opinions on carpet. I've sort of learned to let Stella make those calls. She cares about stuff like

Nanci Kincaid

that. The size of closets, the height of ceilings, how much light comes in windows. She cares about details too, moldings, paint colors, the stain on hardwood floors. So I say, what the heck, let her have at it. If Stella hated the carpet in the Highland Hills house and wanted it gone, I wasn't about to sit around and argue with her. Life is too damn short.

Like a fool, I offered the ripped out carpet to Daddy. He keeps a bunch of rental houses out by the university. He's always needing to replace the cheap carpet the students tear up about as fast as he can put it in. And this stuff, it's a kind of dark mingled color, rust, brown, gold. Won't show much. In fact, Stella says it's called *camouflage* carpet. She says the name alone is enough to make you want to rip it up. So I gave it to Daddy and he was glad to have it.

What I forgot was that since he and Mama moved into that little house on Cobb Road Mama's been wanting new carpet. She's had her heart set on it. I didn't think about that—which Stella says is typical of me. Vaughn and I were the ones that started talking to Daddy first, planting the idea of downsizing, saying "Mama's not as young as she used to be, Daddy. This big house is too much for her." Next thing you know Daddy's ready to put a down payment on the place on Cobb Road. It's a small house on a nice piece of land. He's got lots of room for his garden. Room to put in a tool shed in the back. The yard is what makes the house. And just like you'd expect, Mama said, "If your Daddy likes it, then it suits me."

"You sure?" I asked her. "Daddy's set to put down earnest money."

"All it needs is new carpet," Mama said. "That green carpet won't go with a thing I have."

Daddy promised her he'd put down new carpet throughout. He'd made a tidy little profit selling the old house too, more than enough. So Mama picked out what she wanted at *Carpet World*. It's called *Desert Sand*. She's pretty much been waiting ever since. As usual, Daddy had every reason in the world for stalling on the carpet. I got so tired of Mama being embarrassed about that sculptured lime green turf in her house—that I said, what the hell, I'll pay to have some new carpet put in if it means that much to her. But Mama wouldn't hear of it. "You save your money, Son," she said. "This is between your Daddy and me."

Stella fussed at Daddy for making another promise he didn't keep.

Stella and Daddy never have gotten along. Daddy doesn't understand anything about women. It's a point of pride with him. Stella thinks he shouldn't be allowed to get away with never learning anything new. She says he's stupid because we all allow him to be stupid. I've stopped arguing the point.

So what if all Mother's furniture is in the rose family—and the carpet is the ugly green of thirty years ago. He doesn't see what difference that makes. But me and Vaughn and Wallace—we understand things like that. We learned it the hard way, but we learned it good.

***

On the day *Carpet World* is set to come put in the *Desert Sand* carpet Mama goes with Mrs. Pico to the Boaz outlet mall, a senior citizen trip put on by the church. Mrs. Pico said Mama was happy all day, just thinking about coming home to that nice beige carpet, not one thing spilled on it or tracked on it or messing it up in any way. Just new and clean enough to sleep on.

But when she gets home, Lord knows. Daddy has cancelled the order at *Carpet World* and hired the guys that lay carpet for his rental houses and they have sawed, nailed and who knows what to get that ugly Highland Hills mingled camouflage carpet laid down throughout the house. He tried to pass it off as a nice surprise. When Mama called me I thought Daddy had died or something the way she was crying. I didn't know that at the time she was as near to killing him as she'd ever come.

Two weeks later she had a heart attack. It wasn't her first, but it was the worst one so far. She about scared us all to death.

***

When I get to Daddy's house I hear Precious crying at the back door. She's scratching to get out. By the time I get the door open she scrambles past me down the steps into the yard. Precious is pretty old to be moving that fast. She's half-blind. Then I see it, over at the edge of the mingled carpet, a little doggie surprise. It smells too. I imagine Daddy walking by in his slippers and stepping in the stuff, slipping down and breaking his neck. It would serve him right. As far as I know this is the first accident Precious has ever had in the house. "Daddy," I yell while I go to the kitchen for some paper towels to clean things up. "Daddy? You here?"

Nanci Kincaid

I look out in the back yard and see Precious running around in circles, pausing every few seconds to pee. She's peeing on everything. "Daddy!" I holler. I need to get Precious on her leash, but I'm worried something might be wrong with Daddy. He usually meets me at the door. He usually hears the car come up the drive and the door slam. I walk back to the bedroom and see him sprawled across the bed with his shoes off. He's lying face down like he's been shot. "Damn," I mutter and shake him to see if he's alive. It takes him a couple of seconds to open his eyes. They are red-rimmed like he's drunk. But Daddy doesn't drink. Not anymore.

He rolls over and looks at me, "Vaughn? What you doing here?"

"It's not Vaughn. It's me. Raymond. What you doing in bed, Daddy? You okay?"

"What time is it?" Daddy asks.

"Almost six," I say. "Have you been remembering to take Precious out, Daddy? Say?"

While he sits up and gets his shoes back on I go outside and put Precious on her leash. She trembles when I bend down to pet her. She tries to do her business but nothing happens. I take her back inside and notice that her water bowl and food bowl are both empty. Precious noses around them, sort of panicked. "Damn," I say. "Has the old man been feeding you?" I get her *Kibbles* and pour a bowl full. She dives into it face first, slinging dry dog food everywhere. I've never seen her make such a mess. I rinse out her bowl and fill it with water and set it down beside her. Now she is really crazy, trying to decide whether to lap up all the water or devour all the food first. She's frantic, back and forth, back and forth, like she's afraid I'm going to take it away if she doesn't finish it off in record time.

Daddy comes into the kitchen and says to me, "What brings you around here?"

I'm so mad I feel blood pumping upstream right to my head. "Came to see about Precious and it's a damn good thing too."

Daddy looks at Precious like he has just the vaguest notion who I'm talking about.

"You hadn't been feeding her, Daddy. You hadn't been taking her out."

Daddy pulls out a kitchen chair and sits down.

"This is why dogs die, Daddy," I say. "Precious is starved for attention.

Nanci Kincaid

You got to pet her and talk to her, Daddy. You don't want Mama to come home and find Precious dead do you?"

"I was up at the hospital today," he says. "They're talking about letting your Mama come home the end of the week."

"Good. That's good. Are you listening to me, Daddy? You hear what I'm saying?"

The doorbell rings and Daddy gets up to answer it.

I reach down to pet Precious. Wallace and Vaughn and I pitched in and gave Precious to Mama the year Vaughn graduated from college and moved out of the house. We thought it would be good for her to have a dog to fuss over. How long ago was that? Almost thirteen years. Damn. Mama is attached to Precious like she's a child. She and Daddy never go see Vaughn or Wallace without taking Precious with them. I didn't see how Daddy could treat Precious this bad, especially not with Mama in the hospital.

"Look who's here," Daddy says. He's carrying a Tupperware plate with a matching lid. In his other hand is something wrapped in tin foil. "Mrs. Pico," Daddy says. "Kind enough to bring me some supper."

"How's your Mama, Raymond?" she asks me.

"I'm on my way to the hospital now," I say. "Just stopped by to see about Precious."

"He don't trust me to take care of my own dog," Daddy says.

"Your Mama would just die if anything happened to that dog," Mrs. Pico says. "I believe she thinks that dog is human."

"Raymond, you want me to fix you a plate?" Daddy says. "Mrs. Pico brings plenty for two."

"I got to get on up to the hospital," I say.

"Tell your Mama not to worry about Monroe," Mrs. Pico says. "Tell her I'm doing my best to keep him fed."

As I'm going out the back door I see Mrs. Pico bend down and say something to Precious. She puts the leash on her, "I believe I'll take Precious out to walk while you eat your supper," she says to Daddy. "I could use the exercise."

All the way down Cobb Road I can see Mrs. Pico standing in the yard with Precious. First Precious circles Mrs. Pico's legs, then I swear, it looks

Nanci Kincaid

like she sits on Mrs. Pico's foot. Just sits there like she's glued.

***

Mama looks relieved to see me when I get to her hospital room. I haven't missed a night so far, but I guess maybe she worries that I will. "Hey, good looking," I say. "How's the best looking woman in Alabama?"

"I wouldn't know," she says.

"Look what I brought you," I show her the fistful of cut flowers I bought downstairs in the gift shop. I stop there every night too, buy her some flowers like clockwork.

"Looks like a funeral in here," Mama says. "Do you know something I don't know?"

"Heck yes," I say. "I know all kinds of stuff you're too young to know."

"I doubt that," she smiles. "You want any of this Jell-o? I haven't touched it. I never did like the orange kind."

"No thanks," I say. "I'll eat later on."

"I know Stella is not fixing you any supper," Mama says. "Not if she's off at class like you say. So where is it you're eating supper these days?"

"You think I need my wife to fix my supper, Mama? You think I can't whip up something myself? It's a new day. I like fixing my own supper. That way I can have anything I want."

Mama folds her hands in her lap just as calm as anything. I feel a prayer meeting coming on. "Stella came by to see me this afternoon."

Damn, I think. *Damn. Damn. Damn.* What the hell is wrong with Stella? Why didn't she tell me she was going to do this? "Is that right?" I say. "Stella came by?"

"Why didn't you tell me, son? I may not be modern, Raymond, but I'm not dumb."

"Mama, nobody ever said you were dumb."

"I called Stella this morning. Asked her to come see me."

"And I guess she rushed right over?"

"She said she was waiting for you to explain a few things to me before she came, but she guessed you weren't going to—you know, explain anything—so she said she might as well get dressed and come on over and tell me herself."

"She shouldn't be upsetting you. What's so important it can't wait until

Nanci Kincaid

you get home?"

"They're saying maybe I can come home at the end of the week. That new medicine seems like it's helping. My heart has stopped all that fluttering."

"Still, Mama. I don't see what the big hurry is—why Stella has to spill the beans now. We haven't even told the kids yet. We're waiting—you know—until the time is right."

"You mean you're waiting for me to die first?"

"No, Mama. Hell no. Don't even talk that way."

"Stella says the break-up—the *divorce*—is your doing. You didn't leave her any choice."

"We all got a choice, Mama," I say. I don't really know what I'm talking about. Did my choice (Heather) leave Stella with no choice? That's what she says. But maybe she made a choice too, an unconscious choice—and it left me no choice but to choose Heather. Maybe there really isn't enough choice to go around. Some people get theirs—some don't. But I swear to God, it feels to me like none of this is anything I chose. It feels like something that, you know, happened. That's all.

"Used to be people didn't have choices," Mama says. "Not any good ones at least. Back then you just made one choice and that one choice made most of your other choices for you. Nowadays people have so many choices they can't make up their mind what to do."

"What else did Stella tell you, Mama?"

"That you met a young girl that you think you love more than you love Stella. That you've moved in with this ... this..."

"Heather."

"Right. And she has two little boys, too."

"So I guess she made me out to be the bad guy," I say.

"Was she supposed to make you out to be a hero?"

"There's two sides to every story, Mama. Did Stella tell you I tried to come back home but she wouldn't let me? Did she tell you she put the Highland Hills house on the market without even telling me? Did she tell you she's rented a place above Posey's down by campus?"

"That country food place?"

"Yep. Got an apartment upstairs."

Nanci Kincaid

"They have good food over there. Your daddy always liked Posey's for lunch."

The nurse comes in then and takes Mama's blood pressure. I half expect her to shout down the hall, *Code Blue* or something. I think maybe Mama's blood pressure will be skyrocketing in light of all this bad news Stella has dumped on her. But no, the nurse smiles and jots something down on Mama's chart. "You don't stay too long now," she says. "Your mother needs her rest."

I pick up Mama's orange Jell-o and start to eat it. It has no taste at all. "I guess I thought you'd be upset to hear all this," I say. "I didn't want to get you upset."

"Stella seems like she's taking the breakup pretty good," Mama says. "I always thought that if your daddy ever left me for another woman I would just die. Like that." She tries to snap her fingers. I see her do it, but it makes no sound. "I didn't think I could live that down. But Stella. I don't know. She acts like you've done her some sort of favor or something."

"Tell me about it," I say.

"It makes me wonder," Mama says. "If your daddy had left me—you know—what kind of life I might have had. What you think I would have done if I wasn't married to your daddy."

"I don't know," I say. I can't even imagine it in my wildest dreams.

"I would have had some nice beige carpet in my house," Mama smiles. "I know that. None of that camouflage mess. I would have had things the way I wanted them."

***

The truth is I'm not actually living with Heather, you know, permanently. She has two kids that need a daddy and I know she wants me to volunteer. But damn, I just got my own kids reared and off to college. I need a chance to catch my breath. Besides, her kids, I don't know. It's not that I don't think Heather is a good mother. I do. But she's not much on discipline. She doesn't believe in spanking. I tell her I spanked my kids any time I thought they needed it and I believe they appreciated it too—you know, later on. Sometimes when I have dinner over at Heather's house it's about all I can do not to give those boys a good swat on the butt. They need it. They practically beg for it. I swear I think they want somebody to take charge and see to it that they behave. The way it is now they run all over their mother. I can't hardly stand it.

I tell Heather, "My mother took a switch to me and my brothers more times than I can count and we never held it against her. No sir. We worshiped the ground she walked on then—and still do now. The way I look at it, she didn't whip us nearly enough."

Heather likes this story. She laughs. She says, "That's how they used to do things. But now people know better. Hitting teaches hitting."

"Nobody needs to teach boys to hit," I say. "Boys are born knowing how to hit. Somebody needs to help them figure out how to stop."

"They'll outgrow it," Heather says. "The hitting age."

"What about the smart-talking age? Will they outgrow that too?"

"I don't know," she smiles. "You never did."

***

I've rented a little efficiency off the interstate. One of those residential hotels. I hate it. I hate feeling like a tourist in my own hometown. But they have a Cracker Barrel out there and so I can get all the vegetables I want. Stella hates Cracker Barrel. She liked to steam our vegetables. I'm in favor of health as much as the next guy, but damn. The Cracker Barrel cooks the way Mama does—or the way she used to. It's a small comfort, under the circumstances.

When I get back to the efficiency I call Stella on the phone. She has a message on her answer machine that makes you think you've reached a place of business instead of a human being. "You have reached, 732-7301. Leave a message." There is no friendliness in her message, no courtesy. After a woman leaves you, you start to notice all her shortcomings.

"732-7301," I say, "this is 732-2114, formerly 732-1616, remember? Call me. Room 233. Before 9:00." If she wants businesslike, I can give her businesslike.

It's after eleven before she calls me back. I have the sneaky feeling she has been out on a date or something. I have the urge to ask her. But I cannot bear to hear her answer if it is yes. I cannot bear to give her the pleasure of getting even with me.

"Mama tells me you made a visit out to the hospital today," I say. It is not an accusation of any kind. It is more like a question I already know

Nanci Kincaid

the answer to. Stella says those are the only sorts of questions I ever really ask anymore.

"She called and asked me to come," Stella says. "So I went."

"You had to tell her everything? You couldn't wait until she got home?"

"Raymond, you think our split is big news to her? You think she didn't see it coming?"

"I didn't see it coming," I say. "How could she?"

"Don't make me laugh," Stella says. "It's comical, you trying to pass for a victim."

"Well, give me a break, I'm new at it. Unlike you. You've always been a victim. Right, Stella? When I married you I thought that big V tattooed across your forehead meant virgin."

"I'm not going to compete with you, Raymond. Not for the victim award. Not for anything. I don't have to. And I don't want to."

"All I'm saying is, I don't want you upsetting Mama. That's all."

"Why do you think she called me, Raymond? She wanted somebody to verify what she already knew. She said she gave you every opportunity to tell her the truth but it was clear you just couldn't do it. So I did it for you. It's better for her to know, Raymond. Trust me."

"How can I trust you, Stella? You're living a secret life above Posey's Country Kitchen when you're philosophically opposed to country cooking. Your answering machine sounds like you work for the FBI."

"We should never have given your Daddy that carpet," she says. "I told you not to do it."

"How the hell was I supposed to know he would put it in his own house?"

"It's your Mama's house he put it in."

"Same thing."

"It's not the same thing, Raymond. Don't you get it?"

***

It's sick. But lots of nights I call Stella before I go to bed and pick a fight with her or whatever I have to do to get her to talk to me a minute. It's not like I want her back or anything. It's just that I'm so used to her after all this time. Her voice, her complaining and everything, it just sort of soothes me and helps me get to sleep. Besides I can't call Heather late at night because it might wake her kids and they need their sleep, especially on school nights. I have to wait for her to call me. Sometimes she forgets. Sometimes she falls asleep in her clothes and doesn't wake up until daylight. I've got a lot of respect for a single working mother. I mean that.

***

Mama keeps her social security money in a Ziplock bag clothes-pinned to a valve in the back of the toilet. You have to lift the lid off the back of the toilet to find the money. She showed it to me once not long after she moved to Cobb Street, when she'd first started thinking about dying. She had more than a thousand dollars in there at the time. It made me wonder what other secrets she might have. It had never occurred to me that Mama had any secrets.

Today I go by the hospital same as I've been doing every afternoon this month. Almost immediately Mama reminds me about the money hidden in the toilet. "It's almost enough," she says, "to carpet the front rooms of the house."

"Mama, I told you that me and Wallace and Vaughan will pay to put that carpet in."

"Your Daddy is a proud man. He doesn't like his own boys going against his will."

"Oh, but he likes his own wife to go against his will. Is that it?"

"Stella says a woman has a right to be happy in her own home. She says if new carpet would make me happy then I owe it to myself to get that carpet."

"Yeah, well, Stella wrote that book, didn't she? We had houses instead of a marriage. How many houses did we re-do? We had more carpet than we had commitment."

"You talk crazy," Mama says.

"You taking Stella's side, Mama? You blaming me?"

"You're blaming yourself," Mama says. "Don't need anybody else to blame you."

"I promise when you meet Heather—when you get to know her— you'll like her."

"Maybe I will. Maybe I won't."

"You'll try won't you, Mama? Promise me you'll at least try."

"I'm trying to talk about the carpet, Raymond. I want you to get my money and go and have *Carpet World* come change out that carpet. Stella knows the one I picked out. She can show you. I don't want to come home to that mingley, mangy stuff your Daddy has got in there. It makes my blood pressure hit the roof. It causes everything in the house to mismatch."

"If that's what you want, Mama. It's done. I'll get it done."

"Now your Daddy may give you some trouble, Son. You know that."

"So, what's new? I'm not scared of Daddy anymore. I'm not sixteen. He can't whip me with the buckle end of his belt or take my car keys away, can he?"

"Show him respect now, Raymond. He needs that."

***

When I leave the hospital I go by to see Daddy. I want to give him warning of what's about to transpire—carpet wise. I'm planning to be firm, but adamant. I'll convince him that there is no use in putting his foot down on the subject. That carpet is making Mama sick and she needs it to be changed and by damn I'm going to see to it that she gets it changed. I have a real convincing monologue worked up by the time I get out to Cobb Road.

When I drive up to the house there is Precious in the street. She looks like she's trying to do her business in the middle of Cobb Road. My heart jumps. She could get hit by a car coming or going. Damn. She could get hit by *my* car. I swerve to the side of the road. Precious is a house dog. She never goes outside without her leash. Is Daddy losing his mind? Is he getting senile? I call Precious. She just trembles and stays squatted down in the road. I go over, talking soft so I don't scare her. I pick her up. She feels like a sack of bones.

I carry her up to the house and pound on the door. Daddy has locked up the house, which he never used to do. It takes a lot of pounding before he gets to the door. He looks out the window first, like he's afraid of who might be out here trying to bang his house down. He unlocks the door and peeps out.

"Daddy," I yell, "what the hell is going on? Let me in."

Precious is trembling in my arms. I push my way in the house. Daddy looks at me like I'm the pizza delivery boy who forgot to bring the pizza.

"You okay, Daddy?" I say. "You don't look good."

"Spent the morning at the hospital," he says. "It tires me out. I was watching television."

"Do you know where Precious was, Daddy? Say? Do you know Precious was out in the middle of the road when I drove up? What you got to say about that?"

"I don't know how she got out," he says. "I don't remember letting her out."

"Letting her out? Daddy, you can't let her out. You have to walk her. You have to put her leash on, Daddy. You know Precious is a house dog."

"Your mama is the one who looks after the dog," Daddy says. "Usually."

"Well, this ain't the usual, is it, Daddy? This is the *un*usual. Mama is laying up in the hospital. And you're supposed to be looking after Precious."

"She must have slipped out someway," Daddy says.

"You don't want to have to tell Mama that, thanks to you, Precious is roadkill, do you, Daddy? Say?"

He looks like he's thinking this over.

"Look at this, Daddy." I walk over where Precious's water and food bowls sit empty. "Look. You forgot to feed her, didn't you? She had anything to eat today?"

"I feed her later on," he says.

"No you don't," I say. "You forget, don't you Daddy? If I wasn't standing here right now holding Precious you wouldn't have any idea in this world where she was, would you? Dogs need a little love, Daddy. Dogs die without love."

"I'm not going to let the dog die," Daddy says.

"I know you're not," I say, "because I'm taking her with me. I'm going to look after her until Mama gets home. The last thing Mama needs is for Precious to come up dead. That would be the last straw."

"You don't need to take her. Miss Pico will take her."

"I don't want Miss Pico to take her, Daddy. Look at her. Precious is

Nanci Kincaid

scared and confused. She needs to sit on your lap. She needs to sleep in the bed like she does when Mama is here."

"Dogs don't belong in the bed."

"That's why I'm taking her with me. I could use a dog in my bed about now. I love Precious, Daddy. I don't know about you, but I love this dog." I set about gathering up the dog bowls and the dog food and the dog collar and even the little bed Mama keeps in the kitchen. I put everything in my car. Sometimes I don't know how Mama managed to live with Daddy as long as she did. I mean it.

When Miss Pico comes over just as I'm getting ready to go, she sees right away that Precious is trembling. "Here," she says, "let me give her some of this baked chicken. I bet she'll like that." She tears off a piece of Daddy's supper and feeds it to the dog. Precious gobbles it up and I feel a wave of relief seeing her eat like that.

Miss Pico pours me a glass of ice-tea and one for Daddy and her and we all sit down in the den while Daddy eats his supper. Baked chicken, rice casserole, green beans, and cling peaches. It looks good. It looks like Miss Pico could get a job at Cracker Barrel any time she wants to. "Tell me how your Mama is doing," Miss Pico says. So I tell her all I know. Medically speaking.

Before I leave to go home Mrs. Pico says. "It's a shame about you and Stella breaking up. I always liked Stella."

It shocks me that she knows my business. "Who told you?" I ask.

"Well, your Daddy did."

I look at Daddy.

"Stella should have left him a long time ago," Daddy says. "He never did stand up to her. It's a wonder she didn't leave him before now."

"You are a prize, Daddy," I say. "You know that? A real prize."

"My wife never left *me*, did she?" Daddy says. "Did my wife ever leave me?"

***

I sneak Precious into the extended stay hotel with no trouble. I probably could have fit her in my briefcase but it was dark outside so I didn't even try. Precious has never been a barker. I call Heather like I promised and she wants me to come over, but I'm just too damn tired and need to get Precious to eat something and settle down for the night. I haven't slept with a dog in I don't know how long. Since I was a kid. I like another heartbeat in my bed—always have. Precious snuggles up to the hollow of my armpit—sort of like Heather does sometimes—and in no time we are out like lights.

When the phone rings I think it's my wake-up call. I reach across the bed for the phone and feel something wet. "What the…?" Then I see Precious rolled into a little knot of fur and remember that I'm not alone. She looks like some kind of damp winter hat. Damn, I think, Precious wet the bed. When did she start wetting the bed? I grab the phone and expect to hear the recorded message, *This is your wake-up call.* It's pitch black outside.

"Raymond," the voice says. "She's gone."

For a minute I think it's a wrong number, then I realize that the heavy breathing at the other end of the line is Daddy's. He's crying.

"I'm coming, Daddy," I say. "I'm on my way."

***

Mama's funeral is a bad dream. I'm a grown man. I ought to have some composure at a time like this. But I swear—maybe I should be—but I'm not ready. I'm not prepared. Vaughn and Wallace and their wives are handling the arrangements—and I'm letting them. Maybe it's easier to lose somebody you only visit twice a year.

I'm sitting here between Stella and our three kids—who are not kids anymore—on one side—and Heather on the other. I hold Heather's hand one minute and Stella's the next. I'm so torn up over all this I can't get ahold of myself. I know the people around me are saying, "I never knew Raymond was so close to his Mother." Until right this minute, I didn't either.

When we're leaving the church my daughter, Susan, puts her arm around me and says, "Daddy, cry all you want to. You probably got a lot of things you need to cry about."

I look into her serious red-rimmed eyes. "Is that what your Mother says?"

"Yes," she nods.

***

Nanci Kincaid

Mrs. Pico stays home during the service in order to get all the food organized for when people come by the house afterwards. The women from the church and all Mama's friends brought so much food the last two days you couldn't even walk through the kitchen without bumping a casserole or knocking a plate of deviled eggs to the floor. But by the time everybody gets back from the cemetery Mrs. Pico has the dinning room set up buffet style—even puts out Mother's good dishes that she never used and her linen napkins. The kitchen is organized too, everything labeled in masking tape. I don't know why that gives me a moment's relief, seeing the food labeled as to contents and dish owner. It gives me a little peace of mind.

"I put Precious in the back room," Mrs. Pico whispers to me. "I believe her eyesight has got worse. I almost stepped on her half a dozen times."

"Thank you," is all I can think to say.

Wallace and Vaughn are courteous to people. I'm not. I'm a zombie wandering through the crowd, looking at my own kids like I hardly know them in their dark suits and adult bodies. My daughter hugs me every time she walks by. My sons pat me on the shoulder and look away from my grief-puffed face. I never loved them more. I notice that they're not particularly friendly to Heather, but that's all right because Stella is. The two of them stand for the longest time eating coconut cake and whispering in the sort of way that ordinarily would scare the hell out of me—but today, all I know is, life will never be the same again.

Somebody accidentally opens the door to the back room and Precious runs into the crowd. People *ohh* and *ahh* and say, "Cute dog." Daddy is slumped on the sofa in a daze. Mrs. Pico has fixed him a plate, but he says he's not hungry. I watch Precious weave her way through the roomful of high heels and wingtips. She sniffs the feet surrounding her. Then she pees on a man's shoes. The man doesn't notice. Before I can make my way to pick her up, she pees twice more. Here. There. "It's a good day for camouflage carpet," I say to no one in particular.

I lift Precious and carry her back to Mother's bedroom. Daddy has made the bed and it looks like it. Stella says you can always tell when a man makes the bed—and it's true. I get a towel out of the bathroom and lay it out on the bed and sit Precious there so she can feel close to Mama.

Precious can't get off the bed by herself. It's too high. I talk a little dog talk to her and close the bedroom door.

Heather brings me a glass of red wine and says, "I had a nice visit with Stella. Did you know she's been dating a divorced gynecologist?"

"Really?" My blood pressure surges momentarily.

"He's a menopause specialist," Heather explains. "She was referred to him. He took her off hormones and put her on soy. Then you know—lightning struck."

"Lightning?" I repeat.

"You know, as in *when you least expect it.*"

Ordinarily I'm not clumsy. Maybe somebody bumps into me. Maybe I lift my wine glass too fast, but next thing I know it flies from my hand and sloshes all over Heather's dress and splatters on the carpeted floor. People jump back, dodging the spill. It should look like a blood stain where it lands, a full glass of red wine, but it's like the carpet drinks it up, mingling it with the rest of the mingle.

Heather's dress is another story. It's splattered. She looks like somebody shot her. A woman hands her some club soda and she begins dabbing it on the stains with a paper napkin. Before she leaves for the bathroom to deal with the mess I've made she smiles at me. "This has been a pretty rough day, huh?"

***

The grief doesn't hit Daddy full force until a couple of weeks later. Until recently—in my whole life—I'd never seen Daddy cry before. Not once. I gave Precious back to him. I had to. For one thing he was so alone. And he swore he'd treat her good. For another, the maids found Precious in my extended stay room. She'd made a mess of the place and they turned me in. So I didn't have a choice. Now I stop by to see about Daddy and Precious every afternoon when I get off work. Daddy and I don't have a lot to say to each other, but we try. Suddenly he's taken a great interest in the photo albums Mama spent years putting together. It's like he recognizes the faces in the photos for the first time, understanding that the people smiling at the camera are connected to him in some way. He looks at pictures when Wallace, Vaughn and me were kids and bursts into tears like he misses us so bad and wonders where the heck we've gone.

I try to hug Daddy when he starts the crying, but he goes stiff. He doesn't like men hugging each other. He doesn't believe in it—never has. "I should have done better by your Mama," he sobs. "I wish I could tell her that."

"She knows," I say.

***

When Daddy marries Mrs. Pico I'm not all that surprised. A man's got to eat. A man gets lonely. Daddy's too old to change his habits. Mrs. Pico watched Mama try to stay married to Daddy for the last fifty-six years. I don't guess he's got her fooled. Mrs. Pico is dressed-up in a pink lace dress and a hat with fake roses around it. She says, "Raymond, I told your Daddy before I agreed to marry him that there were two things he needed to know. Number one, I am not your Mother. I am Mildred Pico. There's a difference. Second, I told him I cannot think straight with that crazy carpet he has everywhere. That carpet has to go."

As far as I know Daddy didn't argue with her on either point. Two days after Mrs. Pico issued this statement Daddy had that camouflage carpet ripped out and the beige Mrs. Pico wanted put in. She didn't pick *Desert Sand*. She picked *Le Neutral*. It looks the same.

The wedding is in Daddy's living room. Wallace and Vaughn neither one come for the spectacle. "It's too soon," they said when I called them. "We were just down there not two months ago putting Mother in the ground."

So besides the preacher, there is nobody but Heather and me to stand up for the happy couple. Daddy thought maybe Stella would want to come too. But she didn't. I guess she's so busy these days with her new boyfriend, the menopause expert, that she can't be bothered with an old man's wedding. Daddy cries through the whole thing. Maybe that should satisfy me, but it doesn't. Mrs. Pico keeps dabbing at Daddy's eyes with her handkerchief. The preacher pauses a couple of times to be sure Daddy isn't on the verge of a heart attack himself.

During the whole so-called wedding Precious lies on the new carpet at Daddy's feet. As blind as she is she knows where Daddy is in the room and tries to stay near him. She jerks a few times during the ceremony, like she's dreaming of falling off a high place. When the ceremony is finally over Daddy is so emotional Mrs. Pico has to sit him in a chair to keep him from keeling over. It's then we notice Precious has peed where she lies on the *Le Neutral* carpet. She can't seem to get her legs back under her to stand up. The puddle is dark and Precious seems panicked trying to lift herself out of it.

Mrs. Pico has made a red velvet wedding cake. She cuts everybody a slice and Heather pours ice-tea all around. The preacher, no spring chicken himself, is beginning to sweat. He gobbles his cake. It's clear he wants to make a run for it without being rude and refusing the celebratory food Mrs. Pico offers him on this holy occasion.

I put Precious on my lap. I try to feed her a little bit of red velvet cake but she isn't hungry. She lies still like she's sleeping, but her eyes are wide open. The wet spot on the carpet is like a message. It's not hard to decipher. I guess Daddy sees that too. Maybe that's part of what has him crying so bad. Me, I'm not sure what I'm so choked up about.

"Precious needs to be put to sleep," I say to Daddy. "Look at her."

"I can't do it," Daddy says. "Don't ask me to do it."

The way Daddy talks you'd think all my life I'd been asking him to do things. You'd think he was just worn out from always having me depend on him for everything. Damn. "Don't worry about it, Daddy," I say. "I'll handle it."

So Precious has to count on me. I'm all she's got. It's a heck of a predicament for man's best friend—or anybody else. But, I swear to God, I don't want to let her down. I want to give her a real good send-off. I guess Precious understands what we're saying too because she looks up at me and licks my hand. Her tongue is dry as a bone.

Nanci Kincaid is the author of five novels, Crossing Blood *(Lillian Smith Prize nominee)* Balls, Verbena, As Hot As It Was You Ought to Thank Me, *and* Eat, Drink and Be From Mississippi, *and one collection of short stories,* Pretending the Bed Is a Raft. *The title story of this collection was*

Nanci Kincaid

optioned by El Deseo Films, under the umbrella of director Pedro Almodovar, and made into the movie, My Life Without Me, *directed by Isabel Coixet, staring Mark Ruffalo, Sarah Polley, Deborah Harry, and others. Kincaid has published short stories and essays in numerous literary magazines and anthologies. While Kincaid considers Alabama her home state, she has also lived in Florida, Virginia, North Carolina, Massachusetts, Wyoming, Arizona, California, and Hawaii. She received a Bunting Fellowship at Radcliffe in 1995 and was recipient of Alabama's Emerging Artist in 1996. (She feels compelled to go on record as having written abundant material that has been rejected over the years and now sits in a rusty file cabinet in her garage awaiting one last—highly unlikely—revision. This is worth mentioning.) Currently Kincaid is collaborating with a Hollywood screenwriter/actor on* Fisher Gets Out, *an independent film based on her unpublished novella of similar title. Kincaid divides her time between Honolulu, Hawaii, and Tucson, Arizona. She is married to former college football coach Dick Tomey. They have a swarm of kids and grandkids.*

Girl with the Flaming Hair

Cassandra King

This piece is from my third novel, The Same Sweet Girls, *which is set mostly in the Mobile Bay area. Because I belong to a group of women who call ourselves the Same Sweet Girls, this was an especially difficult book to write. To me, our decades-long friendship was both unique and universal, so I really wanted to have a go at fictionalizing it. I had to disguise our stories, make composite characters from myriad personalities, and kill one of us off, which was a daunting task. I think it helped to begin small. Since the "real" SSG's had attended Alabama College in the sixties, I began by fictionalizing the school by combining Alabama College, Huntingdon, and Mississippi State College for Women into a college I called "The W." (Thank you, MSCW). That made writing "The Girl with the Flaming Hair" much easier. I simply took a well-known ghost story that all three colleges claim some variation on, and adapted it to fit my characters. Then, I was able to further the plot by having one of the characters, Lanier, relate the story as a means of explaining her reluctance to explore a mysterious light next door.*

It took me a while to get up the nerve to investigate the light at the Pickett house next door, and I didn't go over there until the day before the SSG weekend. Because I've always been so reckless, folks think of me as brave, which is not the same. But my freshman year at The W, during what has come to be called "the incident of the Girl with the Flaming Hair," I found out what a chickenshit I really am.

The senior dorm at The W was haunted. When The W was built there was only one dorm, Wesley Hall, named after the founder of the Methodist church, good old John Wesley. Wesley—the dorm, not the preacher—has these big spooky halls and wings and hidden staircases. Story goes, on a stormy night long, long ago, one of the coeds, candle in hand, goes down a hidden stairway, sneaking out to meet her lover. She's a babe and has this long flowing hair—golden blonde, naturally. Just hearing that, you can figure out what happens next: The long hair catches fire and she's trapped in the stairway, where she burns to death. Serves her right for sneaking out like that, and I'm sure the ghost of old John Wesley nods in approval when she dies screaming in agony. Anyway, the Girl with the Flaming Hair became a famous ghost story in Alabama, and legend at the W was, if you took a candle and went up that stairway at midnight during a storm, you'd meet the ghost coming toward you, her hair on fire.

What kind of nitwit would want to see that sight? It scared the crap out of me to even think about it, but of course, the SSGs dared me. Since I was a bigger fool than coward in those days—not that things have changed much—I took the dare.

Part of the deal involved sneaking into Wesley Hall, which was hallowed ground because the seniors didn't allow us lowly freshmen there. One November evening when it started thundering and lightning like crazy right after supper, we knew this was it, the night the daring Lanier Brewer of the newly formed SSGs, camera in hand, would make freshman history by taking pictures of the Girl with the Flaming Hair.

Sneaking out of the freshman dorm, Tutwiler, was much easier than getting into Wesley Hall because of a weird feature of the W: spiral fire escapes. Each dorm had them, enclosed fire escapes that you slid down like slides, making fire drills a hoot. They were off-limits otherwise, but that never stopped any of us from taking a joyride every now and then. Problem was, there was no way to stop your fall, and you came barreling out right on your ass. The first week of school, Dixie Lee, braying like a donkey, came flying down the fire escape and landed right at the feet of the college president, Dr. Lumby. Dr. Lumby, acting quickly, put Dixie Lee on room restriction for a whole week. Byrd was far enough behind her that she could wedge her feet against the sides of the fire escape tube and crawl back up, which is exactly how we figured we'd get into Wesley.

At midnight the SSGs dressed in black and slid down the fire escapes of Tutwiler without a problem. The storm was keeping everyone in, including, we hoped, the seniors and the campus security force, all two of them. We ran across campus to Wesley, where we proceeded to crawl *up* the fire escapes. The rain had us wet enough that the slide was slippery as snot, but we made it, me and Byrd and Dixie Lee and Astor and Julia. I should've suspected something when Corrine wouldn't come with us, claiming she was claustrophobic, but I was more trusting in those days.

What I didn't know was, as we sneaked in Wesley on one side, Corrine was crawling up the fire escape on the other, her long, white nightgown under her raincoat, and with a flashlight covered in red crepe paper, designed to hold under her chin and look ghostly when she met me on the hidden stairwell, long hair flowing. Although she was already pale as a haunt, she'd put white makeup on her face and ringed her eyes in black. The SSGs had planned their little dupe of me carefully except for one thing: At the time, they didn't know what a chickenshit I was. We sneaked into the hidden stairwell; I slung my camera around my neck and lit my candle. Then, with the SSGs on the landing waiting for me, I began to creep my fanny up the stairwell, scary-looking as the halls of hell with only the candle to light my way. Soon as I turned the bend where I could no longer see the SSGs, I looked up into the darkness. Sure enough, a ghostly figure in white appeared above me, with a zombie-like stare and long hair in flames. I let out a screech, then proceeded to faint dead away, falling over and rolling down the staircase. I could've become a whole new legend if the candle hadn't gone out.

The SSGs managed to drag me to the fire escape, still out cold, and we made our getaway before the seniors caught us. Problem was, we got our asses out of there so fast that we forgot Corrine. When the seniors, in their gowns and curlers, came running to investigate the bloodcurdling scream and the strange noises, Corrine had no choice but to stand her ground, looking ghostly and holding the flashlight under her chin. The seniors who ran up the dark stairwell went into hissy fits, screaming their fool heads off as they scattered like baby chicks, which gave Corrine the chance to make a run for the fire escape, back to Tutwiler. The next day the whole campus talked of nothing but the appearance of the Girl with the Flaming Hair. My candle was found on the stairwell, proving once and for all that the ghost really did exist. When the story was picked up by the *Birmingham News* and reporters swarmed the campus, we met in my room and swore to never tell *anyone* what really happened that night.

Since then I've had better sense than to do anything that stupid, till the other day. The very next night after I see the ghostly light in the Pickett house, I can't help myself—I get up and look to see if it's still there. Sure enough it is, dim but definitely *there*. Only way I can get back to sleep is with two double vodkas, straight, and the next morning I go to work with a hangover. When I drive back on the island at sunset—no dolphins greeting me today—I pull into the driveway of the Pickett house next door. I don't get far. Sure enough, the gate to the property, which I remember as always flung wide open, is padlocked.

At home I get out of my uniform and into my cutoffs and a T-shirt. Without noticing till I had it over my head, I'd picked up one Lindy gave me for Mother's Day last year that says, "If Mama Ain't Happy, Ain't Nobody Happy." Pain hits me like a punch in the stomach, tears sting my eyes, and I jerk the T-shirt off and poke it in the back of the drawer.

After pouring a glass of Kendall Jackson Chardonnay (from a bottle I'd hidden from myself in an attempt to save it for the weekend), I head down to the pier. With the seagull shit gone, it's sure nicer sitting out here and watching the sunset. Still no dolphins. Hope it's not my bad karma acting up. When the sunset's gone, I start back to the house before the lights come on on the pier. One of the last things Daddy did before his heart attack was to rig the string of lights along the pier to come on at the same time every night. I'd like to stay down here at night and watch the lit-up boats on the bay, but I need to get a couple of loads of laundry done before the SSGs get here tomorrow.

There's only one place on the pathway down to the pier where you can see the Pickett house, through the branches of the water oaks. I'm not even looking on purpose; I just happen to see it. It's still daylight, yet there it is again—the weird light in the house. Looks like it's not an electric light but a candle. Suddenly, I'm transported back twenty years, and it's the Girl with the Flaming Hair all over again.

I don't know what makes me do it, any more than I know what made me go along with the idiotic idea of seeing the ghost in Wesley Hall that night. I cut through about a million snakey-looking ferns under the water oaks until I reach the fence separating our property from the Picketts. Grabbing a supporting post, I clear the fence easily, though my days as a jock are long gone. I only want to peek in a window and see if I can tell what's going on. What if a devil-worshiping cult is using the deserted house, burning black candles and chanting while they sacrifice virgins or something? Well, if that's the case, I'm perfectly safe.

Unlike Dolphin Cove, the Pickett house is their family home, a really cool-looking place. Much bigger than ours, it sits in the middle of palms and water oaks, with big old porches in the back, facing the bay. From the looks of things, no one has been here for a long time. It's definitely deserted, the lawn overgrown and creepy looking. Like most of the houses in this area, part of it is elevated on stilts to protect against flood waters, and under the house on this side, I spot just what I need, hanging with the crab traps and fishing poles: a stepladder!

Scanning the yard to make sure no one's here, I place the ladder against the side of the house, under the window where a light glows. It's been many years since I've been in the Pickett house, but I'm pretty sure this is the kitchen. Maybe the devil worshipers use the stove to boil their cauldron of toads and spiders and stuff, or whatever it is that makes up a witches' brew these days. No standing and stirring over a campfire for modern witches, I'll bet. They may even use a microwave, for all I know. When I climb the ladder, which is much ricketier than it looks, I see why the light has looked so dim—the window's filthy. Finding a Kleenex in my pocket, I spit on it and clear a little peephole in the dirt, then strain my neck, trying to see in. I don't exactly hear anyone come to stand underneath me on the ladder, but I sense it, and the hairs on my neck stand up. My heart pounding, I turn and look down.

At first he doesn't say anything, looking up at me with his hands on his hips, his legs apart. Then he squints and says, "Still spying on your neighbors, Lanier?"

I'm so surprised that my legs give out and I sit down on the top of the ladder, staring at him with my mouth wide open. It's been at least ten years since I saw him last. "Jesse!" I gasp. "Jesse Pickett—my God—is it really you?"

"Don't get so excited at the sight of me that you fall off the ladder and bust your ass," he says dryly. "Which looks pretty good for a fifty-year-old. I got a real good view from here."

"My ass is not fifty for two more years, when yours will be sixty, if I remember right." I start down the ladder backward, still staring at him. "Jesus, Jesse, this is unreal. What are you doing here?"

When he rolls his eyes and hoots, I say sheepishly, "Guess you're the one who should be asking me that question, right?"

"Lanier, honey," he drawls, shaking his head, "nothing you do can

Cassandra King

surprise me. I admit, seeing you on a ladder looking in my window ranks, but hell, I've caught you doing it before."

I jump to the ground and go into his open arms for a hug. My face buried in his neck makes it easier to hide my shock at his appearance. "I was only twelve last time I peeked in a window at you," I say, hugging him tight and patting his back. "But I will admit that I was trying to see you naked."

I expect him to laugh, to keep up our bantering. But with his arms so tight around me that I can hardly breathe, Jesse Pickett, known to his many fans as Jesse Phoenix, world-famous balladeer and songwriter, says, "Thank God you're here." Then he breaks down and cries like a baby.

By holding him up like an old man—which is what he looks like now—I manage to get Jesse into his house, him still boo-hooing, those harsh, racking sobs that men do. What I see once we're inside shocks me speechless, not the usual state for me. We climb the back steps and past the porch, going into a large, open living area that's instantly familiar to me, though I've not been in it for years. I half drag, half pull Jesse until I manage to get him to a couch. For such a slender, wiry man, he feels heavy as a walrus. All the time, I'm speaking to him in a calm voice, saying things like, "Hey, it's okay, Jess, honey. Let's just get you inside. I'm going to help you; lean on me and I'll help you." I've seen plenty of patients lose it, even seen some have what my mama called a nervous breakdown, but even so, I'm scared, not so much by Jesse as by the condition of the house. Something weird is going on here.

When I get him on the couch, Jesse lets go of me and buries his face in his hands. Because it's almost dark, I ease over to turn a lamp on but nothing happens; I'm not sure if the electricity has been cut off or if the bulb's just out. Half-burned candles are on the wicker coffee table in front of us, the candlelight that I've been seeing at night. A box of matches is there, too, but I don't want to move far enough from Jesse to light a candle. Not yet.

I lean over Jesse and put my arms around his shoulders, laying my head against his. His once-dark hair is thin and gray-streaked now, the back part long and pulled into a little ponytail. He looks real bad, almost like a street person. *Homeless.* Maybe that's what he feels like, with his mama dead, all his family gone. "Jesse?" I whisper. He's quit his boo-hooing but still has his face buried in his hands. I've always liked his hands, so strong looking, with long slender fingers. I notice he has on a hammered silver ring with a turquoise stone, but no wedding band. Last I read about him, seems like he'd remarried after his divorce to another singer, but I'm not sure. "Jesse?" I ask again.

His voice is muffled. "Guess it'd be better if you go home, Lanier. Looks like I'm not in any condition to see anybody after all."

"I'm not leaving you like this! I'm a nurse, Jess. I can help you."

His laugh is bitter, but he raises his head and fumbles in his jeans pocket till he pulls out a handkerchief and wipes his eyes. Then he blows his nose and puts the handkerchief back into his pocket. "Can't nobody help me. I'm too fucked up."

"Amen to that," I agree. "What in hell is going on?"

Instead of answering me, he rubs his face and looks around. "Is it dark already or have I gone blind?"

I smile, lighting a couple of candles on the coffee table before easing back beside him on the couch. "My guess is, with no one living here, the electricity's been cut off."

He nods. "Hadn't even thought about that."

"Jess, how long have you been here?"

He shrugs wearily. "Hell if I know. A week, maybe?"

With the candles giving some light to the dark room, I dare to look around. Beer cans and whiskey bottles are everywhere. Empty whiskey bottles. Stinky old cigarette butts are all over, squashed out in ashtrays. "You been alone?" I ask.

He chuckles. "Oh, yeah. Just me and old Jack Daniel's."

I keep prodding, even though he won't face me, looking down at the floor instead. "You eaten anything today?"

When he doesn't answer, I put my hand on his arm and shake him. "Jess? If I go to my house and get something, will you eat it?" Still no response, and I shake him again. "Come on. Do it for me, for old times' sake." Kneeling in front of him, I make him look at me. His eyes are bleary, and it's obvious he hasn't shaved in days. His face looks like he's been living the sad ballads that have made him famous. "Jess? You know what? You're the first boy I ever loved." I knew from the first time I saw him that Jesse Pickett was something special, sitting out on the pier playing his guitar and

Cassandra King

singing his mournful songs.

To my surprise, this brings a halfhearted grin. Smiling, he looks like the sweet young man I had such a huge crush on as a kid, before he left home for good, setting out for Nashville to seek his fortune. I've kept up with his career, attending his concerts when I could, going backstage a couple of times and meeting his band, reminiscing about the good old days on Dauphin Island. I took Paul and the kids to meet Jesse following a concert in Biloxi. That was the last time I'd seen him, over ten years ago now. He found both fame and fortune when he left Mobile Bay for good, but from the looks of things, he's sure not found much happiness.

A native of L.A. (Lower Alabama) and a graduate of the University of Montevallo, which awarded her an honorary Doctor of Letters in 2013, Cassandra King currently lives in the Low Country of South Carolina. Her latest book is The Same Sweet Girls' Guide to Life: Advice from a Failed Southern Belle *(2014). King is the author of five novels, most recently the critically acclaimed* Moonrise *(2013), her literary homage to* Rebecca *by Daphne du Maurier. Much of King's fiction is set in her native Alabama:* Queen of Broken Hearts *(2008) in a fictionalized Fairhope, and* The Same Sweet Girls *(2005) largely in Montevallo, with many of her actual classmates as characters.* The Same Sweet Girls *was a #1 Booksense Selection and a Literary Guild Book-of-the-Month Club selection. Her second novel,* The Sunday Wife *(2002), set in Birmingham and perhaps her most autobiographical, received wide acclamation, including* People Magazine *Page-Turner of the Week, Books-a-Million President's Pick, and South Carolina State Readers' Circle selection. In paperback, the novel was chosen by the Nestlé Corporation for its campaign to promote reading groups. King's first novel,* Making Waves in Zion, *published in 1995 by River City Press, was reissued in 2004 by Hyperion. King's short fiction and essays have appeared in numerous journals and anthologies, including* Callaloo, Alabama Bound: The Stories of a State *(1995),* Belles' Letters: Contemporary Fiction by Alabama Women *(1999),* Stories From Where We Live *(2002), and* Stories From The Blue Moon Café *(2004). Cassandra King was married to the novelist Pat Conroy, who died in 2016; they met when he wrote a blurb for* Making Waves in Zion.

How's England, Missy?

Kerry Madden

"How's England Missy" is a chapter from my novel, Hop the Pond, *about three generations of women—grandmother, daughter-in-law, and granddaughter. I spent my junior year at Manchester University in England and became enamored with Boy George and George Eliot and all things British around the time of the World's Fair in Knoxville. Although neither of my grandmothers ever visited me, I imagined qualities of both to create Granny Mame. I see this novel as a kind of* Trip to Bountiful *meets* Wuthering Heights *meets a twisted* My Fair Lady. *Fifteen years ago, I wrote it with only the girl's voice and it came close at publishing houses, but the YA editors said it was "too adult" and the literary fiction editors said it was "too YA." I'm very glad it was never published then, because I've been able to recreate my long dead grandmothers and send them on a trip they didn't even know they wanted along with a fascination of the Bronte Parsonage. There are also three men's voices weaved into the narrative as flash fiction, and they include Granny Mame's brother, son, and grandson. Addiction ran in the Bronte family as it does in the Hazlett family, which is another theme in the novel. The chapters go back and forth between East Tennessee and Manchester, England as Granny Mame makes the decision to see something besides East Tennessee before she dies, although the family tries to thwart her trip at every turn. I think it's really a story of a journey that stretches from the Smoky Mountains to the moors of Yorkshire.*

September 30, 1981
Dear Shelly-Grace,

How's England, missy? Have you found a Catholic Church? What's the name of it? This is the first letter I've ever sent to a foreign country. Wonder how long it will take to get there?

Well, I got your letter, and I'm tell you this right now, Lady Jane. Don't move out of the dorm into a "flat." That's crazy! Stay with the Americans where you have a meal plan, and I'm not fooling around. Don't forget who you are—an American Exchange Student, thanks to me and your daddy so generously footing the bill.

And what is this about you drinking hard cider? You'd better be minding your manners, sugarpig. And I'm <u>NOT</u> calling you by your "new name" of "George." I don't care if George Eliot or Boy George hung the moon and stars. Your name is <u>Shelly Grace</u>. Who are they anyway? Never heard of either one.

Good news, honey! I like my new job doing accounts at "Cherry Bear Books & Things." Easier than working for your father—I needed a break from the exterminating mess, and I don't mind driving over to Knoxville from Maryville. It's a cute little store off Kingston Pike not too far from the "Pick & Grin" where you and Dean took those ill-fated guitar lessons many eons ago. The owner, Mary Alice, sells way more fancy potpourri than books and also keeps highfaluting teddy bears in stock that cost upward of fifty dollars. Folks scoop out that potpourri mess like ice cream flakes and weigh it on an old fashioned ice-cream scale in fancy paper bags with ribbons. Can you imagine? And they buy those damn teddy bears on their credit cards. Blows the mind. "Scarlet O'Beara" and "Chef Bearnaise" and "Rhett Beartler." Nonsense! Don't you dare get a credit card, missy!

But you'll love this. The bestseller here is: <u>AN ENGLISH WOMAN'S GARDEN</u>. There is another hot ticket item called <u>AN ENGLISH WOMAN'S COTTAGE</u>. Thought you'd like those, but I'm not buying them or anything else in this overpriced bookstore even though I get a ten percent discount. Maybe I'll write one and call it <u>A MARYVILLE WOMAN'S SHOESTRING</u>. HA!

In Jesus' Holy Name,

Momma

P.S. Old Deuteronomy and Grizabella miss you, honey. Our dear pot-bellied pigs know when things aren't right in the home, and you are missed by the two and four-legged creatures around here. And why are you talking funny in your letters? It's like you are writing with an accent. It's me. Momma. And no ma'am, I don't "fancy" sending you any money or quids or whatever you call it.

Maybe I'll start talking British too. How would you like that, MADAME? Don't get all hoity-toity just cause you live with Brits. In my day, it was boys who went off, and the daughters who stuck close to home. A mother needs her daughter close by—as for her son, especially when he's raising all kinds of hell—not so much. You'll only know when you have children yourself and they go off and leave you.

I think Granny Mame and Aunt Bernadette are taking old Uncle Gudger's death pretty well. It's almost a relief. Is that a terrible thing to say? I know he was their only brother, but he wore everybody out except when he didn't, bless his heart. We'll have the memorial when you get home. Pray for Gudger's pitiful soul wandering around purgatory. Sometimes prayer is all we got. Your daddy goes to church everyday to pray for us all, since it's pretty clear your brother might be following the outlaw path of Uncle Gudger to a T. Do I need to say it again that I need my daughter close to me in this time of strife? If that's wrong sue me. You could come home in the spring and get you a job at the World's Fair. It opens in April and it's the biggest thing to hit town! "Knoxville's Energy International Exposition." They'll have all kinds of jobs for students. They're already playing a song on the radio: "The 1982 World's Fair—You've got to be there!" Catchy.

P.S. AGAIN: I almost forgot: Whatever you do, DON'T CALL HOME COLLECT! International rates give me heartburn, and I already have enough to contend with when the hot flashes hit. It's like my hair's on fire and the sweating, Lord have mercy. When they hit at work, I duck behind a shelf of books and suck on ice. Sometimes I'll just slip an ice cube right down the back of my shirt. Talk about relief. It's not pretty.

Anyway, once again, Shelly Grace Hazlett, do not be asking me or your daddy for more money. Do you think we're made of money? England was your grand idea, don't forget! Live with it, Lady Jane! Oh yes, Tennessee plays Alabama on Friday. Go Vols! Everybody's gearing up for the big game. Wouldn't it be a miracle if we could beat that sorry Alabama for once? Lordy. Can you get the football scores in England? I can start sending you the sports page if you want. Miss you, sugarpig! Granny Mame wants to know if you've been to the Bronte Parsonage yet? Write me back. Bye!

Kerry Madden

Kerry Madden-Lunsford is the author of the Maggie Valley Trilogy, *which includes* Gentle's Holler *(2005),* Louisiana's Song *(2007) and* Jessie's Mountain *(2008). Her first novel,* Offsides, *was a New York Public Library Pick for the Teen Age and has been released on Kindle by Foreverland Press.* Up Close: Harper Lee, Booklist's *Ten Top Biographies of 2009 for Youth and a Kirkus Pick for 2009, was re-released in 2015. Her first picture book,* Nothing Fancy About Kathryn and Charlie, *was illustrated by her daughter, Lucy, and published by Mockingbird Publishers, is about the friendship between Alabama storyteller Kathryn Tucker Windham and folk artist Charlie Lucas. Her newest picture book,* Ernestine's Milky Way, *will be published by Random House Children's Books in 2018. She has written stories for the* Los Angeles Times, LA Weekly, Five Points, Shenandoah, Salon, Redux, *and the* Washington Post. *She appeared in her first indie film, "Little Feet" as a bag lady, directed by Alex Rockwell. Kerry will begin directing the Creative Writing Program at the University of Alabama Birmingham this fall and has been the editor of* PoemMemoirStory *at UAB. The mother of three, she divides her time between Birmingham and Los Angeles.*

Clara, Part One:
Single Familiar Object
Pat Mayer

The two stories included here, Clara One ("Single Familiar Object") and Clara Two ("Last Gleaming"), are the final stories in my collection, Two Legs, Bad. *I placed them at the end because I wanted the reader to take away Clara's voice most of all, when the stories were told and done. Although both stories involve the narrative of a quiet traditional marriage in its last days, there are stark contrasts between the two. I've always liked stories within stories, and characters as story tellers, so in Clara One, I chose the intimacy of a first-person narration as Clara tells us about the outrageous Jackson brothers, their scandalous "non-marriage" and their exhibitionist offspring. This leads to her memories of a deadly feud over a raccoon. Around these tales of strippers and killers, Clara wraps the story of her life-long affection for her husband, Eugene. In contrast, Clara Two is told in third person so that we watch her, literally from a distance, as the story opens. Clara doesn't speak to us directly any longer. She's become insulated. All we can do is watch and wait. It's been my experience that grief is a learning process filled with anger and stumbling, and Clara is made clumsy by rage. The slow building of rebellion and frustration warps her judgment, but we finally regain our connection with Clara in our final glimpse of her, as she raises her hand to the night sky in a single wave of defiance. She'll never go quietly. I don't think any of us should.*

We were driving in the countryside, Eugene at the wheel, me beside him with Skippy on my lap. Lord, that dog surely loves a car ride. Eugene and I were quiet with each other the way people are after forty years. Not silence, because silence comes at you from outside. We were enjoying quiet that comes from inside, roomy and comfortable. That's where we stayed most of the time, unless something came up and we needed to discuss it, and that's what happened that day. Something came up. It came right up.

Delta farmland is flat and empty and as old as time. The air's so thick with history that sounds ride for miles on the shoulders of ghosts. We're a whisper away from the afterlife, with our haunted battlefields and mossy cemeteries. There's an unchanging permanence, so when something new appears in the countryside, it's more than shocking; it's revolutionary. The damn thing dominated the flat horizon. It was huge—gigantic, in fact—and as we moved closer, it loomed over us, towering by the side of the road, bigger than a dinosaur and as much out of place. I said to Eugene, "Look at that."

Eugene craned his neck and said, "Wow, Clara."

We pulled over and gawked, and even Skippy put his little paws on the dashboard and craned up at the enormous billboard on a single round steel leg, like a Popsicle on a stick. I believe billboards are an abomination, I certainly do. I'm grateful that St. Bernard councilmen don't allow the damn things, but here it was anyway, next to the road, a few yards inside the town line. Later, we found out that the councilmen had erected the damn thing. I guess they wanted to get a last-minute message to young people on their way into town to raise some hell. The billboard had a picture of a giant marijuana leaf inside a red circle with a red band across it, and at the bottom it said, "Dope! Don't Smoke It!"

For a long time, the councilmen had been worried about our kids and marijuana. (This was coming from middle-aged hypocrites who, in their day, raided cow pastures for mushrooms and cooked LSD in college dorm rooms.) "Oh, that'll really stop the kids from smoking, for sure," Eugene said in that sarcastic way he could put things and make them funny.

Marijuana? Hell, we were flower children of the sixties, me'n Eugene. We'd come of age in a waving sea of it. Dope fueled our dreams of a floral universe. We tried it all and saw it all, including JFK's promise—manned space flight. It was the ultimate psychedelic rush, watching Neil Armstrong step out on the moon on a snowy TV screen while we passed around a big doobie on the couch. There's not much wonder and amazement in the world today, but we made it happen back then. Everything was new and the future was rosy, even for a couple of kids from the swamplands.

Eugene said, "Yeah, kids, don't smoke it. Eat it. Those brownies are gooood!"

He started giggling and got me going too, so we drove the next few miles laughing because the councilmen didn't have a clue about what went on in the world. They thought they could make something go away by posting a twenty-foot picture of it. That billboard wasn't a deterrent; it was a giant spliff, a sales pitch, a love letter to hooch. The biggest publicity shot of all.

"Clara, that puts me in mind of the Jacksons," Eugene said.

"Ahh," I said, "Right."

Elvis and Otis Jackson were local boys, identical twins, and our unofficial village idiots. They made their living as country and western singers touring the fairground circuit, state to state, like the Everly Brothers, only more matching. Being twins, Elvis and Otis shared everything, including the same woman. She'd shown up in the audience one night, a typical stage-side groupie in a fringed leather jacket and snagged leopard leotards dented by panty lines, and she took up with Elvis and Otis in tandem. The twins looked so much alike that the woman could barely tell them apart, so after a while she stopped trying.

Eventually, after routine congress with one twin or the other, she gave birth to a son. A year later, she birthed a second son. Being deeply celebrity-crazed, she named her first-born Michael Jackson and her second-born Jesse Jackson. Nobody, including the mother, knew which twin fathered Michael and which twin fathered Jesse, but the fine points seemed to be hypothetical. They all settled into a peculiar three-parent family unit that was so bizarre it freaked out the other seasoned musicians on the music circuit, even those performers whose stock and trade was wholehearted exhibitionism.

After a few years of swinging from Elvis to Otis and back again, the Spandex groupie finally realized the difference between fertility and futility, so she abandoned the toddlers and their twin daddies. Elvis and Otis were forced to give up their music careers and settle down to raise their sons Michael and Jesse, but over the years they continued to fondly mention the joys of bonding with the audience.

When we considered the show business atmosphere of their formative years, we weren't surprised that Michael and Jesse grew up and took jobs in the public's eye. I'd seen them at work, which was dancing nearly naked, so naturally I'd seen quite a bit. They were a cheap variation of Chippendale male dancers, but taken to the next level, which was the final step to

Pat Mayer

which it could be taken, short of being arrested. They called themselves Chipmunks and worked up a synchronized dance, mostly sweating while thrusting to music. They wore clip-on pointy ears and snap-on tails. Their business card bore a tacky logo of a gyrating squirrel in a G-string.

At first, they played to ladies' birthday parties, bridal showers, and girl luncheons and business flourished. Eventually bookings fell off sharply when the local ladies became saturated in what the Jackson boys had to offer. Sweaty imitation lust and clumsy dancing simply couldn't sustain genuine interest. As for their masculine attributes, we'd witnessed the organic gifts of Jesse and Michael so regularly that those parts grew commonplace. If the boys hadn't looked so much alike, they might've held more fascination, but they were too similar for any defining novelty. The exhibitionism business continued to decline, so Jesse Jackson took a job at the chicken packing plant and Michael Jackson hired on with a house roofer.

After a while, Michael's boss, the house roofer, took his family to Disney World and Michael had a few days unencumbered by shingles. Spare time had never sat easy with Michael and he tended to stray into mischief and nonsense. In practically no time at all, he stumbled across that human skeleton in the woods.

The Jackson property abutted a stretch of woods where the sheriff had recently discovered and destroyed a crop of damn fine cannabis secreted among the trees. Michael sprawled in a lawn chair in his littered yard and guzzled beer while the last of his dope smoldered between his fingers. He gazed into the woods, pondering if any of that destroyed crop was self-seeding and might've grown up wild and unclaimed. He phoned his brother Jesse at the chicken packing plant and told him to come over after work and help search the woods for weed. Jesse, being agreeable, showed up as soon as he'd packed his quota of fryers.

As Michael later told the police, he and Jesse were making their way along an animal trail when a covey of quail fluttered out of the bushes and startled them. Michael fell sideways and tumbled downhill into a soggy creek bed. He rolled over and came face to face with the empty eyeholes of a skull buried up to the cheekbones in mud. Screaming and scuttling ensued, after which he summoned the law. Michael stuck to a wide-eyed claim that he and Jesse had been bird-watching in the woods, albeit without benefit of binoculars or any workable knowledge of fowl except for the fact that Jesse packed them.

Yellow caution tape was strung among the trees and the skeleton was excavated amid a mountain of paperwork. TV news reported on the bones, which meant the Jacksons were suddenly thrust into the spotlight without having to undress. They granted an interview with the press, but it only solidified the conclusion that any intelligent discovery the boys made must've been accidental.

The cops said the skeleton was probably a nameless drifter and the cause of death was pending, but the coroner wasn't ruling out foul play. Anyone with information should notify the police. I went to the phone and told the girl on the police switchboard that the coroner was too young to know local history. "If he did," I said, "he'd realize that the skeleton is probably a Koonts or a Tarbuckle. They were feuding, you know, and shooting each other in those woods."

"A feud, ma'am?" the operator drawled, "I ain't never heard of no feud."

"Of course you haven't. How old are you? Eighteen? It started with a fight over a raccoon, thirty years ago; Junior Tarbuckle's pet raccoon, Bandit Tarbuckle. The Koonts were fond of raccoons too, but preferred them on a plate with gravy. The Koonts were known to be lazy and thieves to boot, so when Bandit's cage turned up empty, the Tarbuckles figured the Koonts had stolen him and served him up with candied yams. The thought of Bandit working his way through several Koonts digestive tracts caused Junior Tarbuckle no small amount of anguish, so to get even, Junior snuck over to the Koonts farm and shot a Koonts hound dog."

"That's fine, lady," the switchboard girl said. "Thanks for calling."

"Wait! That's not all. The Koonts were fond of their dogs to an unnatural degree and bedded down with them on cold nights, so, in return, the Koonts went over and shot a Tarbuckle pig. The Tarbuckles doted on their pigs and had given them all names, so the Tarbuckles retaliated by shooting a Koonts goat. The loss of a beloved goat prompted the Koonts to execute a Tarbuckle cow, which is the largest animal either of them owned."

Pat Mayer

The switchboard girl said, "Ma'am . . . please."

"Naturally, there was nowhere to go but bigger and better, but neither clan owned an elephant, so the Tarbuckles settled for an unfortunate Koonts cousin. This led to the shooting of a Tarbuckle cousin in fair return. Since there were ample worthless cousins on both sides, the clans simply buried the unlucky cousins in the woods and neither clan reported the murders to the law. Of course, by then, both sides were much too fond of the feud to end it."

"Buried cousins in the woods, ma'am?" she asked. "I don't reckon so. I know them Koontses and Tarbuckles. I doubt they kilt any cousins."

"Well," I said, "you only know tame Koontses and Tarbuckles. They were wilder back then, with low thresholds of boredom, too much pride, and nothing to be proud of. Tell the coroner to compare the skeleton's DNA with samples from both families, if they've finally evolved to the point where they actually have DNA."

She scraped up the grace to thank me for my input and again attempted to hang up, made hums and hahs, but I wasn't through with the disrespectful smart-ass. "Hold on a minute. Better to be buried in the woods," I told the little twit, "than to die shut up in your house, rotting away undiscovered and smelling to high heaven."

She agreed with me and redoubled her effort to cut me off.

I said, "Junior Tarbuckle was so deconstructed by the loss of Bandit that he turned to a life of crime. He was the first outlaw to plant a fine crop of weed in the woods where the dirt had been enriched, I suspect, by the buried cousins. Luckily, Junior had a green thumb and both Koontses and Tarbuckles harvested dope until they were so laid-back that they forgave each other, except for Junior who refused to put Bandit behind him. He dropped out of the world and smoked himself to death with his own product, alone in his house, quite mellowed out."

The switchboard girl said something like well thanks and goodbye.

I said, "Dead two weeks before they found him, alerted by the stink. When they picked Junior up, their fingers went right through his rotten skin, just like punching through an overripe tomato. They brought his swollen, leaky remains out in a giant zip-lock bag."

"Bye, lady," she said, her voice quivering.

I paused to light a cigarette, drawing out the time like the actress Bette Davis. Bette knew a few things about timing. That's why Bette always smoked in her movies. Each puff was an elegant pause, a three-count. I blew a smoke ring and said "Windows of his house were black with flies. Can you imagine the smell?"

The little switchboard bitch was silent now, defeated.

I finished, "But that was Junior Tarbuckle, a rotten old toker to the end."

The phone clicked and hummed.

"Ahh," I said, smiling.

The skeleton found by Michael and Jesse Jackson had been unearthed because the four elements—wind, water, earth, and fire—don't combine very well in the Delta where we live. Those elements are always at war, and it skews everything a little bit off the natural plane. Winds howl across our fields, shearing off layers of topsoil, fanning wildfires and spreading sparks. Soil and water are at odds, too, like alien life forms thrown together. We had torrents of rain that spring and great sections of wet earth began to move. The topsoil melted into a wide river of mud sliding slowly through lowlands and down Michael Jackson's creek bed, groaning like a beast, knocking over everything in its path and bringing that skeleton along for the ride. That's my opinion, but I've lived a long time on this odd, spongy soil, and I've seen things get up and move, even after they've been properly buried.

Michael and Jesse never found the wild weed they were seeking that spring, but their luck changed with the coming of summer. The spring rains tapered off and the earth stopped sliding and our woods exploded in rich, vibrant, self-seeding summer green which must've included marijuana because the Jacksons showed up in town with a supply of freshly harvested weed and were promptly arrested. The judge gave them six months of picking up roadside litter, as a method of educating them. Eugene and I passed the boys on the side of the road many times. We laughed and honked, and they smiled and waved and kept on cleaning up trash, but I doubt they learned anything.

Pat Mayer

Some things can't be taught. Once, Eugene gave me an empty bird nest he'd found. He said, "Clara, I got two hands and I couldn't create this amazing thing and I sure as hell couldn't make it with my pecker, like the bird did." Simple creatures often do complex things, but some complex creatures can't even learn the simplest of things. The Jackson boys would never walk a straight line down the middle. Their feet didn't move that way.

The skeleton Michael found was never identified. Guess there wasn't enough human DNA in the Koontses and Tarbuckles to lay kin. The bones couldn't be buried because the case was still under investigation, so the coroner stored the bones in a drawer, hoping the future might shed some light.

I told Eugene, "I feel bad about those bones. No matter what happened to that cousin, the poor soul deserves to rest in peace, but now his bones are sitting in the coroner's drawers."

Eugene said, "Not really, Clara. It doesn't matter what happens to his bones because his spirit's moved on. He's walking strange territory now, waiting for the rest of us to catch up. We'll all get there eventually, because we're just cosmic travelers in time and space. Space isn't such a bad place to be."

My gray-haired flower child waltzed me around the living room like he did sometimes, singing our special song, "Moon River." He knew all the words. Skippy yipped and danced around our feet and we had to shuffle, catching each other, to keep from stepping on him. "One small step for man," Eugene laughed, and scooped up the dog. "Clara darling, let's fly to the moon!"

"Oh no, Eugene. I'd be too scared."

"Everybody's scared, Clara, all the time. Strange territory always terrifies us. We just shut the door on it and go on living." He laughed at the doubt on my face. "Courage is simply ignoring what's on the other side of the door. Come on, Clara, or you'll miss out. The moon's the greatest show spinning in the heavens."

He held Skippy in one arm and me in the other, and the three of us spun around and around. Then, he sat down, panting. "Chest hurts," he said.

The next day, Eugene died.

Pat Mayer

That was the day that our shared quiet ended and my isolated silence began. My ears ring with it. I hurt, and that hurt is forever collapsing inward with sharp edges. Our old local landmarks are shuffled. I'm disoriented. The familiar is indifferent. I keep forgetting what comes next. I have a new understanding of the word *constant*. Eugene's under my skin like the watermark on stationery. Nothing washes off. It can't be shrugged away.

I need the courage Eugene talked about. Not enough courage to go to the moon, just enough to stay here on earth without him. Native Americans hereabouts say that grief leaves us through our mouths. We have to talk it away, but those hated words hurt me, cutting me on the way out, so I push them down and keep them behind my throat, below my eyes. I don't have the courage to say them. Not yet.

Eugene is somewhere else now, in strange territory, branching out. He's still here too, in spinning eddies of air, as though he just brushed past me. He is constant.

When astronauts become disoriented in space, they're taught to focus their thoughts on a single familiar object; a fishing hat or coffee cup, a soft tee shirt, something well known and constant. They find their equilibrium this way. So I sit on the porch at night and scan the heavens looking for— what? A familiar object? Well, why not? Plenty of familiar constellations. I tip up my chin and starlight falls into my eyes. Eugene was right when he said that space isn't such a bad destination, once you master the concept of neverending.

I see pinpoints of light, diamonds on a black blanket, spheres of erupting mystery . . . expanding . . . hypnotic. The stars are slowly dying, every single one, but even when their end comes, we won't know it because the light that reaches us was sent out millions of years ago. In our brief time, the stars will always seem forever constant, the place where all creation began, serving us, each to our own heart's purpose.

Reflecting in a lover's eyes.

Shaping an astronomer's constellations.

Guiding a sailor home through troubled seas.

Granting a dreamer's wish.

My sweet Eugene, some nights I dream of an Arctic glacier. Miles down in the glacier is a layer of snow that fell forty years ago, on the same

Pat Mayer

night you first took me to bed. The earth would have to be destroyed in a rain of fire before that deep layer evaporated, but if I were still around to breathe the mist of that ice, with my last breath I couldn't give up the joy of that night with you. There should've been only a faint memory, or at least embarrassment, but the remembrance is there, sensual and sharp as if it had happened yesterday.

Wrapped in a dream of ice, we are warm.

We are constant.

Clara, Part Two:
Last Gleaming

Here, then, is a muffled world in dripping suspension. Misty rain, sky the color of an aluminum washtub, no birdsong, no cars passing, nobody. On closer look, there's meager movement. An old woman, Clara in Eugene's oversize galoshes. She wades slowly through standing water . . . schlop . . . schlop . . . down her driveway toward the back door. Clara's much more stooped these past few months.

Eyes down, she sees a metal sky reflected in puddles; sees her neglected lawn, shabby along the edges of the concrete where prodding tendrils of yellow centipede snake onto the pavement. Eugene never tolerated a shaggy lawn, but he's been gone for months. Seasons have passed, and he's still dead.

Didn't come back, no, no.

The Britt boy cuts her yard for money, shitty little thug. He says he trims the grass along the concrete edges, but he doesn't. Not an inch. He thinks she's old and won't notice. He takes her money with a grin, without conscience.

"Ahh," Clara says, when she sees the shaggy edges.

Let the boy spend her money, he can't buy his way out of being a liar. It's only grass, trying to grow and spread. Holding grass back seems unnatural to her, always did. It was Eugene who thought that nature could be disciplined.

Her house needs paint, but paint's unnatural too, covering the beauty of wood with a coat of phony color that flakes away in the sun, some garish shade of the Caribbean, in this place, nowhere near Jamaica.

Oh Jamaica, where they never worry about the next meal. Plenty of food in their trees, in their nets, they've no need to be intense, those gentle ocean grazers, laughing and barefoot, prying open oysters on the beach. Clara's seen the Gulf a few times, but didn't like it. She likes easy oysters from the supermarket, slick in a plastic tub, floating in cloudy brine.

Sometimes her thoughts spin beyond control. She knows her words are hazy and unreasonable, even as she says them, but she throws them out like anchors at the end of long ropes. She says any inane or shocking thing to preserve her importance so others can't ignore her. She knows she's pure and wise; her words have weight, so she says them, and it's as though a breeze has drifted past, no substance, no snagging anchors. In the ache of her loneliness, she wraps herself in a silent pout and the silence rings.

Ah, here's her back door, where it ever was.

She's forgetful since Eugene died; forgets where she needs to go, or the day of the week, or where she put something, but she can still make her way to this door with the conviction of a spawning salmon. Purse over her arm, she shifts her umbrella to grip the handrail and she sees it, a tan-colored blob on the ground under her dripping rose bush.

What the hell . . . ?

She uses the umbrella to lean upon, to tilt a line of sight through the leaves. He comes into focus, her ancient little dog Skippy, wet and dead against the root crown. He must be dead; he wouldn't tolerate such a soaking, otherwise.

"Skippy, oh Skippy, come here, boy!" she calls.

No response. Just the wet rose bush, dripping. Wet ground. Wet dog, unmoving.

Clara straightens and blinks. "Ahh."

She's swamped by immediate sorrow, bewilderment, piercing loneliness, not in a mature fashion, but disorienting and alien, as a

Pat Mayer

child might experience it. There are things she should do now, with this discovery. The dead always leave us with chores. There'll be cleaning up, words to invent, the work involved in a proper funeral, be it man or beast or sodden, aged dog. She lived with Skippy many years, longer than she lived with a lot of things, except Eugene. Now, there's only this chore, this enormous task, in the way.

She briefly considers wrapping Skippy in newspaper as though he were a dead fish and storing him in the freezer until the Britt boy, the little cheater, can dig a hole, which is not a bad idea. But like a ripple on a pond, the plan moves smoothly to the edge of her mind and bumps against a stubborn shore of resistance. The kid is a rotten apple, a mean little shit. He hated Skippy, and the sentiment was mutual. Skippy barked at him, an unyielding yip-yip. Once, she watched through the window as the boy kicked the dog. Another time he swung a rake, making Skippy howl with pain.

Even more than the little thug's meanness, she can't stand the idea of her Skippy wrapped in newspaper, stiff and frosty in the freezer while she eats her supper alone at the kitchen table nearby.

Eugene spoke of the olden days, when bodies of dead Vikings were burned to ashes. She may not be able to dig a grave, but she can still build a fire, so why not?

It's decided; cremation, the ancient Viking way, the funeral pyre, on a raised platform between heaven and earth. Skippy liked warm places. He slept on the heated bricks of the fireplace on cold days.

She'll need a proper location and a hot fire to do the job. Eugene had built a cooking fire, two years ago or more, burning meat on a cheap crusted grill. The grill was red and rounded on the bottom like half a cracked egg, lidless, with rubber wheels. As far as she remembers, that grill's still around, rusting in her potting shed. The open area behind the shed would make a good setting for the funeral pyre, near the compost heap, so she could simply tip Skippy's ashes into the compost to be spread upon her flowers. The little thug will spread Skippy around and never realize it, and Skippy won't mind. She scooped his dung for years and tossed it into the flowerbeds as fertilizer. No freezer for Skippy then, no crook's hole in the ground. Her loving companion will nourish the flowers, the roses. A comforting notion.

She stands in the yard, drizzle-soaked, rubbing her wet forehead with age-misshapen fingers. There should be procedure; there must be combustible fuel, at least at first, to ignite the body. That stack of yellowed newspapers in the shed will do nicely. Dry, brittle newsprint, fuel enough for a little pup. She hooks her umbrella and purse over the handrail of the back steps.

She's thirsty, always favors a beer in the afternoons, looks forward to it on the walk home. She often takes a few shots of good Russian vodka, a community cup of sorts, because she shared it with Eugene with a bit of ceremony and juice. Now it gives her solace almost every day.

She goes to the potting shed, pulls open the scraping door, rotten at the bottom. Ahhh, there's the grill. She stacks dusty newspapers on the grid and rolls it to the open space behind the shed, beside the compost heap. The grill is shaky, so she braces it against the shed's back wall and covers the grid with a thick layer of newsprint. Then, it's back to the rosebush, back to Skippy.

The body is deep beneath thorny limbs, so she uses the hooked handle of her umbrella to snag his collar and pull him out. Skippy slides on mud, surprisingly weightless, and his lightness twists her heart with guilt. When had he become so thin and frail?

She plucks a couple of roses and shoves the blooms into her pocket and begins to pull the dog behind her. She whimpers as Skippy bumps along, sodden and limp and open-eyed, with the tip of his pink tongue protruding. It takes both hands and all her strength to lift and lever the umbrella high enough to unhook Skippy awkwardly above the newspapers. He drops with a thud upon the classifieds. She shreds the roses and scatters petals over him, sobbing now, recalling Skippy napping in her lap, snoring softly, his pink belly warming her wasted thighs.

"Skippy, you're a bit soaked, so you may be hard to light." Her quivering voice, the sudden sobbing breath, surprise her. "I have to find some fuel, boy."

She searches the garage for charcoal lighter, preoccupied and sobbing less now, brushing at her wet eyes. Eugene probably used it all and didn't replace it. Not replacing, leaving her stranded, one of his bad habits.

Pat Mayer

"Ahh," she growls, and puts her face in her hands.

Eugene had laughed so hard every time Skippy stood, hind legs in Eugene's lap, front legs on Eugene's collar bones, bumping Eugene's wrinkled face with a wet nose, dog Eskimo kisses. Clara suspends her search and hauls herself up the back steps to have a shot of vodka. She keeps a bottle in the freezer, where she refuses to put Skippy. The cap unscrews with an effort. She pours two fingers of vodka into a jelly glass, lifts it and sips. The familiar distraction of heat. "Ahh."

She looks over her pantry for something flammable to boost the cremation, turns and sees the vodka bottle on the counter. She takes it in her hand uncapped, finds the matches in a drawer, teeters outside.

"Here Skippy, my friend. Let's share this."

She douses him with cold vodka. After several arthritic attempts, she strikes a long match, holds it aloft. All hymns of her childhood escape her, so she hums "The Star Spangled Banner" as she touches the match to Skippy. Vodka flares like a torch. Flames shoot up five feet as fire quickly leaps to the potting shed. The old porous wood expands with a *whomp* and a sudden expulsion of air as the shed's back wall ignites.

"Bad dog! Just look what you've done!"

Clara backs away from the heat and shuffles toward the house to make an emergency call; almost yells for Eugene in her confusion. On the way, she stops to catch her breath, until the crackle of burning wood and smell of charring dog remind her to hurry. "Ahh," she says in frustration, hits her forehead with the heel of her hand as she climbs the steps and goes into the house.

Eugene had posted the number for the fire department, but she can't find it, so she calls 911 and explains that her dog has set fire to the potting shed. The dispatcher asks if she's sure about that.

"Oh, yes, dear. And he smells damn awful too, you know—burning fur. I basted him in vodka."

The dispatcher suppresses a surge of nausea. *"What?"*

"Well, hell, he was too wet to light, and you can't cremate a dog that won't light."

The dispatcher, fully repulsed, sets the mechanism of response into action. Her report dutifully includes dog and vodka.

Hook and ladder and pumper trucks pull up in front. Fat white water hoses soon criss-cross the street. A fireman named Charlie LaForce, a Cajun fellow whose dog Lucky Jack can talk when he pleases, is on duty that afternoon.

"What cause dis fire?" Charlie asks another fireman.

The other fireman answers, "That old lady was trying to cremate a dog."

Charlie asks, "Was the dog dead?"

"Jesus, I hope so."

Clara taps Charlie LaForce on the shoulder. "Are you a fireman?"

Charlie turns. "Beg pardon, ma'am?"

"Are you a fireman?"

Charlie grins. "Me? Yessum, most certainly am."

"Skippy died. He's on the barbeque grill. Can you put his ashes in my compost heap? I want that little bastard to put him on my roses."

"Sure can, ma'am, now would you go on the porch where it safe so we can put out dis fire?"

"Okay, but I'm keeping an eye on you. Tend to those dog ashes, you hear?"

Firemen feed hoses onto the property. One of the men says, "Seems like she would've buried the dog. Old people love funerals."

Charlie grins. "Who need a pet cem'tery when dere's a barbeque grill?"

Clara yells at him from the porch, "What are you laughing at? I'm watching you!"

The potting shed is extinguished and rendered to a dripping shell. Charlie approaches Clara on the porch. "Ma'am, we found your dog. He still whole, no ashes. What we do wit him?"

"There's still something of him left?"

"Yessum. You burnt mostly shed, vodka, and fur. Dere still more dog'n you would imagine, given what he been through."

"You boys got a shovel?"

"We gotta buncha shovels, jes not much time." Then, Charlie softens. "Where you want the hole dug?"

Clara, smudged and sooty, ashes in her white hair, picks a spot and Charlie digs a hasty hole under her supervision. He summons the other

Pat Mayer

firemen and they assemble around the grave as he lowers Skippy with the shovel, fills the shallow grave, and pats the mound with the back of the spade.

Clara glares at Charlie expectantly, as though he should say a few words of comfort. He glances at the other fireman, sighs, and begins, "Lord, please take—"

Clara interrupts, launching into an off-key National Anthem. Firemen snatch their helmets from their heads and hold them over their hearts. Clara finishes: . . . *homer the braaaavveee* . . . holding the last note for a surprisingly long time. Without a word she turns and goes into the house, slamming the door. The firemen shrug, load up, and drive away.

That evening, Clara steps out on the back porch, beer in hand, and almost calls for Skippy, but then she sees the remains of the shed and remembers. She bumps her forehead with her hand. "Ahh."

Clara tips her chin to look at the stars, dependable constellations from the beginning of time. A soft night breeze touches her lined face. She flutters pink-rimmed eyes. The scent of a recent wood fire drifts from the shell of the potting shed. Such a comforting smell, a primeval reminder of warmth, light, food, companions. Clara smiles in response, bends and carefully lowers her backside to the step as she did when Eugene was there to sit beside her, when Skippy dozed at her feet.

"Eugene, I almost forgot. Skippy's with you now."

The sultry night wraps her like a shawl. She's comforted by the familiarity of her own back yard, and she relaxes into trickles of silent tears. The human soul, a cup of sadness. Clara's soul must be almost full by now. *Dear God, it has to be*, she thinks and clears her wet eyes with the back of her hand.

She talks to the scraps of Eugene she can see . . . his lawn, his flowerbeds. Her voice dissolves into the warm evening air like sugar in tea. "I'm leaving this old world, a slow piece at a time, Eugene, yet I wake up every day, still here. I'm tired of loneliness, and . . . and . . . I'm so pissed at you all the time for leaving me. It's embarrassing, Eugene, being the last one, still here, like I have nowhere to go, like I don't know how to leave.

Why can't I be with you and Skippy, like we used to be?"

No reply, only crickets, those night chirpers, and a flutter of moths at the porch light. Clara looks at the tipping cups of the big and little dippers. At the edge of her vision, the fiery August star Sirius flickers and burns. Stars are untainted by eras; they spin in peace and endless time; origins of light in the cold ether of space. As with Eugene and Skippy, they're pure mystery now.

Her memories are clear and dramatic. She's a sum, the total of his years plus her years braided like a rope, a lifeline. The cadence of a waltz begins to throb, softly at first, then unfolding in a pulsing orchestra of memories. Violins swell and surge, a stream of rhythm. Moon River, Eugene knew all the words. Humming the melody, she sets down her beer and rises on shaky legs, lifts a twisted hand to the heavens, and waves.

Pat Mayer is a life-long resident of the Alabama Gulf Coast. She's the author of two novels, Terminal Bend *and* The Cannibals Said Grace, *both set in the Alabama delta. A fan of comedic verse, Mayer was awarded first place in the 2007 International Limerick competition. Her short stories have appeared in four anthologies of southern writers and she has twice been nominated for the Pushcart Prize. She was a finalist in the ninth Tartt Fiction Award and won the tenth Tartt Fiction Award for her dark comedy short story collection* Two Legs, Bad. *Mayer and her husband, Paul, live in the port city of Mobile, Alabama, in a house they built to repurpose and preserve salvaged local architectural relics.*

Pat Mayer

The Communion Plate

Jamie McFaden

I wrote "The Communion Plate" based on an experience my parents had in trying to find the perfect servingware for their local church's communion. While the names were changed, the characters are all based on church members that I myself grew up observing. I'm from a small, Southern town on the Georgia-Alabama line that's filled with interesting personalities. The church setting ended up being ideal for the circumstances on the whole as it manages to contain the reality of companionship, faith, and the bits of hypocrisy that lie between the cracks of life. I hope readers will find a bit of themselves in the main characters as real people doing the best they can to make themselves and each other happy.

Ed Walden knew exactly where he could get a new communion plate for the Epworth United Methodist Church. The question was, how much would it cost him? Walmart had nothing but plastic trays that looked like they belonged on a rickety picnic table in some redneck's back yard. Big Bob's Thrift World had plenty of plates, but Ed hated Big Bob on account of Big Bob being on the city council and voting against the bill that would've finally allowed the sale of alcohol on Sunday. Big Bob made it a no-go five to four, and now Eufaula, Alabama, would remain booze-free on the Lord's day until the Lord killed off all the current council members in, oh, say about 20 years. So Ed took his '94 baby blue Chevy Cheyenne to the best option in town, Satterlock's Jewelry.

Now normally, Ed wouldn't be caught dead in a hoity toity joint like Satterlock's. All those damn Main Street Eufaula stores overcharged like crazy. "That damn Jaycee Breeland charges thirty dollars for a Bama t-shirt I can get at Walmart for seven bucks! What the hell would make a cotton shirt with a pocket be thirty dollars? Must've imported the cotton from Bear Bryant's private estate," he'd exclaim after returning from Dixie Delights, the corner boutique on Main Street that sat directly across from Satterlock's. Fat Jaycee Breeland was a good friend of Ed's wife, Philma, though, so from time to time, he'd make his way in to see if there was anything good to get Philma for an anniversary or birthday. Today, though, all Philma wanted was for Ed to get a new communion plate for Pastor Jeffrey's upcoming Church Homecoming Extravaganza.

She had been too busy coming up with a cheer for Epworth's youth group for the Extravaganza to pick one up herself. And she'd waited until the last minute—again. Leave it to Philma Walden to volunteer for everything in the world and then launch into a full-fledged hissy fit the day before when nothing was ready.

"What's that for anyway?" Ed asked her as he watched her press one finger to her temple while she stared down at the yellow legal pad in front of her, scribbling words then scratching them out. She sat at the big wooden kitchen table, surrounded by painted antique saws hanging on the painted-over wood panel walls that were the color of the inside of a blood orange. Years ago, when Ed painted it for her, it was supposed to have been a bold ketchup red, but according to him, the sorry bastards who mixed the paint at Marvin's messed it up and now they had orange-red walls. He swore no one in town—hell, maybe no one on the planet—had a kitchen with walls that shade. Philma had grown to like it, though. What she hadn't grown to like were the overfed deer that looked more like fat dogs or small bears with antlers positioned dead-center on the wall on the largest of the cylindrical antique saws—one of Ed's prized finds from the Shady Oaks Flea Market. For years the chubby deer had overseen dinners of spaghetti with hamburger meat sauce and chicken-a-la-king made in Philma's cast iron pans; they had witnessed every argument and every game of Balderdash, their black handpainted eyes some small-town, downhome Alabama version of Dr. TJ Eckleberg's bespectacled stare.

"It's a cheer for the youth group to perform at the beginning of the Homecoming Extravaganza. Pastor wants them to all come up to the front and holler out what 'Epworth' stands for to kick things off. I'm stuck on about half of what the letters should represent."

"Why didn't he come up with it himself if it was his stupid idea?" Ed still couldn't believe Philma had taken on yet one more thing. Home daycare mother by day, water aerobics instructor at the local community center at night, and now she was the superintendent of the children's church department at Epworth. At 58, most people were starting to slow

Jamie McFaden

down. Not his wife—their two daughters left for college and she decided to become Mother Teresa. He had seen a coffee mug at Dixie Delights a few weeks back featuring an old woman with frizzy white hair and a frazzled expression that read, "Stop Me Before I Volunteer Again." If he knew it wouldn't piss Philma off that the cartoon woman looked so damn haggard, he'd bring her that mug home sure as God made little green apples.

"That's not nice. And he did come up with what the letters should stand for. They're just not very good. Like, he wants E to stand for 'Enthusiastic Christians loving the Lord.' That doesn't exactly roll off the tongue."

"Oh, yeah, that's shit," said Ed, now peeking over her shoulder to see what she'd written down. Philma glanced over the top of her readers, shooting him a warning with her narrowed blue eyes. He quickly recovered with, "Well, what have you got so far?"

"E. Everyone's welcome. P. Prayers work. W. Okay, I'm stuck on W."

"What the hell else you have better to do on a Sunday?" Ed answered, laughing at his own joke.

She exhaled loudly through her pursed lips and said, "That's not helping. Get out of here, if you're just going to mock me."

"Wonders of Christ witnessed daily?" he said.

"Now don't even—" she started, then paused and cocked her head to the side, staring at him, "Actually, that's pretty good."

"Of course it is. I'm a goddamn genius. Or did you forget?"

"Oh, sure. And don't use that word when I'm trying to come up with a cheer for the church youth group. Got anything for H? I'm stuck on H, too."

He took his crimson Alabama baseball hat off, smoothed the thin strands of light brown hair down on the top of his sparsely coated head with a calloused hand, then gently pulled the hat back down on his head. He grabbed the pen from off the table and pulled the legal pad away from Philma. Using one hand to cover as if he were trying to thwart an attempt at cheating off a middle school test, he took a few moments to write his response beside the H in his all-capitalized hand. Looking satisfied, he sucked on his dentures making a wet clacking sound and scooted the pad back to his wife.

It read: Hell yes, Methodist.

She laughed and shook her head. "Now, you know good and well we can't use the word 'Hell.' But that is pretty good, Edward, I gotta give it to you." Philma Walden was the only person left on the planet earth that called him by his real name. Because, according to her, "Ed" made her husband sound like a damned redneck trucker. Despite a CDL, her man was no redneck.

"Why not? It's in the Bible."

"Yeah, well, I don't think that's the message the pastor wants to get across. Especially not out of the mouths of babes."

"So say, 'Heck yes, Methodist.' Ain't that legal?"

"Maybe. I'll think about it. We're not tryin' to look like we think we're better than say the Baptists or Presbyterians. Besides, what if there are visitors of other denominations? They could get mighty defensive about that. It's supposed to be welcoming. I'll figure it out. What I need for you to do is take your butt to the store and find that communion plate we talked about last week. Pastor just wants something simple to replace the one that Dusty broke Sunday before last."

"Why'n the hell would they let a retard do the communion anyway?" Ed asked, reaching for a bag of Lay's Potato Chips in the basket on the side counter.

"Don't eat those. I'm gonna have lunch ready by the time you get back. There's a turkey in the oven right now. He wasn't doing the communion; he was just helping move it under the cupboard where it goes. Myrtle's husband—I can never remember his name—left it out by the sink in the church kitchen after the last communion and he knew it didn't go there. That boy's nice as can be. Just a little slow. They probably shouldn't have had a ceramic platter anyway," she said, now doodling a box within another box on the legal pad next to what she had written down.

He grabbed a handful of chips out of the bag anyway. He looked into the palm of his hand where he held the crispy pieces and then handed a folded one to Philma, saying, "Here." The folded chip-giving had been a love token between them since they first got together.

"I love you, too. Now get out of here and let me think," she answered.

Jamie McFaden

Ed parked the truck directly in front of Satterlock's. As he shut the truck door, it made a loud, high-pitched squeak that caught the attention of an elderly man in a faded Auburn hat and pleated khakis. "How 'bout it now?" Ed said to him, not really expecting a response.

"How 'bout your Crimson Tide this season? That black quarterback can't throw no bomb like your last guy. Think Florida's gonna give you some trouble."

Ed felt the right corner of his mouth turn up just slightly as he answered, "He'll be alright. Saban'll have him in real good shape come next weekend. You just worry about those little orange and blue kittens. Or are they eagles? I can never remember. What're they supposed to be anyway?"

"We'll just see," said the old man, turning away to go into the Old Mexico next to the jewelry store.

Ed knew more about the Alabama Crimson Tide than most people knew about their own family. He always had a response ready for naysayers. Feeling victorious, he tugged on the door to Satterlock's, feeling the cool air from the store mix with the stifling Alabama humidity as he walked inside.

"Hey, Ed. Long time, no see. Whatcha thinking about the Tide this year?" asked the chubby thirty-something behind the counter. Ed had coached him in little league. He had been one of those kids who picked dandelions from the grass in the outfield, never paying any mind to what was going on during the game. Ed liked him, though. He was a nice enough kid. Uncoordinated as hell, but nice.

"They're gonna get to rollin'. No doubt about that. Hey, my man, you still have that plate you showed me last year? The one they messed up engraving?" Ed asked, careful not to get too close to the display cases. He knew if he knocked anything over or broke something, he'd have to damn near take out a second mortgage on the house to pay for it.

"Sure do. Don't nobody want that thing. It's scratched up all to hell in the center. You know how folks are about their silver around here. Gimme a sec," the man answered, making his way to the back of the store.

A few moments later he returned. Ed had been looking for a tray for Christmas dinner the year before and had seen this very one. It wasn't really their style with the mother-of-pearl inlay and the gleaming silver surface, but for the church it would be perfect. Certainly nicer than that last plate they had. The Powers woman had ordered the plate a while back special as a wedding gift for her daughter. It had been damaged when the lady in the back who does the monogramming put the wrong last name initial. The poor thing had put the bride's first husband's moniker in a rushed moment, then made matters worse when she tried to scratch out the mistake, giving the center of the plate a tarnished look. Ed didn't see what the big deal was. Hell, you put stuff on the center of the plate to cover it up anyway.

"How much you want for it? Philly wants it for the church's communion plate," he said, letting his fingers fall along the raised edges where the mother-of-pearl shone under the special light of the jewelry store.

"Twenty bucks. No tax since it's a donation for the church and all," the man answered.

Ed nodded and whistled as he blew out a little gust of air. "Sure is pretty. Thanks, my man. Appreciate it."

Philma saw the Satterlock's gold embossed logo on the white bag Ed held before she noticed her husband's proud smile.

"Oh, Edward. You went to Satterlock's? Why, they charge an arm and a leg!" she said, taking off her glasses to get a better look.

"Now, just wait a minute, Philly. I got it for twenty bucks," he said, easing the plate out of the bag to show her. He held it up to her narrowed eyes, sticking his chest out a little and pulling his shoulders down the way he always did when he knew he'd done well.

She gasped, bringing her hand to her cheek. "It's beautiful!" she started, "But I don't know. It might be too fancy. The pastor just wanted a plain old plate. Like a plastic lunch tray. You could've just gone to Walmart."

"What do you mean? This is a damn fine plate. And it is the Lord's supper, after all. Don't you think the body and blood of Christ need to be served on somethin' a whole lot nicer than a Walmart dish?" he answered, indignant.

She paused for a moment. Her eyes darted back and forth the way they always did when she was thinking long and hard about something. She ran her fingers over the plate. Then, she looked at her husband, shaking her

Jamie McFaden

head. She bounded toward him suddenly, wrapping her arms around his chest in a big hug. "You sweet man. Of course we'll use it. It's perfect. I'm sorry I'm such a cynical old woman sometimes." Even as she spoke, she had a tinge of wish to keep the plate. After all, it was pretty. They hadn't had a nice cheese plate for Christmas Eve in years. The hunks of pepper jack could go on the right side and the Wisconsin extra sharp could—but no. Even born-agains knew better than to press their luck with the Big Man upstairs. Keeping it for any reason at all at this point seemed almost categorically to go under "pressing your luck."

Ed interrupted her rapid-fire thoughts with, "Hell, I'm used to it. Is that turkey ready yet? I'm 'bout to perish over here."

"Yes, it is. Go wash your hands and I'll set the table," she said. As she moved the plate to the top of the china cabinet on the back wall of the kitchen for safe keeping, she silently counted her crimson-clad husband among her favorite blessings.

Two weeks later, Philma walked in to church carrying her canvas tote bag featuring the Very Hungry Caterpillar filled with this Sunday's children's church Bible lesson (Jacob steals the Blessing) along with construction paper, glue, and a snack of apple juice and Cheddar Blast Goldfish. She positioned herself next to Ed's cousin Polly on the third pew at Epworth United Methodist Church—the same seat she'd been taking for nearly twenty years on at least three Sundays out of the month—Polly poked out her Avon-brand Berry, Berry Nice-lipsticked lips, a sure sign she had some kind of good gossip to dish. Philma braced herself for it, even though it made her uncomfortable and fidgety. Just last Sunday, Polly had claimed to be "a clairvoyant" after all. Philma thought she was nuts. Couldn't pick your family, that's for sure, she thought. Polly didn't care if it was God's house or the White House, when someone was getting divorced or going to bed with someone else's husband, she had to say it then and there before it burned a hole right through her tongue.

"Hey dar-lin," she drawled, opening her pudgy arms to embrace Philma. Philma hugged her back, feeling a little guilty for just thinking she was batshit crazy. She smelled like too much Far Away Gold perfume and Aquanet.

"Good to see you, Polly. It's a gorgeous Sunday."

"Sure is. Oh, girl girl, let me tell you somethin'.'"

There it was. Not twenty seconds in and good ol' Polly of Eufaulie, as Ed called her, was proving she much preferred gossip to the gospel.

"What's that?" Philma asked, humoring her.

Polly lowered her voice, dropping her head slightly. "That purdy plate Ed had brought for them to use during communion is just'a collectin' dust over in the fellowship hall kitchen. Old Jim Briarton and Gary Oakley said it was too heavy for 'em to hold up for that long. Can you believe that? They usin' a lunch tray from the Walmart instead now."

"Oh," was all Philma would reply. Maybe that would be her cheese platter this Christmas season after all.

"Where is Ed anyway? Sleeping at home?"

"Oh, no, he's up at four o'clock every morning. He wanted to get the pool opened up for summer. With as many leaves as we have on top of that cover, it's gonna be an all day job."

"Least he's not lazy as all get-out like my Grady. Lordy, but that man can lay around. But, anyway, Ed done good with that plate. Such a shame. Sure is a purdy thing. Shines like diamonds," Polly went on. Just as she was about to tell Philma about how Carol Sims' daughter got caught kissing on a black boy at Old Creektown Park, the piano music started. Philma breathed a quiet sigh of relief that she wouldn't have to be subjected to the most recent rumor this morning.

After children's church dismissed and the kids ran back to their parents and grandparents, Philma hung back a second. If they weren't going to use the damn plate her husband had gone through so much trouble to get for them, she'd get it for herself. It surely wasn't stealing if they were the ones that had bought and paid for it and it wasn't even being used! She peeked her head out into the hallway. Everyone had already filed out of the sanctuary and into the bright May sunshine. She tidied up the bits of cotton balls that had fallen while the kids had been making their own "fur" to relate to the Bible story they had discussed. It was convenient that they did these lessons in the fellowship hall—now she had access to the kitchen cabinet where the pastor kept that communion plate (soon to be cheese plate). Quickly, she opened the cabinet under the sink and saw it—not even wrapped in the felt bag it had come in. She could feel herself shaking

Jamie McFaden

her head in disgust.

"Don't be that way. You're in the Lord's house," she whispered to herself. She snatched the plate up and wedged it down in the canvas tote bag.

When she got back home, Philma saw Ed out back by their pool, a can of Busch Light glinting silver in his hand under the sunlight. Without taking the canvas bag off her shoulder, she walked out to where he stood. He had gotten the tarp pulled off the pool quicker than she'd expected. The water wasn't as mucky as it had been last year.

"How was church?" he asked.

"Oh, it was fine. Good turnout of kids today. Got another one of those for me?" she said, pointing at his can of beer. They made sure to buy up enough beer on Saturday to make it through the Blue Law's attempt to dictate a sober Sabbath. For Ed and Philma, it had become tradition to crack a cold one on the warm days of summer right after church let out. Philma didn't see a thing wrong with it, either. After all, Jesus' first miracle had been turning water into wine.

"Of course," Ed answered, turning to walk into the pool house where the fridge was.

"Wait just a second. I've got to show you something," she said, pulling out the communion plate.

"What do you have that for? I got that for the church," he said. She could tell he was more confused than upset.

"Oh, those old men were griping about it being too heavy. They went with a lighter, plastic one instead. I think it's too pretty to just sit under a sink. We can use it for Christmas, anyway."

"Whoever heard of a plastic communion platter? That's just . . ." he paused a moment, thinking of the right word. "It's lackluster is what it is!" he finally exclaimed. He took a sip of his beer.

"You don't mind, do you?" she said.

"Nah, I don't mind. It's their loss. Now, we're big time with our fancy plate."

"I guess we are," said Philma.

Ed walked to the pool house and brought out two more beers. When he walked back to where she stood by the pool, they popped their tabs together, creating a fizzing hiss that reminded Philma of all the times during their first years of marriage when all they could afford was cheap beer. Just silver cans and each other—that's all they'd ever really had back then. Their penchant for both had managed to stick. Ed wrapped his arm around her shoulders as they stared out into the blue-green pool water, sipping Busch Lights in the Sunday afternoon heat.

Jamie McFaden holds her M.A. in English with a focus on creative nonfiction from the University of Alabama-Birmingham. She has called Birmingham home for most of her adult life, but hails from the speed bump on the way to the beach otherwise known as Eufaula, Alabama. Jamie has had articles published in Birmingham Home and Garden, Sense Magazine, Mobile Bay Monthly, *and* Alabama Seaport *and her flash fiction has been published in* Cease, Cows *and* #thesideshow. *A former Thomas H. Brown Scholarship recipient, she deems her family's Southern-fried dysfunction the best possible source material. When she's not in the word vortex, Jamie can be found teaching ballet barre fitness classes or seeking out the newest food trucks and mixology bars in the Magic City.*

Jamie McFaden

Flight of Angels

Mary Elizabeth Murphy

The story is loosely based on my Aunt Gene (Geneva), mom (Berniece), and grandparents. Aunt Gene was considered a rebel in her time, who dared to live life to the fullest and despised hypocrisy. She was a teacher and principal for many years, eventually discovering she made a great deal more money working for the railroad. Aunt Gene quit teaching and moved to New Orleans, living there the rest of her life.

The colored preacher refused to visit during daylight hours, walk the long gravel drive from the road between fields, or use the front door of the Simmons place to avoid trouble for them, a white family known for kindness to all. Such boldness would have been frowned upon in rural Marion County in Alabama, and generally the entire nation, in 1935. Not on this farm anytime, but especially on this Saturday morning, when the sun had already cleared the horizon. A time considered late for farmers and early for the sick. Leading mule teams and wagons of his congregants, they had come to show God's love to those who practiced mercy, when others had failed.

Rapping on the screen door, Reverend James heard the footsteps of Geneva on the other side. She, twenty-two and the oldest, and Berniece, the youngest, were the only ones in the family without the malaria. All the rest—Mr. and Mrs. Simmons, the three boys and three girls were fevered.

As Geneva opened the door and stepped outside, the church women begin to file by with platters and pots of food, along with mops, buckets, brooms, and rags for cleaning. The female elder, Mrs. Norwood, led the procession. "Gene, we're dressed and ready for work. You go on out on the porch and take a break. We've brought hot coffee and I'll bring you some in just a minute."

Stunned, the school teacher could barely speak as the Lord's servants passed, each stopping to say "Good Morning" along with various phrases of endearment, from "Love You" to "It will be all right." Hugs and occasional cheek kisses with Geneva, their balancing whatever container of food. Three middle-aged men stood beside the minister, waiting for the ladies to enter, then followed saying good morning and shaking hands. When the spring on the screen door pulled it shut, Geneva turned to the preacher. "What in the hell have you done? Mama and Poppa are going to have a fit. They don't do charity."

Reverend James pulled the left strap of his faded overalls a little further over on his shoulder. "I keep praying for God to do something with that mouth. By the way, Yvonne told me to send her love and she'll be by tomorrow with the next bunch of people. She and some of the others are sitting with the children—ours and the members, over at the church. We all decided this was a work day, but the children needed a play day. So there are all types of championships going on—checkers, horseshoes, and baseball."

James turned and started walking away, with Geneva following him down the porch toward the steps. "Adam, now…"

"There will be someone here all week for the house and fields. I don't have time to stand here and listen." James held the step rail as he walked down, petting the old mama dog with hanging tits at the foot of the steps, having never barked and wagging its tail. "You're welcome, Gene."

Geneva stood on the porch and looked at the twenty or so men working the fields. The food crops—peas, beans, tomatoes, okra, and especially the corn had to be brought in, along with the first rows of cotton ready. The realities of the Great Depression made the foolishness of pride even more dangerous. Watching as the men moved between rows and started gathering, Geneva realized how close to destitute they all were.

Just then, she heard Mrs. Norwood speaking to her. "Gene, I just went ahead and put cream and sugar in your coffee." Turning, she found the woman with two of the everyday cups, chipped and cracked around the rims. She handed Geneva the lighter colored one, before sitting down in one of the dozen rockers scattered across the house length porch, all rooms side by side and with screen doors to cool.

"Gene, we're going to sit here a while and visit. The men are bathing the men and changing sheets, while some of the women are doing the same for your mama and the girls. As soon as they're all finished, we'll

Mary Elizabeth Murphy

start up the laundry. Did you know Rex is already shadowed lip? In another year, he'll be shaving. He might be the youngest brother, but I think he's going to be the hairiest."

Geneva heard the process of cleaning—dishes being washed, brooms moving across the flowered linoleum, and the harmonizing of spirituals so loved by the congregation and her parents. Mrs. Norwood continued. "I'm so glad the ladies decided to fill their pails with water before we came in. It's like Sister Ag said, 'There's no need to walk by the well and then walk back.' Do you know that stubborn mama of yours was going to try and get out of the bed to help ... and don't even think it yourself."

Geneva smiled as she took a sip of coffee, hating to admit how good it tasted and how good to just rest. After a pause, she looked at Mrs. Norwood. "I'm embarrassed."

The elder laughed and leaned back in her rocker. "I thought you were smarter. Gifts are to be accepted with delight and freedom. You know, like when we get new schoolbooks for all the children every September. Not the fifty-year-old throwaways more tape than cover ... if the school board even remembers to do the ragged. Every fall though, some angel leaves a box at the school door. Our angel's left six regular dictionaries; a Webster's a foot thick and all type of fancy, all grade levels of textbooks, chalk, notebooks, colors and pencils."

Geneva crossed her legs, realizing she hadn't even bothered to put on shoes yet and her red toenail polish shined brightly in the morning light, a growth line of nail barely showing. "Mrs. Norwood, I think that's called a thief."

"Angel gathers all the textbooks back every May. We put them out in a box, just like they came. I think that's called borrowing."

"If I remember my Bible correctly, I do believe Satan was an angel."

Mrs. Norwood took a sip of coffee before answering. "Yes, yes he was. A peacock that so wanted to preen. But our angel is modest and hides ... and is interesting."

"Really?"

"Yeah. Ours drives ... and sometimes weaves back and forth on those center road lines."

"Do tell."

"Uh-huh. Sometimes Angel's walk is a little wobbly … and sometimes it's almost getting up time before feeling the call of home."

Geneva looked down and then back at Mrs. Norwood. "What else about Angel?"

The elder looked at the fields where the men were working. "They're doing well. The farm will look like a farm at the end of the day."

"Mrs. Norwood, tell me more about the angel."

She looked back at Geneva. "Sometimes she has a companion that does look like Satan. Good looking, like a movie star … and he can steal a soul and make you glad about it."

"Stars have fire."

Mrs. Norwood laughed, her perfect store-bought teeth pearly white and almost dropping loose, with her covering her mouth to prevent embarrassment. Whipping her lips, the older woman continued. "Yeah, fire can warm … and it can cook. Lord how it makes something so cold so scorching … and it can burn and scar … and kill."

Geneva studied the features of the gray haired woman in front of her, their eyes looking directly at each other.

"Mrs. Norwood, you sound as if you know things."

The woman's face grew serious, the crease between her eyebrows deepening. "We survive this world by knowing … especially if you are of color. When people don't think, really don't think of you being someplace … existing, you can learn a lot. Maids hear a lot at work … serving at teas and dusting at the right times. Fly, my Angel, fly as far and as fast as you can from here. Fly while you still have wings."

Active in the writing community and health field for many years, Mary Elizabeth Murphy is a diverse writer. An English Instructor at the University of South Alabama, she has presented her poetry at the Library of Congress Poetry at Noon Series and the Alabama Book Festival. Her collection of poetry Blama: Sound

Mary Elizabeth Murphy

of the Wounded Word *(Negative Capability Press) dealt with her mother's battle with Alzheimer's and the complex emotions one goes through in the role of caregiver. Mary Elizabeth also published a series of in-depth articles with* Sense *magazine about local health care facilities in Mobile. She has presented academic papers at the United States Air Force Academy, the University of Louisville, and Marquette University. She is now in the editing process of her next collection of poetry.*

How Do You Do, Mister Cat?

Sena Jeter Naslund

When a black cat crossed the path of my somewhat superstitious aunt, she would politely say, "How do you do, Mister Cat?" My story title derives from her gentle effort to defuse the possibility of bad luck. Originally published as a short story in the Georgia Review, *this piece later became a chapter in my second book, a novel,* The Animal Way to Love. *The character Wanda has come home to Alabama after resigning as a professor of botany in order to protest her university's unfair treatment of another faculty member. "Mister Cat" is a rather philosophical story partly about the problem of evil: how do we account for it and how should we respond to its existence? Wanda tries to extend sympathy to others, even at her own expense, but where does one draw the line? She experiences a spiritual conflict between her fundamentalist upbringing and a broader sense of spirituality rooted in the natural world and aesthetics.*

I, Wanda, wanted to know at an early age if there was a moral order, to the universe. That there was some sort of order was as clear to me as a sliced onion. I remember the paring knife and the sound of the blade slicing through raw food, and my mother, mischievous and merry, glancing down through her bifocals at me. She held matching onion halves, exposing their order, in front of my eyes and nose and said, "If we planted this, all these fleshy layers would nourish the little plant in the center." I smelled the fleshy layers—stacked together, translucent, white, juicy—my nose and eyes turning juicy, too.

"Tulips are like this," she said, "and lilies, and all true bulbs." Her hands were dusted with flour.

It meant that things were planned.

And now I am home again, a jobless adult—and I witness the special order that my parents have imposed on this land. Their garden steps down in terraces, each level lush with vegetables. The adopted children usually work in couples among the crops. Now I can see Laura whose spine is fused, lying on a platform nimbly weeding onions. Could she marry? I see no reason why her disability would preclude sexual union.

Onions can be hoed between the rows, but in the row you must weed by hand. Billy who is pulling the platform has no fingers, but rounded nubbins, like peas, the buds of fingers that never grew.

From my thinking chair on the back porch, I can see the blind twins: albinos, almost sixteen. Terry and Gerry wear short-sleeved, blue-plaid shirts, and they are pushing twin wheelbarrows. Most teenage girls, even a woman like myself, would think them attractive; they are tall and well-muscled; their pink faces and white hair are ultra-vivid; someone who painted portraits in acrylics would be fascinated by them. They are building a path, and Bridget, the little humpbacked girl, directs them.

When I look at Bridget, at any of these children, I want to pray. Most of the time now I have no belief in God, let alone in the efficacy of prayer. Yet sometimes I have religious moments, and they surprise me, flame suddenly, like a burning bush on a bleak and natural hillside.

Here in Alabama, I can continue the project that I started at the university. It is June, and nothing keeps me from continuing to think of my research. My present project involves the production of a gargantuan rose hip, and it will have genetic implications for apples which are of the same family. It is a project that pleases me more than any other that I have worked on because it combines so perfectly the considerations of aesthetics and nutrition, of beauty and of goodness. When I look at my rose hips, I think of the clay fertility dolls with the exaggerated buttocks that primitive people revered.

A beautiful deaf child—a boy who is part Japanese, part black—helps to tend my roses. He is ten years old, a child with no sexual identity, at the height of childhood. The deaf child is kneeling before the oldest rose— *Rosa gallica*. He works with no shirt on, and he wears a smooth steel cross on a chain around his neck. His eyes are very quick. Now, when I lift my hand to wave at him, he sees me and drops the pruning shears, smiles at me and waves. His waving hand looks like the bill of a bird, of a brown crane opening and shutting its mouth. Now he goes back to work, and I can see from the way that he tucks his chin down and holds up his bare chest that he is pleased to have been noticed. Derek is my favorite of these children.

This terraced garden is like a purgatory, but the children can never be purged of their handicaps. It is time to stop thinking now. The long red wave of the setting sun seems to ignite the red of my roses. The purple-red stems of the beets on the top terrace are also glowing, and the purple eggplants gleam like lumps of amethyst. It is a moment without morality, religion, or science. It is a moment of beauty.

A young man named Tom is gathering up the garden tools and trying to balance them over his shoulder. He is really twenty, but he looks older. The lines of his face are always taut because he has cerebral palsy. He does not speak clearly, but he thinks that he has a great sense of humor. I do not especially like him. He lurches along, the spades and rakes and hoes jangling together.

On the bottom terrace, he puts down the tools; he is trying to check the corn. He wants to roll back the shuck near the tip of the ear; he wants to see if the kernels have filled out and if they are soft and full of milk. His hands shake badly and the whole cornstalk is vibrating. It is too early—the silks have not turned brown—but Tom is full of curiosity.

He looks at me with the same curiosity. He wants to handle me, to undress me, to see if I am ready. I hate it when I have to be close to him; I hate it when he puts his shaking hand on my shoulder.

The other children, some holding to each other, are coming up from the terraces along a path. They are singing "Now the Day Is Over."

But the day is not over because after supper, my mother will have them all study. She will help them, and I will be there to answer questions in science.

Supper is miserable because I have to sit next to Tom. Worse, my uncle has been invited from next door to eat with us, and my father is away, as he often is. When I have to look at my uncle, I think, *How do you do, Mister Cat?* As loudly as I can.

I remember my uncle at my father's used car lot:
Come sit in the backseat of this Packard, Wanda Mae. This is real mohair. An old lady had this car, first thing she did with it was cover up the seats. Now just feel that. Good as the day it rolled off the line. Here let me

Sena Jeter Naslund

show you how. Why, I can't even see your little hand under my big hand. Soft as a little bird. Want me to catch you a little pet bird someday? There was one here yesterday on the lot, and I almost caught him, a little robin redbreast, but he scooted right under that Studebaker over there before you could say howdy-do, but I might catch him next time for you, if you would let me run my hand right down here, right in down here where your little tummy is.

With other children, I had been a superb fighter, though thin. I could easily subdue any child I knew. They were afraid of me, and it was only because I didn't like the word *bully* that I restrained myself at all. I wondered if the universe would punish me for my sins, and I found that it did. I observed a moral calculus at work: if I badly assaulted another child, then would I fall into disgrace on the first round of the spelling bee? If I shared candy, would I win later at Monopoly? Yes. Though I believed in this moral order, though I carefully assigned numbers to represent the degrees of guilt and punishment, or kindness and reward, I was still terribly tempted, and from time to time I succumbed to putting my knee in the small-of-the-back of some unsuspecting girl. While she lay on the pavement, I stood over her and laughed nervously. This impulse to bring down other children must have been like the compulsion dogs have with sheep, that my uncle had when his finger tasted the slick place under my skirt.

Where was my father when my uncle lured me into the Packard with the inviolate mohair seats? My father got sudden urges to go on buying trips for the car lot. Sometimes, he picked out a car and took it to Natural Bridge or Moundville, without Mother and me. Now when my faith suddenly flares, I remember how, just so, his urges inspired him to travel or caused his temper to ignite.

I remember being suddenly spanked by my father for what seemed to me to be no reason at all. Dawdling, perhaps. I was sitting in front of the fireplace and slowly eating my grits: I remember yet the fantasy that he interrupted—the pat of butter in the middle was a snowbound house, yellow from lamplight, and my spoon was the snowplow coming to free the family.

Suddenly I was turned upside down, my skirt curtaining my head, and angrily spanked.

I held grudges when these spankings occurred, and sobbed and sobbed. Sometimes the next morning when I woke up, my father would have left a stuffed stocking beside my pillow, as though it were Christmas. His thin maroon sock would be distended with apples and oranges—very old-fashioned presents, I thought, but I knew that, as a boy, he had prized them, so I accepted them and forgave him.

This afternoon, July, I am working again with my roses, with Derek. Sometimes when Derek is not looking at me, I talk to him because I know that he cannot hear me. I try to explain to him, to me, why I am here.

While I am speaking, the quivering shadow of Tom falls across us. He puts his finger under my chin, the tip of his finger jiggles into my flesh; he lifts my face.

I close my eyes. He releases me. I hear a stem snapping. I know he is biting off thorns—he slides the wet stem over my ear, into my hair. He leaves us.

How can I reject his need? I stare stupidly after him as he lurches away.

Derek's eyes are full of rescue. He snatches the blossom from my ear, throws it onto the mulch and stamps on it. Derek would have bitten my uncle when he moved his hand over my bare belly and then down. Derek would have kicked my father when he held me upside down in front of the fireplace with my skirt making a circle of curtain around my head.

At night Bridget with the bowed back comes to my bed and asks, "Please, can I sleep with you?"

I hold my arms out, and she puts her head on my shoulder just as I used to put my head on my mother's shoulder. Bridget lies on her side, with her face turned away from me and her humped back snuggled against my ribs and breast. She asks if I think her hair could grow as long as mine.

I tell her that hers will be nicer because it's already so thick and such a nice color. Her hair is the color of taffy candy, thick, slightly crinkly, and cropped short.

She says, "Let's pretend that your hair is my hair."

I bring my hair around so that it lies over the side of her head and

Sena Jeter Naslund

down her body. She draws her knees up, and I spread my hair over her knees, too, so that she is enveloped in a cocoon of hair. She strokes the round of her knee, overlaid with my hair, and I hope that it feels silky to her.

She says that she is a princess now, and Terry and Gerry are building a road to her castle that will take exactly one hundred years.

Then I have a vision of my own, and I tell it to Bridget.

I see myself living in a little dugout house. We could dig it into the side of the hill, below the roses and beside the vegetable terraces. The dugout will have a many-faceted glass roof. At night, when I lie in bed, I will look up through the glass at the stars. I will live in the center of a giant eye, whose socket is the earth.

When Trixie, my friend who still teaches at the university, writes to me, she only wants to know one thing: exactly why I resigned my job. When I think of my lost job now, my tears fall in warm splatters across my knuckles. I lift my hair from Bridget's back to dry my face, but the hair sticks to my cheek and has nothing of the absorbency of cloth.

Bridget asks, "Why are you so sad?"

I lie and say, "I'm not sad."

Bridget says, "Are you afraid you'll have to marry Tom?"

"Yes," I answer.

"Then we could all be your children forever," she says happily.

But it is not possible to be anyone's child forever, I remind myself.

This morning Billy is pulling Laura's platform, and she is lying so that she can scatter 10-10-10 fertilizer on the vegetables, their August side-dressing. Billy suddenly arches over and unfastens his harness with his teeth. He walks to Laura's box of fertilizer and plunges the nubbins of his fingers into it. She understands at once and rubs the fertilizer over his tiny, stunted arms.

The other children see this, and they drop their tools. They run to bathe in the fertilizer. Sharon rubs it on her mulberry birthmark; Kimberly rubs it on her shins between the straps of her braces; Doraldo rubs himself all over, a cloud of dust covering his ugliness, and he rubs Bridget's hump so vigorously that he shoves her down. Gerry and Terry are holding their full wheelbarrows and calling to Bridget to find out what is happening. Derek is kneeling among my roses but he stretches his back and neck to see. The steel cross gleams on his brown chest. He looks quickly at me, and I shake my head *No*. He tosses his hair like a raven's wing and bends over the roses again.

Tom runs to them shouting, "Yaw top it. T-T-Top it!"

Tom is an adult. He has given up the wild hope that some miracle will pass over him, will baptize him with immaculate selfhood.

As much as these children, when I was a child I felt the need to be given a second chance at being a child.

I knew my soul was besmirched, misshapen. When another child offered to take me to "Happy Hour," a children's Bible class, I approached the meeting with my heart full of hope. I was greeted by Mrs. Jones whose gray hair was in pin curls, fastened with crossed bobbie pins; she had the serene face of a saint.

I knelt on the gray concrete of her basement floor, and the bench in front of me was gray with the same paint. The basement was hushed with gray. Kneeling in front of me was Linda Brady whose red-plaid dress was buttoned down the back with three tiny heart-shaped buttons. I wanted to have those buttons. I wanted to pull them right off Linda Brady's dress and leave the thread dangling. But we were praying not to be tempted. Was it wrong to pray in Jesus' name when I didn't understand yet?

There was a girl who stole a doll, Mrs. Jones told us. A rag doll stuffed with corn. The girl was afraid that if they found her with the doll she would be punished so she dug a hole in Mexico and buried the doll beside a bush. During the long winter she forgot the doll, and the ground beside the bush was covered with snow. But in the spring, up came the corn, and everyone saw. They saw the green corn spring up in the shape of a doll.

So because a corn doll grew up, green as guilt, in Mexico, because my nervous hands wanted to assault, I knelt in the basement and said those simple words that promised relief: Please forgive me for my sins. I am heartily sorry. Please forgive me, please. I believe that Jesus is the son of God.

Sena Jeter Naslund

And I felt saved.

But Jesus was not part of either the order of the onion or the arithmetic of moral order that I had found to exist relentlessly. I had given up both my mother's botanical order and the faceless calculus that I had discovered, for Mrs. Jones and Jesus. I did not want my mother with her merry glasses to know of my new piety. At home I prayed in the bathroom. There the small, white octagonal tiles were cold under my knees and the altar rail of the bathtub was cold against my forehead.

Sometimes, I prayed: Help me, O Lord, to speak out.

Now I have spoken out to my colleagues in the botany program, and after the speaking out came the deed of resignation. But speech and deed have left me only this misery of isolation and the faces of orphans for colleagues.

Now, as in Mrs. Jones's gray basement, I have radically changed my life: it is my own root—no, all that I have grown to be, stem and branch— from which I sever myself.

After my salvation, familiar objects became signs. In the kitchen, Mother's tomatoes in the quart jars looked like a collection of hearts. I knew I should collect hearts for Jesus. I should lead others to the basement to be cleansed of sin and then offer their hearts to God. Through the glass sides of the jars you could still see the nourishing veins. Store up treasure for yourself, not here on earth—where moth and rust doth corrupt—but in heaven. When my first period came, it was like a rust stain on the crotch of my panties.

Once my parents were sitting at the kitchen table and playing a card game they had invented themselves. On the table was a mixing bowl full of diamond-shaped baklava. All day, on every flat surface in the house, finally even on waxed paper on the floor, my mother had rolled out the thin layers. Now the honey oozed through the layers, and they ate pastry while they played, licking their fingers to keep the cards clean.

I sat on a stool and watched them. I had eaten as much of the baklava as I wanted. I said it reminded me of stained glass.

The room was quiet except for the shudder of the refrigerator going on and off. Out in the driveway, four used cars were lined up like a train in the dark.

"Do you know how stained glass is made?" my father asked me.

"Let's add a checker board," my mother said.

A slow smiled curled on my father's face: "All right." He got the board and the pieces, chanked them through his fingers. "Read about stained glass," he told me.

I went into the dark living room where the encyclopedia was kept. At the end of the alphabet was my Bible. I stroked its soft spine and whispered, "How do you do, Mister Cat?"

Then I pulled down *G* from the encyclopedia and found the *glass* place as I walked back toward the lighted kitchen. It was a Friday night, and the tires of some rowdy teenager's hotrod caterwauled on the asphalt. I was having my period and I felt dizzy.

"Let's see," my father said. He quickly glanced at the article. "It's not too long. Read it out loud." I climbed up on the stool and leaned my back against the refrigerator.

"There ought to be colored illustrations for stained glass," said my mother.

"Grocery-store encyclopedia," he responded.

He turned over a nine of clubs and skipped a checker across the board.

I began to read: "'Stained glass is like the blood of Christ. It suffuseth the church with its power; it sufficeth for thee. In troubled water I will send my glass.'"

Both my parents jumped up. They stood close to me on either side of the stool, like judges. My father took my shoulders in his hands; his face, swinging into mine, seemed to be breaking like dried honey: "Wanda Mae, darling, what's the matter?"

I hung my head. A tear dropped onto the article, and I closed the book. I remember my mother got an ice pack and put it on my forehead. She put me to bed by myself.

I turned my face to the wall where I had written my name in red lipstick before I found Christ and goodness. *I layeth my face turned to my name which I maketh when I was little.*

The printing looked like a smear of greasy blood. I held up my hands

Sena Jeter Naslund

and with the Friday light coming through my bedroom window, I made the shadow of a bird swoop across my name. A black bird had flown in front of the Packard. My uncle had pointed at it through the windshield with his bloody finger. On my bedroom wall, I made the shadow of a rabbit. Then a howling dog.

Big as a house, Mister Cat came to me in the night. He stood over me and I lay between his four feet on the ground. Like trees, his black-fur legs soared up.

When I got out of bed in the morning I saw that some of my blood was on the sheet, and the marks looked like the print of a giant cat's paw.

That Saturday my father came home from the lot at noon for lunch. While he made himself a peanut butter and jelly sandwich, he said, "Tomorrow I want us all to go to church."

My mother must have known already; she just said, "All right, Horace."

When the altar call was made, I willed my parents to go forward, but they did not. This was not the true Basement Church, but it was better than none. Afterward, we had a big noon dinner, like other people who have gone to church, and before we ate, my father said grace. His voice sounded like he knew what he was talking about, as surely as the minister.

But my mother wouldn't eat the Sunday dinner, though she had cooked it. She took a spoonful of grape jelly—it stood on her toast like a tiny stained-glass mountain. With the back of her spoon, she spread a purple stain over the toast as though this were any breakfast instead of Sunday dinner.

It is almost September, and, thanks to neighbor Babiak's backhoe, my dugout house has become a reality. The room is dug into the hillside, and the roof is a geodesic dome, each section an equilateral triangle of acrylic. I have sunlight, moonlight, starlight, my kerosene lamp. The room is not wired for electricity. I have left the earthen walls in the back uncovered, and my place is rather like a monk's cell. I think of Mendel, who, after all, was a monk, who taught high school, and who had no place in the university—he couldn't pass the exams in botany any more than I could pass their test for institutional immorality. I have even planted some peas in front of my place, and I will repeat Mendel's experiment that led to the rules for the occurrence of dominant and recessive genes.

It is very quiet here in my dugout room in the evening, but I can hear someone walking on the terraces. From his lurching gait and the clanking tools, I know it is Tom. I feel afraid and hope he will go away.

The light from my kerosene lamp throws my shadow on the back of my cave. I can see the orange color of a root that was skinned in the excavation. I like it that my wall gives me a cross-section of the roots, of underground.

With the geodesic dome, it is easy to imagine that I am inside the world of a miscroscope. The stars examine me.

My floor is a smooth layer of white sand. I have one large rock in here, as a decoration, and I have planted a fern in one of its cavities: *Polystichum acrostichoides*, the evergreen Christmas fern. I have a table that Tom made for me; it is rough boards nailed together. He wanted to smooth and paint it, but I wouldn't let him.

The front of my den is made of earth bricks. I have a board door barred with a heavy wooden arm. I have visitors at my door.

Not Tom, but my favorites come, Bridget and Derek. They bring me a bouquet of my apothecary roses.

Bridget says, "We saw Tom walking on the terrace."

Derek mimics Tom's walk, pretends he is carrying tools over his shoulder. I should reprimand Derek for his cruel imitation of Tom, but I put my hand lovingly on his shoulder.

Bridget says, "Tom's started to smoke."

Derek puffs at an imaginary cigarette, mocking Tom's gesture of adulthood.

I hug them both and turn them toward my door. "Run fast as rabbits back to the hutch," I say.

I love the silence they have left.

Looking only at the roses, I know that I cannot resist their order. My heart turns into a rose, and I am grateful to God who has made such beauty.

Their color is bruised rose red, their stamens golden and gathered in the center in a crown. Not only is God there, but all the universe is

Sena Jeter Naslund

centered in this color and perfume.

It is the moment of the burning bush—it flares! And goes out.

The night my father came home a converted man was the October I became fourteen. We hadn't turned the furnace on yet, so I had suggested to my mother that I build a small fire in the fireplace in the living room. She sat in her rocking chair close to the fire, but she was still chilly, and I got her one of the quilts she had made and bundled it around her.

For a moment I went back into our kitchen, and I could hear my uncle next door calling in a forlorn voice, "Kitty kitty kitty." I knew he was standing on his back porch and holding the chipped blue china bowl with milk in it.

When I came back from the kitchen, my father was kneeling beside my mother with his head down in the quilt on her lap. I had not heard him come in, but there was a fresh October smell in the room as though the door had been opened.

She was looking down at him, sadly, not touching him; her plump arms hung down on each side of the rocking chair.

He lifted his red face to me and said that his life was changed. He said that his faith had been reborn. He said that he would study and work to become a full-time evangelist for Christ. At the first moment, I felt joy sweep over me. I knelt at our hearth and prayed with him. Soon I felt like a foreigner.

At breakfast my mother told me that we were going to adopt some children. She said that that had been part of my father's message from God. He was to be a traveling preacher. She and I would take care of the adopted children while my father was on the road.

My mother does not move quite as briskly now, but really she is just the same as before the other children came. They are handicapped, but she has kept them busy working in the vegetables on the slope. She had the children build the garden terraces. They did it by hand, like the Indians used to do, carrying the earth in baskets. There are always ten children. Now they are Derek, Bridget, Billy, Laura, Sharon, Kimberly, Doraldo, Terry, Gerry, and Tom. When one becomes twenty-one and is self-sufficient, he or she must leave home, and another child or teenager is adopted. Any of us can come back to visit any time.

Tom will not be twenty-one till the day after Christmas. I think he will be glad. I know he wants to be a man—officially, if the world will not grant his palsy any other maturity. Here in late summer, he stares at me and watches me. I can see that he is working up to something. While he stares, he tries to move his jaw, silently exercises his tongue.

My father has changed. When he sold used cars, he was a mild, quixotic person, except for the surges of bad temper. Now he is a flashy dresser, and his complexion is permanently florid. He is full of gusto and enthusiasm. When he preaches, he stabs the air with a finger that is so red it is almost purple. He has turned the business over to his brother to manage.

Yesterday, when I walked past the used-car lot, my uncle crooked his finger at me and said, "Come here, Wanda."

I shouted at him, "How do you do, Mister Cat?" I would not set foot on the lot alone.

I find that my own religion changed slowly in a vague way. When I went to college, I become more and more interested in botany. Imperceptibly my zeal for Christianity was converted into a zeal for work with plants. For a while I prayed with a green tomato clenched in each fist.

Good work must be done: no matter under what banner.

I think that I can get a job here teaching high school. I believe that I am at peace about leaving the university. I have buried personal ambition beside some bush.

Still, I have strange dreams of metamorphosis: my father has turned into my uncle; my mother and my uncle are standing in a field of lavender thistles, and he is lewdly stroking her forearm with a pudgy finger. In my dream, I am not in my cell but back on the porch sitting in my thinking chair.

Now we are well into fall and thinking of winter. I sit in my cell with my kerosene lamp, and I warm my fingers against the chimney from time to time. If I go to my door, I can see that only pumpkins are left on the terraces, shelved on the next-to-the-top level, where they seem to glow.

Sena Jeter Naslund

And I can see down the dark terrace steps to the meadow, and across the meadow to the other side which is far enough away so that the light from Babiak's square window looks round.

The summer is over now, and I feel like a creature who ought to migrate, but where to go? The high school did not need another botany teacher here. My rose-hip studies have not gone well, but I have roses in my cell. I am giving a party in my cell.

Here are the purple and lavender roses—Heirloom, Angel Face, Paradise. In the old orange-juice bottle are some of the reds—Mister Lincoln, Crimson Glory, Christian Dior. The white roses sit in fluted milkglass on the rock above the fern: John F. Kennedy, Evening Star. And the yellow roses, here on the table next to me and next to the yellow glow of the kerosene lamp: Oregold, Golden Showers, New Day. Derek has picked so many for me because tonight may be first frost.

Tom came to my cell tonight and asked me to marry him. His face looked carved in the lamplight, and the words seemed articulated by a hinge. I was not afraid, though he knelt down on the sand and pressed his head against my rock. I told him that he should work and become self-supporting, and then he should marry Sharon whose face is splashed with the mulberry birthmark. It was wrong to name Sharon, but this was a right thing to do, at least: to say No to Tom. I know that my flesh was not made for the nourishment of his flesh; my pity for him is not love. I will celebrate my No with a party, and he is invited.

My uncle also stood at the door of my cell and knocked. I went out to him and talked with him though I have shunned him for twenty years. He asked me why did I shout and call out across the lot at him, *Mister Cat?* I told him because he had made me afraid when I was a child. He pressed his hands together and could not speak. I believed that he wanted to say that he was sorry, that he was ashamed. He didn't know why he had treated me that way. Then I held him in my arms and kissed his cheek.

And this was a right thing, to say Yes to my uncle, Yes I forgive you. Because I was not guilty, any more than these children are deserving of their afflictions, I forgive you.

Because summer is over, I have invited all the children and my parents and my uncle to come to my cell tonight. They will be here soon and will bring cushions and sit on the sand. My mother will bring hot fresh bread, and my father will play card tricks. Finally we will turn out the kerosene lamp and watch the stars beyond my clear roof. We have discovered that Bridget has a beautiful voice, and we will say softly, one and then another, "I wish you'd sing for us," and "Please, Bridget, do sing," and "Sing now, Bridget," and "Stand here, in the center, and sing."

Sena Jeter Naslund grew up in the Norwood area of Birmingham and graduated from Norwood Elementary, Philips High School, and Birmingham-Southern College. After teaching Latin, French, and English at E.B. Irwin High School, Centerpoint, she studied at the Iowa Writers' Workshop, earning the Ph.D. Having taught at the Universities of Montana, Indiana, and Louisville, and in Alabama as a Montevallo University Vacca Professor and a University of Alabama-Huntsville Distinguished Eminent Scholar, she founded and continues to direct the low-residency MFA in Writing at Spalding University, Louisville, where she edits The Louisville Review *and the Fleur-de-Lis Press. She received the Alabama and Southeastern Library Awards for Fiction, the Harper Lee Award for Fiction, the Hall-Waters Prize from Troy University, and a 2011 Alabama Governor's Arts Award; most recently she was inducted in 2015 to the Alabama Writers' Hall of Fame. Sena is the author of nine books, including* Ahab's Wife; Four Spirits *(set in Birmingham during the Civil Rights Movement); and* Abundance: A Novel of Marie Antoinette. *Her fiction has been translated and published in eleven foreign countries. In recent years, she has enjoyed residing and writing at Wolfe Cottage in Fairhope, Alabama, and she is on the Advisory Board of Negative Capability publishers, in Mobile. She is currently at work on an American Civil War novel.*

Something Temporary

Jennifer Paddock

My story is based on my time working in Washington for Senator Dale Bumpers from Arkansas. Senator Bumpers (DB we called him) was amazing, always fighting for the underdog, and that spirit ran through the office. Everyone working for him wanted to do good. This story is more specifically about the first time my heart was broken. I guess enough time has passed—about twenty-four years—that I can admit that it's mostly true. The person who broke my heart has remained a friend, remained an advocate for the world's poor, so I believe his heart was true. We were just young, and we did have bad timing. His favorite writer was Raymond Carver, and then Carver became my favorite writer, and I remember reading Will You Please Be Quiet, Please? *at my desk and feeling like such a rebel. I moved back home to Arkansas shortly after and took my first creative writing class. About eight years after that, my novel,* A Secret Word, *was published, and this story was a chapter. I happened to be in Washington for my book when former staff members were having a reunion dinner for the senator. And I got to go. I remember shaking hands with Senator Bumpers outside the restaurant. He said to me, "Jennifer, I read your book. I had no idea."*

This is the first time Scott Foster has ever talked to me. I'm sitting at my desk in the mailroom, sorting letters for Senator Blair, the senior senator from Arkansas, when Scott hooks his hands around the door frame and leans in. "Do you want to go to the Senate floor?" he says. "I have to meet the Senator, and since you're new to the office, I thought you'd like to come with me."

Scott seems so cool, relaxed. He's wearing a softly wrinkled shirt with the sleeves rolled up. I feel his eyes looking me over. "Yeah. Sure," I say.

We take a subway only for senators and their staff from the basement of the Dirksen Building to the Capitol. We flash our IDs to an elevator operator, then to a woman at the cloakroom where the Senator is waiting for us. Scott hands him a chart and some papers. I shake the Senator's hand. "Good to see you, Chandler," the Senator says. He turns to Scott. "I know her father, Ben Carey. She comes from good stock." I smile. I picture my father in his lawyerly suit and wire-rimmed glasses. I am glad the Senator thinks of me as my father's daughter. I want to say something about my father or growing up in Arkansas or at least about my best friend, Sarah, his niece, who got me the job. I just want to say something, but I freeze. I feel scared and elated being so close to the Senator. He smiles at me and puts a hand on Scott's shoulder and says, "Scott, my old boy."

On the way back from the Capitol, on the Senate subway, Scott sits across from me. He leans toward me, looking into my eyes. It's something the Senator does, something all politicians do, part of their magic. They look at you like you're the most important person in the world, but Scott is telling me about his girlfriend. And I almost believe he's talking about me.

He and his girlfriend are going to travel through Asia for six months. She's already quit her job and is living with her parents in Connecticut. He's quitting his in a month.

Ever since reading *The Ice Storm*, a novel set in Connecticut, I've been intrigued with the place, and Scott says that both he and his girlfriend grew up there. I imagine him coming from an upper class Northeastern family, living in a tasteful house in a clean and rustic neighborhood, taking the train into New York City.

In the mailroom, the fax machine always hums, voices rattle. It's easy to fall into a daze opening, stapling, and sorting envelopes. I touch Scott's name on his box and trace each letter with my finger. I like how the two T's feel connected.

The Senator said I came from good stock, which I guess is true. I went to college at Sewanee and majored in English, and I'm a good writer. The administrative aide, who hired me upon Sarah's recommendation, told me I was overqualified for the mailroom, but if I worked hard, then I could move up to legislative correspondent. It was just a matter of someone leaving.

I start dropping by Scott's office, which is not much bigger than a cubicle. There's a small TV in the corner, and taped on the walls are quotes in his own writing and a map of the world. I find any excuse to talk to him, acting interested in his issues. He's the housing aide and is working on a rural homeless bill.

"You'd be surprised," he says. "They're living in chicken coops, under

Jennifer Paddock

overpasses. There are no funds for the rural homeless."

Scott eats lemon drops from a package on his desk.

I reach for one in a casual way and look at one of the quotes taped to the wall.

He who learns must suffer. And even in our sleep, pain that cannot forget falls drop by drop upon the heart, and in our own despair, against our will, comes wisdom to us by the awful grace of God.

"Do you like that?" Scott says. "That's the ancient Greek playwright, Aeschylus."

"I do," I say, but I'm embarassed that I've never heard of Aeschylus. I look at the map and finish off my lemon drop. "I'd like to go to Indonesia."

He looks at me and smiles. "You should go."

I fold my arms across my chest and shift my hips to one side, swaying slightly. "I still haven't really seen Washington. I've only been to museums and receptions on the hill. I don't even know anyone who's not a staffer."

"I know a lot of great places," he says. "Have you been to Garret's? It's kind of a neighborhood bar in Georgetown."

"No." I take another lemon drop and pop it in my mouth, then look his way. "Would you want to go there for a drink after work?"

For a moment, he cocks his head at me. "Yeah, okay," he says. "Okay."

Garret's is crowded, and Scott and I sit at the bar. We drink gin and tonics and listen to the Stones' Hot Rocks CD playing on the jukebox. I want to talk to him about work, but it's too loud for a real conversation.

After our third drink, he rubs his hand on my wrist. "So, what do you think, Chandler?"

"It's great," I say. My head feels light. I'm leaning close to him, my leg brushes against his. "Georgetown's a great neighborhood. Do you live near here?"

"I live back by the Capitol. Do you want to go there?"

That isn't really what I'm asking, but it's what I want to happen.

He makes a move to leave.

I put a hand on his leg. "Do you like your job?"

"Of course," he says. "I'm afraid to leave. I've worked hard on that bill for three years. I want it to pass."

"Do you think I could do your job?"

He pauses a moment and shrugs. "Maybe."

In his bathroom, I notice a ponytail holder and a red barrette on the floor behind the toilet. I look under the sink and find an empty box of Tampax and a woman's disposable razor.

He waits for me in the bedroom. A pair of running shoes and a headband are sitting on top of a big cardboard box marked Claire. "Who's Claire?" I ask. But I know who she is.

"My girlfriend," Scott says.

"She's a runner?"

"Yeah, marathons."

He pulls me toward him and kisses my neck, then my mouth. I feel his tongue, soft and wide, and a shuddering passes through me. We move onto the bed. In a quick sweep, he has my blouse off my shoulders and my skirt and underwear down, moving them off my ankles. I open my legs, and he pushes himself inside, making me jerk at the suddenness. My eyes are open, but I can't look at him. My gaze is fixed on the running shoes and headband on top of the brown box. I imagine Claire in a warm-up suit watching us, her head tilted to one side, crunching on an apple.

Scott strolls into the mailroom the next morning as if nothing has happened. "Hey, Chandler. How are you doing back here?"

I keep my head bowed and slice open an envelope.

"Do you want to go downstairs for some coffee?" he says.

After I left him last night, it was late and dark and nobody was on the street. I was afraid walking alone, not quite sure where I was going until seeing the dome of the Capitol and knowing Union Station was not too far away, and I could get a cab there to take me home.

"No, thanks," I say.

"How about lunch?"

I clutch the stack of letters in front of me. My hands feel wet.

He says, "We could go to Union Station."

"Listen," I say in a soft voice. "You don't owe me anything." I turn around in my chair to look him in the eyes, like politicians do. I want to let him off the hook if he wants to be off the hook. "It was my fault as much as yours. We both had too much to drink."

Jennifer Paddock

He looks away from me, though doesn't turn his eyes completely away, as if he were studying the part in my hair.

"Don't worry," I say. "I won't tell anyone what happened."

Scott leans over me. His voice is soft, too. Everyone in the office knows about Claire. "I had a good time last night. I like you. I've been thinking about you all morning." He runs his hand down my arm. "Did you have a good time with me?"

I nod.

He smiles in a sly way. "So how about lunch?"

"No. I don't think I'll have time. Too much mail."

He looks down at his shoes. "Are you doing anything tonight?"

I say, "I don't know." And I don't know what I want.

"After work we could get take-out and rent a movie."

"Well," I say. I *love* movies. "If I can pick the movie."

He smiles. "Deal," he says, and my eyes stay on the doorway after he leaves. I think about the evening before, riding with Scott past the White House. The sun was setting, a yellow glow between us.

In front of Scott's apartment, a homeless man asks Scott for change. Scott doesn't give him any, but he speaks to him, saying he's sorry.

"I can't afford to give them money every time they ask. But I always talk to them," he says. "So they know they're alive."

I'm not sure how to respond. He sounds condescending, like many members of my country club back home talk to the black people who serve them. But I know he has good intentions.

Scott lights candles, opens red wine, and we eat Thai food (my first time, but I don't tell him that). After dinner, watching my favorite Woody Allen movie, *Hannah and Her Sisters*, I lie on the couch, and Scott sits in the chair and laughs in all the right places. The first time this has happened for me on a date.

"Do you want some more wine?" he says.

I run my fingers through my hair. "Please."

He takes my empty glass and goes into the kitchen.

"Hurry up," I say.

He yells over, "Nobody, not even the rain, has such small hands," a line from an e.e. cummings poem that is a line in the movie.

I answer with another line in the movie, "If Jesus ever came back and saw what was going on in his name, he'd never stop throwing up."

"Yeah, I love that actor. He's in a lot of Bergman films."

"Max Von Sydow," I say, feeling smart.

"That's good," he says. He hands me a full glass and leans toward me and stops smiling to kiss me.

I pull away.

He bends down on one knee. He looks at me. "I thought about you all day."

"You did? How so?"

"We only have one month," he says. "I don't want to waste a single minute."

In his bed, after making love, he rubs my back. His hands move down my arms, then again to my shoulders.

"I'm nervous about the trip," he says. "I don't know how I'm going to act with Claire."

"What does Claire look like?"

He moves to get up. "I don't know."

I grab his shoulder and pull him next to me. "What does she look like?"

"She's tall with long, brown hair," he says.

I lift my head up from the pillow and turn toward him. "Tell me about her."

"She's a lot like you. Pretty, intelligent, athletic."

I stretch my legs out as far as I can. My knees lock. I think about walking with my roommate, Stacey, whose legs are much longer. I have to move faster to keep up. "I'm not athletic like Claire's athletic," I say.

"Oh, I thought you were."

"I play tennis. I don't run marathons." I lean back against the pillow. "I used to have long hair. It was to the middle of my back."

Scott closes his eyes. "I love long hair."

We lie still. After a moment, I say, "Send me a postcard."

"Oh, yeah," he says. "I'll send you postcards and gifts all the time. Maybe some jewelry from Bombay. A necklace or something. Or silk pajamas from Singapore."

Jennifer Paddock

When Scott is in the mailroom sending a fax, I feel his eyes wander over my face, my hair, my dress.

He calls me from his desk and tells me to meet him at the water cooler. "I just want to be next to you," he says. "We don't have to talk."

I walk down the long hall, past his office, past the reception area, to the water cooler. I pull a paper cup from the dispenser and wait for him.

I watch the thin blue lines on his oxford shirt as he bends over to fill his cup. I sip my water until he turns to leave, until I feel him brush against my linen blouse. This is what I remember from the beginning: waiting at the water cooler and imagining how the lines on his shirt would feel against my fingers.

Scott and I go to movies he wants to see before he leaves. In the movie theater, my mind doesn't register the images flashing across the screen, and I never hear what the characters say. I turn to Scott, but he looks straight ahead, watching the screen. He's in another world. He doesn't reach for my hand.

At a dark, quiet restaurant, we sit in the corner by a window. Our table is small and round with a white tablecloth. We have already eaten, and our plates have been cleared. A candle fluttering in the center casts off an orange glow, shadowing Scott's face, making it flawless. I hope that mine looks the same. I stare at his brown eyes.

"Do you have to go on the trip?" I say.

"I'm coming back, though. I'll see you when I get back."

I run my fingers along the rim of the glass holding the candle. "What about Claire?"

He looks off a moment. "I don't know."

He reaches for my hand, but I pull away. "You really have to go?"

"We've been planning this for a year. Claire quit her job." His voice grows faint. "You know that, Chandler."

I look at him. "So, is this it?"

He turns from me to look out the window at people walking by in raincoats and under umbrellas. "I really care about you," he says. "We care about each other, right? I'll see you when I get back."

I think about saying, I think I'm in love with you. I could be falling in love with you. I'm scared I might be in love with you.

Outside it's raining, and it seems perfect. Like a scene from a movie. Water will drip down our faces. My mascara will run.

"I love you," I say.

He opens the car door for me. "I love you, too," he says. "We just have bad timing."

The image of Claire looms everywhere. Sometimes I think of her in bed with us, the ridges of her running shoes pressing against my ankles.

After awhile, we stop going out. Scott says he has to save money for his trip. "Every dollar I spend here is forty-six rupees I can't spend in Bombay," he says.

Every day work becomes more tense. Sometimes when I pass him in the hall, he won't look at me. He even turns his shoulders to one side to make sure he doesn't brush against my sleeve. He stops coming back to the mailroom, so I have to take him his letters at the end of the day. He doesn't stop typing when I set them on his desk. But still, each evening we leave together.

I follow him up the stairs to his apartment, my heels clicking against the wooden floor. "Why do you not speak to me all day, but then wait for me after work in the reception area? Why not sneak out the back door? Everyone in the office knows we leave together."

He closes the door behind me. "I don't know. Maybe they think I just give you a ride home."

"I know what they think." My voice is almost a whine, but I can't help it.

Scott paces, staying close to the door. "I'm sorry. I'm just confused. We have to stop sleeping together. I'm sorry. I'm not going to be able to handle it when I see Claire." He stares at me. "I have to spend six months with her."

"Fine. I'll get my things and go home."

"Chandler." He speaks to me with a gentle voice. "Is that all right?"

I nod.

"I'll take you home. I'm sorry. Sorry for everything."

On the way to my house, it starts to rain. He turns on the windshield wipers, but water still runs in rivulets down the front window. The only thing he says to me is that it is hard to see.

Jennifer Paddock

I run up the sidewalk, gripping my bag with yesterday's skirt and blouse and bra and underwear and mail for the Senator that should have been opened. I peer through the screen door, and my roommate Stacey is ironing and watching television. C-Span, of course. I go in.

"Chandler Carey," she says. "Finally coming home."

I sort of smile and rake water out of my hair.

"Senator Blair was on the floor today," Stacey says. "He was all alone, giving this impassioned speech to nobody, only to me, watching from the gallery."

I drop my bag and sit on the couch. She's ironing between buttons on a navy dress.

"He was great, going on again about that stupid mining law. Did you know that it dates back to 1872 and was signed by Ulysses S. Grant, intended to entice people to go West and settle?"

She doesn't notice that I'm upset and might cry. She's moving the iron faster than before, with bursts of steam and spraying starch.

"That archaic law permits mining companies to gouge billions of dollars of gold and silver and platinum from public lands without paying one cent to the American people, the real owners, the taxpayers, and we're required to pay billions of dollars to clean up the environmental mess left behind. It's an outrage." She sets the iron on the edge of the board and looks at me. "But I guess you know that."

"I've heard of it," I say. "And sometimes I get mail about it."

"Oh, and you have a letter from your dad, I think," she says.

I walk over to the kitchen table where we keep the mail. The table is actually an old door that Stacey found and sanded and made a base for out of two boards, crisscrossing them, and painted white. It looks pretty good.

"And your mom called again," she says.

I hold the envelope. This is the first letter I've ever gotten from my father. I open it, and there's a check and a short note written on law office stationary.

Dear Chandler,

You got it done! There you are in Washington, D.C. working on Capitol Hill. It fills me with love and pride. Let's you and I try to correspond often. Your news will be more interesting than mine, but that's what happens to old folks. I wish I could swap places with you.

Enclosed is a little walking around money.

Love, Dad

I fold the letter, with the check, back into the envelope. I'm glad he's in Arkansas and not here, seeing the place I'm in.

The next day at work the administrative aide calls me into her office to tell me I will be taking over Scott Foster's job. I will get a big pay increase, and I will have my own office. She tells me Scott has come in several times to talk about me. Scott wants to make sure the rural homeless bill gets passed. Scott doesn't want all his hard work to go to waste. I am smart and care about the issues, Scott has said.

I walk down the corridor, past the water cooler, to Scott's office. I stand just inside the doorway. The walls are bare. He sits in his chair, cleaning out his desk drawers.

He sees me, points at the TV. "There's a chance the rural homeless bill will be up."

I watch for a moment. The Senate chamber is nearly empty. Nobody cares about the bill but him. The Senator isn't there, and the bill is certain to be pushed back until after the August recess.

"I got your job," I say.

He grins, pushing to his feet. "That's great. I knew it would work out." He walks over to me. "You're not going to let me down, are you?"

"No," I say.

He brushes my hair behind my ear. "I'm sorry things got so bad."

"Me, too," I say.

"I want you to take over for me," he says. "You'll be my connection to the office."

Because I have his old job, I have his old connections. Every time I call HUD someone always tells me what a great guy Scott Foster is. I tell them he helped me get this job. "We are close friends," I say. "He's probably trekking in Nepal right now." I'm telling them more than they want to know, but I can't help myself.

A postcard addressed to the entire staff is passed around the office. It's of a man and woman running down a white beach in their bathing suits. A deep blue ocean is in the background. They are holding hands.

Jennifer Paddock

BALI BALI BALI in red letters lines the bottom. "All this and a hut for only five dollars a day. Wish you were here, Claire and Scott." The letters are small and slanted to the left. Scott's writing.

On the corner of 27th and P, I think I see him. A man in a raincoat with his head down. Scott didn't even own a raincoat, but there is a striking resemblance. Barely slumping shoulders. Light brown hair.

I begin to take in a lot of movies. I need them. I pay attention to what the characters are saying, attaching significance to every word, trying to understand what I'm feeling.

When I think back to those weeks, to why I felt what I did, I recall the excitement of not knowing what would happen. I kept thinking that for him, it was just an affair. Something temporary, to fill in time. But for me, it was different, I think. I felt a different way, and it had to do with him, but also with the not knowing. Uncertainty quickens the heart, fools you into believing what could never be true.

At lunch, I walk on the Mall and sit on the edge of the reflecting pool. I see my face in the dappled water, strewn with Popsicle sticks, wrappers, coins. A man sits, maybe twenty feet away, in old clothes with a stack of newspapers and smiles at me, and I smile back.

On the steps of the Capitol, there is a girl wrapped in a green pashmina shawl who's crying, and a guy is down on one knee looking up at her. I can't tell what he is saying, but it's not a *marriage* proposal. He's got the tone of voice of someone trying to make an excuse for something. She's crying hard, not caring who's listening. I have to turn away, and I see the man in old clothes has folded one of his newspapers into a boat and is cradling it with both hands. He is smiling, but not at me, not at anyone.

Jennifer Paddock is the author of the novels A Secret Word, Point Clear, *and* The Weight of Memory. *She received an M.A. in creative writing from New York University, and her short fiction and nonfiction have appeared in* Stories from The Blue Moon Cafe, The North American Review, Other Voices, Garden and Gun, Mr. Beller's Neighborhood, *and* The New York Times. *She lives in Point Clear, Alabama, where she is a tennis pro at The Grand Hotel.*

Jennifer Paddock

313

Good Measure

Wendy Reed

Here's the thing: there was, once upon a time, a rented U-Haul in the parking lot of Bates' House of Turkey in Greenville, Alabama. There was no Mildred, no author writing about his marriage in a book of essays, no Sea Doos, no mistletoe, and no kiss. I made those up, conjured them deliberately, except for the kiss, which happened out of nowhere. I was as surprised as the characters, only I felt disappointed. I fancied myself to have a certain style—Beckett bleak and O'Connor absurd—not Lifetime Channel cheesy. Yet there it was in all its sentimental glory, and despite several revision attempts over several months, I could not make the kiss go away. Finally I declared the story a failure, relegated the file to a folder deep within my computer's hard drive, and gave up. A few years later a Book Arts student asked to use one of my stories for her thesis project—the only criterion was that it had to involve a sea shell, the image she'd designed for the cover, which her advisor had already approved. "Feel free to change the ending," I said when I sent her the story. "I can't seem to get it right." Instead she made 35 copies of a letterpress edition printed on Niddegen mouldmade paper and wrapped in Indian Khadi handmade paper and, as a thank you, gave all but one of the 35 hand-numbered copies to me. Not a single change had been made. I'd like to think there's something more to this story but maybe there isn't. Maybe what's here is what matters. Maybe that is enough.

When I drive to Destin, I like to stop in Greenville and eat at Bates' House of Turkey. If you aren't from the area, Greenville is about an hour south of Montgomery in what we call Harper Lee Country. The famed author still lives in these parts, lending an aura of elegance to the real life Southern Gothic that is live and well. Out back of the restaurant— the emergency exit alarm won't go off though it says it will—two gazebos have gone up so you can eat outside with the flies and smoking employees. Unless it's raining too hard. The roofs leak. Gazebos, like love and underwear, wear out.

Rain, here, is like everything else in the South—unpredictable. Some say it's because of the Gulf of Mexico's close proximity. This area gets the cast-off storms from the hurricanes, storms with just enough time to change into tornadoes as they sweep into the Black Belt, pelting the Black Angus chewing their cud in the pastures, and flooding the catfish ponds. But often these storms forget what season they're suppose to occur in. I worked up quite an appetite driving through one with worn out windshield wiper blades a few Decembers back. I meant to go to Autozone first, to buy refills, but my truck stopped at Bates'.

"Turkey's up," Mildred said. Mildred smiles like Carol Burnett.

I'd plunked myself into one of the rockers at the side of the restaurant and was watching three mockingbirds try to decide whose turn it was to be "it."

"Would you like to eat out here?" Mildred asked. I couldn't think why not, so I said yes.

Have I mentioned that on Sundays the vegetables are candied yams and green limas? Mildred brought my milk first. I like a tall glass of sweet milk with any kind of bean. That's when I noticed the young woman, probably near thirty, though she might have easily been eighteen, get out of a U-Haul. I mean she was the driver, not the passenger, and it was odd to see a little thing like her jump down out of a seventeen-foot rental truck by herself. She wiped her hands down the sides of her jeans and locked the door with the key. She looked at her watch and disappeared inside. I didn't see her again until I was halfway through with my cobbler. She must've ordered the turkey dinner special, too, because she walked like she was full. I watched her unlock the orange door and climb up into the truck. She didn't start the engine. Instead, she wadded something up, probably a sweater or sweatshirt, and wedged it against the window to prop her head. She was settling in for a nap. I myself was in no hurry to hit the interstate again, but I didn't consider Bates' a particularly good place to nap. I usually saved that for the beach. I tipped Mildred $5, three times what I should have, and went to the take-out side of the cash register to order a smoked breast to eat on for the rest of the weekend. I hate to have to go out and fight Destin's restaurant crowds. When I came back, the woman was still there and still napping.

"Mildred, what's that woman doing?" I asked. Mildred drives a moped even in the winter. I believe that gives her psychic powers.

"Sleeping."

That Mildred's quite a seer.

"Yes, but why's she sleeping in the parking lot of a turkey restaurant?"

"I've never seen her. She's not from around here." Mildred tucked her straight hair behind both ears and adjusted her name tag. "You want me to go ask her?"

"Mildred," I scolded, "you cannot just go wake up a napping woman when she's in a U-Haul."

"What?"

Mildred says "what" like she's loading a .22.

"Why not? Will Sheriff Goodlow come charge me with obstruction of U-Haul peace? Believe you me, that woman may be asleep but she's not peaceful. Women know things about women. You can write all you want about finding truth at the beach for that book of yours, but it won't help you know a thing about women's needs."

I'd told her about my book, the reason for my bi-weekly trips, not to brag, but to make sure she didn't get the wrong idea about me stopping through so much. But it was Mildred who told me I was fooling myself. "You aren't writing no book about truth. Anybody been alive as long as you have knows truth is a tool. Some use it for a weapon. Others cling to it like some kind of Coast Guard approved flotation device. I'm not saying it can't be useful. I'm not saying that at all. I'm just saying it's funny that you're lying to yourself about your truth book."

"I'm not lying to anybody. Truth is a gift, I think, the way to real life. I'm merely exploring the necessity of truth in what I hope to be a collection of reflective essays."

"Necessity of truth my hind end." Moped women have a way with words.

"I'm calling it Listening to the Shells: Truth from the Sea."

"How about calling it *How to Get Back at My Wife and Get Away with It!*"?

It was then that I knew Mildred had the powers.

Maybe I'd mentioned in passing that the wife and I'd signed papers six months ago because she was cheating on me, but I didn't tell Mildred any details.

"You signed those papers, relieved that you could finally blame the divorce on her." I hate women who ride mopeds.

"That woman, by the way," she pointed with an eyebrow toward the U-Haul, "is going to need a friend."

"Now or in the future?"

She raised her other eyebrow like it was an antenna. Imagine Carol Burnett with feelers.

"Both."

The woman was obviously heading somewhere, but she slept, face lodged against the glass, as though she'd already reached her destination. I, on the other hand, as Mildred has told me repeatedly, don't know where the hell I've been much less where I'm going. So I decided not to rush off. The beach would wait a while, and the turkey was on ice, so I settled back into the rocking chair with a toothpick. The back and forth creaking reminded me of wooden waves.

"Excuse me," her voice was little girl high, slow, but definitely not from Greenville. Her Braves' baseball cap cast a shadow over her face. "I was wondering if you would watch for my husband while I run inside." She blushed, unsure whether to tell me why she was going inside, though it was so obvious by the way she was fidgeting that she had to go to the bathroom. "He'll be here any minute and I don't want to miss him."

Something in her eyes looked hopeful, or maybe it was the way her small pupils seemed to float to the top of her milk-chocolate irises.

"What kind of car does he drive?"

"An Expedition. White. And he'll be pulling a Sea-Doo."

"I'll be happy to." A piece of the toothpick lodged between my top front teeth.

"If he comes," she hesitated and I thought for a second she might have tried to hold it too long, "just knock on the ladies room." She went inside and left me to wait.

Well, he didn't come. And she was back out before I'd gotten the toothpick out from my teeth or developed a decent line of questioning.

"You're fast at that for a woman," I told her. I didn't mean it as a compliment, but she took it that way. The little ridges on the side of her face from sleeping against the window spread across her cheeks as she smiled.

"Sometimes speed counts, I guess. Sometimes, no matter how fast you are, though, it's the timing that's important." Her grin made her top lip disappear. I expected her to tag such a statement with a question of agreement like "Don't you think?" Or at least a "Right?" But she didn't. She let what she said lay there between us like something newly planted, something plain, like grass, that neither one of us should step on.

Her top lip reappeared and she examined her fingernails by pushing the cuticles back with her thumbnail.

"I'm surprising him."

I glanced up at the U-Haul. The mockingbirds had made their peace and stared back at me from the overhang. "It was easier to rent that one way than to rent a car," she said, turning back to be sure I was listening. "I can leave it here." She pointed next door to the Citgo where a fourteen footer was parked. "Avis has a drop-off in Greenville, but it's on the other side of the bypass."

I nodded as though Avis's rental car locations had thwarted my intentions one too many times, too.

"I've made him a cake. A chocolate three layer. His favorite. I called him on his car phone and told him on his way home to stop and pick up a Bates's turkey for supper tonight. That's how I know he's going to stop by here. And I'll give him the cake." She glowed but not just from pride in her plan. Something else burned beneath this cleverness. "When he gets here," her eyelids rose and fell rapidly and I wondered if she was catatonic, "I'm going to give him his cake, chocolate's his favorite, did I mention that, and then ride back the rest of the way with him because I've got something to tell him." She eyed me to see if I had figured out what the news was, but I managed a blank expression. These days and times it could be anything from a negative AIDS test to leukemia remission.

"I'm pregnant."

"Well, congratulations," I said. "He's a lucky man. I'm happy for you both. What a nice Christmas present." I'd once wanted children, but they never happened. My wife said I fathered one too many stories, and it reduced my sperm count.

"I hope he's half as happy as you." What was the right thing to say in a situation like this?

She finished her cuticles. "At any rate, we'll have a couple of hours to talk on the way back. Just the two of us with no interruptions. That should be time to decide some things."

I scanned the sky, Rorschach-style, to see if any of the clouds had meaning. Maybe I'd see a stork. Or a wise man. I made out a cyclops. "I hope it works out like you want."

This seemed to be right enough, and she extended her hand. "I'm sorry. I didn't introduce myself. I'm Mindy."

Her hand was even tinier than I expected and much smoother. She wore a cluster engagement ring with a plain gold band.

"Billy'll warm up to the idea, I think. He's a great dad. We already have three. I thought I couldn't have any more children. Apparently I thought wrong." The cyclops winked and turned into a funnel.

So much for her being eighteen. She seemed too fresh to already be the mother of three. Not that children rendered women ugly or stale. They just had a way of toasting a woman around the edges sometimes.

"Why don't you sit in this rocker rather than out in that truck while you wait?" For December it was overly warm, but the humidity was what was so bad. An hour earlier the wind had whipped everything in its path into submission, and now the stillness felt like a shroud. I could have breathed easier in my Wet/Vac.

Mindy seemed unaware of conditions not related to her husband. I tried to talk about something else, anything, but she always steered the conversation back to him or their family. I did find out that she'd gone to junior college but didn't finish. That she'd married during her senior year of high school. That her father worked at ACIPCO, a pipe company in Birmingham where she and the kids still lived. Billy had started commuting to Mobile at the end of the summer to work on the Bay Bridge renovation project. Santa was bringing the Sea-Doo as much for Billy as the kids.

"It's working out fine," she said of the commute. "The time away makes us miss each other in a way our ten-year marriage needed."

She listened to me as I told her about the book I was writing, about wanting to find metaphorical buried treasure at Grayton Beach, and hoping that truth was at least part of the package value.

"Do you think there's real treasure buried there?"

"I think there's treasure everywhere if you've got the stamina to keep digging." Eat your heart out Helen Steiner Rice. If the book failed, I started thinking, I could do greeting cards.

She kneaded her stomach through her "Sweet Home Alabama" t-shirt. "Here." She reached over, took my hand, and placed it under "Alabama." "Tell me what treasure is hidden here."

I wondered if she had stretchmarks. I wanted to press harder with my fingers, but the top of her jeans got in the way. I let my pinkie drop as low as possible.

"I won't get big for six more months."

She waited patiently for me to say or do something, but this was not what I expected, and I had no idea what to say or do next. I wanted someone to elevate my feet and throw a warm blanket over me. I wanted to lecture her on candy, and strangers, and flying reindeer. I wanted her husband to pull up with a Scotch Pine tied to the luggage rack in exchange for the cake and whisk her off to Wal-Mart for extra strands of blinking lights. I wanted to kiss her.

Instead, I gave a mini lecture on short story writer Raymond Carver's definition of love. I was summarizing his famous cardiologist's dialogue about the different phases when I got carried away and bit my tongue. Blood started running down my chin before I figured out what I'd done. In a flash she had an ice pack and towels doctoring me up. Something about her attitude reminded me of Marcus Welby—only with hips.

"Have you thought of going back to school and becoming a nurse?"

"In all my spare time? Besides Billy says there's no money anyway, even if there was time. My job is at home right now. Maybe later." She made me bite down on a huge piece of ice. I had no idea the tongue's vascular system was so rich.

"Be right back. I'm going to rinse these towels out in the bathroom."

Billy's Expedition pulled in, (and two Sea-Doos, not one) a shiny, brand new model, white with the tow package. I strained to look through the windshield glare and see what a man lucky enough to land this Mindy Angel might look like, but it wasn't Billy's looks that surprised me. It was

Wendy Reed

the blonde sitting in his lap. He stopped the truck, and she sucked on his Adam's apple before he got out.

"Mildred!" I yelled. She was on the phone. I motioned to the other waitress standing beside her. "Take the man in the white truck a turkey. And tell him it's been paid for."

Mildred handed the phone to the other waitress. "You got the last smoked one."

"Then give him mine. Now! And hurry it up." My tongue throbbed with the urgency I felt. The restrooms were at the back of the restaurant, down a narrow hallway—right under the Turkey Commandments sign. She hadn't come out yet. I could hear Mildred at the front explaining to Billy that the turkey had been paid for. Her voice was fading, so I knew she was guiding him outside.

I pushed against the door right as Mindy went to open it. There was a second of confusion and she waited for whoever was at the door to move. She pushed again, and again I pushed back.

"Is that you?" I hadn't realized that I hadn't told her my name. "Is he here?" I let the door go and it opened. She was holding a slightly pink towel in one hand.

How could I tell her a man in a white Expedition had come, but it wasn't the man I was expecting? I had thought discovery was the only vehicle to truth, that digging below ground was where real treasure lay, but it was Christmas time, and there were three kids. Truth seemed like anything but a gift. What she needed now was something I didn't have to offer: faith.

She must've read my hesitation as a yes because she started around me. "Mindy," I said not knowing what to say or do but aware that Billy's truck would be visible through the front windows. That's when I grabbed her shoulders and kissed her. I kept squeezing her hard and pressing her into me because I expected her to resist. But she didn't. She went slack, and after a bit I thought she might faint. I counted to fifty wondering how long it took to shove a turkey at a man and send him on his way. I swept aside a piece of hair that had got caught between our lips and kissed her again. This time she stared at me. I wondered if I had stopped bleeding.

I pointed to the ceiling tile. "Mistletoe." I've not believed in miracles very often, but there really was a Styrofoam ball sprayed green and covered in artificial mistletoe hanging from the drop-in ceiling tile exactly where we needed it. On the ribbon was a bell. I rang it and smiled.

"Forgive me," I said. "It's tradition in my family that all beautiful ladies must be kissed or its seven years bad luck."

"I think you're confusing mirrors with mistletoe."

"Confusion comes," I stuck out my tongue and winced, "with trauma, you know."

We rocked away two more hours, much of it deciding whether I needed stitches, the rest in silence before the frosting started to run.

"Here. You keep this." She scooted the Tupperware cake-container behind my rocker. "I guess he didn't want turkey for dinner after all."

I watched her drive off in the U-Haul. I think she was right about timing. It's important. Even as it concerns truth. So often we think time is a measure. Maybe it's more of a dimension. She would discover in time whatever she needed to know, I suppose, the way we all discover what we need to. I went on to finish my book—an eventual collection of essays about faith, Gifts and the Giver. On the cover is a U-Haul.

As for the cake, I gave it to Mildred.

She said, "Thank you." And I knew she meant it.

But she said it again.

*Wendy Reed is an Emmy-winning public TV producer (*Bookmark *with Don Noble and* Discovering Alabama*) and author. In addition to publishing stories and essays, she has written* An Accidental Memoir *and co-edited, with Jennifer Horne,* Circling Faith *and* All Out of Faith*. The Alabama State Council on the Arts fellow teaches in the Honors College at the University of Alabama and lives with her husband in Hoover.*

Wendy Reed

Thelonious Rising

Chapter Eight

Judith Richards

I fell in love with New Orleans when I was fifteen years old. A summer job as a waitress twenty miles from home meant renting a room, living away. Late one lonely night, I discovered WWL Radio, a clear channel AM station broadcasting beautiful music from the Blue Room of the Roosevelt Hotel in New Orleans. Although 700 miles away, I was transported to the exotic and elegant ballroom in a city I would come to love. Leap forward to 2005 and 40 years of living on the Alabama Gulf Coast. I've experienced several major hurricanes, but none so emotionally devastating as Hurricane Katrina. One year after the storm, my husband, C. Terry Cline, Jr., and I traveled to New Orleans to see first hand the changes to my adopted city. Terry had been plotting a suspense novel set there and knew he could not write it without including the impact of the storm. But almost immediately upon arrival we realized that "something" needed to be written that would capture the heart and soul of the city, the heartbreak its people had suffered. In unspoken agreement we began to plot a story built around an innocent. Thelonious Monk DeCay was born; a nine-year-old boy who has lost his home and family to Hurricane Katrina. Monk's heroic effort, not only to survive but rise from the tragedy, to find his father and a life again filled with music, is meant to represent the struggle and triumph of many native New Orleanians.

Donna Marie DeCay had read studies about the psychological connection between twins. Identical, that is, not fraternal. And yet, all her life, whatever trauma her twin brother experienced she felt also. When Dean first went to prison, any confinement made her claustrophobic. Even a blanket on the bed at night left her choked for air, thrashing for more space. She entered therapy. The psychiatrist said her anguish was a response to the distress of a loved one.

"Empathetic reaction to the troubles of others is not unusual," the physician had said. "A wife's pregnancy might cause a husband to suffer morning sickness. In extreme instances he may develop a bloated abdomen and crave odd combinations of food. He may even believe he has felt the baby move. You have imagined your brother's suffering and it has caused a sensitive response in your own mind."

During the terrible months after Dean's conviction, besieged by anger and disappointment, she lost weight and couldn't sleep. Finally, as he must have accepted his situation, so did she. She threw away tranquilizers and concentrated on teaching eighth grade students at Central City Junior High School in Atlanta, Georgia.

Then last night she started thinking about their childhood. Not bad memories, those she could handle. It was the happy times that hurt her: Dean helping her learn to roller skate, building an ant colony between panes of glass for a science class. He taught her how to embrace a boy when dancing, a clever hold that pulled him close and held him off at the same time. The memories brought a smile and tears of remorse.

Plagued by these thoughts, she fixed hot tea spiked with rum, lemon, and sugar, soaked in a tub of warm water, and suffered reminiscences even more painful: the evening Dean announced his engagement to marry Donna's best friend, a girl loved by the entire family; then when he broke up with her to marry an African-American girl in Louisiana.

Donna returned to bed and lay awake staring at the green glow of her luminescent bedside clock. With the approach of daylight she got up for good, bone weary, and went into the kitchen where she brewed a pot of strong coffee and waited for a call she was sure would come.

Later that morning the telephone rang. Collect call from Angola Prison. "Hey, Donna."

"Hello, Dean."

From his end of the line, she heard the hollow sounds of men confined. Their voices echoed, and metallic things rattled. It must be a jarring environment, awful for a man who treasured silent contemplation and time to compose.

Their conversation began with tight amenities:

"How's Mom?"

"Fine."

"Dad?"

"He's all right."

"You, too, Donna?"

"Yes."

Without further preamble, Dean said, "I need your help, Donna."

"If I can, Dean."

"There's a hurricane bearing down on New Orleans."

She'd seen it briefly on the news, but normally Louisiana weather was of little concern here in Atlanta.

"At seven o'clock this morning," Dean said, "the eye was 250 miles out in the Gulf of Mexico. They predict it'll come ashore in twenty-four hours as a category five, which is a killer storm, Donna."

She could tell he expected to be rebuffed. He acknowledged objections before she mentioned them. "I know this is a busy time of year for you," he said. "School starts in a few days."

"Actually, classes began last week."

"The thing is," he persisted, "my son's grandmother has no transportation. I'm not sure she'd leave New Orleans if she could. Mrs. James is a large woman. Moving around is a problem for her."

Donna heard raucous shouts and wondered how Dean could hear over the turmoil around him.

"If the grandmother won't leave, what can anybody do?" Donna asked.

"She'd have to be convinced," he said. "Have you been keeping up with what's happening down there?"

"Not really."

"I was listening to our radio station."

"Your radio station?"

"We have our own radio station here at Angola," Dean said. "KLSP, 91.7 on the FM dial. We call it the 'incarceration station.' " He laughed, a sound so precious Donna almost sobbed. "It reaches about five thousand inmates, staff, and visitors. We play gospel, blues, rock 'n' roll, jazz, and country; anything but rap. I have a sixty-minute program once a week. Four fellows and I put together a jazz ensemble. We were six, but our sax player got paroled. We lay down some mean sounds."

For an instant this was the brother she'd always loved, upbeat, happy, productive.

Then his voice fell. "There are probably a hundred thousand people in New Orleans who will not evacuate for one reason or another. They don't have the money or the means, and they won't go. CNN says the Superdome will be opened as a shelter of last resort. They say it's built to withstand winds of 200 miles per hour."

He spoke aside to someone, "Back off, pal!" He cleared his throat. Prison racket had filled the void. He returned to ask, "Are you still there, Donna?"

"I'm here."

"My son, Thelonious, is nine-years-old, Donna. His grandmother doesn't have a telephone."

"I'm a long way from New Orleans, Dean."

"I know you are, and I wouldn't ask you, except there's nobody else I can turn to. I tried to call an old friend, but he's out of pocket."

"What do you expect me to do?"

"I don't know. Just—just—I don't know. Go there and get them if you can."

"Dean, I've never met those people. I can't show up and tell them what they should or shouldn't do. Maybe they've gone to the Superdome."

"I hope they have," he said. "Do you know someone in New Orleans who could check on them?"

"Not a soul."

"If I could reach Quinton Toussaint, I know he'd take care of this for me. You remember Quinton?"

"No."

"Years ago, he produced my first records. Didn't you meet him when we came through Atlanta one time?"

"I don't think so."

"He's a sweetheart of a guy," Dean said. "Gentle, wonderful friend. He keeps me posted on Thelonious. He says the boy is smart and talented."

"How could he be otherwise?"

"Let me give you Quinton's phone number and address."

Looking for paper, she added his message to a scant grocery list of items she intended to buy this week: yogurt, brie, croissants, and Toussaint. Sunlight cast the windows in shades of gray. Donna wrote down the information Dean dictated. In turn, she gave him her cell phone number.

"It's difficult to make calls out of this place right now," he said. "You have to constantly dial a number to get past busy signals at the other end. Every man is lined up to call his family about the storm. We're on a timer to keep conversations short. Donna, I know this is an imposition."

"I'll see what I can do, Dean."

"Thanks," he said, and then she lost the connection.

It occurred to her she hadn't told Dean she loved him, or that she missed him and thought of him every day. She forgot to ask if he needed any personal items. How was his health? Was he still composing music? It had been five years since she last heard his voice when he called to tell her he'd been convicted and wouldn't be eligible for parole until 2017. Given the opportunity this morning, she failed to say anything heartfelt. He must wonder if anybody cared for him anymore.

She studied her notes. Quinton Toussaint: an address on Esplanade. Diane James and her grandson lived at the corner of Andry and Royal in the Lower Ninth Ward, but there was no house number.

She dressed in loose slacks and a cotton shirt, called her principal, and then drove to his home on Decatur-Flat Shoals Road in Dekalb County. She and Bob Miller had gone to the University of Georgia together. They dated one another until the news broke about Dean's arrest. She wasn't sure which of them had withdrawn, but the relationship stalled.

Perhaps it was just as well. Poor literal Bob Miller was not blessed with Southern wit. She once told him a joke about a girl in Hahira, Georgia, born with breasts on her back—a tragic story—but she made a great dancing partner.

"Breasts on her back?" Bob was horrified. "There's no surgical procedure to correct that, is there?"

Donna telephoned Bob to say she was coming, and when she arrived at his house he met her with an awkward hug. She came straight to the point. "I have a family emergency. I need a few days off."

"Your father?"

"No."

"Your mother?"

"No. It's—"

"Dean," he guessed.

"He has a nine-year-old son in New Orleans," she said. "I can proba-bly go down and be back in a few days."

"Right here at the beginning of our school year," Bob worried. "Well. It can't be helped. Trouble rarely makes an appointment. Have you called the Louisiana state police? I heard on the news that all major highways in New Orleans are now one way going out to facilitate evacuation."

That was only one thing she hadn't thought of. It was Sunday; she couldn't go to the bank, so she had to withdraw cash from an ATM. She packed a pair of jeans, shorts, underwear, and polo shirts, gathered a few toiletries and stuffed them into an overnight bag.

By the time she was ready to leave, it was almost noon and she hadn't eaten, which made her think, with thousands of people fleeing south Lou-isiana, would restaurants have food? Could she get fuel for the car? She decided to carry twenty-five gallons of gasoline in plastic containers she bought at Wal-Mart. Throughout the preparations, every fifteen minutes she redialed her call to Quinton Toussaint in hopes she wouldn't have to go at all. There was no answer.

At last, she was on her way, driving west into the sun and south toward the storm. Had she forgotten anything? As she drove, she tried Quinton Toussaint again. The circuits were busy.

Even though all the windows were opened, the smell of gasoline fumes from containers in the trunk filled the car.

She stopped in Montgomery, Alabama, for dinner, and from there, telephoned her parents back in Atlanta.

She kept it light. "Mom, I'm on my way to the windy city."

"Chicago?"

"New Orleans."

She could imagine her mother stiffening. "What for, Donna?"

"Dean called. He wants me to check on his child and—"

"Donna, really now. Don't get caught up in that mess."

"He's worried about his son and the boy's grandmother."

"I saw on the news there's a six p.m. curfew down there. The storm is due to reach land early tomorrow morning. You should wait until it's over, and then call somebody. Shame on Dean for putting you in harm's way."

"I'll be all right," Donna said.

Her mother dropped the receiver and yelled, "Alfred! Pick up the phone. It's Donna. She's going to New Orleans!"

Donna heard him answer on the kitchen extension. "Bad time of year for a vacation in Sin City."

"I figured the room rates would be reduced."

"That storm has winds of 155 miles per hour," her father said. "It's nothing to fool around with. Wind of that velocity will bring a huge storm surge. Do you know New Orleans?"

"It's somewhere in south Louisiana, right?"

"Wait until the thing blows over," her father counseled. "Then you should take along ice and drinking water. They'll need it. Come over to the house and we'll discuss it."

"I'm in Alabama, Dad. On my way there."

She heard her mother, "Dear God, Alfred, talk some sense into that girl."

But Dad said, "Be careful, sweetheart. If there's anything we can do, let us know."

"Thanks, Dad."

"So we won't fret needlessly," he added, "let us know where to hunt for your body. Do you have your camera?"

That's what she forgot. "I never go to a disaster with proper equipment, Dad."

"Stay safe."

Paying the bill for dinner, Donna heard someone say, "Every motel is booked in Louisiana and Mississippi. Now they're coming over here."

She dialed around on the car radio for news.

"Katrina is 226 miles southeast of New Orleans," a reporter said. "She's a category five with winds gusting at 202 miles per hour. There's lots of pre-storm excitement in the Crescent City."

Looking through the windshield, a few clouds blocked the stars. Traffic increased in Mississippi as refugees from coastal areas inched north in search of safe haven. Every motel displayed a "No Vacancy" sign. She pulled into a service station to top off the fuel, but on each pump a paper sack covered the nozzle with a note that advised, "No Gas."

At a roadside picnic area she took two five-gallon containers from the trunk and poured petrol into the gas tank. A sudden breeze swept her hair and cooled her skin. But then it was gone, and a deathly still remained. She watched the last peek of stars disappear behind clouds. She put the gas cans in the trunk again.

Back roads were her best routes to avoid slow-moving traffic. In small towns the stores were closed, streets empty. A light drizzle dampened the pavement, raising oil, which made the surface slippery. She had to slow down.

South of Hattiesburg police cars blocked the road. Flashing lights made a mask of the trooper's face.

"I need to get to New Orleans," Donna explained.

"No ma'am. They're about to have a hurricane."

"I have to check on a child and his grandmother."

"No one is allowed in, ma'am. Turn around, or park across the street at the mall."

Using her cell phone she tried again to call Quinton Toussaint.

No answer.

All she could do was pull off the highway into a strip mall parking lot crowded with other cars. A family with several children had set up a charcoal grill. As the father cooked supper, the youngsters ran between cars yelling and laughing. In a car next to hers, Donna heard an apocalyptic weather advisory that locked her heart.

"Devastating damage is expected," the radio newsman said in a monotone. "Large areas will be uninhabitable for weeks. Half of well-built homes will have roof and wall failure. All windows will blow out. Persons, pets, and livestock exposed to winds will face certain death if struck by airborne debris; damage will be widespread."

A bank clock sign said the temperature was 90 degrees, humidity 90 percent. Her lips were chapped from gas vapors seeping out of the trunk.

"At this hour," the radio continued, "nearly ten thousand people have taken shelter in the Superdome. The French Quarter is empty. It is quiet and warm here in New Orleans. The most recent advisory on Katrina reports winds have diminished to 160 miles per hour. We have been warned that most parts of the city will lose electricity around five o'clock this morning. This is a safety precaution to prevent electrocution from fallen power lines."

Donna dialed Quinton Toussaint.

The circuits were busy.

*****

Mosquitoes pestered her, and Donna endured them because it was too hot to sit in the car with windows closed. She tried to get some sleep to compensate for last night, but it was not to be. Her clothes were soaked from perspiration, and she itched for want of a bath. Somewhere in the parking lot a baby cried. From the roadblock, revolving lights of police cars threw red and blue reflections onto dark windows of the strip mall shops.

I wouldn't be sitting here if Dean had married Gail.

The thought brought renewed regrets.

If he had married Gail, he'd be living the good life in fashionable Buckhead, north of Atlanta. His son would be—white, and out of danger.

Donna slapped an insect biting her ankle.

The memory of an argument she had with Dean was as painful now as if it happened yesterday. He had taken her to the Varsity Drive-in Restaurant near the campus of Georgia Tech in Atlanta. It was Saturday night, following a football game. Cars circled the lot trolling for parking space. Students blew their horns and shouted at one another. Dean said, "I've decided not to marry Gail."

"What?" Confounded, Donna said, "But, Dean, you've always loved Gail."

"I did. I do. I still have tender feelings for Gail, but I love another woman more."

The other woman was Elaine James. He met her while playing a gig in New Orleans. He'd known her for one year.

"A year? Dean, you and Gail have been going together since high school. Gail is my best friend. We always planned to be bridesmaids at each other's wedding."

"Yeah, I know, Donna. I'm sorry."

"I can't believe it," she said, hotly. "When will we meet this woman?"

"That brings me to the second part of this confession." He tried to grin but the expression came off anguished. "Elaine is not Caucasian."

"She's—"

"African-American," Dean said. "She's a beautiful woman, Donna. Talented, intelligent, a great singer."

"Is she pregnant?"

"No, no. Thank God. No."

"Have you told Gail about this woman?"

"No."

"Gail will be devastated, Dean. Her parents and our parents—they'll all be devastated."

"I know that. I need you to help break the news gently to Mom and Dad."

Then Donna said something totally out of character for her. She said, as though making an announcement to people in the circling cars, "Folks, my twin brother is going to marry a Negro!"

She wasn't a racist. At least she'd never been before. "What kind of people are her parents, Dean? I mean, other than the obvious."

"Her mother is a well-known singer. Her father is deceased."

"Did he die of natural causes, or was it during the commission of a crime?"

"Okay, you're angry." Dean stiffened. "Because I won't live my life by your conventions, you're upset. Well, here's the way it is, Donna. I'm going to marry the woman I love. Take it or leave it, I don't give a damn."

He got out of the car and slammed the door so hard the carhop's tray fell off the window. His last words to her were, "Take the car. I'll catch a bus."

That had been ten years ago.

Donna slapped another mosquito and then pressed redial on her cell phone. It rang, and rang, and rang. "Come on, Quinton Toussaint," she snarled softly. "Answer."

A man and two boys came by with boxes of Krispy Kreme doughnuts offered at a dollar apiece. Despite the outrageous price, they were selling briskly. Donna wished she had a cup of hot coffee. Another slap sent a bloodsucker to insect heaven.

She asked a man in the next car, "Do you have a Louisiana map?"

"I do."

She spread it on the hood of her car and studied the roads by flashlight. "I've got to get to New Orleans," she said. "I'm worried about a nephew living in the Lower Ninth Ward. Do you know that area?"

"Yes, I do," he said. "You know about the storm?"

"Of course."

"Then you don't want to go tonight," he said. "You're liable to get stranded somewhere. Are you by yourself?"

She hesitated. "I am for the moment."

He extended a hand. "I'm Barry Hampton, reporter."

She laughed. "Donna DeCay, educator."

She turned off the flashlight. In the dark, he said, "Who do you educate?"

"Junior high students at Central City School in Atlanta. Whom do you report for?"

"The *Probe*, a maligned and underappreciated periodical that keeps tabs on extraterrestrials, birth anomalies, celebrities, and oddities of human nature."

"Is that the *Probe* I see displayed on grocery counters when I go shopping?"

"One and the same," he said. "Our entire staff has vacated the premises in New Orleans, gone to Houston from whence they will put together future issues until they can return to the French Quarter."

"You didn't go with them," Donna noted.

"No. I was left to guard our offices. However, the storm predictions became so dire, I borrowed this automobile from a used-car dealer who was anxious to sell before the storm arrived. I told him I wanted to take a test drive, and here I am. The car did not pass the test, incidentally. I got this far when it quit."

He refolded the map and gave it to her. "Keep it. Obviously I won't be going anywhere for awhile."

"You know this area?" Donna asked.

"Like my own navel. That might not mean much to you, but as a student of Eastern religions, I practice omphaloskepsis, which is contemplation of one's navel as the center of the universe. I know my navel. Are you looking for a guide?"

She had no reason to trust this man, but Donna said, "Could you find a way into New Orleans tomorrow?"

"As a matter of fact, I should be there in the morning to protect the assets of my employers. While we wait out the storm, would you like to share a twelve-dollar box of day-old doughnuts? I also have a thermos of coffee, sans chicory. I live in New Orleans, but I'm not a native. Chicory is for Cajuns."

She sat in her car and he sat in his, doors open, talking in shadows. The police lights shot red and blue daggers of light across their windshields.

He was fifty years old, Barry said, a would-be novelist who had lost his way. He'd been writing quirky stories for the *Probe* most of his adult life. He described himself as a dropped ball before the bounce. "Since my wife died, I have fallen from a lofty height," he said, "but the peak of the rebound will define me as a man. Toulouse-Lautrec was a slave to absinthe; Arthur Conan Doyle was hooked on opium. My addiction was my wife, and I had been on a twenty-year high when I lost her."

He talked constantly and made her laugh; Donna needed to laugh.

"Most people think what we publish in the *Probe* is a pack of lies," he said. "Actually, we do not knowingly publish anything untrue. We merely look at truth from a different perspective. For example, the cover photo might be a strange creature with pointy ears and fangs, and the headline says, 'Bat Boy Brings Luck.' You read the article and it's about a winning streak a ball club has had since they hired a new bat boy. Or a story may be ludicrous, only meant to be funny. One of my favorites was the picture of a woman holding a very large child. 'Two Hundred Pound Newborn and Ninety Pound Mother,' the headline said. Read the article: the baby was an orphaned elephant being bottle fed by a lady at the zoo."

They ate doughnuts and sipped coffee. His wife had died in surgery five years ago. "It was a routine procedure," Barry recalled. "Appendicitis. Go in today and be home day after tomorrow; nothing to it, they said. For some reason, my wife's heart stopped beating and they couldn't get it started again."

Judith Richards

To ease the moment, Donna asked, "What's the best story you ever wrote?"

"My favorite would have to be, 'Baby Born with Bungee Cord Umbilical.' The kid kept going back where he came from."

Donna turned on her car radio and Barry Hampton came over to sit in the front seat beside her.

A news report said Katrina had weakened to a category three and was about to hit southeast of New Orleans. "That's good for us," Barry remarked, "and bad for the Mississippi Gulf Coast. The west side of a hurricane is the weakest. Maybe New Orleans will dodge the bullet."

Donna tried Quinton Toussaint's number and listened to the burr of an unanswered phone.

"I've been calling this man for the past twenty hours," she complained.

"If he has any sense," Barry said, "he left town long before now."

The breeze picked up and with it came a patter of rain. It was too hot to raise the car windows. Mosquitoes buzzed around her ears. Donna put her head back and closed her eyes.

Here she was trying to get to a hurricane and about to share her car with a man she'd just met. Had she lost her mind?

An actress once said she'd never met a dumb comedian. Donna had always been a sucker for wit, and she admired intelligence. With humor, Barry Hampton had lifted her spirits, and he wasn't stupid. Conversation ranged from politics to haute cuisine. "With me it has been less haute and more cuisine," he patted his middle. "I've gained thirty pounds in the past few years."

Sitting beside her, he'd fallen asleep. She heard a crude rhoncus. Okay, he snored. Nobody is perfect.

From the radio came another report, "Katrina has reached the south Louisiana coastline pushing a storm surge of fourteen to seventeen feet. If you ain't out, baby, it's too late to go."

In a car sharing the parking lot there were now two infants crying. Donna heard a woman cursing. "I need help with the babies, damn you!"

"What do you want me to do?" a man replied.

"Change a diaper," she replied. "Feed the baby."

"Hell, woman, the baby is breast fed."

"The other baby, you ass!"

Donna slapped another mosquito and stared into worsening weather. What was she doing here?

Judith Richards grew up in the tri-state area of Arkansas, Missouri, and Southern Illinois. She moved to Montgomery, Alabama in 1968 where she met her mentor and future husband, writer C. Terry Cline Jr. It was Cline who inspired Judith's interest in writing. From Montgomery, and later, Dothan, Alabama, Judith traveled for three years to schools throughout Mississippi, south Georgia, and central and south Alabama, working as a lecturer for the Colonial Educational Exhibits, a public relations program conceived by Terry Cline. Using live animals as visual aids, Judith taught students anatomy and psychology of different animal groups. The experience, meeting children and educators and visiting small Southern communities prior to the integration of schools in the South, was profound, and later influenced Judith's writing. Among Judith's six novels are Summer Lightning *and* Too Blue to Fly. *Both won the Alabama Library Association Award for Fiction, in 1978 and 1998. Too Blue to Fly was nominated for the Lillian Smith Award. Judith's most recent novel,* Thelonious Rising, *set in New Orleans at the time of Hurricane Katrina, is under option for a film.*

Judith Richards

Scales

Michelle Richmond

"Scales" grew out of an assignment of sorts. John Klima was editing an anthology called Logorrhea: Good Words Make Good Stories. *Each writer was asked to select a word from a list and write a story based on that word. The word I chose was logorrhea, which means "a tendency to extreme loquaciousness." So I set out to write about a character whose life has come undone because she can't stop talking. The story begins, however, with the woman walking out onto the Fairhope pier on a moonlit night, falling instantly for a man whose scaled body she finds mysterious and irresistible. Where did the scales come from? I can't exactly remember. It is difficult sometimes in hindsight to recall how a story came together, but I do remember writing the first sentence, in which a man appears on the pier, and it seems that the entire story laid itself out from that sentence. At some point the man's scales came to embody the truth we all learn at some point: there is no love without pain.*

Before we met, he had passed a decade of bachelorhood in a small house in Fairhope just steps from Mobile Bay, with the aid of a trusted assistant who did his shopping, ran his errands, and occasionally shared his meals.

And then he found me. Or, it should be said, I found him. On the Fairhope Pier, on a typically moonlit night. He appeared to me first as a statuesque figure at the end of the pier, dressed in a long-sleeved shirt and linen pants. I was having a difficult time of it, having recently lost, within the span of a few weeks, a decent job and a beloved pet, not to mention a boyfriend, when I saw him standing there, so still and silent he did not seem real. I stepped off the warm sand onto the pier. When the boards creaked beneath me he turned, and only then did I understand that this splendid creature was alive.

For several moments I hesitated. Someone standing in such a way, at such a place, on such a night, surely does not want to be interrupted. Then the moonlight hit his face, and a flash of multicolored light shot off the tip of his elegant nose, and I found myself walking toward him, as the old pier wobbled and groaned.

"Stop," he called out.

It was a slightly scratchy voice, halting, as if it was out of practice.

"Why?" I called back.

"Because," was his reply.

"It's a public pier," I said.

To this, he had no answer. He turned back toward the water and took a step. For a moment I thought he might jump. But he didn't. When I reached him, he kept his back to me and muttered, "I came out here to be alone."

"Me, too. I won't bother you." Then I moved to stand beside him, and he lifted a gloved hand to shield his face.

"Please," he said.

But by then, I had already seen.

We stood for a minute or two in silence before I said the only thing I could think of to say, which was, "You're beautiful."

"I'm ghastly," he replied.

"Not to me."

He produced a small paper bag, and when he opened it I could smell hot spice and salt and the sea. It was a strong, wonderful odor particular to the Gulf Coast, and immediately I was happy to be home again, after a long time away.

"Crawfish," he said.

"I know."

I reached into the bag, took one of the hard little shells, and twisted until the tail came clean from the head. I sucked the head, something I hadn't done in years. But the juice was delicious, even more so than I remembered, tangy and sweet. The shimmering man followed suit, and it occurred to me that the boyfriend who had just kicked me out of his stylish apartment in the stylish city that had never really felt like home would never have done such a thing. I squeezed the tail end of the shell until the tender pink meat came out and popped it into my mouth. Only after I had swallowed did I have the good grace to thank him.

"No, thank you," he said. "One should never eat crawfish alone. I've been doing it far too long." The combination of the words and the way he looked at me, as if we were complicit in some dream of love, seemed

Michelle Richmond

to cast forward into a future when we would do this together frequently, would, in fact, do many things together. It would not be an exaggeration to say that, at that moment, I understood that the thing we were going to share would be nothing short of a life.

We sat down on the end of the pier, removed our shoes, our feet dangling in the water, and ate. He produced a couple of warm beers, which seemed to materialize from thin air. We drank them in silence. When the crawfish and the beers were gone, he began to talk. He was three years old when the scales began to appear, he explained—on his upper legs, at first. Tiny, half-moon shaped bits, hard and thin, the edges paper-sharp. Eventually the scales began to thicken and to stretch up his body—to his groin, his stomach, his arms, shoulders, neck, and, at last, his face. "The doctors could do nothing," he said.

Once he started talking, it was as if he couldn't stop. And I, who had driven away my last boyfriend with the sheer volume and excess of my words, sat and listened. For the first time in my life, I found listening to be effortless. Every now and then I'd feel a school of tiny fish moving past like a gentle wind, the mouths nibbling at my ankles.

"No one has ever loved me before," he admitted, by which I understood him to mean that no one had ever made love to him.

When he was finished, I said, "I have something to tell you."

"What is it?"

But when I opened my mouth to say it, the words would not come out. Why mar this perfect evening with my confession? I would be for him, that night, the ideal companion. I would let him think that I was the kind of woman a man might be lucky to have. You'd be a real prize, my ex had said, sliding his hands over my breasts, my hips, my thighs, if you had your mouth surgically wired shut.

"It's nothing," I said. "Never mind."

He shook the last bits of crawfish shell into the water and put the empty bottles into the paper bag. "My house is just down the beach," he said. "Do you want to come home with me?"

"Yes."

In hindsight, I understand that when he removed his glove and took my hand in his, it was meant as a silent warning. Though he held my hand as gently as he could, I could feel the scales cutting into my palm and fingers. I wondered, but did not ask, whether the affliction covered his entire body. Later that night, pressing my face into a pillow to squelch my screams, I understood that it did.

***

That first time, I was covered with lacerations. Tiny red marks all over the front of my body, like thousands of paper cuts, and also on my back where his arms had embraced me. All through the night I kept waking in pain, the fresh wounds damp with blood, my body sticking to the soft flannel sheets. Beside me, he slept soundly, his scales wet-seeming in the moonlight, his face the picture of peace. I couldn't help but feel, somehow, that I had saved him, although it would occur to me later that it was the other way around. In any event, that first morning-after, when I woke to the sound of his scaled feet clicking softly against the tile floor, I knew that I would stay with him. That I would make a home there in that house by the bay. Maybe it was the disfiguring effect of our first attempt at love—after all, I had never been loved so dramatically. More likely, it was the fact of his having accomplished something no other man had ever been able to do: with him, I had fallen easily, happily, willingly into silence.

I can say without reservation that the weeks that followed were the best weeks of my life. Days, I went out looking for a new job while he concealed himself in the house, making notes for a memoir he planned to write. He was very secretive about the book, would not let me see so much as a single page, kept the steadily growing manuscript locked away in a file cabinet. It was a house of secrets to which I was not privy, but I had my secrets too. I did not mention to him the flaw that had brought all my previous relationships, romantic and otherwise, to an abrupt and tearful end. I did not tell him that I had laid cruel waste to a long cadre, of therapists, professionals who, though trained to listen, could not bear to listen to me. Or that my second-to-last boyfriend had been so put off by my incessant talking that, following our break-up, he'd taken up with a woman who rarely spoke, who made her living as a mime on the streets of New York City. I did not tell him that my own mother would not take my calls.

He had fallen in love with a certain girl, the one he met that night at the end of the pier, the one who sat silently and listened to his stories. In order to keep him, I would remain that girl. It was easier than I could have imagined: he held my rapt attentions, and I, miracle of miracles, held my fevered tongue.

***

Following that first night, we went an entire month without making love, during which time my body slowly healed. Mornings and evenings, he dressed the wounds with salve. Of course, he had to wear gloves, but even so, I felt that I had never been touched so gently. Some nights, while he was sleeping, I stood in front of the bathroom mirror, peeled back the bandages, and examined my shorn skin. It was a source of fascination for me, this pain that made me feel, at the same time, horribly wounded and deeply desired.

Then, at the beginning of our second month together, I came home from work—by then I had landed a gig as a docent at the maritime museum—to find him dressed head-to-toe in a suit of clean white felt.

"Feel," he said, holding an arm out for me to touch. "It's impenetrable. I had it custom-made. The felt is the best one can buy, hand-beaten by Tuvan women in the village of Tsengal in Mongolia."

I stroked his moon-white arm. "So soft," I said. "It's beautiful."

But what I was thinking was that I missed his scales, the way they captured and reflected light, the way, when he moved across a room, he looked like a human chandelier.

Have I mentioned that his scales twinkled? Have I mentioned that, after bathing, while he stood in the middle of the tiled kitchen floor, dripping dry to avoid shredding the towels, he was like a fountain of light?

"There is a necessary flaw in the suit's design," he said, leading me to the bedroom.

"What's that?"

When we reached the bed, he turned to face me and unfastened two buttons on his groin. A flap of felt fell away to reveal that most beautiful part of him, of which I had been in awe from the beginning.

It was average in size but exceptional in appearance, covered as it was with scales of many hues, ranging from the palest white to the deepest blue. When in repose, it lay against his body like a cylindrical jewel. What cruelty, to be blessed with such a thing of beauty, but to be unable to share it with the world!

That night, separated from him by a layer of plush white felt, it was like making love to a pillow, or a human-shaped yurt. Except, of course, for the one part. Our way of making love was to be very, very still, to let the closeness of our two bodies be a substitute for motion; even so, I came away from the event cut and bleeding. Afterward, it wasn't too bad as long as I was sitting or standing still. But walking around the maritime museum, instructing eager third-graders on the mating habits of stingrays and jumbo Gulf shrimp, proved excruciating painful. In a way it was terrible, but in another way it made me feel as though I had happened upon an exceptional love. He was like no man I'd ever been with. I could search for years, and never find anyone like him. It was satisfying to think of the women I knew at work—the secretary with her portentous hair, or the events planner with her eternally disappointed air of someone who has just missed out on a very good party—passing through the days with their ordinary loves, while, in the little house by the bay, my own love waited, freakish and beautiful.

***

As it turned out, the suit was only an early prototype. Over the months and years it would be followed by many others, each one hand-sewn by a celebrated textile artist across the bay in Mobile, each one an improvement upon the last. An improvement in that each new suit was less obvious, more natural-looking than the one before. The white felt gave way to something thinner and somewhat flesh-colored—also smooth, but with the faint hint of human hair. He gave the textile artist photos of himself as a very young child, before the scales began to appear, and gradually, the color of the suit came to resemble, more and more, the color his skin had been prior to the affliction. That's what he called it, in his more depressive moods, when the memoir was going badly—his affliction—and I didn't have the words to tell him that it was the affliction that drew me to him, more so than his personality, which, I came to realize, was rather ordinary, or his intelligence, which tended toward the esoteric, or his humor, which could be cruel.

The suit's hair, too, became more supple and fine, placed discriminately in the appropriate places—thicker on the legs and upper arms, a lighter patch of it on the chest, and only a few stray hairs, for authenticity's sake, in the small of the back and on the wrists. By and by, the suit began to look alarmingly realistic, so one had to examine it closely to see that something was amiss, that he was wearing not his skin, but rather a suit of simulated skin, designed, ingeniously, to bruise upon impact and to emit faint odors reminiscent of the wearer's last meal. Under the proper conditions, the suit was even designed to sweat.

The suit was so realistic, in fact, that he gained a kind of confidence he'd never known before. Over time, as the suit improved to near perfection, he began to go out in public, to socialize with ordinary folk. Eventually he got a job. He kept his hair long and always wore a hat and scarf, even in the merciless humidity, in addition to a thick makeup that had been designed by a friend of the textile artist. With all of these precautions, he was able to keep his face pretty well concealed.

But at night, when he came home from his job at the finance company—something he'd dreamed of his whole life, not least of all because it smacked of normalcy and unobtrusive prosperity—he allowed me to unzip the suit and peel it off of his shimmering skin in the pastel light cast through our windows by the sleeping Gulf, and to rinse the makeup from his face, and to do the one thing I desired most, the one thing that, unbeknownst to him, kept my love for him alive: to look at him, in all his scaled and glittering glory. When he was naked, stripped of the deceptions he had so meticulously acquired in order to pass in polite society, he was nothing short of beautiful.

When it came time to make love, I willingly zipped him into the suit again. With my job, it would have been difficult to endure the all-over scarring that would have occurred if we made love without the suit. Not to mention the fact that some genetic code was at play, some peculiar aging process was afoot, so that, while his suit grew softer and more pliant with each mutation, his scales grew sharper and more pointed.

During all his time, the suit's one supposed flaw remained: one key part of his body had to remain exposed during lovemaking. According to the textile artist, it had something to do with the chemical makeup of the fabric, which could not sustain exposure to certain types of bodily fluids.

So it passed that, year after year, my feminine parts bore the brunt of our lovemaking. As a result, I felt that I belonged to him, as if our union had been purified by fire: for what is love if not sacrifice?

And then, one Friday afternoon nearly a decade after that night meeting at the pier, my husband—by then, we had walked down the aisle of a non-denominational church by the sea, and feasted on champagne and crawdads while a local Zydeco band inspired the small group of wedding guests to flail about in the sand—came home to me and said, "It's been solved."

I was sitting at the kitchen table, reviewing the literature for a new live specimen the maritime museum had acquired, the *Tonicella lineate*, or lined chiton, a prehistoric-looking mollusk with a single large foot whose tongue, or radula to be precise, is covered with iron teeth. I suppose I didn't properly hear him, or didn't note the enthusiasm in his voice, because rather than asking him what exactly it was that had been solved, I was moved to share with him an interesting fact I'd just discovered in my reading. "It says here that the lined chiton can travel up to three feet on the ocean's surface to scrape algae off nearby rocks. Then it returns to its home scar, which is a depression in its own rock that is, get this, shaped just like the lined chiton." I shoved a potato chip into my mouth and kept talking. "I mean, the chiton has used his iron-coated teeth—they get that way, the teeth I mean, by a complicated chemical process called biomineralization—to shave away the rock until it fits his body just so. Like a glove! Like a lover!" I exclaimed, taking a swig of my beer, for by this point I had really made myself at home on the Gulf Coast, swigging beer and sucking crawfish heads with abandon, occasionally even attending a tent revival, forgetting that I'd ever lived in one of the strange cities of the North or that, in a past life, my logorrhea had made me intolerable.

"Says here that chitons have flexible shells," I said, "composed of eight articulating valves, which are covered with thousands of tiny eyes call aesthetes. The largest chiton in the world is the Cryptochiton stelleri, or gumboot, which can reach thirteen inches and has valves shaped like butterflies. Butterflies, mind you! Never say there isn't poetry in the sea."

My husband, at this point, was staring at me in stunned silence. And why shouldn't he? I'd never strung so many words together the entire time

Michelle Richmond

I'd known him. Something strange had happened that long-ago night on the pier; I had, without warning or effort, been cured. What I'd believed at the time to be a temporary reprieve from my own affliction had turned out to be permanent. Weeks turned into months, months to years, and I did not feel the need to talk. Quite the opposite, I felt compelled to silence, so that by the time I returned home each day from the museum, where it was my duty to speak at length about the wonders of the sea, I had little desire to say anything. Instead, I listened. In truth, I could not help feeling that some important part of me was missing, that I was somehow less than I had been before.

"Didn't you hear me?" my husband asked, taking a seat beside me at the table, and looking with some disgust at the oily stain the potato chips had left on my paper plate. "I said it has been solved." He was wearing Bermuda shorts, a T-shirt, and thongs—Fridays were mandatory casual day at the finance company and his suit was so excruciatingly skin-like, so perfectly fitted to his body from neck to fingertips, that, had I not known better, I might think that he had been cured. By this point we were making love infrequently, and the intimacy we'd once shared had begun to melt away. He had taken to wearing his suit round-the-clock, even to bed, so that I rarely experienced the sweet thrill of disrobing him in the evening after work, peeling away his outer layer to reveal the man I loved.

At that moment, I felt that I was sitting across the table from someone no more familiar to me than the paperboy or the clerk at the 7-Eleven. Then, mercifully, he unwound the scarf that covered his chin, and took off his floppy hat, and brushed back his long hair, and I felt enormously grateful for this glimpse at his private self, this glimpse he allowed to no one but me.

"What's been solved?" I asked.

"This."

He stood and dropped his shorts. And there before me stood an entirely natural-looking man, adorned in curly pubic hair and dangling flaccidly in the heat, the scrotal sack appropriately wrinkled, the whole package dismally common.

"How did he do it?" I asked, reaching out to find the zipper.

At which point he began to swell at my touch, saying, "Baby, there's no zipper."

"Well then, how do we get this damn thing off?" I said, tugging at it in a completely utilitarian way, which he mistook for an erotic overture.

"There's no taking it off. I've been sealed into the suit. I can bathe in it, exercise in it, even make love in it."

By now I was using my teeth, trying to tear the wretched false skin away.

"It has to be removed once a year so that the skin can go through an aging process and any necessary alterations can be made," he panted, as if this thing I was doing with my teeth had something to do with sex, as if it were not a desperate attempt to reveal that most beautiful part of him, that most real and multi-colored thing, which was a specimen in its own right, deserving of its own field of scientific study, not to mention an entire school of experimental art and a movement in postmodern literature.

But I was no match for the suit, this soft and lifelike armor. I did not find what I was looking for.

That night, we made ordinary love. While he thrashed and thrusted above me, I faked an orgasm for the very first time. And when it was over I had nothing to say. My speech on the mighty chiton, that master of disguise who carved for itself a home in the rock and looked, to any possible predators, like nothing special, like a part of the rock itself— my speech had been a one-time thing. My logorrhea really was gone, relegated like the ex-boyfriends and the therapists and the big city to my distant past.

Before long, the textile artist came up with a way to disguise my husband's one remaining feature, his face. He fit in so well, even he seemed to forget that the skin he presented to the world was not his own. Eventually he got a promotion, and we moved across the bay to a restored antebellum home in downtown Mobile, keeping the little cottage by the bay for the sake, I suppose, of nostalgia. Mornings, I'd drive the Causeway to the maritime museum in Fairhope, watching the sun blaze over the silver bay. Afternoons, on the return trip, I'd catch a glimpse of the old warship, the U.S.S. Alabama, sitting placidly in the water, a gigantic relic of some bygone glory, its dull gray cannons barely hinting at the

Michelle Richmond

violence they'd once wrought upon the world.

Nights, my husband and I would sit together in our well-appointed living room, reading: he read biographies of captains of industry, while I buried myself in colorful textbooks detailing the wondrous creatures who made their home in the sea: sharpnose puffer, ocellated frogfish, mushroom scorpion-fish, flying gurnard, dragon wrasse, leafy seadragon. There were pictures of sea stars and urchins, mollusks of many varieties, crustaceans of indescribable beauty.

My husband had long since given up his dream of writing a memoir. After making several attempts to break the lock of the file cabinet in which the manuscript was concealed, I finally called in a locksmith. Upon opening the drawer I saw that the book had never really been started. It was little more than a list of potential titles and chapter headings, accompanied by a few photocopied documents from the medical files of his youth. These documents were characteristically clinical in nature, but among the dull listings of medications and false diagnoses, recommended treatments and such, a little light occasionally shone through. Upon removal of a small sample of the scales, one doctor had typed, the subject bled profusely. Close examination of the scales under a microscope revealed a range of exceptional colors not found in nature. And then, in nearly illegible handwriting in the margin was a note the doctor had apparently scribbled to himself, an afterthought: *Rare opportunity to witness a thing of wonder. Thanked his mother profusely for bringing him to me. No diagnosis possible. Very clearly one of a kind.*

I returned the files carefully to their places and had the locksmith conceal any sign that the lock had ever been compromised. I did, however, steal from the files the one piece of paper on which the doctor had allowed himself a moment of professional awe. I keep it hidden in a secret place. Every now and then, when the ease of our ordinary lives becomes overwhelming, when I think I cannot pass another day in the shadow of my husband's brilliant disguise, I take the paper from its hiding place and review the doctor's words, and I think of the treasure I found that night on the pier in the moonlight. It is almost close enough to touch, this treasure. Sometimes I dream of some point in the future, when some ordinary disease or accident will take my husband's life, and I will lay him down in the good light of our little house by the bay, and I will go exploring. With my fingernails, my teeth, my eyes, I will search until I find his secret seam. Then I will open him up like some splendid fruit, like some creature from the depths of the mysterious sea, and behold, once again, his beauty.

Michelle Richmond was born in Demopolis, Alabama, grew up in Mobile, and studied creative writing as an undergraduate at the University of Alabama. She is the New York Times *bestselling author of four novels, including* The Year of Fog *and* Golden State; *and two story collections, including* Hum, *winner of the Catherine Doctorow Innovative Fiction Prize, and* The Girl in the Fall-Away Dress, *winner of the Grace Paley Prize. Her novels have been translated into thirteen languages. She lives with her husband and son in northern California.*

Michelle Richmond

The Sadness Of
The Sadness of Elephants
Lauren Goodwin Slaughter

I hope that "The Sadness of The Sadness of Elephants" wavers between hilarity and despair as it dramatizes a question everyone must deal with: what does it mean to be, and how does one function as, an individual within a family? I tend to read quite a lot of Flannery O'Connor with my students—her stories and also her dead-on essays about writing—and so I happened to be thinking about how she uses, and how I could use, various kinds of disfigurement to emphasize the attributes of my characters as well as more global themes. I also made the mistake, long ago, of offering my real email address to advertisers. It's terrible. I am particularly distracted by those emails from certain political or environmental groups that want me to get behind issues in which I really do believe. But they nag, they hassle, and they badger. And this compels me to do nothing. Or, at least, not enough. Thus: I feel guilty.

Suri, a 36-year old elephant born in the wild on the African savannah, was dying of sadness. She'd been eating her own excrement and swaying her head and trunk from side to side—typical signs of elephant depression, according to the article. The article said Suri's companion, Kayla, died recently and this was the cause of the sadness. Also, Suri didn't have enough room in her enclosure, which was a mere 1,200 square yards. An internet campaign organized by savethecreatures.org kept Hanna updated via email and was circulating a petition to have Suri moved to a safari park in Madrid where she could have more room to roam with other elephants. "Suri won't last," the most recent email assured, "unless you help us, *Hanna.*"

So of course Hanna signed the petition and sent in a hundred bucks—not nothing for an adjunct instructor. This contribution designated Hanna a "Changer." Fifty would have made her a "Helper," but that sounded too pejorative and she simply could not afford to become an "Enforcer." But because she felt guilty about not doing enough, she kept finding herself at the Springfield Zoo, leaning against the guardrails staring at Nori and Joni, instead of at Nathan's basketball games or picking him up on time at school or practice. Joni and Nori were 10-year-old elephant sisters who transferred from the San Francisco Zoo two months ago. As Hanna observed them cram hay into their mouths, or twitch their tails, or flap their enormous ears, she tapped notes on her cell phone for the story she planned to write this summer called, "The Sadness of Elephants." *Paintbrush eyelashes. Hay looks like pool hair.* So far she had not noticed any excrement-eating, but she was especially keeping an eye out for that.

Today, finally finished with her end-of-the-semester grading, Hanna planned to spend the whole afternoon with the elephant sisters until she had to go get Nathan, who still had a few weeks of school left before break. She packed a tuna sandwich, a Coke, and even applied sunscreen to her freckle-dotted face—too much sun and the dots merged. But just as she began to record a lengthy description of Joni's ears—in this late April heat they billowed behind her like those rainbow parachutes Nathan and his friends used to love—she received a call from Coach about an "emergency regarding your son." After Hanna's gasp he qualified, "He's okay, Mrs. Wheeler—we just need to talk."

Still, Hanna rushed out of the zoo trying to fight that drowning-flashback-feeling, past the orgasmic-sounding Gibbons, the zigzag flamingos, the kaleidoscopic line of kids waiting to ride the choo-choo. "Work!" she commanded her mini-van with the unreliable starter; her hands shook as she wrenched in the key and the engine engaged. *Parachute ears, parachute ears,* she repeated under her breath, trying to shake the replay of her son's half-blown-off face—the way it looked before all the surgeries. But soon she'd made it across town to the YMCA where Nathan played on a basketball team with other kids with mental and physical challenges. She whizzed through the Y's maze of base-pumping fitness classes, the oof-ing old men of the rusty weight room, the screaming childcare center, the somber closed door of an AA meeting. Her heart knocked against her ribs: *Na-than, Na-than.*

Coach's "office" was the former Men's locker room and it still festered with the vinegary pang of man stink. Hanna forced back a gag as she

Lauren Goodwin Slaughter

walked through the open door, stepping over a frazzled volleyball. A boy of twenty-two-ish with a reversed baseball hat pressed into his shaggy blonde curls scowled into a phone that emitted vague battle sounds. Somebody seemed to be getting killed. "One sec," he said, rapt by the device. This was exactly the kid Hanna encountered in her English 101 class—a too-cool Facebooker who made her feel jittery and self-conscious. It was the wrong shirt to wear, this REI "Good Life" tee featuring a cartoon dog catching a cartoon Frisbee.

An explosion-sound crackled. "Die, zombie fuck-head!"

Coach put the phone down. As he swiveled towards Hanna on a mauled, detective-seeming chair, his demeanor was discordantly grave. "It's his attitude, Mrs. Wheeler," the kid said, gesturing for Hanna to sit. The only option was to squeeze into one of the children's school desks that had been pulled in there along with a catalogue of deflated rubber balls, Pac-Man-bent hula-hoops, stacks of card tables and other homeless apparati. She jammed her ass into the miniature chair, letting her knees fall uncomfortably to the side.

"I'm running late for an appointment with my assistant," she announced. She had no appointment and no assistant.

Ignoring her remark, Coach explained that Nathan, whose interest in basketball had been "not-so-awesome" over the past half-year, no longer simply refused to practice—he was now openly combative. Once committed to mastering the foul shot—often staying late with Coach to work on his form—these days, Nathan's goal was to hurl the ball at the backboard so hard it ricocheted to half-court. His once wimpy picks were now body-slams and on the out of bounds plays he was checking his own teammates, often while snarling or barking like a dog. But worst of all, he'd taken to referring to the other boys as "mutants" or even "freaks." Kyle, their best shooter who suffered a rare dermatological condition that gave his skin the appearance and texture of tree bark was so irritated by Nathan's insults that he'd been itching too uncontrollably to dribble the ball. The point guard, Jerry—by far their best player—stormed out of practice yesterday, the middle finger on the remaining hand of his remaining arm jammed skywards in a defiant *screw you*. And Mason, who had the build of a linebacker but no longer spoke after years of sexual abuse by a neighbor kid's father, was starting to protect his teammates by beating Nathan up.

"But those bruises are because of Nathan's hustle and scrappy playing style," Hanna interjected. It was what her son had been telling her. She recalled that Lyle, her elusive, soon-to-be ex-husband had been suspicious of Nathan's injuries—but she'd long ago stopped listening to him.

"You have to understand, Mrs. Wheeler," Coach coaxed as he swiveled to the edge of her tiny desk and looked down, "these kids? This is their one place to be normal. They have to deal with this shit day in and day out, at school and everywhere else." He paused as if to study the threadbare pull-down map of Pennsylvania that dangled precariously off one of the lockers—someone had Sharpied boobs over Harrisburg. "I just can't have one of their own doing this to them."

Coach's earnest tone was infuriating; as if she'd never had to comfort Nathan through another round of teasing, the other children calling him "Razor Face" or "Claw Head." As if she didn't constantly have to deflect the gasps of passing strangers with a corny joke or some other sugary pacification neither she nor her son believed.

At first there had been the endless lasagnas, casseroles and soups that appeared on the porch in disposable aluminum containers; each meal came with a yellow post-it note scribbled with heating instructions and a catch-all phrase of encouragement: *Hang in there ... Thinking of you ... Here if you need anything.* But people have short attention spans for the disasters of others. Now, instead of frozen chicken tetrazzini there was a mournful, knowing look or a flabby, on-the-go 1/2 hug from a 1/8 friend. Even Hanna's own mother, who for a time kept flying in from Cincinnati, called infrequently now. Hanna suggested they Skype, but her mother complained the camera thingy on her computer no longer worked. And when her mother bought a new computer, it was too fancy and she didn't know how to operate it and just gave up.

The waning support of family and friends was a primary topic for the parents as they huddled in the bleachers to watch their mutilated sons compete against the able-bodied boys. It would have seemed cruel, the proximity of these flourishing kids to their band of curiosities, if all the boys on the floor weren't having such a good time. The opposing jocks on any other day might be the swaggering loudmouths who taunted

Lauren Goodwin Slaughter

the "Badgers" team members, but they were composed and cordial for the games. They'd been prepped—or, likely, threatened—into behaving themselves. When the opposing team shook hands after the games they always, inevitably, won, Hanna could discern not a slip of spit on a palm.

Marguerite Fowler, Jerry's mother, was on the national board of the Y.M.C.A. and had rallied to put the Badgers together the summer Jerry lost his arm. Marguerite was frantic for things to remain as normal as possible for her son, and a week after his slaughter by lawnmower this basketball team was already in the works. Jerry played point and was by far the strongest player—even with one arm. He was also resilient, upbeat, and physically strong, with a quarterback's good looks and charm. Before the accident, he had been on track for a basketball and baseball scholarship at John Carroll High, and though that was now impossible he still had the same blonde girlfriend with a smile that ate her whole face. She was always making brownies or cookies for the team and delivering the goodies to practice wearing white short-shorts that encouraged slight scoops of her perfectly round ass to peek out like presents. An example to the other players, Jerry was the team member who gave the locker room pep-talks, called the plays, and otherwise motivated his mostly untalented and morose teammates. He'd come up with a wide variety of modifications for playing with one arm and because he had large enough hands to palm the ball, could manage dynamic dribbling and accurate, breakneck passes.

Nathan, unfortunately, was the target of many of those passes down at the post or at the top of the key. At 5'6" and 140 he made a puny forward, but because of damaged eyesight—a little teacup flap of eyelid still eclipsed the vision in his right eye—he needed a position that did not require much dribbling or play-calling. Forward was an especially bad place for him on offense; his shots forever got blocked as he attempted to pick off boys with fifteen pounds and multiple inches on him. On defense, though, he was quite capable, especially when playing man-to-man. A stellar jumper, he could hone his focus to follow the ball in his opponent's hands. *Ball, ball, ball, ball, ball!* The synthesis of Nathan's throaty screaming and hacked-up face proved too much for many kids he went up against; they found a way to let their arms go wobbly and the ball get loose.

Dear Hanna,

Thank you for your interest in Suri and for your recent contribution to savethecreatures.org. We are hopeful that Suri will be moved to her new home in Madrid soon. Suri's keepers have been telling her about the many generous donors like you, Hanna, who have taken an interest in her situation and as a result she is no longer eating her own excrement. Well, sometimes she eats just a nibble, but mostly there is almost no excrement-eating. Just thought you would want to know.

A yoga-mom clone popped her head in the room. "Hey, guys! Sorry to interrupt—sorry, am I interrupting? Listen, sorry, but Gary's back is out again. Coach, can you do Bootcamp today?"

"Not a problem, Marlene," Coach replied, igniting a smile. Marlene had shiny tan skin and the hyper-toned thinness of a stay-at-home mom with a live-in nanny. Blonde streaks flashed through her chin-length bob. "You are a lifesaver, Coach!" she cried, doing a little clap that revealed quivering muscle definition, "I'll tell the other girls!"

Coach. What kind of a person doesn't even go by a real name? Hanna was getting that bread-clogged feeling—motes of perspiration clustered on her forehead and chest. Now "Coach" was inquiring about "Nate's support system," but she was preoccupied by the enormous framed poster above Coach's collection of gleaming athletic trophies that seemed to represent random, non-existent sports. In yellow capitals the poster read: THE KEYS TO SUCCESS. The image depicted a loopy antique key and these commandments: *Expect more than others think is possible; Dream more than others think is practical; Risk more than others think is safe.*

Not safe, Hanna thought, feeling a sweat dribble make its way down her neck. She thought of Suri, alone, dying. She thought of the hole of Nathan's face. She remembered her wedding day—the too florid lily bouquet, the suffocating veil, how she couldn't quite meet Lyle's eye as she managed, "I do."

We are not safe at all.

****

"No one remembers being born," confirmed Mr. Burgess, his back to the class as he scribbled *FERTILIZED EGG* above a chalk *O*. "But thank you for yet another interesting question, Ms. Martin."

Lauren Goodwin Slaughter

Ashley Martin was always interrupting Mr. Burgess with ridiculous questions. Yesterday, she wanted to know why she couldn't find her cat's penis. Amid the ping-pongs of teenage twitter around the room, Mr. Burgess simply suggested she stop looking. Only Nathan laughed at his teacher's remark, but he was careful to do so only in his head. He felt oddly protective of his biology teacher, even though Mr. Burgess kept giving him C's and D's. Mr. Burgess seemed sad and Nathan was sad, and so there was that between them.

Swimming across the chalkboard, a pink cross-section of the fallopian tube—the tube's fingers reached for the fertilized egg with wavy arrows. As Mr. Burgess turned back to the board after answering Ashley's dumb question he brushed the chalk uterus and spread it into a wind-smeared cloud. "You wrecked the uterus," Ashley taunted. Nathan fought the urge to get up out of his seat in the back of the class and walk straight over to the bitch and ram his lead pencil right through her tarry, mascara-ed eye.

The yellowing wall clock circa 1980 read 3:05, its broken second hand jolting into the three unceasingly. Mr. Burgess continued his lesson, writing *endoderm, ectoderm, mesoderm* on the board while noting that at this point in the fertilization process the genetic code of the father becomes "fully involved." Nathan doodled a game of Hangman to himself, pretending to guess an unknowable word; so far, the man was an empty circle staked on the end of a rod. Its disappeared face could just as well be his father's; a halo of nothing. This was the opposite of Nathan's monster face that broadcast itself like a scream.

After the accident, when they finally got home from the hospital, Nathan's father moved to the couch; nights, his blanketed bulk glowed green by the light of the mossy, one-fished, aquarium. Instead of zooming around town in his Geo "nerd-mobile" doing freelance computer repair, he remained cloistered in his office navigating the morass of eBay, placing low bids on high-end scuba equipment even though he'd never even been scuba diving and was in fact inept and bulky in the water; summertimes at the pool, attempting to keep pace with the other dads, he would cannonball or jackknife off the diving board but then land awkwardly on his side like a flank of beef slapped onto a plate. On the day he left for the first of many extended stays at the La Quinta by the interstate, he sat on the edge of Nathan's bed and squeezed his son's foot much too tightly. "Hang in there, buddy" he said, like a bad T.V. version of a dad, before he departed in the clinkering car Nathan could not watch sputter away because the helmet-cast they'd wrapped around his head made it impossible to move to the window. From the other room he'd heard his mother lock the door and say nothing at all.

In the months following, his father showed up for the occasional McDonald's or movie outing but even at those times he seemed to be off in the distance somewhere, planning his escape. Then, for a time, when Nathan got home from school he'd find his dad on the couch watching war on the History Channel, the house saturated with coffee and bacon smells. Then, his dad was back at the La Quinta. He was there, he wasn't, and was and wasn't until finally he just wasn't and his mother used the word *divorce* and Nathan unplugged the fish tank. Chester, the goldfish, rose belly-up to the top. His mother blamed herself, of course—she guessed her frenzied vacuuming nudged the cord out of place.

The placenta is a veiny blob. According to Mr. Burgess its blood vessels, supplied by the fetal heart, are "literally bathed in the mother's blood." Nathan drew capillaries, like spider webs, across the hangman's face, adding a cape labeled with a capital N. He filled the thought bubble poised above the man's head with *BLLAARRRRRGH!!*

Dear Hanna,

Today, Suri seemed to enjoy the sunset. Like, really enjoy it. The way the sky turns into a smear. She blew a trunk full of water into the air, which we assume means she's feeling more upbeat. We find out about Madrid soon. Fingers crossed.

And, as always, additional contributions are welcome.

Hanna shifted in her squished seat as Coach informed her of Nathan's punishment for being "so uncool" to the other boys; he was hopeful that a suspension for the summer season would provide some "much-needed chill time" for "Nate." But this was supposed to be Hanna's summer, a "season of much-deserved personal renewal and healing" as Dr. Huoi, her

Lauren Goodwin Slaughter

therapist, put it just last week. The new juicer, sleek as a Ferrari, was on order from Amazon and she signed up for an all-female book club that met Tuesday mornings at a local coffee shop. Balance: her double latte would be "skinny" but topped by a cloud of whipped cream. According to the schedule, the theme of Carnal Desire in *Anna Karenina* would be first on the agenda. Various freelancing projects were also in the works in addition to her elephant story and the hours of research that involved. Her plan for the summer: read for book group, spend time at the zoo with Joni and Nori, write rigorously. For exercise she would swim in the local pool or work in her garden using her new, wood, long-handled gardening trowel—the kind with the perfect forest green metal spear. It would be corn, peppers, a butterfly bush. Meanwhile, various basketball camps and summer tournaments were set to take up the better part of Nathan's weekdays and even some weekends. The carpooling schedule was recorded on her calendar, her days highlighted in fluorescent orange. The novels she would read during those practices and games were already smoldering expectantly in a Barnes and Noble bag in her trunk.

After Nathan's accident Hanna felt simultaneously depressed and supercharged, motivated by a rush similar to when Nathan was an infant and only adrenaline could have propelled her through each day's marathon of feedings, changings, naps, store-runs and the glimmering, all-consuming anxiety produced by each tiny decision related to those activities. Placed on his stomach, Nathan would sleep—but everyone knew that position caused SIDS. And if he did happen to nap on his back, her tiny baby would wake with ice-cold hands because the blanket that would warm him could kill him. The weight of a thousand conflicting opinions—of friends, family, the smirking authors of her stacks of baby books—was more than she could bear. But no one else was going to wake up with her son at his 2:00 a.m. feeding, feel the warm jolt of her body kick in to feed the person it concocted from a weave of cells and blood and, as some said, God.

After Nathan was released from the burn unit to recover from home, Hanna, and Hanna alone, read comics by his bedside, parachuting army guys into his line of vision—for he could barely move—or diagramed the solar system of foam balls positioned around his room. He was a brave, kind boy and Hanna knew he kept asking the same questions about the rings of Saturn because it was the planet she knew the most about. In the beginning they were going to physical therapy twice a day, she herself throwing him the lightly weighted medicine ball that he mostly dropped and timing his circuit on the stationary bike; when he got tired, she would bend down and move his legs for him. Set to its lowest setting Nathan still had to strain to reach the pedals. In the evenings, after the bath he insisted on taking behind a closed door and without her help, she would tell him the corniest knock-knocks she could think of as she reapplied the bandages on his face. One night she found herself humming the nursery rhyme she used to sing him when he was a baby, closing her own eyes to obstruct the tears she refused for Nathan to see no matter what.

But that was then. Now, Nathan was fourteen and she was forty-five. Their energy for these efforts had been dissipating for some time; since Lyle finally left for good she could feel herself giving in to her son's gloomy disposition and also to her own. She routinely polished off a bottle of red wine before popping her Ambien, and Nathan's door was X-ed with bright yellow police tape that read CAUTION! DO NOT CROSS THIS LINE! New duct tape kept getting reapplied and she didn't even know where it came from. Each morning over the Pop-Tart or Cap'n Crunch breakfast Nathan refused, his eyes drove a laser right through her forehead. Their 20-minute commute to school was terrible—a monologue of her flaccid, prying questions. She said she was curious about his friends, girls, classes, as if she was some distant uncle who didn't know the first thing about him. And when he gave in and let something slip she clung to the most minor detail, nurturing it, cultivating it, until it grew to represent a whole chunk of his life that she was missing.

Dear Hanna,

Did you ever get the feeling that everything was finally settled only to have it all explode into your face? We've hit a snafu with Suri and Madrid. Something about international animal-handling? Something about who would own Suri? Something about WTF? It doesn't look good, Hanna. Not good at all. And this, after Suri's special sunset …

Additional contributions needed A.S.A.P.

Lauren Goodwin Slaughter

Nathan collected his books and shoved them into his gargantuan backpack. P.E. was the next class block, but he was considering ditching it to smoke on the corner with the other rejects. Today was rope climbing and his shaky, Play-Doh arms wouldn't be up to the task. Anyway, last week's waltz lesson was bad enough; without the guts to choose a partner he'd been paired with Barbara Hogan—the fattest girl in the 8th grade. She wore a too-small Hello Kitty baby tee warped by the bulk of her breasts and stomach. Uneven rows of tiny plastic barrettes notched her slimy brown hair. She smelled vaguely of bathrooms and cheese. And yet it was Barbara who seemed disgusted by Nathan; as they circled around the gymnasium with the other stumbling teenagers she kept her eyes crinkled shut. His right toe still ached from her missteps.

Nathan felt in his pocket for the pack of Camels he'd been nursing for two weeks, anticipating the warm, bitter kick of smoke. The hall between classes was a coagulation of body spray, phone beeps, jock greetings and girl giggles and as he made his way through the mass he was careful to stare straight ahead. Dork. As long as he kept to himself this horde of hormones rarely even looked at him anymore; but Nathan got that—he tried his best not to look at himself, too. The novelty of his fucked up face had passed and now he was just another. Inconsequential. Dork.

As he worked his way to the exit, Nathan found himself behind a t-shirt advertising "Naked Co-Ed Hacky-Sack" showing two nude students with red cups positioned over their junk. This was Ashley Martin's shirt, of course. She had three older sisters and for years had been emulsified with layers of gluey make-up and fashioned in inappropriate hand-me-down sorority tees that commemorated a seemingly endless catalogue of luaus, spring flings, and pimp and ho extravaganzas.

"What do you think *you're* looking at?"

Ashley stopped in the hall to convene with her girlfriends and without realizing it Nathan stopped, too. She turned to face him and the three triangle Tri-Delt insignia on her chest seemed to throb: *wah … wah … wah.*

"Hello? Freak? I asked you what you were looking at."

Though he was trying, desperately trying, Nathan was stuck, eyes frozen on Ashley Martin's big triangles.

"Check it out, people! People? This freak is totally molesting me right now!"

The commotion of the hall ceased and Nathan could feel himself getting checked out. "Seriously, shouldn't you be saving this for your Barbara?" Ashley went on, "Her boobs are even bigger!" A cacophony of *naws*, *oohs* and snickers burst from every corner as Nathan felt the fangs of feral anger bite through him.

"Grrrrrr" he snarled, beginning to thaw, "grrrrrr…ruff! Ruff, ruff, ruff!" Ashley took a step back. New Nathan devoured Old Nathan as the animal edged closer and closer to the ditzy bitch, gnarling his face into an even more grotesque contortion. "Grrrrrrr … rwwwwwww!"

He bared his teeth.

Something was going to happen. Nathan could feel it about to happen and took off running down the hall past the howling and pointing mob, the whirring soda machine, the shimmering trophy case, the graffitied lockers scrawled with obscenities, and past kind and steady Mr. Burgess who must have been on hall duty today and met Nathan's wild visage with horrified concern as the quiet, deformed student became a black blur straight through the jangling doors of Saint Joseph High School.

"Get out of here, you freak!" Jeremy, his team captain cried after him, "And don't even think about coming back to practice!" Jeremy, dressed in a globe-blue Lacoste polo the color of eyes slightly obscured by just-too-long hair looked so normal, Nathan thought, whizzing by. Looked so … lovely.

****

The zookeeper tossed apples and carrots to Joni and Nori; the veil of dust formed from the activity seemed to place the elephants in a dream Hanna was having of the present moment. But wasn't it time to get Nathan from school? Why was she back at the zoo again? How had she left it with Coach, and his robot-fit sidekicks?

"These girls have been spoiled out there in Fog City," the keeper commented, launching another apple through the bars to the sisters. Joni's agile trunk curled around the fruit and urged it to her whisker-rimmed mouth. "They keep asking for guava and wheat grass smoothies! Ha ha!"

Yes. The zoo. Hanna remembered now. Just as she was leaving to pick up Nathan she'd received yet another email update from savethecreatures.

org. It seemed Suri had taken a turn for the worse and was more depressed than ever—she hadn't touched her hay and was refusing water. The excrement eating had resumed. But another contribution would allow the organization to help pay for Suri's increasing medical expenses, the email explained. (Would you help us, *Hanna*? Do you really have what it takes to change things?) So one minute she was digging through her purse for her credit card and the next she was back at the zoo, monitoring Joni and Nori, taking notes. *Eat apples and carrots. Moms and kids. Dust everywhere.* The detour meant she would be 20 minutes late picking Nathan up, but so what. He was fine. He was punished. He could wait on her for once.

Gathered behind the guardrail, a small crowd of mommies and toddlers held out their hands as the zookeeper passed around the feed bucket so the kids could take turns tossing in the elephant's lunch. "I wish my kids ate like that," one mom voice lamented. "Tell me about it" another responded. Hanna remembered it well, those endless days alone with Nathan—they, too, would go to the zoo; and then the park, the grocery store, the pool—each activity geared toward tiring Nathan out long enough for Hanna to take a shower or cook dinner or rush through a superficial house-cleaning. Looking around at the mothers, Hanna knew them. She was them. But she was also struck by their youth; did she really look like that fourteen years ago? One mom chatted into her glittery cell phone, oblivious as her pig-tailed daughter devoured her share. Another mom, with superhero strength, balanced each of her fat, Disney-clad twins as they dove in the pail. Another boy—bigger than the rest—four years old, probably—greedily snatched and grabbed a fistful and then broke loose from his mother, sprinting right up to the guardrail and hurling the apples and carrots towards Nori and Joni's pen. Much to the kid's frustration, the toss came up short of the elephants' reach. Like dethatched creatures, the trunks probed, wormed and huffed, but even fully extended through the bars could not snag a piece of the accumulation the boy had sent their way.

"Urgggghhhhhh!" The boy squealed.

"Please, use your words, Jackson," his mother coaxed. Her skin was still smooth and cheery. Everything she wore seemed hempish and handmade. "Now, do you need help? Jackson, honey—would you like Mommy to help you?"

"Urgggghhhhhh!"

The zookeeper, trying to keep things cool and harmonious, commented that the elephants were also mommies and this meant they had learned to be very, very patient. They were happy mommy elephants. They could wait for their lunch. They could wait for their special helper. The zookeeper offered a knowing smirk to the moms as he went into the bucket for additional carrots and apples so Jackson could try again.

"Okay," Jackson said, appeased, calm, rubbing his eyes. Hanna noticed his yellow ring of tangled curls, dizzy-blue eyes, red popsicle mouth, flushed cheeks. His skin was so polished and milky—like a veneered egg.

And suddenly she knew what was going to happen.

That drowning-flashback-feeling.

As the zookeeper held out a handful of apples and carrots for Jackson, in an electric flash the kid dashed to the other side of the guardrail, slipping his slim body through the wide metal bars to retrieve the misthrown produce lying in the soot beyond the elephants' reach. Only Hanna felt the air turn to glass, noticed the trees suck all the oxygen—and so she began to float up, above the impossible tragedy about to occur. Jackson's mother was not yet crazed, did not know what she would know five minutes from now—that darkness saves its sharpest claws for children. She did not see Joni and Nori's eyes turn to bolts. She only called after her son in a slack, lazy way—the way she might to encourage him to pull up his pants or come inside for Goldfish crackers, his favorite.

"Jackson, honey …"

And even though the zookeeper digested enough of this moment to try to scramble his way to the kid, it was too late and the disaster had already been put in motion and the adults were too distracted and slow and Jackson, instead of throwing the apples and carrots to the elephant from his relatively safe spot, wriggled through the second set of bars which were very close together, but still wide enough for him to slip through. Like a feather through a grate. Now, just feet from Joni's gargantuan column-legs, the look on Jackon's face could only be described as ecstatic. This was the coolest thing that had ever happened to him—way better than cotton candy at the circus, way better than squawking like a chicken off the diving board, way better than going to the NASCAR race with this dad, propped on those strong, bony shoulders as the cars shot past them faster and louder than anything he'd ever heard or seen and ever would now and and all the women started screaming.

Not safe. Not safe at all.

****

Dear Hanna,

Remember that even if this whole thing with Suri doesn't work out, plenty of others need your help. Best not to get too attached, believe us. Consider making a donation to the choking sea turtles of Palm Beach County who keep ingesting plastic grocery store bags. They think the bags are jellyfish! Imagine that. Click here to contribute to our sea turtle rescue efforts.

Nathan pictured it: his mother would pull into the carpool line just as he staggered out from the bushes where he'd been hiding to avoid his classmates. They would both notice that the other parents, in their vans and station wagons and SUVs, greeted their children with obscenely joyous exclamations, like caricatures. These parents were happy because their child was not Nathan. It didn't take long after the accident for him to realize his repulsiveness made others appreciate their own good fortune. "Makes you feel so lucky" the moms and dads would whisper, "so blessed."

Just trying to find a Frisbee for a younger kid, Nathan would say as he appeared out of the ivy. It would be important to gain his mom's good will because by now she and Coach would have talked. She would know about Nathan's abhorrent behavior, the way he'd been wildly snarling at his teammates and generally acting like a lunatic. Last week he stuck his hand down his throat in the middle of an out-of-bounds play and threw up his peanut butter sandwich all over Kyle because in addition to having lizard skin Kyle was also allergic to peanuts. Why? His mom was sure to ask that—why?—and what did he have to say for himself and when she did he might just have to start crying. For effect. But the truth was he couldn't explain it; he had no idea why he'd been acting this way.

Once Nathan finally made his way to the car, looking as pitiful as possible, the first words out of his mouth would have to be, "sorry." But that wouldn't quite work because his mother could answer it was not she who needed the apology, Nathan, but rather your teammates whom

I frankly cannot believe you've treated in this manner. Looking at her son with shivering, translucent eyelids she would say she was not only disappointed, but concerned. It was just that she was wondering what kind of person her son was becoming. And because it was not in the best interest of playing Mortal Kombat II later that night to do it, Nathan would not ask her why she was the weirdest of all moms on the planet, or why she wore those stupid sandals and what was she was doing all day at the zoo with those stupid elephants or what did she do to finally make dad leave for good. Instead, Nathan knew that if he could keep his mouth shut and just sit there dolefully for long enough, listening to All Things Considered, sooner or later she would turn the blame inward and enter an embarrassing stupor about what she could have done differently. For Old Nathan, this would generate in him so much sorrow and regret that he really would be sorry, would want to inhale an enormous, impossible breath and take all of the awful things he had done and said back. He would say, and mean, I love you Mom. But for New Nathan, now would be the time to go in for the manufactured hug because that was how to get what he wanted. The hug would have to be more than his usual, stiff, Frankensteinian squeeze, though—this situation called for a full-out embrace that if he could stand it must be endured for ten whole seconds accurately measured using Mississippis. Eventually, she would break away from the hug, slightly tearful, before adjusting their driving route to swing by Blockbusters on the way home for Soldier of Fortune. Later, it'd be Sloppy Joes with a brownie sundae for dessert.

Except that's not how it went. Nathan waited, itching in the bushes for two hours without a single call or text from his mother. The question mark and where r u, mom texts went unanswered. So when all the yellow buses vanished from the parking lot and the world dissolved into purple-dark, Nathan put his hood in place and started the three-mile walk home.

Like a red strobe, the swarm of fire trucks, ambulances, police cars. But the zoo was oddly silent—no Gibbon screams, no macaw gawks, no train toots, no kid groups, no sound at all from anyone. For Hanna, it was like a gluey Ambien trance; she was here but not here, hovering, tingling. As the men with beeping equipment ran to the boy who lay unmoving on

Lauren Goodwin Slaughter

the ground in a cloud of filth, they were movie versions of themselves running, running. It was so exhausting and unnecessary.

No one could have saved the boy.

Dear Hanna,
Suri didn't make it. Sorry, but thought you would want to know.

Lyle waited in the shadows like he did so many evenings, his junky Geo parked behind the Wilson family's fully-outfitted, double-back, Eurovan Volkswagen camper. The Wilsons were always headed out to this nature preserve or that wilderness refuge, returning with gargantuan pinecones, expertly whittled walking sticks, even raccoon pelts, distorted and apricot-rank. Lyle was convinced that the boys displayed the hides on their back porch as a kind of secret message to him—it meant this is how you raise a boy, you embarrassing, fat, dead-beat. Tonight, he could see the foggy outline of Mrs. Wilson floating through her kitchen. The pie smells that fluttered from their home into the air also seemed like a kind of message, though of what he wasn't sure. He cracked his window and inhaled. Pecan?

8:45. Late. Tonight it was taking longer than usual for a glimpse of his family. Basketball games were Tuesday nights but this was Thursday. Tae kwon do? No, Nathan abandoned that last year. Something at school? But as far as Lyle knew, Nathan wasn't involved in a single extra-curricular. "How about the chess team?" Lyle suggested the last time they went for Big Macs, but Nathan just rolled his eyes. It was a dumb suggestion anyway. And the PTA meeting was last Wednesday: he'd offered to give Hanna a ride, and came home early from his new IT job at the same community college where she worked with enough time for a quick jog and a shower, but then he just stood there, naked, in front of the mirror for who knew how long, ignoring her battery of phone calls. But you promised, Hanna would say if he picked up. Par for the course. Still, Lyle kept thinking each new call would be the one he would answer to say sorry, Hanna, I am so very sorry, I'm on my way right now—just running a few minutes late— been putting in some extra time at work, oh, didn't you know I was in the IT department now, yes, it's great, we should meet for lunch sometime, until the calls finally stopped and he collapsed on the couch with an enormous bowl of Butterfinger ice cream.

Through his rearview Lyle saw the dark shape approaching, a form of Nathan's build and height with a hood pulled over its face. His son. Lyle crouched down in his seat to hide as Nathan skulked by the car, missing his father completely.

"Son!" Lyle whispered into his coat as Nathan kept walking.

Then, Lyle saw two headlights race through the night, one brilliant white, the other yellow. He identified this as his wife's car; together they put in the wrong bulb and neither of them felt it worthy of fixing, so just left it alone. Just as Lyle was making a mental note to swing by the hardware store he saw Nathan fly off the sidewalk and into the car's trajectory, waving his arms. The car skidded to a sideways stop and Hanna—wild, possessed—threw open the door and got out in the middle of the street.

"Get!" She screamed, "Get out of the road!" Her arms were a seizured blur as she ran to her son. Meanwhile, Nathan, oddly calm and slow, bent over the small squiggling shape illuminated by the beams. It was covered in blood.

"You killed it." Nathan said, looking up at his mother. He could see her forehead rivers, her breathing gray eyes, the magic mole. She seemed to settle. In the beams, the little creature curled and squirmed.

"It's not dead, Nathan," she said. "Look." They both looked. Then, leaving Nathan alone in the headlights, Hanna disappeared down the driveway to return with the long-handled garden trowel she'd planned to use for a butterfly bush. As she raised the blade to strike the animal, Nathan stood there staring. She could do this. The metal was shrill on the road as Hanna lifted and struck and struck again, efficient and cool as whatever had been the squirrel changed into something else entirely. She kept at it until, gently, Nathan put his hand on her shoulder to indicate that now it was his turn with the shovel. The curious neighbors who flipped on their porch lights or tucked back their curtains would see Lyle exit his car and rush toward his wife and son to try to join in.

Lauren Goodwin Slaughter is the recipient of a 2012 Rona Jaffe Foundation Writers' Award and author of the poetry collection a lesson in smallness *(The National Poetry Review Press). Her fiction and poetry have appeared or are forthcoming in venues such as* Carolina Quarterly, Crab Orchard Review, Drunken Boat, Five Chapters, Eleven Eleven, Kenyon Review Online, Valparaiso Poetry Review, *and* Verse Daily. *She is an assistant professor of English at The University of Alabama at Birmingham where she is also the Editor-in-Chief of* PoemMemoirStory, *a literary journal that publishes writing by women.*

Desire on Domino Island

Lee Smith

Some summers back, my friend Katherine Kearns, who was pregnant and bored at the time, decided that she wanted to write a romance novel. So she sent off to Silhouette Romances for guidelines, temporarily abandoned her pursuit of the Ph.D. in English at the University of North Carolina, and set to work. Some of the guidelines follow: Our Heroine is, preferably, an orphan. She is alone in the world. (Note: A brother is, in some cases, permissible, but only if he is retarded or has not found his way in life.) Our Heroine appears frail, but looks terrific when she gets dressed up. She is, of course, a virgin. She arrives alone in the lush, romantic Setting, where she encounters our Hero, who is preferably dark, brooding, and mysterious (although we have had some luck recently with stern Nordic sorts and hunky redheads). The initial encounter is tempestuous. Sparks fly, yet there is of course a mad, underlying attraction. The Other Woman will be beautiful, desirable, and wealthy. She is, of course, a bitch. The Other Man will be nice, boring, well-meaning, intent upon saving our Heroine from the clutches of our Hero and the dangerous contingencies of the Plot. (Note: No other main characters will be permitted in this novel, especially children. Any necessary others, such as a faithful housekeeper, should remain as stereotypical as possible, so as not to detract from the romance.) The Plot will ensue, with the ten chapters growing increasingly shorter as tension mounts. At the climax, our Hero and Heroine realize that they are made for each other after all. The novel ends with their passionate embrace. (Note: At no time during this novel will they or anyone else ever actually do it, nor will any specific body parts be mentioned.) My friend Katherine did not sell her novel to Silhouette Romances, even though she came up with a wonderful heroine who inherited an old inn on Pawley's Island, South Carolina, and a mysterious saturnine artist who painted there. Her novel, A Certain Slant of Light, *turned out to have two qualities that are not permissible: symbolism, and semicolons. But I, still intrigued by the guidelines, wrote this Silhouette Romance.*

CHAPTER ONE

As the sleek motorboat slices through the aqua effervescence of Domino Bay to approach the pearly brightness of the beach, Jennifer surveys the lush scene before her with no small trepidation, and a hint of dismay creeps into her normally dulcet tone as she exclaims, "Captain! Oh,

Captain! Why are you docking here in the middle of nowhere? Is there no settlement of any sort hereabouts? I had expected . . ."

But the captain won't say a thing! A native Georgian with an unfortunately cleft palate, he shoots a dark glance from beneath his surly brow at the clearly frightened young woman and mumbles something indistinguishable into his dark facial hair. He throws her bags on the beach. He heaves his bulk around.

Jennifer drums her small fingers rat-a-tat-tat on the hull of the shiny craft. Is it all a huge mistake, her coming here? But what else could she have done, considering the terrible fire that swept the home of her guardians (since her parents' mysterious death some twenty years ago, Jennifer and her retarded brother, Lewis, have been most carefully raised), killing both Aunt Lucia and Uncle Norm and destroying the entire perfect loveliness of their antebellum mansion, leaving Jennifer with only her small inheritance, her paltry background in microbiology, and the hunting lodge somewhere deep within the fastnesses of this fabled island.

"I had hoped . . ." But Jennifer's words are lost in the slap of the waves and the oddly shrill cries of the brilliant birds that wheel in the hot blue sky. Parrots and shy tropical creatures peek out at her from the shiny green leaves of the junglelike vegetation which threatens to engulf the beach; the shriek of an apparent panther is heard.

"Harg!" the captain barks. Clearly he wants to be quit of this spot before dark, wants to be back on the mainland hefting a brew with his rustic buddies.

Jennifer mounts the dock with a sigh, traverses its rotting length, and turns to wave a reluctant farewell to the enigmatic captain, who even now is rounding the great Grey Lady rocks which mark the harbor, slipping from her view. Well.

Although she is petite and somewhat fragile in appearance, a spark of mischief in Jennifer's eye belies the seeming frailty of her frame. Actually Jennifer is not frail at all! She's strong as an ox, and also she looks terrific when she gets dressed up. But right now she wears a lime-green T-shirt, a khaki wrap-around skirt, and espadrilles. Her wispy brown locks are caught fast in a gold barrette which used to belong to her mother. Jennifer hoists the weight of her luggage and trudges through the wet unwelcoming sand

Lee Smith

across the narrow beach and up a faint trail into the very jungle, vines slowing her progress as she bites her lip to hold back her brimming tears, as night begins to fall . . .

CHAPTER TWO

Plucky Jennifer manages to set up her tent in a clearing beneath a giant live oak, where she eats a granola bar, lights her Coleman lantern, and soon is competently ensconced in the jungle wilderness.

But suddenly we note the rustle of palm fronds, the swish of savannah grass, the warning chorus of tree frogs. Footsteps are heard on the path. Jennifer, who was very nearly asleep, stands to face the invader. Jennifer's teeth clatter helplessly in the tropic night.

"Yes?" she cries bravely into the darkness. "Yes? Who's there?"

"Rock Cliff," comes the terse reply.

"I don't believe I have had the pleasure!" Jennifer casts open the tent fly.

Light streams out to reveal the rugged virile form clad in well-worn (tight) blue jeans, cowboy boots, and an old torn Brooks Brothers shirt open almost to the waist, unveiling the wealth of dark hair on the broad, muscled chest. Beneath the sable sweep of unruly hair and the decisive black line of his eyebrows, Rock Cliff's dark eyes flash fire above the prominent jut of his cheekbones. There is a touch of world-weariness in the little lines that web the marble wideness of his brow, a suggestion of tenderness and compassion which is offset by the fleshy cruel sensuality of his mouth, his strong white teeth. All his muscles bulge.

Now we are getting somewhere!

"Miss Jennifer Maidenfern?" he inquires rudely in deep masculine tones which send an unwonted tingle up Jennifer's spine.

"I beg your pardon!" she rejoins tartly.

"I received a communication from a Miss Jennifer Maidenfern not long ago, insisting that I vacate immediately the premises of Domino Lodge, where I have been in residence for the past ten months while finishing my novel," Rock Cliff continues. "I have now vacated those premises at enormous psychological cost, as I now find I am unable to complete my novel in any other surroundings. I urge you to reconsider."

Lee Smith

It all comes back to Jennifer now. "I sent a letter to the occupant . . ." she says slowly.

"I am the occupant," states Rock Cliff.

"I see." Jennifer realizes she is in danger of losing herself in the fiery depths of his eyes. "I'm terribly sorry," she says with an effort, "but that's quite impossible. I intend to stay."

"I am independently wealthy," asserts Rock Cliff. "I will pay any amount of money to purchase Domino Lodge." There's a sudden unaccustomed tremor in his voice now and we can tell how much this means to him, how his life of rich playboy decadence has left him empty and unfulfilled, how the completion of this novel will bring back his faith in himself.

Jennifer presses her trembling lips into a firm line. "Goodbye, Mr. Cliff," she says. Attempting with shaking fingers to refasten the tent fly, she stumbles over a tortoise and falls backward suddenly, upsetting the lantern. The ever-alert Rock Cliff springs forward into the tent. Quickly he lunges past the terrified young woman to right the lantern and finds himself there suddenly on the tent floor beside her shy vulnerability and sweet trembling lips which he cannot help but cover with his own. The tent fly drops silently behind him.

So I can't see a damn thing! I want to be in that tent; I want to see it all. I want to know where he puts his hands. But here I am, reading, and there they are inside that tent, black opaque shadows moving against the flap, moving and thrashing and moving until at last he emerges with a muttered oath and stumbles off into the night.

CHAPTERS THREE, FOUR, AND FIVE

Are a drag. Nothing much happening here except that Jennifer finally finds Domino Lodge (after several wrong turns, lots of boring flora on the trail) and meets faithful Irish housekeeper Mrs. O'Reilly, an amusing old alcoholic fond of misquoting familiar sayings, as in "Don't put all your eggs under a basset," page 62. Mrs. O'Reilly takes a liking to Jennifer right away, fixing her a hot buttered rum, some scones, some fig preserves. Jennifer eats with interest. Mrs. O'Reilly explains the blood feud which has always existed between the Maidenfern family and the deRigeurs on the other side of the island: an insult, a slight, a missing emerald. Mrs. O'Reilly praises the exemplary conduct of the recent occupant Mr. Cliff

(Ha! Ha!), relates the complete history of Domino Island, and is working up to its geographic configurations when thank God she is interrupted by the surprise entrance of Charles Fine, the young Episcopal rector from the mainland, who has sailed over in his lovely sloop *The Dove* especially to bid Jennifer welcome.

"Welcome." He smiles.

"Why, thank you," Jennifer returns.

Jennifer cannot fail to notice this young bachelor's peaches-'n'-cream complexion, his lithe body, the warm sincerity of his soft blue gaze.

"If there is anything I can do to assist you," Charles Fine offers as he prepares to cast off, "anything at all . . ." His voice rings like a bell.

"I'll let you know," responds Jennifer. She watches him sail away until his boat is a mere black dot against the shimmering sea; she approves of him, Jennifer does, with all her fluttering heart, and she cannot understand the recent blush that climbed her features unawares when Mrs. O'Reilly mentioned that blackguard Rock Cliff. Oh! A hand flies up to Jennifer's mouth. It is, of course, her own.

CHAPTER SIX

So Jennifer settles in. The island sun paints a glint of gold on her plain brown locks and a dusting of freckles across the bridge of her nose. One morning she's hard at work refurbishing all the furniture in the east parlor when who should arrive but Rock Cliff! Jennifer—caught barefooted, no makeup, in one of her oldest frocks—tries to flee the parlor, but he blocks her way with his muscled girth. "Not so fast, young lady!" drawls Rock Cliff. He actually appears to be amused; how dare he? "I've been thinking it over, and I feel I owe you an apology."

"I should say so!" snaps Jennifer. And then somehow she finds herself weakening, smiling up into those eyes. She can feel his breath on her skin. He leans down closer, closer, closer . . .

Breaking free with a momentous exercise of pure will, Jennifer evades the virile visitor and commences to wash the woodwork on the other side of the room.

"Now Jennifer," he entreats, following her slim figure. "I want to make it up to you, Jennifer, if I may call you that. I'd like to take you out

Lee Smith

to dinner tonight."

Furiously, silently, Jennifer scrubs.

Rock Cliff edges even closer. "Come on now," he implores. "I feel a real connection between us, Jennifer. I sensed it from the first. I'm sorry I lost my head, but your nearness combined with the hot charm of the night . . ."

Rock Cliff has edged so close to Jennifer that she has been forced to retreat still further, has in fact climbed upon the windowsill itself, a precarious perch.

"Please, my dear," he begs passionately.

"I'm warning you, Rock Cliff!" shrills Jennifer, but then she tumbles— scrub brush, water pail, and all—straight onto the wide-planked cypress floor, overturning a handsome old desk, an ottoman, and Rock Cliff himself, who sprawls violently beside her in the sudden sea of suds.

Jennifer giggles infectiously. Rock Cliff catches her merriment and guffaws heartily, then turns to her with yearning eyes and clasps her wet torso firmly in his rippling arms. "My dear," he says.

"Oh Rock," yields Jennifer, as . . .

CHAPTER SEVEN

I might have known!" cries Monica deRigeur. "Look at you, Rock Cliff, down there on the floor all wet and unkempt in a compromising position!"

"Now wait just a minute," drawls Rock.

But Jennifer sees the emerald engagement ring on Monica's tapered digit.

"No!" Jennifer leaps up and stamps her petite foot. "Don't wait at all! Just leave! Both of you! I see right through you, Rock Cliff, you and your fashionable fiancée!"

Monica, by the way, is a real bitch wearing a low-necked blue-flowered voile dress which does nothing to hide her voluptuous form. White high-heeled sandals and a strand of priceless pearls about her swanlike neck complete the ensemble. Her upswept coiffure is elegant, implicit, or imminent, or something. I give up. "Move it, lover boy," she directs haughtily.

Lee Smith

"This is all a terrible misunderstanding," Rock states, but the force of Jennifer's grief ejaculates them both from the room.

CHAPTER EIGHT

Jennifer sends for her retarded brother and adopts a wild raccoon which she names Bruce, then nicknames Posy. (?)

CHAPTER NINE

Jennifer and Lewis are sunbathing on the secluded pink shell beach when here comes Charles Fine in his nautically white sloop, ready to propose to Jennifer. "I need a helpmeet," he explains earnestly, holding Jennifer tight in his strong ecclesiastical arms where she sheds a single tear upon realizing who it is she really loves.

"The cat is out of the bag now, I guess!" and, oh no, it's Rock Cliff who has been concealed behind some hydrangea bushes observing this tender scene. Rock Cliff's statement about the cat confuses Lewis, who becomes quite frightened and begins to weep openly. As Jennifer rushes to comfort her poor brother, helpful Charles Fine attempts to explain things to the irate Rock Cliff.

"You must not misconstrue . . ." Charles Fine begins.

"Misconstrue, hell!" shouts Rock Cliff, his fiery temper erupting totally since he has just broken his long-standing engagement to the beauteous Monica deRigeur only to find his dream girl in the arms of another man. Rock Cliff stalks off into the jungle just as lightning splits the summer sky and thunder rolls off the horizon, signaling the oncoming hurricane. A distraught Jennifer resists the fervent pleas of Charles Fine and Mrs. O'Reilly. She insists upon setting off immediately in search of Rock Cliff, and there she goes, accompanied only by her pet raccoon, into the dark wild jungle, into the eye of the storm.

CHAPTER TEN

Just goes on and on! Jennifer is lost in the swamp, buffeted by the hurricane, set upon by wild dogs, defended by Posy, and drenched to the skin. Night falls. Jennifer finally takes shelter in a cave which strangely enough turns out to contain her parents' grave (!) as well as a sealed cask holding some long complicated To Whom It May Concern letter implicating the deRigeurs in her parents' death and explaining the curse of the emerald. *Who cares?* Jennifer tosses and turns in a restless doze yet feels strangely warm because of her parents' presence. At the first blush of dawn she sallies forth and retraces her steps through the jungle until she spots Domino Lodge at last through the dense fronds.

"Posy, we're home!" Jennifer tells the exhausted raccoon.

"And it's about time!" cries Rock Cliff, who has thought better of his hasty actions and has been scouring the jungle all night long for Jennifer. The bedraggled lovers rush toward each other and meet in a passionate embrace on the pink shell beach. Their clothes are all torn and wet, revealing their contours anew in the paleness of dawn. They kiss hungrily as Mrs. O'Reilly, Lewis, and Charles Fine steal out to the edge of the beach to share this happy moment. "Well, it's an ill wind which blows nobody," Mrs. O'Reilly observes with a chuckle, and Charles Fine reveals that he plans to teach Lewis to sail. Rock Cliff casts the unlucky emerald into the waiting waves; Monica deRigeur flies past in her private plane, bound for New York; Posy heaves a sigh of relief; and again the lovers embrace as, behind them, the sun rises out of the sea.

And that's it! I shade my eyes against the brightness of this sun, the glare off the water, but in vain; all I can see is the silhouette. Jennifer and Rock have nothing, nothing left—no faces, no bodies, not to mention fear or pain or children, joy or memory or loss—nothing but these flat black shapes against the tropic sky.

While Lee Smith was still a little girl growing up in the Appalachian town of Grundy, Virginia, her mother would send her to visit her "lovely aunt Gay-Gay in Birmingham, Alabama, every summer for two weeks of honest-to-God Lady Lessons" including table manners which were "tested by fancy lunches at 'The Club' on top of Shades Mountain." Lee, born in 1944, would attend Hollins College and after winning the Book-of-the-Month Club contest with her novel The Last Day the Dogbushes Bloomed, *which would be published in 1968, moved to Tuscaloosa with her husband, James Seay, where she worked for the* Tuscaloosa

Lee Smith

News. Dogbushes *was followed by* Something in the Wind, *and then* Fancy Strut, *set in Tuscaloosa during the sesquicentennial. Smith has gone on to write 10 more novels, most notably perhaps The Last Girls, a best seller,* Oral History, Fair and Tender Ladies *and recently* Guests on Earth, *which features Zelda Fitzgerald as a character. She has four story collections; "Desire on Domino Island" is from* Me and My Baby View the Eclipse. *Smith's work has been honored with an Academy Award in Fiction from the American Academy of Arts and Letters, The Robert Penn Warren Prize, the John Dos Passos Award and the North Carolina Award for literature, among many others. Retired from teaching at North Carolina State University, Smith lives with her second husband, Hal Crowther, in Hillsborough, North Carolina.*

Lee Smith

Angels Came Down

Patricia Lou Taylor

While teaching registered nurse students, I went every winter for twenty years to a state psychiatric hospital. It was my favorite part of teaching as I loved the patients and wanted to help the students develop empathy for people with mental illness. I think for the most part I was successful, and this story is my way of trying to extend that search for caring to people who enjoy literature.

"We have been redeemed. Some cherubs found us and realized that we had been left behind," Jerry says as he looks earnestly into my face.

"Uh huh," I respond, nodding encouragingly and meeting his eyes. He looks ahead and is quiet for a few minutes, apparently satisfied that I have heard and understand. We are walking a tree-lined path that leads to the recreation area of the old state mental hospital. Green leaves are starting to appear and flowers are budding. It's cool, sweater weather, and sunny, and it feels great to be outside after the cold, wet winter. It doesn't get really cold in Alabama like it does other places, but it still feels pretty miserable to us just the same. Jerry and I both watch as a cardinal flits.

"My mother was told that if she had me she would die," Jerry suddenly pronounces.

"That must've been awful for her." I give him what I hope is a sad, concerned look.

"It was, I am alive but her spirit was split into pieces and she is everywhere. I feel her around me all the time." He smiles as he motions with his hands and arms to indicate her presence around his head and body. I'm happy for him that this seems to be a peaceful delusion. In the past I've known him to be agitated and fearful, needing to be restricted to his unit because of his idea that the devil was manifesting himself in other people.

We enter the courtyard to the recreation area and join several people, some dressed oddly, standing alone or in groups, or sitting on benches at picnic tables. It is early, the patients have just begun to fill this popular area and they all are smoking cigarettes. Some hold sodas from a nearby machine. The only patients in conversation are two who are sitting by nursing students, and they seem to be enjoying the extra attention. One young woman holds a small pink radio from which rock music blares. No one moves to the music, but no one seems to be bothered by it either.

I say Hello as we approach the group and every one nods or returns the greeting. They know that I am the nursing students' instructor; they have seen me here every week for the last two months and some have seen me every winter in this capacity for many years.

Jerry immediately pulls a cigarette from his pocket and asks Bob, a young man sitting on a bench with a student, for a light. Bob holds his cigarette out and Jerry lights his cigarette from Bob's. This is one way that I've noticed that the patients take care of each other. They don't have lighters at their disposal but they manage to keep each other's smokes going all day. I guess a staff member starts the first one in the morning. I've also noticed a lot of sharing of sodas and snacks, cigarettes, and small change.

We sit down beside Bob and his student nurse, Ben. Bob is a handsome man of about thirty with sparkling dark eyes. He wears jeans that are too big for him, without a belt, and two pullover sweaters that seem too tight; the top is red and the one sticking out from under is purple. He wears a large yellow comb stuck into the top of his short stiff black hair. He occasionally takes it out and sweeps over his head with comb and hand, like an Elvis impersonator. We all sit without talking. For several minutes Bob looks at us and laughs out loud, a Ha-Ha-Ha laugh, and Ben and I smile back nervously. We aren't sure what he is going to come out with. Jerry and the other patients ignore Bob. In the past Jerry has called Bob 'crazy.'

Suddenly Bob yells at me, "Willie, you caught up with me."

I nod. He turns to Ben, pointing at me, "I know her, she is my wife," then jumps up and points at another patient on the other side of the courtyard, "That man over there. That man owes me fifteen thousand dollars. I'm her pimp." He laughs again, Ha-Ha-Ha, and pulls at his jeans that have fallen below his navel. Ben and I laugh too. Bob is always outrageous in his beliefs and comments. For that reason he is normally not allowed outside his unit without supervision. We are happy that the staff let us bring him here. Ben asks him to sit down, and as Bob does so, Ben tries to distract him by starting another conversation. I turn to Jerry.

"Is this your last day?" Jerry asks, grabbing my hand.

"Yes, I'm sorry. I'll miss you." And I really am sorry; I always hate it when the end of our rotation comes, and I know I won't be back for another ten months.

"Will you take me home with you?" he asks, as he has asked every day that I've spent with him.

"That would be nice if I could, wouldn't it," I reply as I have every day that I've spent with him. I smile and squeeze his hand.

"I have been discharged. I can go anywhere I want to." I nod, knowing it's best not to argue. "I've been kept here prisoner but I've served my time. Angels came down and said 'Jerry White, you can go free.'"

I smile and nod again. There is absolutely nothing to say to this that would be helpful. We sit quietly for awhile. The rock music continues to blare from the pink radio. We've been able to talk, but it would be so much more peaceful without it. Still, I think that it helps to calm the voices for a lot of the patients, so it works that way.

While we sit and listen to Bob talk excitedly to Ben over the din of the radio, I feel again my rising frustration that Jerry and a lot of people like him are doomed to serve a prison-like sentence for the rest of their lives because they have brain disorders like schizophrenia, bipolar disease, and severe depression.

In institutions most people are admitted for acute exacerbations of their illness, are stabilized on medication, and then sent out into the community within a short time. Most live in the community in some fashion, ideally with family, group homes, or individual apartments. But we do not have adequate community resources anywhere in our country, and a lot of patients spend more time in jail or on the streets than anywhere else.

For people like Jerry who don't respond to medicines at all and are a danger to themselves or others, this hospital is their home for a great deal of their lives. It is awful for the students to realize this, but I say that at least these patients have a safe environment, shelter and food.

I'm interrupted from my reverie by Bob. He jumps up and down while he shouts, "I'm a white Canadian Egyptian pharaoh!" He pulls at his pants that are falling again while he hops around the picnic table. "They dipped me in shit to make me black and that's why I'm a warrior." He laughs his strange laugh, and Ben tells Bob to quiet down. Ben knows that Bob won't be allowed to come out with us if he gets too disruptive.

Jerry ignores Bob and asks me if I'll buy him a cup of coffee. I slip him fifty cents. We are not supposed to buy things for the patients, but I figure they have so few pleasures that a little spoiling won't hurt.

Later that morning, ten nursing students meet me at the entrance to the chronic woman's ward. It is blocked by a large grey locked metal door. The hall to the unit is painted a dull white with no relief from pictures, murals or plants. Paint is peeling around the top of the door. I knock and stand on tiptoes to see through the small unbreakable window. Finally a staff member sees me and slowly heads towards the door with her keys in tow. When she opens the door, we all enter as a group carrying a cooler of sodas and ice, bags of chips, cookies, and paper plates and cups.

About fifteen women patients crowd around us; there are too many to count or to really talk with individually. They all speak to us at once, and touch us, and ask what we have brought them. I recognize most of these women from each year that I've visited; they are like Jerry in that they have no place else to go. Most of them are so unstable that they are not allowed to walk the grounds with the students. So we have brought a party to them.

While we head to a small closed-off room with table and chairs to set up the snacks, the three staff members dressed in pink scrubs yell at the patients not to get too close to us. They are not nurses; in fact I never see nurses on the unit with the patients. The nurses sit on the other side of the locked door in the nurses' station with their charts. The staff members with us are unlicensed personnel and are responsible for direct around-the-clock-supervision of the patients. A staff member yells again, and the women hold back and let the students pass into the room furnished with tables and benches.

As the students set up the goodies, I stay outside with the patients. Chairs too heavy to lift are arranged in long rows that face a television behind a heavy bolted piece of plastic. The staff settles to watch a daytime

Patricia Lou Taylor

soap opera, and the patients clamor around me again.

Julie, a blond petite woman who looks like she should still be on the adolescent unit, tells me she is Snow White and Grace Kelly. "I have a mansion in Beverly Hills filled with gold and silver. I'll give it to you if you get me out of here," she says. Shonna, a large black woman, over six feet tall, with scars across her forehead and cheek, laughs and tells me not to pay any attention to Julie. Julie starts to cry and I put my arm around her and she stops crying. Bobbie, with dyed blond hair and dark black roots, wears Big Bird slippers and calls me Mamma. Shonna tells Bobbie that I am not her mother and Bobbie cries. I pat her on the hand, as Maggie, who wears a baseball cap and jeans, asks if we can play cards and can she lead the Hokey Pokey.

Shonna says she wants to sing for us. Cheryl, who is sixty-something, gets close enough to tell me that she birthed thirty-three babies last night and just found out she is pregnant again. Shonna laughs and calls Cheryl crazy. Mona, a heavy-set woman in a purple nightgown, laughs at Cheryl too and then tells me she herself is not sick like everyone else here, but is a secret undercover agent for the CIA, and asks if I can get a message to them.

I see Karen across the room sitting near a staff member. She wears a motorcycle-like helmet to prevent her from hurting her head when she bangs it against a wall. Now she rocks back and forth. I catch her eye and wave and she waves back, but does not get up to approach me until the students announce that the refreshments are ready.

Twenty women, everyone on the unit except one woman who has slept cramped on a too small couch since we entered, find a place at one of the picnic tables in the room. They eat and drink everything set in front of them and then keep all ten students and me busy with their requests for more: "More Coke, please, more Cheetos, Are there more cookies? Did you bring candy?"

Shonna sings "Amazing Grace" in a deep throaty voice and we all clap. Several women tell dirty jokes and all the patients laugh uproariously while the students and I roll our eyes. Bobbie keeps yelling out "Mamma" at me, and Shonna and Maggie tell her to shut up. Sue, a young black woman who never speaks at all, starts to sing "You light up my life." Suddenly the room is quiet except for her beautiful perfect voice; for a few minutes everyone looks at peace. Then Bobbie starts to sing along with her and several of the woman and students join in, all sounding terribly out of tune, but joyous.

The party ends with the Hokey Pokey, led by Maggie, and we all put our butt in and shake it all around. As the students clean up, I play a game of Spades with Maggie. Others hover over me and continue to talk, while Maggie yells at them to leave us alone. She wins the game.

The students and I finally say our goodbyes and Bobbie clings to me yelling "Mamma," and is pulled away and held comfortingly by Shonna.

The students leave the facility to go out to lunch. I sit in my car, too tired to go anywhere or to talk to anyone for an hour.

I've finished lunch and am waiting for Jerry outside the recreation hall. We agreed earlier to meet here so we can go to the weekly record hop together. This is the most popular event of the week and patients are streaming towards the ear-splitting recreation hall from all directions.

Bob and Ben show up. Bob says he wants a cigarette before he goes into the dance, so he gets a light from another patient and they stand with me. Bob is very quiet for a few minutes, cocking his head and smiling at no one in particular. Ben and I eye each other. Suddenly Bob yells, "I went up there and there were vampires and wolves." He starts to dance around with his arms out in front of him like he is boxing, while his pants fall down. "They were fighting and baring their teeth." Bob grins at us viciously. "There were red vampires and white wolves. I'm not going there no more." He shakes his head back and forth emphatically.

Ben asks, "Where?"

"In the sky!" Bob answers indignantly and glares at Ben, as he crushes his cigarette under his foot.

"Oh," says Ben and looks at me sheepishly.

"Bob, are you ready to go inside?" I ask.

Bob is quiet and looks like he is starting to turn and walk in the direction of the music when he abruptly stops and points to another patient. He pronounces, "That man is thirty-five million years old. He doesn't have to worry about money. He doesn't answer to anyone."

Ben starts to walk, encouraging Bob to follow him, but Bob continues talking to another patient. "You owe me sixty thousand billion dollars for her." He points at me. Ben takes Bob by the arm and tells him it is time to leave.

Bob follows passively, saying to me, "Goodbye, sweetheart." Luckily, the other patient has totally ignored Bob; he sits staring into space.

I sit on a bench beside Luther. Luther never talks unless spoken to and sits with his head in hands, his forehead creased. Luther has always refused to spend time with a student because he says he has things to work out. And he doesn't go to dances either. Normally, I can barely follow him. His speech is always so rushed and pressured.

"I'm waiting for the canteen worker, Peggy, to get back from lunch, she's my best friend, I'm gonna make her a pillow a yellow one with blue trim, I've been invited to the White House, I can't get hold of them, I need someone to take up for me, I contacted the Secret Service and hope they'll help me, I've got to get out of here, I need someone to know that I'm pregnant; it's twins I'm worried how they'll get out I need an ultrasound, they'll have to go out my bladder and that will hurt, can you help me?"

"You sound like you are having a really bad day," I say inanely. Of course, being a male, pregnant with twins, and needing to get out of here and to the White House, with no one to help you would be worse than having a bad day.

"I am. I need to be left alone to work this out." Luther bows his head again and I leave him alone.

Jerry shows up saying he overslept at nap time. He grabs my hand as we head towards the dance. The patients are not allowed to touch us, or anyone else for that matter, but I believe that they need the feel of another human body; isn't that a basic human need for all of us?

We slow dance and I let him hold me just a little closer than I should. He is a big muscular man with a mustache and beard. He looks and feels great in his leather jacket, jeans and cowboy boots.

"Will you take me home with you?"

"That would be nice, wouldn't it?"

"I've been kept prisoner but I've served my time. The angels came down and redeemed us and set me free."

I'm exhausted; I've danced every dance. But the music has finally stopped and it's time for us to go home. Students and patients alike lined up to do the Macarena and the Electric Slide that have recently become popular. I dance on the periphery with patients like me who can't follow the line dances. We hold hands and sway or twirl each other around. I know the students think I'm corny and that's O.K.

The patients crowd around us all, asking for goodbye hugs which we freely give, despite disapproving glances from the staff. Jerry waits till last and gives me an especially long close hug. I tell him I'll see him next time I bring students.

I head back to my life with no locked doors, with a job and an affectionate family and a car and Cokes and cigarettes and cookies any time I want them. On the way home I think about Jerry and Bob and Julie and Shonna and Maggie and Cheryl and Mona and Karen and Sue and Luther. I pray that the angels will come down and realize who has been left behind.

Patricia Taylor has been a nurse for 40 years. She worked in various settings, including teaching psychiatric nursing at the University of West Alabama, and also working at Bryce Hospital in Tuscaloosa. She is currently retired, works geri-psychiatric nursing part time and is completing a collection of nursing stories. She has had stories published in Belles' Letters, The Sucarnochee Review, *and* Healing Hearts, *a nursing journal.*

Patricia Lou Taylor

Envenomation

Kathleen Thompson

The summer I studied fiction writing with Mary Clyde at Spalding University, I listened like a gardener hoping for rain. Ripe stories with first lines as juicy as watermelon hearts inundated me. In retrospect I realize that my use of a pseudonym, V. Hasseltine Taylor, was the sheerest of curtains that somehow furnished me great psychological license in theological issues of free will / chance. These themes continue to saturate much of my writing: just how free is our will? Theologian Paul Zahl suggests that our free will can be stripped from us by depression and addiction, as well as by worry and mourning. "Envenomation" explores an ancillary question: how can coincidence or a single happenstance shape a life? The seed for this story was planted by my father-in-law, Meron Thompson, an inimitable oral storyteller described by his own discerning pastor, David Hodnett, as "one not burdened by political correctness." Irreverence is not intended toward any religion mentioned, although my characters may embody that trait. My brother-in-law, George Smith, a physician, confirmed the possibility of the snaky happenstance I envisioned. The first line was inspired by a comment from my October 2002 workshop leader, Ellie Bryant, high on the speed of cyberspace: "I'm an e-mail slut." Silas House, an author also in that workshop, called my dialogue "pitch-perfect." He wrote, "Your use of the Southern vernacular is absolutely perfect so don't change any of that no matter what anyone says." I'm still listening. No wonder my preacher got a new name: Silas.

Who pities a snake charmer when he is bitten, or all those who go near wild animals?
—Sirach 12:13

My daddy handles snakes and my mama is an e-mail slut. That's how Mama puts it. Even to my boss who's a preacher. And Daddy just grins. You tangle up Mama and Daddy's gray heads and you've got about as odd a lot as two snakes mating. Now, don't take what Mama says to mean Daddy is a member of the snake-handling church where I work, because he's not. He's legally a Methodist, and what happened was a pure mistake, but a living sin all the same. Daddy keeps snakes. He actually breeds them. Just to tell you the God's truth, it's much more than that.

Snakes are his true religion.

Whether it was the snakes or my brother Slim I don't know, but Radio never would spend the night here in Anniston. My skirt-chasing husband never did hit it off with Slim. But no wonder. Slim is nearly as bad as Miss Mullinax when it comes to Mexicans. And Slim high-hats Daddy's job, too. Herb's Herps. But I say, pot can't call the kettle Blackie. Slim works with nerve gas down at the Anniston Ordinance Depot. Talk about an edgy job. One little mess-up on his part could wipe out Calhoun County.

Me? If I see any crawling thing longer than a lizard, I run. Daddy knows that, and if he ever knows you're afraid of snakes, you'd better watch out. More than once I've started to get into my car and found a rat snake or a black racer coiled up in a little pile under the steering wheel. Daddy wants me to love his snakes inside and out the way he does, but I don't care for snakes at all. And living in this house with my parents doesn't help matters any. The second night I was here, I got up to use the bathroom and stepped on something in the hallway. I nearly jumped out of my skin, and they probably heard me screaming in the next county. The funny thing is how I knew immediately what it was. Some things you can know without knowing you know. Daddy ran out of the bedroom and flipped on the light. I was like a rabbit in headlights.

"Ooh, wee, look at the size of that beauty," Daddy said, whistling low and moving like he was stalking a deer. He just had on his skivvies and a tee shirt. Mama was right behind him.

"Lovie, you just freeze right there, little girlie," he said in a real steady, even voice, never moving his eyes from the snake.

"Temp, you go get me a pillow case, quick."

"What in the world?" grumbled Mama, belting her robe.

"Cottonmouth. Must be at least four foot." Daddy's voice was still even and low.

The cottonmouth lay coiled up with his mouth wide open looking at me, and those fangs flicking around like two deadly needles. I flattened myself against the wall like a calendar in December. Daddy's hand was as fast as a snake's strike. He got that cottonmouth from behind on either side of the head.

"You see this, Lovie? He's got a pointed head."

Kathleen Thompson

Daddy flipped his tail over and said, "One row of scales, too. That's how you can tell he's a hottie."

When I got back into my bed, I had the shakes so bad that if the pink and green wedding ring quilt had been real rings, they would've been jangling. It took me a while to stop seeing snake scales and pointy heads and that gaping white mouth. Daddy somehow wrestled the snake down into the pillow case and tied a knot at the end. He swore this was not one of his snake tricks and left his little package on the porch swing. He was snoring again in no time. Mama said since she was awake she was going to check e-mail. I had a bad case of the big eye. I lay considering what crack that cottonmouth had slithered through. And did he have a mate?

Sometimes when I lie awake in my poster bed staring up at the white canopy, listening to the regular swish, swush of the fig branches against the clothesline outside, I think of what's possible and what's not. Sometimes I wish I'd looked a little harder for work in Birmingham. Or maybe even got a loan and gone back to school. Moved into Isobelle's guest room for a few months like she kept insisting. It was right nigh impossible, though, for me to stay next door to Radio. The only reason Mama ever let me marry him in the first place was because I promised her I'd finish my nursing degree at The University of Alabama in Birmingham.

Me? I would have promised away my life for Radio then. He was driving from Birmingham to give dance lessons on Tuesday nights in the Red Barn Bar not far from here. I liked line dancing and doing the Macarena. Mama wanted to know what dancing had to do with anything in real life. But nursing was her dream, not mine. My real life was my new husband, and he liked the idea of me being his little *nursie* any time he dropped by the house in between installing telephones.

The one thing I did love about nursing school was the babies. Daddy has pictures of me and Slim in the nursery at the hospital, taken through the glass. Rows and rows of babies lined up, wrapped up in receiving blankets like wieners in corn dogs. Daddy said you could tap on the glass and the nurse would roll your baby's bassinet up front. Daddy swore he could pick us out of the bunch by our red hair. But birth pain is kept private now, within four walls, among a family. When our class toured the hospital, we learned all about birthing rooms, but we didn't see one single baby.

Kathleen Thompson

I could imagine me in a room like that, and Mama holding my hand, and maybe even Daddy and Slim both sweating out the contractions with me, but somehow it was hard to see Radio there. He was squeamish about babies and didn't even like it when I brought up the subject, which was about every other day at first.

As a newlywed when I painted my little kitchen yellow, it was fun to think back on my room here at home with its white Priscilla curtains, my red and white pom poms hanging over the corners of the dresser mirror, my framed prom picture with Radio, and my collection of Barbie dolls with her camper and wardrobe and airplane on the shelves. But now I feel like a visitor in some room of a child I used to know.

But sleeping with the Barbies is not the worst part. I'm not supposed to spend time on personal e-mail at church, but I feel entitled, so to speak, if it's urgent. And when Mama has the phone line tied up with e-mail, she seems to forget that you can't have both at once.

I typed, "My idiot uncle has been here to try to sell discounted dentures to the preacher for the whole congregation."

Mama wrote back, "LOL. What else is nu? : >) Gotta run. C U latr."

Honestly, Mama'd rather chat with a rank stranger on a computer than commiserate with her own daughter. That really bothers me. That and bumping into people I went to high school with.

Never mind that I'm thirty pounds heavier. At least I'm not still puffing on Winstons the way of Radio's star Macarena pupil, Scarlet. She keeps one hanging out of her lip. *Ser una vibroa* if I've ever seen one— except on Saturday nights. Then that sneak in the grass regularly crawls out and snakes her old Mercedes into the prime parking place in front of the Ritz Theater. The way she stands there blowing smoke rings, you'd think she owned that parking place. The day I left Radio I hoped I had laid eyes on her red lipstick and her smokes for the very last time.

That was a month ago. I had been over to stay a couple of nights with my parents in Anniston. Mama wanted to show me how to make fig preserves. We've got this huge fig tree that's fairly loaded every year, and Mama has a recipe that makes figs taste a lot like strawberries. After they've cooked down, you can't tell the little bitty seeds apart. She colors them with red food coloring. That's for city folk cousins who may think

Kathleen Thompson

eating figs is foreign.

You get familiar with something foreign and you let down your guard. Like Slim and nerve gas. Or me with Radio Romero. Looking back on it, I gave Radio plenty of rope for a Romeo to hang himself with. He was not expecting me back until the next morning.

Isobelle nearly went with me over to Mama's to put up preserves, but she hated to leave her pets. We're both bonkers about Tom Hanks movies. Whenever I have to help Daddy with his big snake show at the Galleria, Isobelle goes, too. She struts around in her strapless electric blue prom dress. She likes the snakes. I only help to load and unload the crates. I leave the handling to Isobelle and Daddy.

When I got home that day from canning figs, I stopped in my kitchen just to soak it up. It was Isobelle's idea to gather up my hens and roosters and stretch them out along the top of the cupboards. A grouping, she said. Mama calls my kitchen a hen house, but I never saw a hen house like this. I swear I still get a little weak-kneed taking it all in—little green squares shining on white linoleum, vines of ivy curling over the doors. Isobelle is so good with decorating ideas. I took a deep breath and sat down. A bright orange and red and black rooster, and a yellow hen with her brood of three chicks, sit in the middle of the table. It's one of those heavy chrome tables, Mama's first dinette suite. When I was little, I could barely drag a chair out to sit down. But when I got married, I bought new ladder-back chairs, light enough for the smallest child to pull out. They have yellow gingham cushions that match the valance over the kitchen sink. Isobelle's idea again. My kitchen pleased me as much as the smell of teacakes baking.

The smells of your own home can surprise you sometimes when you've been away. I'm a regular Sherlock about my things. I smelled it before I saw it. There it sat, Princess House crystal, kidney-shaped, usually kept in the drawer of the end table in the den, the only ash tray I kept after we both quit smoking last September. It was running over with butts and ashes. Over half the butts were smeared with red lipstick. I looked around. Where was Radio's sticky cereal bowl? His empty Oreo bag and crumbs?

I dreaded going any farther. I gritted my teeth. I wanted to be as mad as a wet setting hen, but it was something else that washed over me, a chill like dipping your toes into Coldwater Creek, or like seeing one lone buzzard circling overhead.

Radio was in the shower; I could hear his music blasting, but he didn't hear me. I've listened to enough Alan Jackson and Faith Hill with that man to last ten lifetimes. His red Roll Tide shaving kit with the elephant was unzipped. My guess was he was getting ready for another little tango away from the house, and we all know how many that dance takes.

I sat down on the fuzzy pink toilet seat. I could see Radio's broad shoulders, swooping and dipping to catch the stream of water. His motion made the rows of pink hearts on the shower curtain quiver. Seeing him like that made something in me quiver. I got up and looked at myself in the mirror. Sometimes I have to talk to myself just like one part of me is my mama. This is one time I'm going to tell Radio off. This is one time I'm not going to let him blabber his way right off the hook. This time I'm going to watch him squirm.

I carefully emptied the ashtray into his shaving kit. Then I rinsed out the ashtray, dried it with toilet tissue, and sat back down on my vanity stool to wait.

He stepped out of the shower and stood buck naked, dripping on the rug. Mama always said he was a Ricky Ricardo made over. He spied the muck in his shaving kit just before spotting me.

"Have you lost your ever-loving mind, Lovelace Lily Braxton?" Radio shouted at me.

Radio then did a rare thing. He reached over and switched off the music.

"You been wearing lipstick when I'm not around, Radio?" I managed to say very calmly.

Radio began screeching and whining like a station trying to cut in on the Grand Ole Opry. Naturally, I didn't hang around to discuss his little *senorita*, and her cigarette butts, or I might not have lasted through one lifetime. I could hear him still hollering out my name and cussing in Spanish as I picked up my keys from the kitchen hook. He shoved through the door with just the towel wrapped around him, but that was one time I was quicker. I scratched off in my red Explorer.

I circled around a few blocks and then drove into Isobelle's back driveway next door. The fig preserves Mama sent to her was my excuse for

Kathleen Thompson

stopping. Or that's what I told her. I really wanted the lowdown on who'd been at my house. Sure enough. Radio was as guilty as sin. Isobelle had seen an old black Mercedes over in my driveway. All night. Or at least it was there when she let Prisspot in at eleven and it was still there at five in the morning when she got up to let Bones out.

Animals can take over your life. I see that now that I'm living back at home. Daddy might as well live down at that trailer with his snakes. It's a regular double wide. Mama wanted it out of her sight so he parked it at the very end of our property. A pine thicket separates it from our house. But Miss Mullinax who lives in the little house with pink siding across the road and catty cornered from the trailer is Mama's Isobelle. Well, she is, but she isn't. She keeps track of every living soul who goes in and out over there, just like Isobelle. She's not Isobelle because Mama can't stand her. Miss Mullinax complains about how the grass is getting plumb snaky looking around at the back of the trailer, and about Tiny. She knows good and well Daddy keeps the juice on all the time for Tiny's electric fence when Daddy's there. When he's not there, Tiny's chained up. But one day when Tiny was barking his head off the way he can do, probably at a squirrel, Miss Mullinax called the Sheriff.

Mama just happened to be down at the trailer when the Sheriff drove up. Miss Mullinax had just finished scraping up a dead armadillo in the middle of the road. She stood propped on her shovel, looking as if this was one big surprise to see the Sheriff. He had pulled in up close to the door on the grass. His blue light was whirling and Tiny had his front legs up on the window with his teeth bared. The Sheriff lowered his window just a crack.

"This damn dog gonna gnaw my leg off?" he yelled to Daddy who was standing in the doorway.

"Naw, he's done had breakfast."

The Sheriff wasn't laughing.

"C 'here, Tiny." Daddy whistled.

Tiny ran over to Daddy and started wagging his tail. Daddy hooked up Tiny's collar to the long heavy chain he had staked in the ground, and Tiny ambled over and lay down in his favorite spot, under Daddy's Dodge pickup.

"Better keep 'at Rottweiler chained up so's he don't eat nobody alive," warned the Sheriff.

He got out and turned to spurt out a stream of tobacco juice. He asked a lot of questions and wrote on his clipboard. Then Daddy asked him inside the trailer. Now, Daddy has a desk camouflaged at one end. It's one of those old desks, wide enough to hold his milking equipment. He has a filing cabinet next to that. Daddy keeps good records. I know because I pitch in when he needs me. But stepping inside that trailer for the first time can nearly take your breath if you're not expecting to walk into the Okefenokee Swamp. All it lacks is a few gators. The room has been gutted of furniture. Croaking frogs and buzzing cicadas and crickets hit you first. They're all in there somewhere among the dirt and grass and tree limbs and vines. Mama ordered Daddy a machine that plays rainforest sounds, so every now and then a monkey or a macaw screeches, too. I've saved the worst until last. Daddy lets the snakes take turns crawling free. Some days he lets one snake out, sometimes more. You never know.

The day the Sheriff came Mama said the biggest Diamondback Daddy owns was snoozing right inside the door in a patch of sun.

"Just come on around him," Daddy urged.

"You say you just milked him?" asked the Sheriff.

"Yep. See for yourself." He pointed to a glass saucer on the desk.

The Sheriff started to inch past the snake.

"But that don't necessarily mean he's totally harmless," added Daddy.

The snake commenced to rattle like a dry gourd. Mama doubled over showing me and Slim how the Sheriff did a buck dance past the snake. Then the Sheriff cleared his throat and said, "You got a license for all this, Doc Braxton?"

Daddy handed him a framed certificate: *Board Certified Staff Emergency Physician Envenomation Specialist*. Daddy still had his job at Anniston Memorial then.

That was apparently all the Sheriff needed to see. Daddy tried to show him a few of his prize snakes, but he begged off. Mama said the Sheriff kept his hand near his gun holster the whole time. When he left, he suggested posting NO TRESPASSING signs at all four corners.

He didn't mention Tiny again. Mama said she thinks it was as crystal

Kathleen Thompson

clear as the water trickling down Cheaha Mountain that the Sheriff thought it would be better on any burglar to have to deal with Tiny than to stumble unawares into Daddy's trailer.

It's a place I don't go in very often, but it's enough to give me the heebie jeebies for days afterwards. When I do go in, I feel like a gathering string in a piece of fabric is pulling me over to look at the snakes. Just like when I'm walking across a bridge. Even though I'm scared to death I might fall off, I can't help looking down. Instead of just hugging the inside path, why do I crumple myself up and spit over the edge?

Snakes, bridges, and, I hate to admit it, but Radio, too. He was a regular magnet, always flirting around, calling me by my full name, rolling out the *l*'s, making *Lily* sound as delicious as Mama's Christmas ambrosia. I knew his music and women habits when I married him. Why *did* I marry him?

Isobelle is the best. She talked to Radio over the fence when she was trimming her ivy and he was washing his truck. He had started hooking up these fast lines for computers for the phone company. She still spied on him just like when I lived there, just as if I still gave a flip how many women he had over there and what kind of cars they drove and what they wore and the color of their hair.

Now, color to me in most things is like sugar to a hummingbird. Daddy, too. He lines up the snakes, the Coral, the Scarlet King, and the Scarlet all in a row next to an eastern window, so when the morning sun comes in, their bands of red, black and yellow fairly gleam. Daddy recites this little jingle in his show that lets you know which Coral is hot and which one's not. "Red on black, friend of Jack. Red on yellow, kill a fellow."

Next to them is the Equatorial Spitting Cobra. Now if I were to go to the trouble to put a snake in Scarlet Garcia's black Mercedes to scare her the same way Daddy scares me, I'd pick this one. He's all mean blackness, as sleek and dark as Radio's hair. This one was Mama's idea. She orders things off the internet the way other women do the QVC. He came from Thailand. She got it for Daddy's sixtieth birthday. Daddy fairly slobbered over that cobra.

I could never adore a thing so big it can lift itself up and look you right in the eye, hissing like a moaning feist. And he does spit.

The day after he got that cobra, I saw Daddy leaving the trailer as

I pulled out to go to work. He honked his truck horn, tipped his hat to me, and waved like a used car dealer on a commercial as he peeled off. Lucky there were no cops around. Except our one-woman Neighborhood Watch. Miss Mullinax stood on her front porch with her hands on her hips, glaring. When I got home that evening about five-thirty, the kitchen was cold. That was nothing unusual. Mama often gets to playing Bible Trivia and forgets meals, forgets laundry, forgets everything except that computer screen. Now, this is the very same woman who used to live by Julia Child's motto, "If it isn't butter, don't bother."

"Where's Daddy?" I yelled in to Mama.

Mama didn't answer so I went on into the hall. She uses the living room as her computer room.

"Earth calling cyberspace. Hel-lo. Mama, where's Daddy?"

"Dunno," she said blinking her eyes and rubbing them with both fists like a child first waking up. "What time is it?"

"Suppertime," I said.

Mama had not laid eyes on Daddy since he left this morning to go feed the snakes. He probably went in for breakfast at Hardee's with the boys and no telling what he did after that.

No telling is right. Daddy staggered in just as I was taking the pepperoni and cheese out of the oven.

"Cannat pizza wait five minutes?" he said, beaming the way he did announcing a new snake. We both know you need to eat these grocery store pizzas while they're hot.

"Does our wait have anything to do with a slippery and slimy thing?" quizzed Mama.

"Absolutely not," he swaggered, steadying himself against the kitchen counter. "Come on, you two. Come on into the den. Sit down on the couch."

He made a big sweeping motion for us to sit. We did. Side by side.

"Got another hellevu birthday present today," he croaked, snatching a pink slip from his shirt pocket. "Got laid off."

Mama and I froze like we'd seen another snake in the house. If snakes were Daddy's religion, his job at Anniston Regional was his cathedral.

"Got myself one more present." He started to hum the music you hear on movies when a cobra is being charmed out of a basket.

He jumped up on the coffee table. It's made out of a ship's hatch cover and is very sturdy. Daddy was acting like he was going to charm us, swaying back and forth. Mama had already told us that it's the movement of the charmer, not the music that controls the Cobra. Daddy slowly unbuttoned his shirt as he hummed. Now we must've looked like two slack-jawed cottonmouths. His chest was tattooed from nipple to nipple with a hooded cobra.

"Whaddayathink, Temperance?" Daddy slurred. "Want me to unbuckle so you can see the full coil and maybe another little snake eye?"

"You dirty old drunk. You said this had absolutely nothing to do with a snake."

"Naw, naw, now Temp," he said, wagging his forefinger right and left, "I hate to dispute your word, but I said it was absolutely nothing slippery and slimy."

Daddy's little dog and pony show ended up with me eating cold pizza and him falling asleep on the couch, and Mama totally disgusted and leaving him there all night. Mama did tell me later that the tattoo ended at the waistline. Not that I cared one bit where it ended.

But that tattoo broke something loose in Daddy. Daddy was a man who never would as much as go wading in Coldwater Creek without a tee shirt on. But he started cutting the grass down at the trailer with his shirt off. Just to give Miss Mullinax an eyeful, I guess. Daddy's chest was still muscular, not like what you'd think of for somebody that age. At his next exhibition at the natural history museum, Daddy performed the second half bare chested. Here was Mr. Modest sashaying around a little like Mama's old heartthrob, Elvis, holding a snake like a guitar.

Soon after that, I saw Daddy's pickup parked at the Red Barn Bar once or twice in the afternoons when I got off work. He never wanted pizza those nights, but went on to bed and left Mama up with her e-mail. She had set up her own website and chatted regularly with the wives of other herp handlers. She told me that not a single one of the wives ever mentions snakes. Herp husbands lead separate lives, she said.

I wondered if this might be true of all husbands. Obviously Mama would not notice if Daddy was leading a separate life. The only life she had was in front of that computer while dust balls grew in the rest of the house. I was spending most of my weekends now vacuuming and dusting. I treated myself to a Ritz movie on Saturday nights with a barrel of popcorn and a Diet Coke for supper. Like as not, my Saturday night was tainted, too. Miss Queen of Macarena, you-know-who, was always parked in her ritzy parking place.

~

It was late afternoon and I was the only one left in the church office. I screwed the cap back on my new Mauve-a-Rita, *Por Favor,* and answered the phone, "Sinner's Haven Church, we want to be your haven, how may I assist you?"

"Lovie, is it you?" It was an agitated, squeaky voice I couldn't recognize. "Lovelace Braxton?"

"Yes'm?"

"Lovie, come quick, you hear." It was Miss Mullinax. "Your daddy's left that trailer door standing wide open. Two snakes slithering out right this minute. No telling how many more got out."

I had seen Daddy's pickup parked at the Red Barn Bar at noon. After a full lunch hour with Brother Silas at the new Chinese buffet, the pickup was still there. But I wouldn't give that old hussy the satisfaction of knowing he might be drunk.

Miss Mullinax's squeaking settled some. "There comes another one. Looks like a rattler from here. You better hurry now, or I'm calling the Sheriff."

"You seen Mama?"

"Line's tied up. I've tried her number five times. I've even tried hollering to her."

"Can't you run over to the house and get her?"

"With that Rottweiler loose?"

I didn't say another word but thank you. I dialed Mama. Busy. I dialed Slim.

"What do you mean calling me at work?" growled Slim.

"Emergency. Daddy's left the trailer door open."

"So?" he said.

"So Miss Mullinax acts like the world's coming to an end."

Kathleen Thompson

"Listen, I've got my own emergency here," he whispered. "We're in the middle of a Red Leg Exercise, and it's my turn to drive the forklift. My world could end real quick if anything happens to that fork lift. Can't Mama go see about it?"

"That's just it. Mama's online. Miss Mullinax is afraid of Tiny and won't go get her. Now, Slim, I'll lose my job if I leave this church standing wide open, and I don't have a key. The preacher's visiting at the hospital. He won't come by until five to lock up. Can't you go?"

"Lovie, Lovie, no no, no," he groaned. "Listen to me. My ass is in a sling. We've already had a small leak in a mustard gas igloo the first of this week, and if anything else goes wrong within the next hour, little black boxes are going to be screaming, and you and all the rest of Calhoun County will be evacuating. Besides, it would take me a good two hours to get there from here. You've got to get Mama. Try an instant message."

E-mail. Of course. I hung up without saying bye. I knew the igloos were in a remote area at the Anniston Ordnance Depot, but Slim had never mentioned they were that far away. I waited, tapping my wet nails while my slow-as-mud computer dialed Mama's number.

I eyed the ominous black box that sat on the edge of my desk, so far, mercifully, a little dusty, but silent. This alarm box was part of a kit they passed out to everybody in Calhoun County to educate them about the disposal of deadly war chemicals. As if any of us wanted to know. Twenty million dollars they spent on stuff I crammed onto the top shelf of the janitor's closet—gas mask, radio, tape, and plastic. A drop in the bucket, Slim reminded us. He begrudged the cool billion they spent building the incineration facility when they wouldn't even give him a step increase.

Finally the screen came up. Temptor10 was available for an Instant Message.

"Urgent, urgent! Mama, are you there? Lov"

"I M here, Where R U? : >)"

"THIS IS NOT A JOKE, Mama. Get down to the trailer quick. Miss Mullinax called . . .

"Oh, no. C U latr."

"Wait! Mama?"

I typed it in again.

"Mama?????"

Oh, Lordy, Mama was gone. She thought something was wrong with Daddy. Speed is the main problem with e-mail. Mama might be in la-la land with her computer, but don't mess with her family. If you do, you can watch her grow the horns of a bison hovering over her new baby calf.

I had Brother Silas paged at the hospital. Thank goodness he came on back so I could leave and help Mama. When I got to the trailer, Mama's car was there, but the door was still standing open. I saw an armadillo balled up in the middle of the road but it was too late to dodge it. I winced as it squashed up under my right front wheel. I pulled on in and parked, got out, and slammed the trailer door shut. Across the road Miss Mullinax was sitting in a porch rocker, and Tiny was lying down at her feet.

"Where's Mama?"

"Out there in the pine thicket, still looking for the snakes," she said, picking up her shovel.

I asked her if she wanted me to chain Tiny back up.

"Guess not. He ain't moved a muscle since I fed him my steak leftovers."

Mama wouldn't even speak to Daddy that night. He fell asleep on the couch, and she was still online when I went to bed. The next morning they were both at the kitchen table as usual when I walked in. Daddy was reading the paper. Mama was sipping coffee and staring out at the bird feeder.

"Did you know your mama's got a mean streak in her?"

I went on pouring Half 'n' Half in my coffee. I was not about to get in between those two sparring blue jays.

"She let Miss Mullinax go on thinking the cobra and a rattler were missing."

Mama just sat there grinning. Turned out if the cobra did get out like Miss Mullinax said, he had somehow climbed back into his tank.

"Don't ask me how or why the cobra got back in that tank," said Temp. "It's as spooky as you knowing in the dark you'd stepped on a snake."

We decided to keep this to ourselves. Daddy read that the Sheriff had already put out an all points bulletin for a missing Equatorial Spitting Cobra. Miss Mullinax, I'm sure, called him. Let those two vigilantes go on thinking he was still missing.

~

Isobelle called yesterday at church while I was in the middle of typing the bulletin. It was my second interruption. A secretary had quit at Isobelle's insurance company on short notice. I could move in with her, Isobelle urged. Filling out a job application in Birmingham was the last thing on my mind. I was itching for Isobelle to stop and catch her breath. When she did, I repeated word-for-word the conversation I'd just had with Radio.

"Heard Scarlet Garcia's lassoed herself some high-faluting dude," said Radio.

Radio was scratching around for information like a rooster digging for worms. Can you believe he had the gall to try and gossip with me, about, of all people, his dearly beloved? Brother Silas had already told me that Scarlet and Felix Ledbetter, Jr. were getting hitched right here in the church next Sunday night. So I told Radio that.

"Felix Ledbetter, Jr.? What kinda name is that?" Radio sneered.

I tried to act real cool.

"The name of a God-fearing guy, that's what. His family goes to Four Mile."

"The priest wouldn't marry them, you know," said Radio. *"I heard Felix, Jr. refused to turn Catholic. Stupid bastard. Said he'd be damned if he'd pray to any female idol. "*

"So?"

"So your old sneaky snake preacher at Sinner's Haven is going to tie the knot."

"You'd better wish you were good enough to tie that old sneaky snake's shoelaces," I said. *"Anyhow, sinners come in all sizes and religions. Brother Silas sees a lot of mixed marriages."*

"Quien?" he cackled. *"Like Alabama and Auburn fans?"*

I hung up on him.

Isobelle, naturally, was as disgusted with Radio as I was, but she's a talker. I mean, really. She could start her own talk show. She wanted to take every word he'd said and cut it open like butchering a hog, rip it straight down the belly and drag out the guts and clean them up for cracklings, look at the bladder and maybe fill it up with water just to watch it balloon out, cut it up into bacon and pork chops and liver and pork roasts and hams until nothing is left except the parts you grind for sausage and the head and feet to cook for souse meat. Isobelle wanted to look for clues. Was Radio still seeing Scarlet? Why did they break up? Why did he care that Scarlet was getting married? Why in the world would he call his ex-wife to talk about his ex-lover?

Hog killing day at home always was a bloody day I detested. Just that brief conversation with Radio flooded me with that same sick feeling I got smelling tripe boiling in the black washpot. Anyway, Isobelle's questions demanded more time than I had at the moment.

The preacher had asked me to write up the announcement about Scarlet and Felix's wedding. Sinner's Haven is rightly named. I wondered out loud, given the preacher's fondness for names and snakes, if perhaps he might like to have a small description of the Scarlet Snake, maybe even a tiny blurb on its nature and habits put into "Lov's Notes" right next to the wedding announcement for Scarlet. He said he would like that very much. He and I share an appreciation of little ironies.

Isobelle is not ironic. When she learned that I might need her help for a wedding surprise that I was considering for Scarlet, she literally dropped the phone. When she picked it up again, I explained how simple my revenge on Scarlet was going to be. A joke. A little wedding present. I laid it out for her, step by step. I told her up front that I didn't want us to talk it to death either.

"Be ashamed of yourself, girlfriend," Isobelle said softly.

She thought I was kidding about it. But there's still time before the wedding, and I can be pretty persuasive. And dogged. After I try it on Scarlet, Radio is next in line.

~

"Hey, Temp, come down here quick," Daddy whooped out to Mama up the stair.

On Sundays Daddy reads the entire *Anniston Star* before getting ready for church. I was trying to sleep in, but Mama's hair dryer had already jolted me awake. I'm expecting Isobelle to call any minute so we can do a post mortem of "Road to Perdition" which was the late show we saw at the Ritz. It was too late and Isobelle was too jumpy to talk much last night.

Kathleen Thompson

I got out of bed and tiptoed to crack my door.

"Listen to this headline, Temp:

Cobra Spits On Wedding Plans.

Scarlet Garcia was bitten by a black Cobra in Garcia's car last night at Sinner's Haven Church. Garcia and her fiancé, Felix Ledbetter, Jr., who had planned to be married tonight, were leaving their wedding rehearsal. Ledbetter said, "We didn't see the damned thing until it was too late. Somebody planted it there." An anonymous source at the emergency room reported, "No problem. She'll get the antivenin. We've kept plenty on hand ever since the cobra got loose. I doubt, though, if Miss Garcia'll feel like getting married tomorrow."

"You reckon there are two blamed cobras in this county?" said Daddy. I had not breathed a word to them about what Isobelle and I were up to last night.

Mama just laughed. Then she yelled, "Lovie, oh, Lovie. You awake?" She cackled again. "Guess whose wedding may have to be postponed?"

I eased my door shut and jumped back into bed. I pretended to be fast asleep when Mama looked in on me. Nine o'clock. I've started to compose in my head the regrets that Scarlet's wedding had to be postponed, how I will word it for the church bulletin, the coincidence of her accident, its untimeliness. *Pobrecito!* I can see the little curl of approval on the preacher's lips when he proofs what I've written.

I jerked the phone up on the first ring.

"Isobelle?"

"Is this Lovie?"

"Yes?"

It was the preacher.

"Lovie, I'm in a real bind, and Jesus help me, you know I can't type a lick. But the Lord has spoken. Lovie, the Lord said, Lovie. Over and over your name echoed like a voice from a deep well. Can you help me out, Lovie?"

I said I would. What else could I say if the Lord wanted it? It was a quick and troubling conversation. The preacher still had to get the extra snakes ready for the service, and couldn't linger to explain. I started feeling sick as soon as he mentioned Scarlet's name. I'm having a hard time getting dressed. I'm nauseous, and my head is whirling. I doubt if I can drive. I've let Mama and Daddy go on thinking I might have had too much popcorn last night.

~

Sinner's Haven seemed very different to me as I drove up and stopped in my regular parking place. As different as the way I was feeling. I wondered how I could get through this day. I felt like shame must be smeared and caked all over my face like an oatmeal and buttermilk mask. Who could have guessed Scarlet would be allergic to the antivenin?

I took a few deep breaths. I knew the preacher was waiting inside, but I had to get hold of myself. I looked around to see if anything else had changed as much as I had. Maybe this was just a nightmare. The little old white chapel was still the same, still snuggled up against the woods of large oaks and pines. Before the preacher felt called to come here, just a handful of families came regularly. Mostly folks who lived on social security, folks who knew more about predicting weather from reading the almanac and watching the sky than weather forecasters did. Folks who saved every grocery bag, and every twist'em from each bag of bread—just in case.

My revenge backfired. Scarlet had gone on to meet her Maker.

I left Mama and Daddy in the dark about it. No need to make them sick, too. I called Slim from the car. He can't stand practical jokes, but in the end, he always takes up for his big sister. When I told him how I was responsible for Scarlet's death and how I needed to go to the eleven o'clock service at Sinner's Haven to see if I could feel better, he nearly had a fit.

"Sis, what do you think those holy rollers can do? You think they'll believe it was a joke? How can they change anything? You better keep a low profile. Why don't you go to Four Mile with Mama and Daddy?"

"I'm ashamed for them to know."

"Lovie, this is not rocket science. Sinner's Haven is dangerous. Know

Kathleen Thompson

how the guy died who founded this religion? He got snakebit. Add up the odds. It's one thing to work in the office, but this is not the church you want to be in."

A few cars were parked outside already. One man was taking a wooden crate from his trunk. My office and the preacher's are located to one side in what looks like a utility shed until the preacher gets enough money raised to build us one of those new glorified family-life gyms.

I got out of the car. The same number of steps up to the door. Same fingerprints on the door. My inbox cluttered with Friday's mail. Slim's little black box on the desk. Princess telephone. Pencil cup with all my fine-point ballpoint pens and yellow highlighters. The basket for offering envelopes for Sunday school. As usual the preacher's office door was standing open. On the back side of the door was a large framed cross-stitched quote about kindness by somebody named Will Campbell. The preacher was leaning over his Bible and a notebook on the desk but got up quickly. I guess he forgot himself for a minute. He actually gave me a big hug, just like I was a regular church member. This was something very different. I was surprised by his soapy smell, clean and very faint. I felt suddenly clumsy pressed against his ribs, but he got busy telling me what he wanted on the insert.

I had the announcement typed within minutes and was standing at the copy machine next to my desk listening to its whir. It was a strange thing. I thought I would be typing up an announcement that Scarlet's wedding would be postponed. I thought on the outside chance that if the cobra did bite her, the antivenin would just make her a little sick. Besides, I watched Isobelle milk that cobra. Yet here I was, copying two hundred funeral announcements. I bit my lip so hard it bled, but at least it kept me from squalling out loud.

The bulletins were stuffed, but it was still too early for the church service, so I began cleaning out my desk drawers. I like my things in order, especially when everything inside me is sloshing around like sour buttermilk being churned.

As I separated the rubber bands, gym clips, and thumb tacks into their own little cubbies, I tried to remember how I could have ever dreamed up playing such a trick. Why hadn't I started with Radio? Blaming it on

Daddy's genes didn't really help me feel any better. We both have the same carrot-top hair and the same desk organizers; we both like to keep Mama's freezer shelves stacked neatly; we both want the toilet tissue to roll over instead of under. Genes are genes. But not one of Daddy's tricks, not one, has ever turned into a tragedy.

I lost track of the time. I cleared out all the mail in the inbox. I filed letters in the letter file. I tossed the last of the dry roasted peanuts that had gotten stale in a bottom file drawer. Before I knew it, I heard the congregation singing, "There is a fountain filled with blood, drawn from Emmanuel's veins, and sinners plunged beneath the flood, lose all their guilty stains . . ." I locked the desk drawer where we keep the offering and hurried over to the chapel. I didn't want to miss the altar call.

The church was small but packed, and everyone was standing as they sang. I squeezed in on the last pew. Everyone was so caught up in the singing they didn't notice me. A few of the older women still held to the old strict customs of not cutting their hair, not wearing makeup, and not wearing pants, but the younger ones were dressed about like Methodists usually dress on Sundays. Some women wore floral dresses like mine, and pumps, and a few had on pants suits. The men wore their Sunday suits or at least wore a necktie. The few teenagers were no different from any teenagers anywhere: the girls all wore skimpy little tops that barely stretched over their taut nipples and flat bellies, and the boys all gawked and squirmed.

Brother Silas is careful here not to step on any toes, especially the richer toes. Slim said he was run off from his church on Sand Mountain when one of his members got bit and died. It was too late when they got the man to the hospital. His well-to-do parents blamed the preacher for not having antivenin at the church. His wife had already been fatally bitten three years before. The grandparents were now left with five grandkids to raise.

"The Lord is in this house today," shouted Brother Silas and several boisterous *amen's* went up from the group.

I have to admit just looking around at the faces of these women with no makeup and with their gray hair rolled up in tight little buns, faces totally without malice or deception, I started to feel some presence, some

Kathleen Thompson

possible let-up of my guilt. I felt they could forgive me anyway. I tried to pray for forgiveness, over and over, but the image of Isobelle milking the cobra kept coming back to me. She had had no problem using the hook to still the cobra. She got a good hold on his head. She has helped Daddy milking the hot ones before. There had been no need to use the glass tube with its cone-shaped funnel. We were not saving the venom. She caught the cobra first behind the head and squeezed his jaw shut with her full fist. With her left hand she lifted his body and tail out of his tank. I handed her a little clear glass saucer but my knees were about to buckle under me, and I had to turn my head once she hooked his two fangs on top of the glass and began pressing down.

"They shall take up serpents, and if they drink any deadly thing, it shall not hurt them . . ." The preacher was flailing both arms in the air, holding up his Bible. "Don't take Brother Silas's word. These are not my words. Turn to Mark 16:18. These words are scripture, brothers and sisters."

Loud clapping nearly drowned out the *amen's*. Everybody's hands were in the air and they were swaying in rhythm on the pews like a stadium wave. I didn't want to look stupid so I timidly raised my arms halfway. A woman shrieked from the front right. I shuddered, dumbfounded. It was Miss Mullinax.

"Praise Jesus," she said and ran up on the little stage where several boxes sat. She grabbed a box up and opened the lid. Out tumbled a timber rattler longer than her arm. She draped his tail over her shoulder. She rubbed the snake all over his back and belly, chanting something I couldn't understand.

Another familiar voice wailed. I strained to see around a straw hat.

"I should've married Scarlet. I should've married her. She begged me, but I wouldn't. I couldn't. That baby wasn't mine. Now she's gone. The baby's gone. God help me, it was not my baby. I can't have any babies."

Radio! Babbling about babies! I clutched the back of the pew. Radio had not been to church, not even a Catholic church, the whole ten years we were married. Radio was standing next to Miss Mullinax. Brother Silas was gathering up several snakes from the church's large box. He held four or five in his hands at once, and was pushing this double handful toward Radio. Radio fell on his knees at the altar.

The preacher sobbed and shouted, "Amen, brother. You've sinned. We've all sinned. Tell it to Jesus," said the preacher, waving the snakes over Radio's head.

The pianist took his cue, and the congregation started singing along, "Tell it to Jesus, tell it to Jesus, he is a friend that's well known . . ."

"I've sinned against the church. I got myself fixed so I could fool around as much as I wanted to," wailed Radio. "I got a vasectomy. I've lost my religion. I've lost my wife. And now Scarlet."

Just at that moment one of the snakes slid from the preacher's hands onto Radio's praying hands.

~

The wind was pretty fierce that February day at Noccalula Falls. Daddy and Mama and Slim and Isobelle and Brother Silas were all in Slim's minivan, but I wanted to walk down to where the water was rushing over the rocks and be by myself for awhile. Nowadays, I feel fairly steady.

It felt wonderful to be outside away from brick walls. Being locked up for six months had been as bad as or worse than my guilt. Some nights I felt like I was in a nuthouse rather than a prison. The things those women threaten to do is enough to make you throw up. And if you think they can't get drugs in prison, you're as dead wrong as I used to be.

Some nights I would wake up about to walk into a wall, thinking I was still at home going to my own bathroom. It's a little better now at the halfway house. I'm grateful to God I just got a two-year sentence, and I'm grateful for Brother Silas.

He put in a good word for me to the parole board about working over at the Blue Springs Fish Hatchery on Grant's Mill Road. An officer picks us up at six and drives us there in a white state van. If you walked in at the end of the day when we're taking a little break from sorting out and counting little fish of all kinds and colors, you wouldn't be able to tell which ones of us rode home in the state van. Everybody's tired. Everybody's dirty. Some are catching a smoke. Some are drinking cokes from the vending machine. Some are chatting about the woman outside who has a flat tire. Not too much difference until we walk out to the parking lot, and some of us climb into the state van driven by a deputy with a gun on his hip while others freely unlock their own car doors and drive away.

Kathleen Thompson

The girls are not too friendly to me yet. They think I'm stuck up because on Wednesdays I work inside sending out invoices to Wal-Marts all over the country.

For the life of me I could never have imagined this ending even in the movies. The snake that dropped down on Radio's hand that Sunday was already dead, probably choked to death, but Daddy guessed it was an involuntary nerve that made it nab Radio in the vein. Daddy had seen this happen one other time. A guy had come into the emergency room with a snake attached to his hand, just like they said Radio did. This man had picked up what he thought was a dead snake so he could cut off his rattler. He couldn't get him loose. All the venom in the snake went directly into the man's vein.

The spray from the falls feels cold on my face. A rush of water is tumbling over the rocky ledge. All the leaves are off the trees and the landscape up the hillside is blue sky stained with black branches. Above the gorge some buzzards are circling. I don't ever see buzzards without counting. One for sorrow, two for joy, three for a letter, four for a boy, five for silver, six for gold, seven for secrets that've never been told. The buzzards have settled onto a tree, leafing it with big bloated bodies.

The falls are a fitting place. I remember when Radio and I came here on my seventeenth birthday. We waded in a little pool of water, cooling off our feet. It had been a hot summer and the falls were nearly dried up. I told Radio the Noccalula legend. This Indian maiden and daughter of a chieftain was not allowed to marry the brave she loved because her father wanted her to marry a man he had chosen, a man with more goods. Heartsick that she couldn't marry her true love, Noccalula plunged ninety feet over the falls.

"If she was Catholic, they wouldn't bury her, you know," said Radio.

"Why?"

"Suicide's a mortal sin."

"What does that mean?"

"It means you ain't a good Catholic cause good Catholics don't do it."

"How you know so much about good Catholics?"

"Cause I ain't one. They won't bury me either, so I want my ashes to be spread right over there where Noccalula fell."

Kathleen Thompson   407

"You want to be cremated?"

"What choice does a mortal sinner have?"

It seemed gross and strange to me that anybody would actually want their body burned. That was the first serious conversation I ever had with Radio. I had no idea what his *mortal sin* might be, and was too young to be really concerned with it. Radio lived long enough in the ambulance for one more serious conversation with me, and it was just as puzzling as the first one.

"Why didn't you just tell me?" I said.

"Couldn't. You wouldn't have married me. It seemed easy when I did it. No snotty nosed brats around like me hungry and whining for food. No barefoot kids getting on a school bus and having other kids snicker. When I had it done, I was so young I didn't know it was a mortal sin. One less kid in the world like me made a vasectomy look real good."

Radio's voice was getting weaker.

"The music, my loud music you always hated. . ."

I wiped his brow with a tissue. He struggled to finish the sentence.

". . .when I played it loud enough, it would drown out the guilt."

~

Brother Silas led us in "Amazing Grace" because we all knew the first and last verses. We had clustered near a row of seesaws and swings on the playground for the children of tourists who came during summers. Now it was empty. The monkey bars were rusting, and everything needed a coat of paint. One of the swings was creaking as the wind moved it back and forth. After we'd all said Psalm 23 together, Brother Silas quoted the cross-stitched sign hanging in his office which he said Miss Mullinax made for him.

Then I went on down alone, carefully stepping over large boulders and sharp rocks on the way to the water. Once I slipped and had to grab onto a low bush. I looked back at the row of concerned faces above me. I made the final steps slowly over mossy, slick rocks.

As I opened the little urn of ashes, I gasped at how little was left. Radio's strong arms that used to lift me entirely off the dance floor in one swift move, his lean muscular legs—all reduced by fire to near-weightlessness, no heavier now than an eyelash on my face, a feather on

Kathleen Thompson

my finger, or one fluffy boll of cotton.

The task of a funeral was left to me. Radio's parents had long ago joined up with a group of migrant workers going up around Cullman to pick strawberries. I whispered the preacher's quote as I slung the ashes as far as I could away from me, upon the rushing water. "Be kind, for everyone you meet is involved in a great struggle." I repeated it over and over until I was screaming.

I brushed some of the ashes away from my eye as I climbed slowly back up the steep, treacherous path. Brother Silas reached his hand down for me and helped me make the final step to solid flat ground again. Mama grabbed me and gave me a hug. Isobelle's eyeshadow was smudged and a streak of mascara ran down her cheek. We held hands the way little girls do. Daddy reached over and brushed off a few ashes still clinging to my black blouse. He kissed me on the cheek. I couldn't look at Slim who was going to drive me back over to the halfway house. He was the one who had gone with me to Scarlet's funeral. I needed someone strong with me, someone who lived close to death on a daily basis, who could look death in the eye without flinching. I needed him for another reason, too. I had to twist his arm, but he drove me to the Sheriff's department afterwards where I confessed that it was my idea to put the snake in Scarlet's car. That I was the murderer of Scarlet and her baby.

So I didn't look straight at Slim. I knew if I saw even a flicker of sympathy, I might start crying again the way I did that night at the jail after Scarlet's funeral. This time, not even a cell full of psychologists nor a ton of Valium would be able to stop my tears.

But Brother Silas came over and opened the car door for me. He kissed me on the cheek, and said in a real low voice that didn't really sound like him, "Lovie, want to keep helping me with Lov's Notes by e-mail?" I opened my mouth to answer, but there were no words. I hoped my eyes weren't too watery for him to read my sudden and unexpected joy.

Kathleen Thompson

Kathleen Thompson holds a B.S. from the University of Alabama and an MFA in Writing from Spalding University in fiction/poetry. An avowed genre slut, she has published three books of poetry: Searching for Ambergris, *2002, Pudding House Publications;* The Nights, The Days, *winner of the 2008 Negative Capability Press Chapbook Series Award; and* The Shortest Distance, *2009, nominated for the National Book Award by Coosa River Books. Recent poems are published in* PMS: poemmemoirstory, *and in* 2nd & Church. *"Journey Home" is a haibun published in* Alalitcom *2016. Her prose in manuscript includes two novels and a truckload of short stories and essays. Excalibur Press nominated her short story, "Looking for the Lord," for a Pushcart Prize. Most recently her story "Woman's Wait" was published in* Muscadine Lines: A Southern Journal; *and "Nesting," in* Waypoints: An Online Journal. *Some days, when she is not revising fiction, her hair is afire writing a memoir, sparked by a recent passion for blogging, an old passion for the personal essay, and a Spalding University CNF workshop in Paris, 2012.*

Jim

T. K. Thorne

Jim, a homeless man seen over the years in Birmingham, Alabama, would appear at intersections in different parts of town and stand hunched over in one place, mumbling to himself for a long period before moving on. As the director of a downtown business improvement district (CAP), I received several calls on him from concerned people. He presented a pathetic appearance, wearing the same ragged clothes, shoes with large holes in them, and no overcoat, even in winter. One woman bought a pair of new shoes and asked my staff to deliver them. Jim accepted them, but she called back later, saying she had seen him again, sans new shoes. We discovered the shoes, still in the box, in bushes near where he had been when the shoes were offered to him. Not long afterward, another homeless man was observed retrieving the shoes that were apparently left for that purpose. I approached Jim one day, not knowing what kind of reaction, if any, I would receive. I waited while he mumbled into the air for a while, still facing the intersection, then he turned to me. Many years before, he had been a professor, and we had a strange conversation about physics and the nature of the universe. Politely thanking me for offers of help, he clarified that he didn't want any. For years, I wondered about him—what he was doing and why—and finally decided to give him a story.

A woman wearing glasses brings me shoes. She offers them at arm's length. "If they're not your size," she says, "I can take them back."

She looks down, and I follow her gaze to the hole in my left shoe where a toe protrudes like a ghostly toadstool from the shadows of worn leather. Beneath the shoe, snow patinas the city sidewalk. It doesn't snow often in Alabama, but it is snowing now.

"Aren't you cold?" she asks. "Your coat has a hole in it. My father had a coat that might fit." Her face goes still.

"Is your father dead?"

"I—"

The words she needs to say lodge between mind and heart. I see them through the transparency of her heavy coat and skin, stuck on the bony thorns of her spine.

She pulls her red wool coat tighter. "That's not what I meant to imply."

I haven't moved to take the shoes, so she sets them on the sidewalk, perfectly aligned, the right nestling into the left, curving toward one another with the knowing that they belong together. She steps back. "I meant to say that I noticed you standing on this corner the past few days and saw that you needed shoes."

She is breathless. She walked to my corner as though wading against an undertow. Now she seeks shelter from her deed, a retreat. "So I bought you a pair," she says. "That's all."

"Thank you." I scratch at the thick bramble of my frosted beard.

"You're welcome," she replies crisply, back in her fortress.

When she is gone, I pick up the shoes and put them in the bushes.

#

"Did the shoes not fit?"

She is back. The woman with the glasses.

"I don't know."

She stiffens. Wind slaps a tendril of hair against her cheek. "You didn't even try them on, did you?"

When I don't reply, she makes an indignant sound and stomps away, though the snow eats the *clap* of her boot heels.

#

Two days later, I am deep into my prayers. I feel her at my elbow, but I can't look at her. I haven't finished. The words have to flow all on one breath. If they are not a perfect offering three times in succession, I cannot move on. Across the street there is a bench beside a raised flowerbed planted with purple cabbage. I've been four days here, and I want to cross the street and sit on the bench where I can watch the pigeons and the purple cabbage between prayer times.

"I'm sorry I got huffy over the shoes," the woman says.

Distracted, I miss a word of the prayer. My fists clench. Now, I must stay on this corner another three days. The human part of me wants to shout and shake her.

The divine part turns to her. "You are forgiven."

She blinks. "What did you do with the shoes?"

T.K. Thorne

"I hid them."

She is still for a moment, but I am not going to try to return to the prayers. I must have silence, and she is not going to be silent. Above us, the traffic light changes to yellow. Prayers must fit into the time between their cycling. How would I know when to start and finish without them?

"You don't have to hide the shoes," she says, her voice edged with desperate reasonableness. "If you wear them out, I can bring you another pair."

"You are a good person," I say.

She takes a tiny breath, as if it is all she is allowed.

A car passes close to the curb, splashing dirty snow-mush on us. She jumps back, pushing the glasses back onto the bridge of her nose. It is a well-made nose. Freckles pebble it, though she has tried to cover them with makeup.

"May I ask you something?" she says.

I wait.

"Why are you here?"

I lift my face to catch the whisper of flakes that have begun to fall. "Because I'm not perfect."

"I mean, why do you stand on the corner every day like this?" She frowns. "What do you eat? Can't you go to a shelter or . . . something?"

"You are alone in the dark." I say.

She stares at me and takes a step back. "Christ, I just wanted to give you some shoes. Why do you say something like that?"

I wait.

"You don't know me," she says. "You don't know anything about me."

She is gone again, and I return to my prayers.

#

I notice her the next two mornings. She passes on the other side of the street at a steady, measured clip, her face turned away.

The prayers are difficult today. A man drops a hot biscuit in my coat pocket. It is wrapped tight in paper, so I will eat it later. With a twist of his head, a young boy, attached to his mother's arm, stares at me.

"He stinks, Mom."

His mother drags him away.

That evening the woman appears again, a cop at her side, but it's all right because I've just finished. The prayers went perfectly, even the hard ones wisped from my lips into the ether without a falter, perfect pearls formed in the hard belly of my imperfections.

"This is the man," she says to the policeman.

He smiles. "Hello, Jim."

"Good evening, officer. How is your little girl?"

"Growing," he says. "I got a picture here somewhere." He pulls out a wallet and produces a photo.

I nod, glad my prayers have been heard and she, at least, is safe.

The woman watches with her mouth slightly parted. "You know him?" she asks the officer.

"Sure," he says. "Jim's a regular."

"But I've never seen him before last week and I walk this way to work."

The officer shrugs. "He makes his way around the whole city. It takes a while and the odds of seeing him aren't that big."

"But can't you do something?" she protests.

"You mean about him standing on a corner? He ain't hurting anybody. What's the charge?"

"There's got to be something."

The officer shrugs. "Jim doesn't drink or do drugs; never asks anybody for anything. People just bring him things. He puts most of the stuff in the bushes, and other homeless people get it. They know to look around near wherever he's standing."

She pulls at her coat in offense. The red collar is stark against her pale skin, though the cold has pinked her cheeks and nose. "But he's a *vagrant,*" she says.

"No law against that, ma'am. It was struck down in '63 during the Civil Rights stuff. I'm just a police officer. All I can do is enforce laws, and Jim's not breaking any of them."

Her foot taps the ground, as if it wanted to stamp, but was too well mannered.

"Look at him, officer. He stands on that corner all day in the freezing cold mumbling to himself. You know he needs help."

T.K. Thorne

"Are you kin to him?"

Her eyes dart sideways. "No, I'm not. I didn't even know his name."

"Well, if you were, you could try to sign a petition on him, but you'd still have to prove he's a danger to himself or others, otherwise nobody can touch him against his will."

My eyes close and though my feet remain standing on the sidewalk, I am back in the state hospital:

I shuffle to the glass partition that separates us from the night attendants, pressing my ear against the thick pane to hear the voice inside. The TV is turned so I can't see it, but I hear—an earthquake in Haiti has killed thousands of people; a school in India collapsed in a flood; a child in Illinois found locked in a basement, starved, beaten, and sexually abused. The endless horrors are reported daily, because I am trapped in here and can't say the prayers. I slap my palm against the thick glass.

The female attendant looks up through her layered bangs. The dark roots, bleeding into the blonde ice, are an inch long now, how I measure time. "Go away, Jim."

I slap the glass again. "I can't say my prayers."

She ignores me.

"I can't [*slap*] say [*slap*] them."

Annoyed, she finally looks up. "Do you need a shot, Jim?"

"No."

"What do you want?"

"I have to say my prayers, and I can't say them."

"Why not?" Her gaze drifts back to the picture on the TV that is out of my line of sight. I can see in her eyes the reflection of an overturned bus and glimpses of twisted, burned limbs.

My cheek presses against the glass wall. "The pills take away my prayers," I whisper. "They take away my prayers … and the world is lost."

The voice of the woman with the glasses catapults me back to the corner where I stand between her and the policeman.

"How can you say he's not a danger to himself out here in the cold like this? What does he eat? Where does he sleep?"

"Ma'am, there's simply not enough room in the institutions if judges ruled everyone who was homeless or nuts needed to be picked up. I know you mean well, but Jim doesn't want any help. Why don't you go volunteer at the Firehouse Shelter? They always need people."

"I can't believe this," she says. "What kind of world is this?"

It is my question too.

He regards her. "There's worse cases than Jim all over this city. Most people don't see 'cause they don't want to look."

#

It is evening. I face the west, which makes it difficult to see the traffic light. A man shuffles up to me. "Hey, Jim. I got the shoes you put out, and I was late to the Shelter, so I ate the sandwich too."

I nod, my eyes on the signal light.

He puts a hand on my shoulder, and I flinch away.

"Sorry man, I forgot you don't like to be touched."

The light turns red and I begin.

#

In dawn light that furs the city without warmth, I move with slow, reverent steps across the street. Wind flaps my coat. The light has changed for me, a deep blood red. On the other side, I face the road to say the first morning prayer. Then I go to the bench and sit.

Later, I see her walking up the sidewalk across the street. Her stride is not so confident, so sure of where she is going. Her head lifts in surprise when she realizes I am no longer on that corner, and she looks around before catching sight of me on the bench.

Without waiting for the light, she *tap-taps* across. "I'm glad you're still here," she says. "I thought for a moment you were gone."

I wait.

"You don't care, do you?"

"I'm waiting," I say.

Wind tangles her hair and she tries to tame it behind her ears. "For what?"

I don't answer.

She begins to pace in front of the bench. "I don't know why I came over here."

T.K. Thorne

Snowflakes fall into her hair and glimmer in the streetlight which is still on, fooled by the cover of clouds.

Now she is looking up at the traffic light, which is yellow. Her breath clouds briefly. "I wanted to tell you—"

She hesitates, but I nod. She is dragging up those words that have been caught on the thorns of her pain, but then she tucks her gloved hands under her armpits and says instead, "I don't know why you want to live like this. It's not right for you to be out here. There's something terribly *wrong* that you are."

She takes a deep breath, exhaling another tiny cloud. "I know you're not responsible. You're mixed up and doing your best somehow."

These are not the words that must be said, so I keep waiting.

She sits beside me on the bench, not too close, and takes another breath, reaching through the hurt for the words she must say.

"I wanted to help you . . . because my father died a month ago. It was a long illness, and I didn't—" She looks away and then back at me again, determined. Tears jewel her eyes. "I wasn't the daughter I should have been."

These are the words.

I turn to her, meeting her eyes. "You are forgiven."

She stares at me for a long time and then takes my hand in both of hers. I don't jerk away from her. I let it rest between the soft leather gloves, looking back at the traffic light.

When she leaves, I shuffle to the corner to say the prayers.

A retired Birmingham police captain, T.K. Thorne's award-winning novels, Noah's Wife *and* Angels At The Gate: The Story of Lot's Wife, *fill in the back stories of unknown, extraordinary women in two of the world's most famous sagas. Her nonfiction book,* Last Chance For Justice: How Relentless Investigators Uncovered New Evidence Convicting the Birmingham Church Bombers, *made the NY Post's "Books You Should Be Reading" list. She blogs on her website, TKThorne.com, and speaks on life lessons, her writing journey, and her books.*

Callie

Betty Jean Tucker

"Callie" was written when I was a nineteen-year-old student at Alabama College, now the University of Montevallo, in anticipation of the arrival on campus of prolific British author Robert Payne, who would become chairman of the English Department and creative writing professor. He read "Callie," pronounced the author "a real writer," published the story in a review he founded, and sent a copy to his friend William Carlos Williams, who called the story "brilliant." It was named in Martha Foley's annual list of 100 Most Distiguished American Short Stories. The encouragement from these literary figures was the catalyst which kept me writing stories during rare breaks stolen from a thirty-year career as an English professor. The success of "Callie" (this is the fourth publication in which it has appeared) emboldened me to create more characters to see how they would cope in the hostile environment of depression-era poverty in the deep South. These stories were collected and published in the book On a Darkling Plain *in 2014. I think "Callie" resonates with readers because they understand that the title character symbolizes the indomitable spirit of the South in her struggles against adversity and her transformation through the sustaining virtues of hard work and benevolence.*

My sister Callie was going to be a nurse. That's what she said when teacher asked us what we wanted to be when we growed up. She'd wrap her big feet around the shaky iron desk legs and say right out that she was gonna be a nurse and get folks like Nathan well when they got sick. Then she'd glare at the rows of good little girls who all wanted to be missionaries. Callie didn't care what they was gonna be, she was going to be a nurse and get sick folks well. She just hoped Nathan wouldn't die before she was growed enough to nurse him.

Callie was different. She was big, and her face was kinda yellow with funny looking places on it, and when she scratched, it left puffy looking streaks on the yellow. Her hair was about the color of sun-paled corn silks, and it was so straight it was always falling down over her eyes when she hung her head. She was so rough on clothes, Ma said, and made her wear overalls 'til she started getting a chest like the other girls. Then she looked funny in the feed sack dresses like she had been melted and poured in and was trying to get back out again. She wasn't fat, Callie wasn't, but she was big, and her legs looked like Nathan's with the white hairs crawling out around the freckles.

But Callie didn't care how she looked. She could do more than anybody else, and if they messed with her she'd show 'em, too. She showed Nelda Jenkins one time. Nelda spit on her when they was playing catch-the-fox, and Callie jumped on her and just about beat the hell out of her. And Callie just kept right on laughing and rolling Nelda in the red clay, rubbing her face in the ground and making her eat dirt. When teacher come out the back door and made 'em quit, Nelda cussed. She cussed Callie and she cussed the teacher. Callie just hung her head and fastened her overall strap. I remember the teacher made Nelda whup Callie with a switch, and we peeped in the window and Callie was laughing. She always laughed when she was mad. I guess teacher didn't like it when Callie didn't cry 'cause she took the switch and beat her till she was tired and Callie still didn't cry. She never did cry, not till she got to be a nurse.

I got mad 'cause teacher didn't whup Nelda, and I said, "It ain't fair. She oughta whupped Nelda too," and Cliff said, "She knows not to bother Nelda, or ole man Jenkins'll make her leave."

"But Nelda spit on Callie first," I argued.

Cliff looked down at me like I was dumb 'cause I wasn't as old as him, and he said. "That don't make no difference, Sam. There ain't no justice."

I guess he musta heard his Daddy say that. I didn't know what justice meant, so I hushed.

When Callie got a whupping at school, she got one at home, too. Always the kids that lived in the bottom would stop by our house and tell Ma if Callie was in a fight or anything. When Callie whupped Nelda, Ma took the razor strop and beat her till the blood oozed out around the whelps on her big legs and stuck the white hairs together. Ma grit her teeth and the knuckles on her red hands turned chalkish where she gripped the belt buckle, and she laid it on Callie, talking all the time. "Ain't I told you to leave that Jenkins gal alone? Ain't I told you? Say? Ain't you never gonna learn? Old man Jenkins'll be running us off if you don't leave his young'un alone. You know that, you know it. Why you keep messing with her? Why, why, why…" Ma screamed, crying and beating Callie, till she give out of breath. Ma didn't have much wind and that time she fainted and fell down. Callie just looked at Ma stretched out in the yard and kicked the dirt and watched the dust cake on Ma's arms and legs where they was sweaty. Callie just looked at her like she was disgusted and then walked off to the barn to see Nathan.

I dragged Ma to the chinaberry tree under the shade and got some water to bathe her face. She looked so pitiful in her greasy apron and kinda pretty like that. She was lots better looking than fat old Mrs. Jenkins even if she did have to pick cotton and chop stove wood. I thought Callie oughta wait on Ma if she was gonna be a nurse, but she never did. I guess it was because Ma didn't like Callie, not like she did me anyway. But Callie didn't care, she said so.

She didn't care about nothing, 'cept Nathan and nursing. When Nathan got sick, she wouldn't let nobody do anything for him 'cept her. She was his nurse. I guess, next to Nathan, Callie liked me best, 'cause she let me go with her and spend the night with him one time after he got sick. Nathan lived in the room next to the corn crib, and it was almost as nice as where we lived 'cept in the winter when it got muddy and smelled bad where the cows were. But I guess he liked it. He lived there ever since before I was born, Ma said.

The night we stayed with him, he said he was feeling kinda low. The board window was latched, and we shut the door behind us with a cross-bar. It was still daylight, but Nathan had the room shut up so the light wouldn't hurt his eyes. It was the first time I'd been in the room since he got sick and it was different. In the almost-dark you couldn't hardly see Nathan. His old iron bed was backed up in the corner, and it looked like the cobwebby shadows was eating him up. He had on his long johns and they was dirty yellow where the camphorated oil rags on his chest soaked through. His long brown hands kinda fooled with a hole in the quilt, and they looked like pieces of dried-up cowhide. Nathan was different in the bed. He looked mostly white with his silver hair plastered down across his forehead and his drooping mustache shining like cream. But I could tell it was him. The snuff dripped out of his mouth, and the brown juice matted

Betty Jean Tucker

the long ends of his mustache together and he had on his hat. It was a great black felt hat with a long brim that curled up like his mustache, and there was a little round hole in the top of it. Nathan never did pull his hat off, not even when he went to bed or to the table. I guess he was just old.

Callie set right in and started cleaning up. She swept the floor with the straw broom and covered up the basket full of half-shucked corn with some croker sacks she got out of the barn. Then she got the bowl from Nathan's bed and went to wash it, knocking the flies away from the dried egg yellow on the sides of it. I asked Nathan if he ate eggs at dinner too, and he said no, just at breakfast, and I wondered if maybe Ma forgot to take him some dinner. When I asked her the next day, she said he got plenty for a hired man.

Me and Callie built us a pallet on the floor next to Nathan's bed. The quilt we had over us was the one Ma used to wrap ice in and it stunk. When the red started coming in through the cracks in the logs, Nathan told Callie to open the window. He wanted to see the sun go down, and it made him sad because he said it looked like a man dying. Then it got dark and the crickets chirped and Callie started to light the lamp, but he said not to, it would spoil the effect. I guess he musta meant it wouldn't do no good to try to make the dead man come back alive.

Callie didn't talk much till I went to sleep, least till she thought I was sleeping. The quilt smelled so, and the mosquitoes hurt and I couldn't sleep. Callie slid off the pallet and squatted down by Nathan's bed and told him 'bout selling the boiled egg Ma fixed in her lunch to Mrs. Jenkins for some store candy, and they laughed together.

"If yore Ma found out, she'd lick the tar outa you, honey," Nathan said low, so as not to wake me up.

"I don't care. It don't hurt no longer than it lasts anyhow." Then the toughness sorta slid out of her voice. "But sometimes I want to cry."

Nathan's voice went soft. "How's that, Sis?"

"I just can't remember when it wasn't hard times. Seems like the only way I can stand it is to be hard myself." I couldn't believe what I was hearing, but I felt the same as Callie when she asked, "Is it ever going to end, Nathan?"

"I won't see it end, but you will. Things have to get better, and you'll be all right. You'll be a nurse like you always wanted." His voice dropped into a cough.

"I ain't never gonna be no nurse," Callie said, and I could hear her foot pushing at the floor. "We ain't got no money, and Ma wouldn't let me if we did."

Nathan moved over to the side of the bed so he could see Callie sitting on the floor. "Yore Ma ain't got nothing to do with it." Then he waited a long time, and finally he said, "When I die I don't want you to let nobody else touch me."

The shuck mattress crackled in the dark, and I could feel him pushing hisself up in the bed. "Looka here," he whispered raspingly, "here it is. Put yore hand up here and feel the money. Feel that wad? When I die don't let nobody in here till you get it. You hear?"

"Yeah, Nathan," Callie whispered as she slid back on the floor. "I'll hide it so she can't find it."

I thought Callie oughta tell him he wasn't gonna die, but I guess she knowed he was. She was a natchel-born nurse. For a long time they didn't say nothing, and Nathan kept breathing through his mouth real loud.

Nathan was dead the next morning. His head in the black hat was jammed back against the iron bedstead, and his eyes stared blind at the ceiling. His tongue was big and hanging out and ants were crawling around on the dried snuff on his mustache. I looked at him and got sick. Callie made me go out, and she put the bar across the door after me. She stayed in there all day, and she wouldn't come out when Ma and Grandma come to lay him out. When the sun started down, she opened the window, and at dark she come out and she had the black hat. She had it and we never did see it again, not till she got to be a nurse.

Callie was kinda mixed up from then on, and she had a hard time growing up. She was strong as a ox and stubborn as a mule and everybody said she was mean. But she wasn't lazy and she worked. After school she picked cotton for Mr. Ted, and he give her fifty cents for every hundred pounds she picked. Then she'd come home after dark and hunt the cows and get water from the spring. In the summer she worked in the fields like a man. We had to have a crop or Mr. Jenkins would run us off, and we didn't have no place to go, especially since Pa was off working with the

Betty Jean Tucker

CCC. He couldn't help it, Ma said. I remember seeing him one time when he come home. I didn't like him.

Then Callie went off to school. I remember the morning she left. The black and red store-bought dress stretched across her belly like a drum, and her patent leather shoes cracked across the toes. Ma had rolled her hair up in corn shucks, and the heavy streaked mass twisted around her head, making her look like a porcupine. Her skin was dark brown from the sun, and the white hairs on her arms and legs stood out like bristles; you could see the white strip across her shoulder where the cotton sack hung. The last time we seen her she was walking down the road, swinging the big suitcase with a rope around the middle to keep it from coming open.

The wash-out between the house and the road was just a ditch then. It growed to be a gully before Callie come back again.

It wasn't much different at home when she come back, 'cept for Ma being dead and Grandma and her walking stick living with me, and the gully being bigger. It was August and so hot the house's tin top cracked under the sun, and flies wiggled on their bellies. It was laying-by time, and the evening Callie come home I was stretched out on the porch, watching Grandma churn. She always shooed the flies when she churned, but she forgot to shoo when she looked up and seen the woman open the gate. She looked hard, her eyes opening wide out of the wrinkles, but she couldn't figure out who it was. I knowed it was Callie.

I guessed she was a lady too. She wasn't big any more, and she didn't push her feet along the ground. She walked up the dirt path kinda slow and easy like a lean yellow cat, and she didn't hang her head either. She had on a blue dress and it made the sky around the sun come sliding down, and it looked soft and cool around her. When she come to the chinaberry tree, she reached up and pulled off a handful of leaves, and the full rounded curve of her breasts pushed against the soft dress. Her hair was short, and she had it combed back from her face. Any fool could tell she wasn't hard to look at.

She come up on the wooden steps, and Grandma said, "Well, if it ain't the old cow." Callie kinda smiled a little around the lips. And her eyes stayed blue like the sun shining through water on a knife blade. She hugged us both, and I could feel how hard she was.

I put her suitcase with the initials on it in the front room and then we talked till sundown. She told us she was getting a week off to rest, then she'd go back and graduate in three months. She was going to do some special studying about babies and then go to work in a hospital and just work with babies all the time. She liked babies.

Callie didn't talk much anytime, 'cept maybe to say pass me something at the table or ask about something that had happened while she was gone. Grandma didn't know exactly what to make of her not talking and all. She liked to talk to herself.

I couldn't figure out what she come back for. Nobody asked her. So far as she knowed, nobody cared whether she ever come back or not. But she stayed.

Then one night when the mosquitoes was holding revival meeting so loud nobody could sleep, Ellis come and said Eunice was sick and would Grandma go set with her till he could get the doctor from town. She was in a pretty bad fix, Ellis said. Thought it was appendicitis.

"Appendicitis," Grandma snorted, feeling the wall for the nail where her clothes was hanging. "What the fool needs is a midwife." She kept fussing in the dark, trying to get her dress over her head. I don't know if Callie had even been to bed or not. When I got my overalls on and found Grandma's walking stick, Callie was waiting in the door. She had on her uniform, and she looked so clean and white I cussed out loud. If she stayed here long, she wouldn't be so pretty and white. But I couldn't tell her nothing. She was a nurse.

It was two miles in the swamp to Ellis' house and it wasn't easy walking. Even in the dark you could feel the heavy dust lying still like in the air, and there wasn't a sign of a moon. It was hilly, and the gutted road was rough, but Callie stayed ahead, and her white heels come down hard on the sliding rocks. Grandma grunted and talked. Eunice oughta have to suffer, Grandma said. Anybody that'd run off and leave a house full of young'uns and traipse all over the country with any man imaginable… God oughta let 'em die. Eunice had her belly full of nerve, come poking back here, big round as a cow. She talked on and on, allowing as how she couldn't tolerate such fool trashy women.

Then she hushed, and you couldn't hear nothing 'cept our feet in the ruts and the parched clay cracking under our shoes. Now and then stunted pine trees made a dark, withered outline on the ditch bank.

"Ain't never seen such a black night in August since here I been," Grandma said. "Plague take the devil," she kept saying, "plague take it."

But that didn't help none, 'cause there still wasn't a breeze, just hot lightning bugs and warm dusty air coming up from the baked ground. I knowed it wasn't all that hot for August, but I could feel the sweat run down my legs, and it tickled where the wet made grooves in the caked dirt around my ankles.

Callie kept on walking, faster and faster, and finally we got to the top of the hill where you could look down and see the light from the house at the bottom. The dark path was so gully-washed I just about had to tote Grandma, but Callie kept right on like she knowed just how deep every ditch was, and I thought about all the times she used to hunt the cows after dark.

The house looked like it was a long way off till we got right up on it. It squatted, so close on the ground that a dog couldn't get under it without scratching his back. Everything was so quiet and still in the dark it seemed like we was slipping up on the barbed wire fence, and when Callie opened the gate, you couldn't hear anything but the screeching of the wire over the nail. There wasn't any trees or grass 'cause it was bottomland, and they had a plank across the yard to the doorstep to walk on. When Callie stepped on the hiked-up end of the plank, a dog, with its head stuck out from under the porch, sniffed and barked short in his sleep. Somebody on the porch said, "Shut up, Mary," real low, and when Callie got to the big rock that was the doorstep, a long barefoot boy with his hands in his baggy overall pockets moved into the strip of light from the door. He just stood there looking like a dried-up prison guard in the yellow light. I knowed he was trying to figure out who Callie was. She didn't move, so I said, "Evening, Haskie." When he finally made out who we was, he said, "Evening, Mr. Sam. Y'all come on in," and followed us into the room.

Callie must not remembered how it was. She kept looking and looking. The floor sunk in the middle, there was big cracks in the wall, and they had a quilt stuck in the window where a pane was out. The fireplace looked like a hog wallow, with the hicker-nut hulls and ashes all over the cracked bricks. It was always like that. The twisted fly-specked mirror made the dresser look like it had a broken neck, and the doily on the mantel was dirty and ragged. It was dark in the kitchen, and all you could see was the stove and its rusty pipe going up through the tin top.

The kids all looked alike, so dirty and hungry-eyed it was a sin. Haskie was mighty friendly, but I wouldn't trust a one of them further than I could spit. I couldn't ever remember which was the oldest, Haskie or Sally Mae. I guess it was Sally Mae. When we come in, Callie looked at Sally Mae over in the corner holding the last young'un. She was a thin girl, with big breasts and lips that turned down. Grandma said she was no count. Too many men in pretty cars come to see her.

The cross-eyed twin boys was the ones that did the work of the farm, and I guess the only decent ones in the lot. They was propped against their half full cotton sacks behind the dresser, their crooked eyes staring up at us and their mouths opening in sleepy, twisted grins.

A tired-looking little girl in a dirty underskirt fired the smoke bucket in a corner by the sickbed. Pot-bellied mosquitoes swarmed, and Callie rubbed her eyes when a big gust of smoke filled the room, making the yellow light turn gray.

"How's your ma?" Grandma asked.

"I don't know, Miz Sally; she's been moaning like that a long time," Haskie answered her.

Grandma laid her walking stick down and walked over to the bed, her old eyes squinting down at Eunice. She slid her hands over the heavy breasts, then felt the great bulge under the sheet. Callie watched her, and she watched the young ones staring. They grinned, shamefaced. Callie looked at 'em, and then she went and slung the smoke bucket out of the window. When she turned around, they stopped grinning.

"You'd better get the kids out," she told me. They got up and went out on the porch, and I latched the door after them.

"What about you?" she asked me.

"Think I'll stay," I told her. I didn't like the way she sounded so bossy.

"Suit yourself," she said, twisting her shoulders and listening to the low, bubbling sound from the bed. That's the way it started, a low bubbling sound from way down in the throat, and it kept boiling up and up till the

Betty Jean Tucker

long high scream beat down hard on our heads. I followed Callie to the bed, and when I put my hands on the iron bedstead, pieces of blue cracked paint fell down on Eunice's greasy, gray-brindle hair. Callie put her hands on Eunice's forehead, and the woman opened her eyes.

"Well, bless my soul and body," she said, her jaws sagging. "It's Callie Ford."

"Yes, it's me," Callie said.

"Guess everything'll be all right now. Ain't never had a shore 'nough nurse to wait on me before." She kept talking and kinda grinning while Callie pulled down the sheet. She had on a coarse cotton gown, and her body spread all over the bed. Callie took the hot smoothing iron wrapped up in rags from her side and handed it to me. I went to the fireplace and put it down.

Callie said low, "When you going to stop having babies, Eunice?"

Eunice was breathing hard and jerky, straining to raise her glob of fat up in the bed. The pains caught her, and her face looked like wet ash.

Callie looked at her watch and put her hand on the mound of belly.

"I ain't gonna have no baby," Eunice said.

Callie motioned me to come help her, and she told the woman it wouldn't be long now. We took her out of bed, and there was a huge wet spot on the sheet. I thought about that hot iron she had had in the bed and figgered she had done a lot of sweating. But Callie said, "Her water's broke."

"I ain't gonna have no baby," Eunice gasped. "I ain't gonna have no baby."

Callie told her she was going to have that baby, whether she wanted to or not, that she meant to see to it that the baby was born. She propped up the woman's legs and told me to keep them steady while she examined her. She didn't need a tape measure to know how dilated she was.

"I guess we'd better fire up the stove for some hot water. Right?"

Callie nodded, and I was glad to get away from the screaming.

"Bear down, Eunice. Push hard. It's coming."

Bringing the water, I watched Callie's hands, long and white, pushing up the wobbly legs and reaching in for the baby. She talked to the woman, and her voice was like her hands, willing the baby to be born.

Callie smiled. Smiled kinda glad-like with the sweat running off the sides of her face as her hands come around the baby's head, its shoulders, and finally its long legs. It was a yellow, shriveled-up thing, but Callie's hands loved it.

At first I couldn't make out if she was laughing or crying, but when she moved over to the broke dresser mirror with the baby, the cracked glass and dirt faded, and I could see her face was shining with the crying kind of wet. My sister Callie never did cry. Not till she got to be a nurse.

It come to me then, kinda strange like, that the Depression was over.

Betty Jean Tucker was born in 1931, the very heart of the Great Depression, in the little farming and sawmill community of Octagon in Marengo County, Alabama. For the first ten years of her life, she experienced the Depression up close. Though she was only a child then, the cataclysmic era seared into her memory a dark record of life in that time and place. Moreover, she has drawn on years of narrative handed down by relatives and friends to enrich the fictional stories in On a Darkling Plain. *The author has lived in the Alabama Black Belt town of Linden except for college years at Alabama College (now the University of Montevallo) and a brief stint as a reporter for the* Birmingham Post-Herald. *With a Ph.D. from the University of Alabama, she chaired the Division of Languages and Literature at the University of West Alabama for twenty years and is now retired.*

Betty Jean Tucker

Good Grief

Sue Walker

*The story was based on an actual occurrence in which a high school friend went
out to pick up the morning paper and found in it an article about her demise. Her
picture was on the front page. My story seemed to take off from there. It is loosely
autobiographical since I was an adopted child and later, in adulthood, found my
blood brother. He is responsible for some of the outrageousness that appears in his
letters. I don't have a daughter but Lila Bee stepped into the narrative, and she has
no basis in fact. "Good Grief" makes manifest its southern roots.*

It was in the morning paper how I died. Mama always said not to believe
anything you hear. Daddy said if it's in print it has validity. There it
was—front page of the *Surf Gazette*, Saturday, January 19. "Woman Dies
When Stove Tips On Her." I wouldn't have believed it if I hadn't read it
with my own eyes. Sergeant Conrad who investigated the calamity said
my death was thought to be accidental. If I had been asked, I might have
said that Hiram could have done it. He was my third husband. Rudolph
wouldn't do it. He's my current husband, and he likes for me to wait on
him, and take coffee to him in bed. Bring him hot biscuits even if they're
the frozen kind. Terrance Earl could have done it when he got mad after I
kicked the refrigerator in and trounced out of the house singing "Forever
Goodbye." He was Husband #2. None of that, however, was the case.

The Coroner, Happy ("Hap") Blunt Sr. put in his two cents worth
about the matter. He said, "It appears the deceased fell on the door of
the oven while it was open, which in turn made it lean on top of her."
And if that wasn't enough he had to elaborate about the supposed demise.
"Basically," he said, "the stove burned the woman and pinned her down so
she couldn't breathe."

I couldn't breathe all right. When I picked up the morning paper in
front of my house and saw my smiling face on the front page and read I
was dead, I was more than breathless. I was, as you might say, burned up.
Here I was minding my own business, and I find myself configured dead.

The description of my purported termination was positional asphyxia and thermal injuries. Of all the things I can think to die of, I must admit that this never occurred to me. And it's pretty gruesome too. I know that at age 62, my bones could be brittle enough for me to break a hip and die in surgery, but such a holocaust—no way.

A few years back, I might have died of lung cancer if I hadn't been saved by a faith healer in Biloxi, Mississippi. I might even have killed myself. I tried that once. Rolled up my car windows, put a brick on the gas pedal, and lay down in the back seat waiting to be transported to the Great Beyond. My sister, Peggy Suzanna came by and rescued me. I'm glad, because that good-for-nothing, mule-headed son-of-a-gun I was married to wasn't worth a broken fingernail, much less my life.

18,048 deaths have been attributed to household accidents in the past seven years. Those statistics were printed in the paper. I didn't make them up. 33 percent are due to falls. No wonder Mama always said to look out where you're going. Old people have to take care not to fall down stairs or trip over their dog in the middle of the night.

At any rate, I wasn't back in my house good and the front door shut behind me before folks started arriving. Gilda was bamming the knocker with a bucket of chicken and coleslaw before 9:00 a.m. Irene brought a squash casserole. Cara Nell brought cheese straws and pecans she'd picked up at the Nut House. I tried to tell myself that the names of the dishes weren't indicative of anything. People in lower Alabama are big on grief food. My friends wanted to comfort my dear distraught husband, but when I met them at the door, there wasn't a one of them who didn't scream.

Some folks don't think seeing is believing and doubted I wasn't dead even when I was standing before them. Peggy Suz kept reaching out and touching my arm. "Is that you? Is that really you?" She kept palpitating my flesh like she was a veritable artist at massage.

"Nah," I said. "Who you think I am ain't who I am or ever was."

"Ah, shush!," she said.

Gilda has been a friend for fifty years. We used to double-date and neck out in Hubert's corn field when we were in the 11th grade. "You could sue the paper," she said. "It's not enough they wrote you're burned up in the oven, they put a picture of you on the front page to prove it."

Sue Walker

I think I ought to set the record straight about my life. Here's my story as told by me to a lot of people, some who listened and some who didn't. I loved my husbands. All of them—at least for a time. And even though I've passed through the 50s and have had my share of failed nuptial flourishes, I still believe in love. I got married for the 7th time last July. Mr. Right came up to me in the flea market while I was selling a 1960s settee and stuck a head of silver hair prettier than an angel's halo right in my face, and you know what happened? I fell in love. Mary, my second best friend, doesn't believe I know "Right" when I see it—but what does she know? I mean, really. One body can't approach another body and pretend to know what's right regarding feelings and intentions.

Now here's the truth, and it signifies my attitude toward life. Five years ago, Dr. Block removed a tumor from my lung. Mary came to the hospital and brought me frozen yogurt, and whether or not Dr. Block or Mary or the yogurt was the cure, I was fine up until I married Fred. Anyway, shortly after that knot was tied, another tumor turned up. I flew to Arizona to see the Grand Canyon. Then I came home and had all these high falutin' tests—CT scan, body scan and the like, and it was determined I had two tumors in my right lung, one 11 centimeters. That's when I got a new Chevrolet, drove to Biloxi, and like a miracle, up popped a sign about a revival. I stopped right on the spot, and went and stood before a contingency of fire eaters. They sang and prayed and laid their hands on my head, and when I went back to my doctor a month later, the little tumor had gone and the big one had about disappeared. The doctor said "Let's wait a month and see what happens."

Now that I'm supposed to have died with my head in an oven, it's important to get things straight in my life, say thank you to the people who have been good to me, and maybe forgive some who haven't. If I don't go to Heaven and go to Hell instead, it will be a lesser flame. At least it won't be hotter than the oven.

#

After my purported demise, my head faux-fallen into the oven and that exposure in the paper, Rudolph and I got enough grief food to last us a month. I hadn't been dead even a day. The newspaper posted a retraction and said the woman reported dead wasn't dead after all. Anyway I'm going

Sue Walker

out this morning and get a deep freeze. Can't let anything go to waste. That would be a sin. "Waste not, want not." I'm not quite sure what it means, but Mama used to say it all the time, and she spent a third of her life canning. Put up pickled peaches until two whole shelves in her pantry were covered with them. I always thought they were too sour, but come to think of it, they make me recall resurrection. Those peaches would have fallen to the ground and rotted there if Mama hadn't brought them back and given them a new lease on life.

Yesterday I got a letter from my brother, "T." We haven't spoken since he decided to pal around with my second ex-husband Terrence Earl. He and "T" would go bowling together down on the Gulf highway where people would sit around and pretend they were looking at the two guys bowl when really they were listening to talk about me. I heard "T" told Earl he never knew what he saw in me in the first place. My own blood brother said that. I swear. I was glad he moved off to Florida, and we lost touch. Then this letter turned up:

I am so sorry to hear about your demise. You can't imagine what a shock it was when I opened that letter from Earl and your obituary fell out. Holy Mackerel! I never expected that. My own sister, dead! I still can't believe it, and it has been three months since it happened. I had been in France on some business and Earl had been kinda watchin' my place. I know you don't like him, but he's done me a lot of favors and we just pal-ed up after you and he divorced. He was very broken up and needed someone's shoulder to cry on. He was lonely and since you got to keep the dog, he had nobody. So, I just sort of let him hang around. Anyway, I'd been over in France on a Pickle Canning Photo Shoot contest. It's not much money, only $500 for first place, but it gives me a chance to get my name out in the front, ya know.

So, what was wrong with that old stove you were supposed to have fallen into? I remember Earl telling me about when him and Daddy was moving it into the house. Daddy had bought it from Absolute Antiques, in Foley, Alabama and him & Earl loaded it on Earl's old red pickup truck and brought it home. Daddy said he had one like that when he was a boy, and it brought back so many memories. Well, they was taking it off the truck when the tail gate broke off and the stove fell to the ground on the front left leg which put a crack in it. Earl said he was going to put a chunk of firewood behind the leg to shore it up. I called him when I got back to see what was going on with this obituary thing. He said he is upset with himself for not ever putting that piece of

Sue Walker

firewood behind the leg. I think he still loves you, Sis. I know he is "redneckish," but he has good intentions. He is still very bitter over when you kicked the refrigerator and stomped out of the house. I am sort of caught in the middle here so don't get too upset with me.

Did you ever make out a will? I got me a "Living Will." That's where if you are dying and you ain't quite dead yet and just hanging on, the person you designate (usually someone close to you, well—like you and Earl once was) can direct the doctor to pull the plug on you. It saves all your family and close friends from wondering what to do. I hope you didn't screw up and forget to update your will so that one of them flaky ex-husbands you had doesn't get put in charge of your disposal. You know, your ashes. I know you want certain things done with them and it would upset you if it wasn't done right.

I'm not sure what I'm supposed to think about receiving a letter like that. "T" said I might have invented the whole thing about being burned up in the oven just to get attention, but I reckon I ought to think about my demise and decide what I want done with my body and what I want done with my money and pictures and things. You might say that this experience of passing-on has given me perspective. It seems you never can truly tell about people, and "T" said it wouldn't be beyond the realm of probability if Rudolph, my current husband, had done it—gotten mad because I'd stayed out too late with my girl friends watching the movie *To Kill a Mockingbird*, at the Crescent Theater, and when I was retrieving a rhubarb pie from the oven, he'd taken his knee and given me a little head forward boost into the oven.

#

This morning, I'm sitting on the love seat in my bedroom, looking around and thinking about who ought to get what in terms of my possessions. When Grandma died, folks kept coming over and saying to my father: "Annie said I could have those bluebell plates she's got in the kitchen." I guess Daddy thought if somebody said his mother said they could have something, it was the gospel truth. Anyway, a whole hoard of people made off with about everything in her house, and I only got a cast iron skillet and pot. I still make chicken and dumplings in that pot just like Granny used to do, and I think about her every time I haul it out and use it. It weighs a ton; I can hardly heft it to the front burner. I'm going to scratch Lila Bee's name on the bottom with a finishing nail. She's just recovered from being a vegetarian.

Can't decide what to do with my piano. Mama's daddy played the piano and Mama too. I wish I had a nickel for all the times I heard her sit and play "Darling I am growing older. Silver threads among the gold." I used to feel so bad about her aging, I'd have to hide in the closet and cry. It was like I was to blame somehow because Mama had gained too much weight, and Daddy wasn't really interested in how she looked anymore. It's not Daddy's fault. He's no different from any other man. Mama told me to marry a man who's a lot older, but like about most things, she wasn't right. Marry a man who is twelve years older, and you have to shove him around in a wheelchair in his later days. I have friends who are doing that. Marry a man who is twelve years younger, and rest assured he won't shove you; he'll be out gathering sprouts in a greener pasture. You can't win either way. That's how I see it.

Mostly though I have things nobody wants. A lot of mugs I've picked up on trips to Louisville, Kentucky, or Washington, DC. A poster by Nall, "La Petit Mort": a woman with a sort of flimsy veil on her head with her heart outside her body and a couple of roaches crawling around her feet. We're big on roaches in the South. They don't hurt anything, so I don't see why people are freaked out about them. There's about 4,500 species of cockroaches, and only 30 are associated with human habitations. Poor creatures act like they're ashamed and only come out at night. It's like they're trying to hide themselves from view.

I even have Rudolph's bronze head on a table in my living room. He has a friend who is a famous sculptor and did the likeness. I don't know who might want to house Ruddy when I've passed away. Maybe some of the children by his first wife or some of his grandchildren.

I've got other things too—like clothes I haven't had on since I married the first time. I have this gauzy white creation with rhinestones on the cuffs. I once felt like an angel in it, but I haven't been able to fit in it for at least ten years though I'm on a diet now and have hopes. Maybe I'll have the mortician, or whoever looks after dressing corpses, put it on me when I'm ready to be dispersed with, considering I have a viewing, and folks can come by and comment on how I look.

"T" told me to consider what I wanted when I'm dead. Well, I have

Sue Walker

elaborate plans. Depending on how I appear at the time of my Leaving, I might just wear that white dress and have everyone come bow before me in a silk lined casket of palest blue. I wish I could have my eyes open and observe it all.

I read last week that anybody could get contact lenses that covered their whole pupil and display really enormous eyes. I don't want to be too outlandish, but maybe pretty youthful eyes, all wide open and smiling would be appropriate for a last look-see. Once, when I was in my actual prime, a man asked me if my eyes lit up in the dark. I told him only if he turned them on. I was a looker in spite of what "T" said.

I tend to get off the subject, but that's all right too. I'm not trying to impress. That's one of the smallest good things about growing old; you don't have to lie about liking to go water skiing when you're scared to death you'll drown. I never was good at sports. I had an English teacher who wrote in red in the margins of my papers: "Off the Topic." She tried to get me to outline what I was going to say, but I couldn't do it. I never knew what was going to come out of my mouth, and writing is like talking anyway.

If I do have a Viewing, then I want a Cremation to follow. And I want a proper House, like the little houses of the dead in New Orleans. A Mausoleum. I'm not going to ask for marble. I'll settle for moderate expenditure. I want my resting place to be like a library inside. I want my Urn (Urn, "T"—not vial). Vial sounds "vile," and it's not appropriate to talk about dead people as being vile. My daughter, Lila Bee, got her Master's in English, and she's into poetry. Even writes it. Reads to me when I deign to listen. She says I ought to have a Grecian Urn. "Thou still unravished bride of quietness," she said to me. A line from some poet named John Keats.

Lila Bee gave me a souped-up dictionary last April for turning 62. It's called the OED which is short for Oxford English Dictionary. There's two volumes of it, each one about two feet thick and weighing more than a new-born baby. It has words that are practically as old as the King James Bible. I had to look up "ravished," and it means raped. I thought of "unravished" in the context of "unraped." Same as virgin, I reckon, but then I went and looked the word up in the OED, and it gave a different meaning. It said something about withered. I couldn't really see the tiny type, so I couldn't get at everything that was written, but I could go with being "unwithered" up until the time I'm actually dust. Lila Bee said I have to be careful about using words. She said they're "slippery." I don't think of words as being like oysters or even stewed okra, but it's good to have a child you can learn from.

I want a couple of Lazy Boy chairs in my little Death House, a good floor lamp, and a couple of bookshelves. I want my friends, children and grandchildren to come in and read to me. I saw a Dorcy 41-1090 8D Battery 200 Lumen LED Bronze Patio Light on Amazon for $69.00. There needs to be an end table by each chair in my mausoleum and a note pad so visitors can leave me messages.

My mama gave me two lots in Pine Crest Cemetery. "Who you want to be next to, darling?" she said to me. This has given me pause. I don't think I want to spend eternity in the cold, dark ground, and maybe I want to adorn a monument all by myself. I want Lila Bee to come up with some sayings to put on the outside of where my coffin rests. If I sell one of the cemetery plots, it ought to be possible to build my house. It wouldn't have to be big. I'm not acquisitive, but I'm not ready to go yet, not by a long shot, and I'm working on a living resurrection. Losing weight and getting things propped and altered or at least covered over a bit.

#

I must thank "T" for setting up a website for us: lovingsiblings.org. What I need is an e-mail address just for the two of us to use. I don't want everybody knowing our business. It's enough to have my name in the paper as being dead but the small particulars of someone's life are private.

I'm glad I found my blood brother. He's the boy Mama had before she married my daddy and she never spoke of him until "T" went searching and found me. I need a brother to confide in, tell him that Lila Bee is PG. She told me last night she'd been to the doctor and he said so. And that's not the worst of it. The father is married. And if that's not enough hell to burn in, Rudolph is leaving me. He said he'd had ENOUGH! He said it was enough to tolerate my past—and I only told him about four ex-husbands. I think "T" might remember Henry. He's the husband who stepped on a live wire getting out of his boat in Bon Secour. "T" met him when he came and visited us. Marveled at the coke bottles I hung off the pier to collect barnacles. I used to make enough pocket money every week to keep me in Evening-in-Paris perfume. Tourists came from all over to buy the bottles and take them back to Philadelphia and New York and set them on their bookcases or use them as paperweights. Once I even sold a barnacle bottle to somebody from China.

Rudolph said he wasn't about to hang around and suffer Lila Bee's disgrace. He said she'd really gone and done it this time. Well, she's only been married three times, and she didn't have any children to divvy up between her and her spouses, so I don't know, really, what the problem is except this time it's a married man with children already. He's the Chair of the Communications Department at the University of Missalaflo, not ten miles up the road. Everybody had known for years that the man was given to indiscretions. Peggy Suz told me that when she was in school, a couple of teachers in his department had opened one of his drawers to find a pen to sign a petition with, and there was a pair of panties and a wine glass! Lila Bee thinks he's going to marry her. I told her she was a bloody fool, and she stomped out the door. Would you believe she's happy about the kid? She told me I was going to be a Grandmother—and I shrieked like I had seen a moccasin, his wide-open mouth all white with cotton. "T," I have enough grief to fill a mule wagon. Send me your e-mail address, please. And your phone number. No use trying to hide it. I can look it up on-line. I need to see you, I really do.

#

"T," I'm sorry to hear about your ears. Doctors do make you feel like you ought to feel grateful because you allow them to practice their craft on your body. You didn't tell me how old your hearing aids were when you took them in to be fixed and complained you couldn't hear soft sounds, and sharp sounds hurt your ears. If doors slamming and dishes clattering in the sink disrupt your thought processes for 10 minutes, that sounds really bad. What did you say when the doctor told you to just get used to your old hearing aids, no matter what? You should have told him that he needed to get used to folks complaining. Why weren't you told about the warranty running out? And how is your wife going to learn how to listen and talk to you and give you a list of "do's" and "don't's"? Are you sure

Sue Walker

you heard right? Let me see if I can write some "do's" out for you, and you won't have to hear what I say. 1) Don't throw your hearing aids away. Remember what your mama said about saving and not wasting things? Just because you don't know what use they might serve if they're not in your ears doesn't mean that there's not an answer somewhere. 2) Don't try to answer the phone with your hearing aid poking out your ear so that it slams up against the phone. If the phone won't fit flush with the ear, get yourself one of those phones that are loud enough for you to hear with no amplification. 3) You really can't have put a new battery in your hearing aid if you wore it only one day. Some things are duds, and you must have had one of those. Throw the old battery away or flush it down the toilet, and put another new battery in and see what happens. I'm worried though about your concentration.

#

Dear Sis,

After due consideration I think I owe you an apology. I was thinking that you may have wanted to commit SU____DE (I can't even write that word it is so terrible).

I know what a sensitive subject "wills" are with you, but Earl sent me a sample of one that you might want to peruse. Please don't misunderstand me, but I did meet a fellow at the bowling alley once who had a glass container (vial) with a cork in it that contained his ex-wife's ashes. He said that he was the only living person that was related to her in some way, so they gave it to him. He also had a clear plastic bowling ball that had a human skull in it which he said was his ex-mother-in-law's. I don't know about Earl. I went over to his apartment one time, and there he sat in front of the TV watching "Dukes of Hazard" and sopping up a saucer of beer with his cornbread. I knew he may have a problem with alcohol but, man!

I do have an issue with you over the "Lucifer" comment you made about Earl, him liking cheese grits and turnips. Lucifer is not a Southerner nor a Redneck. He's more like a Yankee and would hate grits. He would probably put milk on them like most people up North. When I was in France, there wasn't a restaurant that had grits or turnips, nor any kind of soul food. It was nice to get back to civilization and get some good vittles.

I'm sorry to hear about your predicament with Lila Bee. I am sure that if you just turn it over to the Lord, He will take care of it.

PS I am attaching a copy of that "Living Will" Earl sent me.

Brother, "T"

#

I got up early this morning to walk the dog. It's supposed to be 96 degrees today. Or hotter. I got in my car one day last week; it was sitting in the sun, and the temperature registered 114 degrees. Nobody can walk a dog in 114 degree heat, that is if the dog would walk. Dogs have more sense than humans do a lot of the time. Pamela Ann sent me an e-mail that her dog had died. It's one of those little bitty dogs that needs its own set of steps to get up on the bed where it sleeps. Anyway, it was on the floor, and when her husband got up in the middle of the night to pee, he stepped on the dog and killed it. Pamela Ann is grief stricken. She said she loved that dog better than any dog she'd ever had. I think she loved the dog better than she loved her husband. Every time I was over at her house, she was kissing on the dog, rubbing noses with it, holding it in her arms like it was a baby, but I never saw her smooch her husband, not one time, and if there was a party, most of the time, she didn't even sit by him. Pamela Ann is having the dog cremated, and they're going to have a ceremony when they put dear Crissy away.

Lila Bee is going to Africa. She said she won't be able to travel much after the baby comes, so she's going to make hay while the sun shines. She's going on a safari with some photographer who is famous and once worked for the *National Geographic.* I said, "it's awful sudden, isn't it Lila Bee—this trip?" She said it depended on what is meant by sudden. She said, sudden is like a stroke or a heart attack that fells somebody standing straight up in their shoes. I said it wasn't like that at all. If somebody had annual check-ups at the doctors, they would know about their cholesterol and high blood pressure, and they could get on a preventative regime.

I haven't heard a word from Africa. She promised to send postcards, but I know they don't have a post office at the foot of Mt. Kilimanjaro or out in the Serengeti. I swear I never know about that girl, but I guess she's a chip off the old block. That's what Rudolph says, anyway.

I wish I was as pretty as Lila Bee when I was 34, going on 35, all that

Sue Walker   439

auburn hair hanging down her back that she swishes about. I have auburn hair now. Didn't used to, but Loving Care can go a long way in erasing the more obvious signs of aging. Which reminds me. I need a new up-lift bra. I'm beginning to sag something terrible. I even have to take my hands and ease myself into the Shirley of Hollywood, size D cups, and jump and jiggle to get myself in shape. Getting old is not a lark, not a walk in the park, not something anybody would want to do if there was a better alternative.

Death, I'm discovering, is Big Business. I just read in *The Week* that a New Zealand man attended up to four funerals a week just so he could eat free food, including "take-out" which he stashed in Tupperware containers. The Funeral Director, according to the report, alerted other funeral homes, and the "Grim Eater" had to find some other food supply.

#

"T," I got your letter. I don't appreciate your comments about Rudolph, even if he has decided to hit the road. There's another angle you haven't considered. Lila Bee isn't Rudolph's daughter. She's either Rich's or maybe Jimbo's. They were sort-of over-lapping in regard to my affections. Nevertheless, Rud and I are reconciling ourselves. He says that when push comes to shove as it is wont to do, he can't see us going East and West apart from each other. He says a body has to tolerate a girl's fanfooting around. I'm going to forgive him his trespasses, and he's going to forgive mine—and Lila Bee's. So you've got to get over yourself too. And don't say any foul words about him. Don't.

And to show you how good Rudolph is being, he told me and Lila Bee to have a good time when we set out for the Alabama Writer's Conclave in Birmingham. We stayed at the Hilton. All kinds of red and white flowers lined up along the road into the hotel. It looked like a picture postcard it was so pretty. And I've never laid down on such a comfortable bed in my life. Lots of fluffy pillows. Lila Bee had her own bed and I had mine. I say it was kind-of good not to have Rudolph stretched out beside me making snorts and snores and throwing his arms about. I slept all night and never had to get up for anything.

Lila Bee read some of her poetry, and though I couldn't understand much of it, it was kind-of beautiful in an unusual way. She read "Burning

Sue Walker

Leaves." My Daddy, not the man who actually sired me, used to have a big barrel out back behind the garage, and when he got all the leaves raked up, he'd set them on fire. Oh, they smelled so good. Lila Bee says she's going to be a poet. I'm so proud of that girl even if she hasn't got no common sense at all.

#

Sis, just wanted to tell you this, I learned that the best way I can help some people is to get away from them, and leave them alone. Cogitate upon that. T.

#

I just went out to get some fast food for lunch. Got to Hardees and a rude-voiced female—after I had been waiting at the drive-up for over ten minutes said: "Can you wait?" I just put the pedal to the medal and hauled out of there. Decided I would come home and open a can of tuna fish.

When I was driving into the yard, I saw our neighbor getting his mail. It's probably the first time I've seen the man in three or four years and we don't live 100 yards apart. I must tell "T" that he's on my list of people to stay away from. We got enough of the Smarts practically from the day we moved in. They accused our builders of killing their grass by stomping on it when they were putting up a fence between our two houses. They wanted us to have new grass put down on their side of the divide. They had a whole passel of dogs what lived in their concrete back yard that they hosed down every morning. Well, those dogs started barking at 6:00 a.m., but they complained about our sweet Baggio. Went and put up a huge sign at the front of their house: Dogs Are Not To Use This Grass. I wrote at the bottom of the sign: " Our dog can't read," but it wasn't until after our pup died and was buried out under the popcorn tree that the sign was removed.

The worst was when Aaron and his friends blew up some condoms, filled them with water, and threw them out the bedroom window. They landed on the Smarts' patio. The boys were thirteen at the time and interested in Kathleen Smart who was seventeen and the girlfriend of Aaron's friend who probably had a stash of condoms for Kathleen's benefit. The next afternoon when I got home from sitting with Evelyn, Mrs. Smart rang our bell, handed me a little paper bag stapled at the top. "I think these belong to you," she said, handing me the parcel. I had no clue, so I walked into the kitchen and opened the bag. There, inside, were three soggy condoms. I can't remember whether I screamed or what, but I don't think Mrs. Smart and I have conversed since.

Soon after the condom incident, Mrs. Smart substituted at Aaron's school. She taught the whole semester, and failed Aaron in math. What kind of neighbor would live right next door and fail her neighbor's son?

#

Lila Bee told me that with my experiences, I ought to set myself up as a Life Coach. "Mama," she said, "remember that time we were having breakfast at the restaurant in Napa Valley looking over the vineyard, and there was this couple at the next table talking about how wine was a passion, and I asked them to tell me about their favorite winery, and we all got to sharing stories about where we were from and what we did, and that woman in a smashing red outfit said she was from San Francisco and ran her own business Life Coaching. Remember how we had never heard of a Life Coach, and you got mad because I asked her to tell me what a Life Coach did. She said Life Coaching was one of the top businesses in America."

Well, damned if Lila Bee might be right. I've been Life Coaching at my kitchen table for years. I looked up the definition, and it said: "Coaching a 'private' individual in the context of his or her personal life." I've been doing that most of my life, only I never got paid for it. If I set up a true legitimate practice, I could make enough money in a year or two, and I could go off on an extended vacation. I might even get to travel around the world.

"Lila Bee," I said. "You got more problems than the gallons of oil that pooled on the bottom of Gulf of Mexico. If you think I'm good at coaching, why don't we start with you?"

"Mama," Lila Bee said, "you've been coaching me for 34 years. I don't know if you want to boast about it."

"And where would you be without me?" I asked. "Maybe I need more practice. Why don't we try?"

"I don't have time this morning, but you read up on the practice a bit. Go to the library. Ask for some books on the subject. Life Coaching will give you a new lease on life. Start by making a list of people you know who need coaching, and you can offer a free trial lesson."

"What will Rudolph say?"

"Never mind him. He could do with some coaching himself. Gotta, go."

Lila Bee always gets something started and then darts off. Maybe that's a good thing. I don't know whether to get me a mailing list or to plaster flyers all over the place. It will beat collecting barnacles, I can tell you that.

Experienced Life Coach
Life Lessons That Will Enhance Your Life

Do you need to change your life? Get out of a relationship? Live more complete and fulfilled?

Let Miss Blossom guide you and help you create a new identity, learn to cope, achieve success, understand the past, and prepare for the future.

Regardless of where you are on your life journey, Miss Blossom can get you out of the woods.

Name _____

Address _____

City, State, Zip_____

Phone_____

15% discount
Call: 1-800-122-2244

#

Lila Bee said my ad wouldn't do. She said it smacked of silly, and upon reconsideration, she didn't think I would satisfy the requirements of a Life Coach. She said that anybody who been knotted with seven husbands might be considered just plain stupid, rather than possessing wisdom of any sort. Now, here I am with my hopes dashed and trying to figure what it is I'm going to do with my golden years. I don't hanker after making pies and selling them in the parking lot of Wal*Mart. I could take in dogs and board them. I have a cookie-cutter dog bone, and I could supply the creatures with specialized awards if they "sit" and "stay" and obey appropriate commands. Just a passing thought, because I know what Lila Bee would say. I don't even have to imagine. I refuse, however, to turn into a crone, sit old and toothless in a corner, and grow meaner by the day. I'm trying to develop the Art of Kindness and pay honest compliments to deserving people. I'm not trying to turn into an aging Pollyanna and say it's good to have gotten crutches for Christmas by mistake and profess I'm glad because I've got two good legs. Mama touted that book when I was growing up, and ranted on about how I ought to develop character like Pollyanna. I wondered why there wasn't a book called Ollieandy for boys. It was just girls who had to espouse gladness.

#

Violet found her baby at the beauty parlor. Her place card was next to mine at a dinner party last night, and she went on and on about how she was sitting in the chair getting color and talking to the woman next to her when she said her baby was due next week.

"I can't keep him," she said. "I don't really care for either of the couples who want him. I just have this gut feeling about them. There's nothing specific, but I don't want to turn 'No Name' over to them. That's what I call him. If I were to give him a name, I'd never give him away."

Violet said it was like she heard God speaking, like He was at her side. She and her husband had been trying to have a baby for eight years. Now, here was a woman, not a curling wand away talking about giving her infant away. Violet said she burst out crying, and the next thing she knew, she and the woman were hugging each other and saying how right it was for them to find each other. Violet said she called her husband right on the spot and told him she had found them a little boy. She said she'd found a puppy dog too. Mavis, who owned the shop, had brought five eight-week old pups to work with her, and by the time she closed shop on the second day, three girls and two boys had been sold for $350 apiece.

#

Oh my—and if I just said shit—that would be most descriptive. "Pal," our current dog has been sick two days. She went out for her walk with me on Thursday morning and had "the runs." Then Pal started throwing up. She would drink water like the ocean wouldn't satisfy her thirst. Then she would throw up again. I had a "Loaves and Fishes," Women's Missionary Union, WMU meeting at my house, and I had to go to a birthday party in the evening. Locked Pal in the bathroom before we left for Sally's, and when we got home, Pal had thrown up some more. Then yesterday, she was better, so I fixed her scrambled eggs for breakfast. She didn't touch them. I went out to Mosely's and bought her some lean ground sirloin for lunch—and she ate that—but when I fixed her some more for supper, she wouldn't eat a bite. I just got up to go to the bathroom, and Pal had had the big "D" all over the floor. Thank goodness, it was the bathroom—and not the carpet somewhere. After that, who can sleep?

Rudolph and I are supposed to drive to Washington, DC, on Tuesday morning. I gave myself this trip for my birthday. Haven't ever been to our nation's capitol. I want to see the White House. I want to walk along where Obama walked with Michelle. I want to drop two pennies where Jack Kennedy stood. That's my two-cents worth. There's a tropical storm in the Gulf called Bonnie that is supposed to blow in tonight. I have to take my car to the shop on Monday at 8:00 a.m., and it's going to start raining buckets the closer Bonnie gets. A sick dog, a car that needs fixing, and a tropical storm—all in a couple of days! And what, pray, is Rudolph doing at 1:45 a.m.? Soundly sleeping. "Yeah, baby! "Everything's Made For Love!"

What've we got lips for? What've we got arms for?
Why do we have stars above?
"Oh you know I know everything's made for love."
What've we got eyes for? What do we sigh for? Why do we say "dovey
    dove?"
"Oh you know I know everything's made for love."

Mama used to play that song on the piano. Daddy said "Everything's Made For Love" is a theological statement. He said it was an extrapolation of First Corinthians, Chapter 13: "If I speak in the tongues of men and of angels, but have not love. I am a noisy gong or a clanging cymbal."

Daddy used to tell tales about Frank Boykin who was an Alabama politician, a fourteen-term U.S. Congressman born in Bladon Springs, Alabama in 1885. Died in Washington, DC, in 1969. "Zest incarnate!" everybody said. Daddy said he was once invited to Frank's Hunting Lodge. You had to be kind-of famous to be issued an invitation. Alabama governors went there: Big Jim Folsom and George C. Wallace.

I think Boykin Lodge is still up on Highway 43 with "Everything is Made for Love" written on the Gate. If love can make somebody a multimillionaire by the age of 21, I think that's quite an affirmation. I don't know where I went wrong. Maybe I wasn't flamboyant enough. Daddy said he went to a political rally where someone bet Boykin would come on to a pretty woman he'd seen in the crowd. By the end of the evening, Boykin was hanging around shaking hands and mouthing, "Everything's Made For Love," and by damn if he didn't go up and kiss the preacher's wife on the cheek. Then he moved his hands comprehensively over her buttock. Frank, it's said, was like Al Capp's Southern Congressman in the "Li'l Abner" cartoon strip, 'Senator Phogbound.'"

And here I am in the middle of the night proclaiming "Everything's Made For Love" while Rudolph sleeps and I'm bent over cleaning dog shit off the bathroom floor. "Everything's Made For Love" all right.

Lila Bee told me to write things down. "Mama," she said, when you're truly dead, we're going to want to know what went on in that head of yours."

Sue Walker is Professor Emerita at the University of South Alabama. She was Poet Laureate of Alabama from 2003-2012. She has published 11 books including a critical book on the ecopoetics of James Dickey. She has edited numerous anthologies that include festschrifts on Karl Shapiro, Richard Eberhart, a critical book on Marge Piercy and has published over 100 critical articles. She has read poetry throughout the U.S. and in Ireland, Great Britain, and Scotland. A new poetry book is forthcoming from Clemson University Press.

Sue Walker

Spores

Theodora Ziolkowski

Like the characters in my story, I visited a gallery of mushrooms when I was a teenager. What I remember most about the outing was my family's enthusiasm that such a gallery should exist, and our subsequent surprise at how small the gallery actually was upon our arrival. Revisiting that space through the point-of-view of a frustrated grandmother was a way for me to reconceive my own memory of the journey to that dimly lit gallery as a kind of fairytale. It is the anticipation of making journeys and the thwarting of expectations that typically propel adults and children alike into the forest.

The gallery was a two-hour drive, and it was too hot to do much of anything else but get out of the house, so I downloaded directions from the gallery's website, packed lunches for my granddaughter Zoey and me in the cooler.

Zoey was a late sleeper—a trait I attributed to her mother. And whereas when she was young I could chide my daughter Brooke for being lazy, I found myself at first unable to be anything but soft with Zoey. Zoey, who I'd find in the rickety guest room bed still sound asleep close to lunchtime, her hair strewn across the pillow like a heap of straw.

I was climbing the stairs to wake her, my knees throbbing with each step.

Surely Zoey would forgive me for yesterday. Surely, she would have forgotten my anger by now.

For up until the day before, I had behaved myself. Let Zoey get away with forgetting to put her dishes in the sink, neglecting to remove her dirt-caked sandals before taking the stairs to her room. I assumed the role of the good, indulgent grandmother I tried to inhabit.

It wasn't until I caught Zoey scooping her hand into the bowl of fresh-cut fruit I had just set out for lunch that I snapped. Later that same night, when we sat in front of the television with our foldout trays like usual, Zoey hardly touched her potpie. Just rolled the peas and carrot cubes around on her plate before she gave me an obligatory peck on the cheek and closed herself in her room.

I caught my breath on the landing, knocked softly on her door and entered.

Zoey was already up, dressed, and sitting with her legs curled under her in the recliner by the window.

She looked like a president's wife, her hair pulled into a bulb on the top of her head, her watermelon-printed dress and rabbit slippers like a coquettish representation of what every First Lady from the 1950's should wear when she rises.

When I asked her to come downstairs, Zoey nodded in what I could only assume was rehearsed solemnity, before padding down after me.

Once she was situated at the breakfast bar, her slippers dangling off the edge of her stool, I told her the plan. We would go for a drive to the mushroom gallery. There was even a gift shop. We could stop, I told her —feeling my annoyance rise again (for Zoey wasn't even looking at me, she was just clanking her spoon against her bowl)—at Pizza Hut on the way home.

Zoey spooned her corn puffs into her mouth and chewed. She slid from the counter, leaving her bowl still filled with the soggy remains of her cereal.

I picked up the picnic basket and my car keys. I walked to the car and hoped she would put on her shoes and follow.

I would pick up after Zoey once we got back the gallery. After the greasy supper at that horrible red-roofed shack I'd promised her.

The drive was long.

Zoey kept kicking the back of my seat and I was too aware of my outburst the day before to tell her to stop.

I'd been to the gallery just once before, when my daughter was a teenager. It was winter when we went, and because I couldn't count on her to do the practical thing, it took some convincing before Brooke agreed to wear a scarf and hat. Getting her to put on her coat alone was like pulling teeth.

Theodora Ziolkowski

But it suited my daughter, that defiant streak. Since she was a child, Brooke always had to be busy, always had to be doing something she made clear was beyond my own realm of understanding. And now as a mother to Zoey, the same was proving true.

For Brooke left Zoey for days at a time at my place. Never mind that I was exhausted. Never mind that I was old and boring for an eight-year-old and that I swear Zoey had become even more lethargic under my care. Brooke was always coming and going. And because she was in a new relationship and didn't think Zoey was ready to meet her new beau, she was, Brooke's words, *in an even greater bind.*

For the most part, I lost myself for a good deal of the drive, though occasionally I did catch Zoey's tired eyes in the rearview mirror. Halfway along, I pulled off to a rest stop and we ate our tuna fish sandwiches and potato chips at a picnic table crusted in the crud of lunches past.

The last leg of the drive was nothing like how I remembered it. Less meandering than the thorny, glassed-over journey I remembered making with Brooke, and more of a straight shot up and canopied with pendulous, blossom-sweeping branches.

By the time we reached the gallery, my legs felt like noodles from either the heat or from having been sitting for so long.

Zoey had fallen asleep after lunch, and so her hair bun was tipped to the side of her head and a red indent from her seatbelt crossed her right cheek when I woke her back up.

I dabbed the sweat from my forehead with the back of my sleeve, got out and opened Zoey's door.

Cardinals filled the trees like spatters of paint, and the ground was speckled in clover, violets, buttercups. The grass was so tall it reached Zoey's knees.

The gallery's windows were all gauzed over; above its rundown door was a hornet's nest I had to resist the urge to punch.

Years ago, when Brooke came with me to the gallery, I'd watched her follow one of the staff members, probably the owner's son, behind the register and into the back room. The boy was around Brooke's age, maybe older, with wiry black hair and big dimples. He wore a sweater as red as the pea coat I had begged Brooke to put on.

Theodora Ziolkowski

After Brooke disappeared, I peered into the dim, cramped displays of mushrooms projecting from mossy rocks alone. They were so rubbery and *phallic,* mushrooms. So many of them seemed to grow toward the center of the room. They clung to the glass like bathtub suction cups or what have you. And there was something absurdly depressing about touring the exhibit on my own, walking about so many spores. It was like I had been enlisted in some sort of fungal porn.

Brooke was no longer wearing her coat when eventually I went to find her behind the curtain. Instead she was standing with her back against a mirror, her earrings shining through her hair, her coat in a red pool at her feet.

She was only sixteen then. Sixteen and triumphant. It had always been hard to talk to Brooke when a fresh argument was ready to come at me like a blow.

I took hold of Zoey's hand and tried the back door. I jiggled the handle again and again.

The high grass rustled and the same wasp kept skimming past my right ear.

—Fuck, I said. Fuck a duck.

Zoey stared up at me, her lips slightly parted and her eyes filled with a blend of approval and alarm.

I tried the door again, bumping my shoulder hard against it. And then bumping it and bumping it some more.

I told Zoey to climb into the front seat.

Not a mile down the road, the wheels got caught in the muck. The harder I pressed on the gas, the deeper we sank. And so I continued to push and push as the wheels squealed into the ground and the mud flecked up. I slapped the dashboard like that was going to do anything, then got out of the car to survey the damage.

We had driven so far, God be damned. Plus, it was so hot and of course all we had with us was a carton of warm apple juice for Zoey and the useless cell phone Brooke had given me for Christmas, a present I'd deemed a nuisance and never bothered to charge.

I was whacking my front tires with a branch when the car door opened and out came Zoey.

Theodora Ziolkowski

My granddaughter looked from me to the branch to the car. She had only just stepped out and was already ankle-deep in mud. She slushed over to my side, picked up a stick, and began banging it against the front bumper.

"God damn," Zoey said, looking excitedly at me to see what I'd do.

Theodora Ziolkowski's poetry and prose have appeared or are forthcoming in Glimmer Train, Prairie Schooner, *and* Short FICTION *(England), among other journals, anthologies, and exhibits. A Pushcart Prize and Best New Poets nominee, Theodora is the author of the poetry chapbook* A Place Made Red *(Finishing Line Press) and prose chapbook* Mother Tongues, *winner of The Cupboard's 2015 contest.*

Editors' photograph: Margaret Raftery

Don Noble is professor emeritus of English at the University of Alabama, host of Alabama Public Television's author interview program *Bookmark*, and book reviewer for Alabama Public Radio. He is the editor of volumes on Harper Lee, Hemingway, Steinbeck, and Fitzgerald and two collections of Alabama fiction, *Climbing Mt. Cheaha* and *A State of Laughter*. He won a regional Emmy for Achievement in Screenwriting with Brent Davis for a documentary on Alabama writer William Bradford Huie and was the recipient of the 2000 Eugene Current-Garcia Award and the 2013 Wayne Greenhaw Service Award from the Alabama Humanities Foundation.

Raised in Arkansas and a longtime resident of Alabama, **Jennifer Horne** is a writer, editor, and teacher who explores Southern identity and experience, especially women's, through prose, poetry, fiction, and anthologies and in classrooms and workshops across the South. Among her books are *Bottle Tree: Poems* (2010), *Tell the World You're a Wildflower: Stories* (2014), and a second collection of poems, *Little Wanderer* (2016). She has edited a poetry anthology and co-edited two collections of essays and currently is at work on a biography of writer Sara Mayfield.

www.ingramcontent.com/pod-product-compliance
Lightning Source LLC
Chambersburg PA
CBHW020828030726
47496CB00001B/141